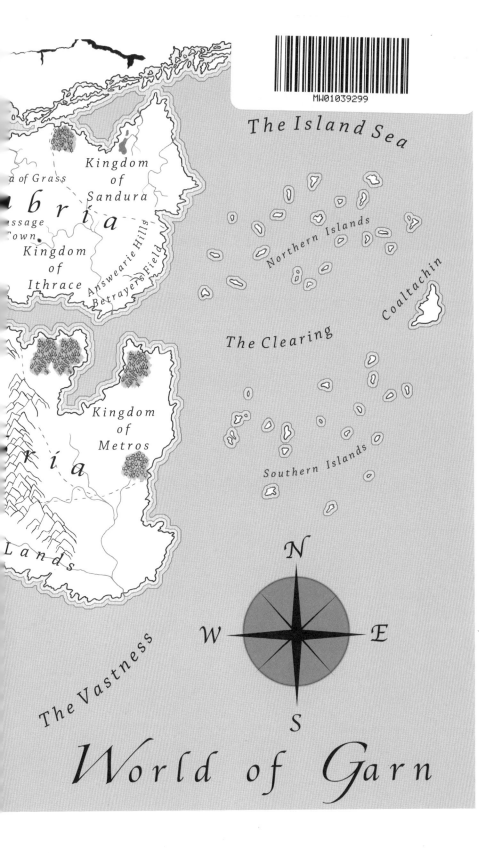

The Island Sea

Kingdom
of
Sandura

d of Grass

bria

ssage
own

Kingdom
of
Ithrace

Answearie Hills

Betrayer's Field

Northern Islands

Coaltachin

The Clearing

Kingdom
of
Metros

ría

Southern Islands

Lands

The Vastness

N

W   E

S

World of Garn

A
DARKNESS
RETURNS

ALSO BY RAYMOND E. FEIST

THE FIREMANE SAGA
Master of Furies
Queen of Storms
King of Ashes

THE CHAOSWAR SAGA
Magician's End
A Crown Imperiled
A Kingdom Besieged

THE DEMONWAR SAGA
Rides a Dread Legion
At the Gates of Darkness

THE DARKWAR SAGA
Flight of the Nighthawks
Into a Dark Realm
Wrath of a Mad God

CONCLAVE OF SHADOWS
Talon of the Silver Hawk
King of Foxes
Exile's Return

LEGENDS OF THE RIFTWAR
Honored Enemy
(with William R. Forstchen)
Murder in LaMut
(with Joel Rosenberg)
Jimmy the Hand
(with S. M. Stirling)

THE RIFTWAR LEGACY
Krondor: The Betrayal
Krondor: The Assassins
Krondor: Tear of the Gods

THE SERPENTWAR SAGA
Shadow of a Dark Queen
Rise of a Merchant Prince
Rage of a Demon King
Shards of a Broken Crown

THE EMPIRE TRILOGY
(WITH JANNY WURTS)
Daughter of the Empire
Servant of the Empire
Mistress of the Empire

KRONDOR'S SONS
Prince of the Blood
The King's Buccaneer

THE RIFTWAR SAGA
Magician
Silverthorn
A Darkness at Sethanon

OTHER TITLES
Midkemia: The Chronicles of Pug
(with Stephen Abrams)
Faerie Tale

A
DARKNESS
RETURNS

BOOK ONE *of* THE DRAGONWAR SAGA

RAYMOND E.
FEIST

HARPER Voyager
An Imprint of HarperCollins*Publishers*

HarperCollins books may be purchased for educational, business, or sales promotional use. For information, please email the Special Markets Department at SPsales@harpercollins.com.

Harper Voyager and design are trademarks of HarperCollins Publishers LLC.

FIRST EDITION

Designed by Alison Bloomer

Maps by Jessica Feist
Sword graphic © Artskrin/stock.adobe.com
Scroll graphics © Shalyapina/stock.adobe.com

Library of Congress Cataloging-in-Publication Data has been applied for.

ISBN 978-0-06-231584-7

24 25 26 27 28 LBC 5 4 3 2 1

ANOTHER FOR JESSICA,
WHO HAS BEEN MORE TO ME THAN A DAUGHTER CAN IMAGINE

ACKNOWLEDGMENTS

I WILL NEVER repay the debt I owe to the fathers and mothers of Mid-kemia, who let me play in our sandbox and acquaint the world with a wonderful place. Now that I'm back there, we part company, at least as storytelling goes. Now that my stories have caught up with the game, the stories I share have nothing to do with the game we played. So, whatever you, gentle reader, love is because of generous people who shared their creativity with me. If you are not happy with the story, put the blame on me.

I've said before, and I reiterate, I'm the luckiest guy I know. I've been allowed to play "let's pretend" in a rich place other people have let me use.

So, to the creators of Midkemia, Steve A., John, Anita, Alan, Steve B., Ethan, Bob, Jeff, Lorri, Tim, and so many others who came and went, but left their mark on the world: thank you. I could not have done this without you. Love is not sufficient to express how I feel, even if I don't show it. I owe everything to your enthusiastic support.

I've had many editors over the years and they have been brilliant. But for this book, I'll single out Jane Johnson as being a shepherd and making me better.

Finally, my daughter Jessica, to whom this book is dedicated, who is better at pointing out where I went wrong than she knows.

Thank you all.

OUR STORY SO FAR

IN THE WORLD of Garn, the Covenant among the Five Great Kingdoms of North and South Tembria is destroyed in bloody treachery. The betrayers, led by the jealous king of Sandura, raze the nation of Ithrace and end the entire ruling Firemane family, save for one baby boy.

Legend tells that a terrible curse will befall all of Garn if the Firemane line should end. Mindful of this, and feeling profound guilt over betraying a man he considered a friend, Daylon Dumarch, Baron of Marquenesas, discovers the surviving heir has been hidden in his pavilion after the battle, and decides to keep the boy's existence a secret.

The baron and his half-brother, Balven, send him to Coaltachin, Kingdom of the Night. It is an outlaw nation of spies and assassins, its location unknown, where the boy, named Sefan Langene, will be raised as one of their own.

HATUSHALY, AS SEFAN BECOMES KNOWN, remains ignorant of his true heritage throughout his upbringing in Coaltachin. He is observant and gifted, his only flaw being a quick temper when he is denied knowledge or explanation, earning himself harsh punishment. He grows to young manhood in the company of two lifelong friends, Hava, the daughter of lowly fishmongers who has become a spy for the island nation, and Donte, the troublemaking grandson of a Master who somehow earns Hava and Hatu's deep affections. Hava's calming effect on Hatu blossoms into a profound love, and Donte remains a friend in spite of their better judgment.

On a journey with Bodai, one of the Masters of Coaltachin, to the City of Sandura, Hatu chances upon a secret meeting with servants of the Church of the One (new to North Tembria, but in control of the distant continent of Enast) and mysterious black-clad figures. Upon hearing Hatu's recounting, Master Bodai names the mysterious figures "Azhante" and quickly abandons the current mission to warn the other Masters of their presence in Sandura.

When Hatu reaches adulthood, the truth of his lineage is revealed to him by Balven: that he is indeed the last of the Firemane line, and that Baron Daylon Dumarch of Marquensas was responsible for his safety. Hatu finds the revelation interesting, but it's as if he's hearing about someone else's life. He may have not been Coaltachin born, but that life is all he knows. He and Hava wish to put that behind them, and decide to return to Beran's Hill, a small town in northern Marquensas, which they had visited before with Master Bodai. Pretending to remain under command of the Kingdom of the Night, Hatu and Hava assume the role of loyal agents of Coaltachin, while living a peaceful life in Beran's Hill.

As the betrayal and destruction of the Covenant unleashes turmoil across North Tembria, Declan, a young smith in the village of Oncon, creates his masterpiece and earns the rank of Master Smith. Declan is the youngest smith ever known to achieve this rank, and is rewarded by his mentor, Master Smith Edvalt Tasman, with the trade secret of crafting noble steel. He quickly earns a reputation as a great swordsman as well as a gifted smith.

Slavers attack Oncon, wearing the colors of the King of Sandura, and are fended off by Declan, Edvalt, and the men of the village. Knowing they will return, the villagers disperse. Declan, who is now expected to establish his own smithy, travels to the town of Beran's Hill, where he strikes up a friendship with Hatushaly and Hava, and falls for a woman named Gwen.

Looking for a way to fit in, Hava and Hatu agree to purchase the inn now owned by Gwen, and they settle into a quiet life in a lovely small town. When Declan announces he is to marry Gwen, the two lovers decide to join in the ceremony and truly wed.

Attacking from across the sea, an army of foreign raiders rages across most of the twin continents. Beran's Hill is overrun, and almost the entire town is put to the torch. Declan's wife of one day, Gwen, is killed, along with most of the townspeople. Hatu, meanwhile, is captured and spirited to safety by two mysterious servants of the Fire Guard, a secret order dedicated to protecting the Firemane line. North Tembria lies in ruin save for the city of Marquenet, home to Lord Daylon.

While being transported to safety, Hatu learns that Bodai is in fact one of the Fire Guard's oldest agents, the only outsider successfully to infiltrate the Council of Masters of Coaltachin. During this revelation, a ship attacks them, and Hatu's rage unlocks long hidden powers. He unleashes a wave of fire, destroying the attackers, and soon realizes he must learn to control his powers under Bodai's tutelage.

Hava, searching in vain for Hatu, is captured by slavers and put aboard a treasure ship. Using her years of training and help from other captives, she escapes and seizes the ship. Reaching an island port near the continent of Nytanny, she attempts to ascertain where Hatu has been taken.

Wounded during the destruction of his home, Declan is befriended by a mercenary and joins his band to find and destroy those who murdered Gwen. Baron Dumarch's family was slaughtered by raiders as they attempted to reach a safe haven, changing everything he and his brother had planned for the future of Marquensas.

THE INVASION AND DESTRUCTION OF Beran's Hill was ordered by the Pride Lords, who control the entire continent of Nytanny. Fearing rebellion, because of the overpopulation of what they call "the slave nations," they sought to conquer new territory and quell any threat from those nations they already control. Hatu's destination, the Fire Guard's community of Sanctuary, lies on an island nearby, hidden by a shroud of mist and by treacherous shoals and currents.

Hava finds Hatu safe there, and learns the secrets of the Fire Guard and their responsibility to the Firemane line. Meanwhile, Hatu has learned as much as Bodai—and a mysterious figure named Nathan—can teach him about his long dormant magical abilities, and his powers have begun to manifest. Together they vow revenge on those who sacked Beran's Hill, the only place that truly felt like a home to them.

Donte wanders the land in search of Hatu, doing odd jobs to get by. He soon falls in with a mercenary company that brings him under the employ of Balven, eavesdropping and decoding secret messages from the Azhante, the mysterious black-clad figures Hatu had encountered in Sandura.

ANTICIPATING A PROLONGED CONFLICT WITH the Pride Lords, the baron orders Declan and Edvalt to create as many quality blades as possible, and Declan travels to South Tembria to secure a large supply of the unique sand needed in crafting the noble steel.

Tribal raiders unexpectedly attack the trading city of Abala, forcing Declan and the company of mercenaries to flee into the desolate Burning Lands. Pushed to the massive canyons known as Garn's Wound, Declan and his men discover a menacing population of cannibals known as "the Eaters." He engineers an escape from the Wound and—with the unknown help of Hatushaly's growing powers and sight—manages to see his men to safety. Returning to the ravaged city of Abala, Declan and his companions find trading goods aboard a ship they can sail back to Marquensas, and along the way recruit other now-masterless crews.

KING DAYLON'S MASSIVE ATTACK ON the capital city of the Pride Lords reveals a startling truth. Rather than being a powerful set of rulers, the Pride Lords are in reality clever crime bosses who have manipulated the entire population of Nytanny into believing they had saved them ages ago from horrible demons, the Dark Masters.

Hatu uses his powers to help Declan and the King enter the Pride Lord fortress, and while using his far-seeing vision, discovers a vast city-like structure atop a massive escarpment in the center of Nytanny.

There, hundreds of statues of hideous creatures stand, soon revealed to be the legendary Dark Masters.

Upon learning of the existence of these Dark Masters, Nathan employs a strange device to vanish from sight. Later he returns with two men he identifies as magic-users, Zaakara and Ruffio, who emerge through a glowing silver oval in the air: a rift.

Once the Pride Lords have been defeated, Declan and his brothers turn their attention to the future of Marquensas. Besides quickly building their defenses against the ascendant Church of the One, they see the need to begin Declan's education as the future ruler of the sole standing kingdom on Garn.

Hatu, with Hava and Donte, journeys to the home of the magicians. There, on a place known as Sorcerer's Isle, they meet two black-robed magicians, named Magnus and Pug.

A
DARKNESS
RETURNS

A DARKNESS RETURNING

In a distant place, a shadow stirred.

It twisted, creating a full circle around a raging center, then found its focus. It continued to turn, gaining momentum, pulsing steadily, a ponderous beat, soundless in a vacuum. At first a quiver, then a quake, it became more frequent, until suddenly it expanded, then contracted, as if a massive exhalation of soundless fury had sent vibrations out in every direction. Echoes of warning sped across the multiverse and awoke those attuned to such mystic energies. Beings of power found their attentions diverted, turning to look first this way, then that, to seek out the odd tickling at the edge of their awareness.

Magnus woke. He sat fully upright and took a deep breath. He let a moment pass in order to reach the necessary level of alertness as he grappled with what had awakened him.

A feeling of foreboding and a dark thought of something oddly familiar were draining away as if a dream was fleeing and would never be remembered.

He shook his head slightly and tilted it as if listening, but now all was still, save for the faint sounds of the night passing and the dawn approaching: a distant bird call, the sigh of a passing breeze and the faint sound of leaves rustling in the garden outside.

He stood and quickly donned his usual black robe, stepped into his sandals, and reached for his oaken staff, taking a moment to let the weight and balance of it settle into his palm—as familiar a feeling as his own arm—and opened the door.

Leaving his quarters, he moved past a large garden at the center of the building. It was a garden that had been tended with care, after years of neglect, and a place where he had been content to sit quietly and reflect on life. As he exited Villa Beata through one of its many large portals, he felt an urge to sit and ponder near a central fountain, but that desire was overridden by the need to find the source of the disquiet that had awoken him.

The villa was ancient and had been expanded several times, but Magnus lived in the quarters once occupied by his parents, a massive square of several rooms surrounding the garden. His sleeping quarters were attached to a large personal library he had inherited from his father. Other buildings sprawled around this one, and over the hill to the east lay even larger buildings, halls, libraries, as well as kitchens and workshops.

Though once it had been home to many, his father had allowed the villa to lie in ruin, for it was here where Magnus's mother and brother had died during a horrific battle. It had taken Magnus years after his father's death to begin repairing all that was lost.

Now, he glanced eastward and could see the sky above the hills begin to lighten. The hint of the coming day, a time of stillness and anticipation, followed swiftly by the false dawn, first light, then the sunrise. It was his favorite time of day, a trembling held breath, a calm, quiet space before the dawn unleashed the day's concerns and problems.

Magnus took a deep breath and savored the hint of sea salt on the morning air. Then he began to walk to the western rise, a spot where he often watched the sunsets.

The darkness of night slowly retreated, and Magnus closed his eyes and sent his mystic senses questing out, trying to isolate and identify the source of his early awakening.

He found nothing.

Something was sweeping toward them, Magnus knew. The morning brightened behind him as he peered into the retreating night's gloom. Something hovered just beyond his ability fully to perceive it, and it was threatening.

He opened his eyes and scanned the distant horizon. Nothing appeared to be out of the ordinary, and nothing echoed the foreboding that had awakened him. It seemed an otherwise normal morning on Sorcerer's Isle.

Hearing the scuff of sandals on the trail behind him, a familiar shuffling tread, he knew who approached. "Good morning, Phillip."

Magnus was the only one to call him by his given name. The man everyone else called Pug approached and replied, "Good morning, Magnus. You rose early."

"As did you." Magnus turned to look at his former apprentice, and asked, "Did you feel it?"

Pug's expression revealed that he understood the question. "Yes."

"Something is coming."

Pug just nodded.

"It's faint and distant," said Magnus, "but it is coming."

"There's something familiar about what woke me. It felt chill, then . . . like a dream barely remembered after sleep."

Magnus cocked his head, weighing what Pug said. He studied his former student's face and recognized an expression from years before he had met the boy Phillip. These subtle reminders of his father contrasted with Phillip's appearance. Taller by a few inches, a little thinner, hair a bit darker and less curly. Clean shaven, where Magnus's father had always worn a beard, but it suited him. Phillip's skin tanned less rapidly, and the sound of his voice was different, though the speech patterns were identical. Most vivid, though, were his eyes. The dark eyes were identical to his father's, as was the cocking of his head when deep in thought.

Conflicting feelings lingered within Magnus, even after all these years together. With absolute certainty Magnus knew that the essence of his father lived again within this man. Even so, he hesitated to fully embrace the idea that Phillip was his father reborn. He felt that if the gods had chosen to return Pug without the memories of his previous life, they had done that for a good reason.

Whatever sacrifice his father had made to end the final attack by the forces of the Void at Magician's End, the gods were not done with him. Not by any measure: of that, Magnus was sure.

As their faith avowed, once dead, a soul was judged and returned to the Wheel of Life owning the rewards or punishments they had earned during life. But this curious rebirth was alien to every tenet proclaimed by any of the major faiths of Midkemia. Even those who followed Lims-Kragma, the Death Goddess, rejected the possibility that Pug could have returned with any prior knowledge from his previous existence. One prelate of that order had even suggested that the returning Pug had earned a far higher level of consciousness than that of a mere human. So, Magnus had kept that faith and denied Phillip any hint of his previous life.

He had wrestled with this dilemma since the day he had first encountered Phillip on a beach near Crydee, Pug's original birthplace, and no matter how many times he returned to the question, he found no easy answers.

He glanced again at Phillip and saw him also contemplating the retreating night. Magnus forced his thoughts away from the imponderable and considered the man before him.

Apart from that lingering conflict, Magnus had grown fond of Phillip, had come to appreciate a unique mind and sharp wit that was different to his father's. This was why Magnus never used the name "Pug," to maintain as clear a delineation between his memory of his father and this man who now stood at his side. It just made things simpler.

After decades as Phillip's instructor and now as his colleague, Magnus had grown comfortable with the duality of the man who stood next to him. Most of the time Magnus focused on what he could deal with, what was before him in that moment, ignoring that complex nature. Whether it was the gods' cruel jest or a second chance, Magnus still did not know; either way, it could occasionally still be haunting.

After a long silence, Pug said, "We'll know soon enough."

Magnus looked questioningly at him.

Pug said, "Too soon. It's coming this way." His tone was certain. Magnus stared at him, and Pug turned to look at the white-haired magician. For a moment they stayed motionless, holding each other's gaze, then Pug added, "I just know."

"How?"

"It's . . . like a forgotten memory, hovering beyond reach until it fades completely." Pug gave a slight shrug, then added, "I don't know how else to put it, but I do know it is evil and that it is coming."

"On that we agree," Magnus said. "The days of a vast cadre of magicians working on behalf of the Conclave are long behind us. Still, we are not without resources, and we have learned from harsh lessons."

Pug could only nod.

"I'll send word to those far away from here, and to our allies at Stardock, to remain alert," Magnus said, "and also to those few priests still willing to speak with us. I'll ask them to let us know of anything troubling, no matter how trivial it may seem at the moment."

"No surprises," said Pug.

"No surprises," agreed Magnus.

"I'm curious. You often come here at sunset, but this is the first time I've seen you here at dawn."

"Is that a question?"

Pug laughed. "I'm curious as to what you hoped to see in the fading darkness."

"Nothing, really," answered Magnus. "I just sense sometimes that something is out there."

Pug looked over his shoulder. "The sun will rise soon, and we need to attend to the newcomers."

"Yes," agreed Magnus.

They turned and walked back toward the villa.

"That fellow, Hatushaly," Pug said at last. "What do you make of him?"

"We had barely an hour last night to chat, and most of what I sensed about those powers of his Ruffio spoke of, well . . ." Magnus looked at Pug and gave a quick shrug. "They are not clear to me."

"If what Ruffio told us is accurate, this fellow is a completely new sort of magic-user."

"He's not a sorcerer, nor a magician of any path. He just seems to do things without using a focus like a Lesser Path, or spells, like a Greater Path. He just . . . does things." Magnus sounded baffled.

Pug chuckled. "There is no magic, correct?"

Magnus almost stumbled. Pug's gaze was trained resolutely forward. Magnus moved to catch him up. "Where did you hear that?"

Pug stopped for a brief second, glanced once at Magnus, then kept on walking. "I don't remember."

Magnus fell silent and nothing further was said as they returned to a community that was rising with the morning's sun.

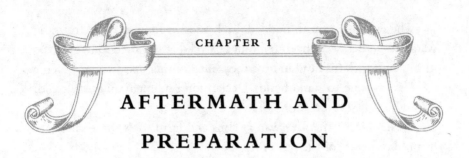

CHAPTER 1

AFTERMATH AND PREPARATION

Declan watched closely as a group of journeymen and apprentice smiths broke apart the clay around a steel blank, the first step in fashioning a sword. He glanced at Edvalt, who gave a slight nod.

A large group had gathered at the main forge of the newly finished foundry built by the king's order next to the armory at Castle Marquenet. It was large enough to accommodate a dozen teams of smiths forging swords and armor. Here worked the best smiths in the kingdom, those trusted with the secret of King's Steel, making the finest blades for the coming war.

The journeyman who had labored to fashion the clay furnace had been tending it for three days, and Declan could see that he was losing focus. Making this quality of steel was demanding, but a master smith needed to stay alert even when on the verge of exhaustion. Declan took down a large water bag which had been hung on a spike in a supporting timber and handed it to the journeyman. "Here, drink," he said.

The well-muscled man looked at Declan and for a moment it appeared as if he couldn't focus on the newly anointed Prince of Marquensas. Then he took the cap off the bag's nipple and drank deeply.

Loud enough for everyone in the room to hear, Declan said, "If you fail from the heat, fail from not caring for yourself first, you fail in this task." He pointed to the crumbling furnace, and the glowing hunk of metal now revealed within it, took a huge pair of tongs from an apprentice, and to the weary journeyman said, "I'll begin." Then, in a tone that was clearly a warning, he added, "And you'll finish."

The exhausted smith nodded, took another long swallow from the water sling, then went over to a water barrel that was used to temper the metal, and stuck his head in for a moment, coming up spewing water.

Edvalt came to stand beside Declan for a moment and softly said, "You think he can do this?"

"If he doesn't then it's wagon rims and farm tools somewhere far from Marquenet for the rest of his life."

"It's as much the heart of the man as any other measure," said Edvalt, clapping his former apprentice on the shoulder, then stepping away. "Still, wagon rims and farm tools put a roof over *your* head for years," he added with a chuckle.

Declan's mood shifted and he relaxed a little. "More than true . . ." He reflected for a moment on the years he had been raised by the old smith and his wife in the Covenant village of Oncon, then added softly, "But we need weapons makers and armorers right now." Being a village smith had been a far simpler life, Declan admitted to himself, never easy, but often pleasant.

A page entered and came to stand before him. "His majesty requires you to attend the council, highness."

Declan glanced at Edvalt, who was struggling to hold back laughter. "I'll be along in a moment." He sighed.

Once the page was gone, Edvalt took a deep breath and said, "One day I'll get used to that."

"Probably not," said Declan, turning his back on his former master, the man closer to being his father than any other. As he left the foundry, he added quietly, "I may never, either."

DECLAN FOLLOWED THE PAGE AND experienced another moment of annoyance. He did not need an escort to the king's meeting room, and certainly not a boy barely twelve years old, in a palace surrounded by an army.

Reaching the door off the throne room that opened onto what used to be Daylon's private study, which had been enlarged by knocking out a wall so he could hold council there, Declan was greeted by three older pages. One held a wash basin, another a clean tunic, and the third a washing cloth hung over one arm and a dry towel over the other.

"Balven," muttered Declan as he peeled off his dirty tunic, which was damp from perspiration and the water he had been splashing on his face to withstand the heat in the forge. When he finished, he noticed a great deal of soot had come away on the towel and judged that Balven had indeed fully grasped the task at hand: of turning an uneducated, somewhat rude, blacksmith into the future King of Marquensas.

Declan knocked on the door and it was opened almost immediately. Upon entering, Declan noticed the recently drawn map of this newly declared kingdom had been pinned to a large wooden board on the wall. He made his way to the chair that had been left empty for him, at King Daylon Dumarch's right hand.

Balven stood at his usual place, immediately behind and to the left of the king. As he sat down, Declan saw everyone he had expected to see: Collin, the king's master-at-arms, General Baldasar, and the former sea captain Kean who was acting as the supervisor of the king's new fleet. The only person he was surprised to see was Bernardo Delnocio, former episkopos of the Church of the One, now a fugitive receiving sanctuary from King Daylon.

Declan glanced at Balven, raising a questioning eyebrow, and his older half-brother gave an almost imperceptible shake of his head indicating that questions should wait.

King Daylon said, "Now that you're here, we can begin."

"Sorry—" Declan began, but an upraised hand from the king stopped him from saying more.

"We're facing many problems," began Daylon. Holding up a finger, he said, "First, we have a huge army scattered around the city, and we can pay them, but feeding them and housing them is an ongoing problem." He looked at General Baldasar.

The old soldier said, "Starting tomorrow, we need to promote some of our better men, and create a group of officers we can place in charge of companies and then send them off to start rebuilding our border garrisons."

"But we need to decide where our borders are," said the king.

Declan looked at his eldest brother and the king returned the questioning gaze, then said, "You came from the Covenant and lived in the far north of the barony, what do you think?"

Declan was taken aback for a moment, then turned in his chair, stood up, and crossed to stand before the map. Quickly he surveyed the marks made by others, then pointed to the bottom of the map, the south coast of what had been the Kingdom of Ilcomen, and said, "Start here. To the east of Oncon, the village where I was raised, is a tapered peninsula, opposite another on the north coast of Zindaros. It is the tightest passage in the Narrow Strait. We quickly build a tor with a supporting garrison on the coast above, equip it with a half-dozen ballistas, and no ship will be able to pass without permission. Add a good-sized garrison that can thwart any force trying to pass on the coast road."

Daylon's slight smile showed that he approved.

Declan continued, "Once you have the south secured, then put small companies in the temporary border posts bam ensas and the current border with Ilcomen. Moving eastward to pacify the western half of Ilcomen and extend the kingdom's border can wait. It's going to take a long time.

"Up in the north, Beran's Hill was the logical place to build a garrison, and you already have that underway." There was something in his tone that suggested he had more to say on that topic, but at some other time. "Everything in between is porous. Right now, it's easy for small groups to slip back and forth. But as we have most of the mercenaries in North Tembria in our service, we only have to worry about bandit companies. Once we get the temporary fortifications situated, then even the bandits will have trouble crossing into Marquensas."

"Until the Church sends soldiers this way," inserted Bernardo.

"Which is why we have to keep paying those mercenaries," said Balven.

"Or swear into service those who are able," added the king. "My preference is the latter, so we can turn fighters into soldiers. Raiding a village or storming a wall is fine for companies like the one—" He waved his hand and looked at Declan.

"Bogartis," Declan supplied.

"—yes, Bogartis commanded," finished the king. "But patrols, defending positions, and long periods of inactivity are not conducive to mercenaries remaining loyal."

"For my men," said Declan, referring to the company he took over from Bogartis, "loyalty is earned, not bought."

Daylon was about to say something but a pat on the shoulder from Balven halted him. Daylon and Declan's half-brother said, "We understand that, highness."

Declan winced at the title.

"We are now a new kingdom," said Daylon, obviously biting back some irritation at his youngest brother's comments, "but we are all that's left for people who do not wish to be ruled by the damned Church!"

Again, Balven put his hand on the king's shoulder, and again Daylon took his meaning. Lowering his voice, the king said, "Very well. We have anchored the north and southernmost corners of the kingdom, but what do we do in between?"

Declan sensed that an argument about mercenaries was not the topic at hand. He studied the map and said, "As you said, Majesty, we must resupply and refurbish the old border garrisons. Then," he added, pointing at the middle of the map, to the east of the old border, "we start moving companies into Ilcomen, and building new garrisons."

King Daylon said, "I'm of a mind that if we add two, maybe three, garrisons at key spots between our existing fortifications, we should have a fairly secure border."

Declan nodded. "Three, I think, should allow for good patrolling, as well as a quick response should any veer to the center." He tapped the marking denoting the massive forest to the east of the city. "Here, in the Darkwood. Build there first."

The king nodded. "I agree."

Declan glanced at Balven as he asked, "I assume we're prepared should someone appear claiming to be the next King of Ilcomen?"

Balven smiled, realizing that Declan had been paying attention in some earlier meetings. "Yes, we are prepared. The portion of Ilcomen we take will be a vassal province of Marquensas, whether some surviving third cousin of the former king likes it or not." He stared at the map, tapping his cheek with his right forefinger. "Once we've dealt with any threats from the Church, we can consider expanding eastward in a few more years."

Declan said, "To that end, we should be planning on a major Church force moving quickly to the Dangerous Passage, or close to it on this side. The mountains become the border between what is now our kingdom and whatever the Church of the One is calling Sandura and Ithrace."

"How big an army is the Church likely to deploy?" Daylon asked Bernardo.

"I can only speculate," answered the disgraced cleric. "There will be mercenaries, of course: all that are not already in your service will flock to the Church, as they have deep coffers. They will also have a large force of common soldiers, mostly garrison troops from Enast. However, at the heart of their forces are the soldiers of the Church Adamant.

"This is an army of thousands. They are all true believers, men who have pledged their lives to the cause of the Church of the One. This is an army that spent almost a century conquering and pacifying the entire continent of Enast. Their presence on North Tembria has barely been twenty years.

"I spent ten years in that army," said the grey-haired cleric.

Declan could barely imagine this older man of faith as a hardened soldier, but he kept silent.

Bernardo saw his reaction. "Ten years, a dozen battles, and countless skirmishes." He paused, and added, "I'll doff my cassock and show you my scars if you like."

Daylon, Balven, and the others also now had their gaze fixed on the shamed cleric. Bernardo said, "If you're a soldier in the Church Adamant there are only three ways out: desertion, death, and taking holy orders.

"Desertion?" Bernardo shrugged. "That's rare. Enast is large, but it is completely under the control of the Church. There are spies everywhere, and very few places to hide. Death is always a soldier's companion. But if promotion to a higher rank is not forthcoming, there are other ways to power." He paused, looking from face to face. "I was a street boy, a thief, and I had to fight to eat, so I had a different type of strength to that of most of those serving in the army. I saw lesser priests content to rest in small churches in little towns, eating too much, drinking too much, and molesting youngsters. Others were devout and tried to be the spiritual leader of their communities. All were unimportant men.

"But I saw that their masters were mostly fat priests and slow-witted prelates in fine raiment with servants and every need answered. Some gained station through family, and others with wealth, but some did it by being clever and ruthless. I judged if they could gain such authority, so could I." He leaned forward and pointed with a sweeping gesture at all in attendance. "Every man here has some ambition in his soul, else he would not be here."

Declan started to object, for he felt he had no ambition, but a quick hand movement from Balven kept him from speaking.

"Every soldier fights for something: for wealth, for women, for a king, or for belief"—he touched the emblem of the Church on his cassock—"but the soldiers at the core of the Church Adamant fight because they enjoy killing for the One.

"Now, to the business at hand," he said, sitting back in his chair.

Daylon took a long breath, then said to Declan, "You know the Covenant better than any man here. Anticipating much of what you've proposed, I've already dispatched a company of builders and guards to that peninsula." He gave Declan a wry smile, and said, "It's pleasant to see how much we think alike. You're right: it's the logical site for a choke point in the Narrows. I want you to travel with another company and see to an adequate fortification as soon as possible."

The king gave further instructions to the others and dismissed the meeting but motioned for Declan to remain.

When there were only the three brothers in the room, the king's voice showed he was near the end of his patience. "I need you here when I need you *here!* Not down at the forge."

Declan's eyes widened and he balled his fists. This argument had been going on since the return of Marquensas's army from the destruction of the Pride Lords.

Declan's voice rose. "We need weapons!"

"But we don't need you supervising every one that's made!" shouted the king.

Declan's face flushed. Balven moved to step between his brothers.

"We don't need another round of the same old argument." Turning to face Declan, he said, "I know a forge is where you are most comfortable, most sure of yourself, and you feel the need to oversee every detail. But surely the man who taught you everything you know is fit to supervise?"

Declan's expression revealed he had no answer to that question.

Balven turned to the king and said, "I know you wish our brother to rise to his place as the future king quickly, but you had a lifetime to learn how to rule. He's had less than two years and most of it has been spent fighting and surviving, not sitting next to you, learning how to be a king."

Balven's voice had now risen as well, but it was not irate; instead, it was more like a teacher scolding recalcitrant students in a cold, commanding tone.

Daylon's face drained of anger as he realized his brother was correct.

Balven took a deep breath and said, "We simply cannot afford to waste time fighting our own."

Daylon glanced at Declan, who after a long moment indicated his agreement. He turned back to Balven with a sigh. "You are again right."

Balven nodded. "The defeat of the Pride Lords was unexpectedly easier than anticipated, which brought us several advantages, but as Bernardo pointed out, we are now the only obstacle between the Church of the One and effective world domination."

"They're welcome to Nytanny, for all I care," said Declan. "Bodai's last message said it's total chaos there now that the Pride Lords have been overthrown."

The king's expression showed he understood Declan's feeling, for both men had lost their wives, and Daylon had also lost his children after the Pride Lords had unleashed a massive attack on the western coast of North Tembria.

Balven looked from brother to brother, then said, "And that would only give them a source for an even larger army to put in the field against us eventually."

Declan sighed, a visible and noisy admission that Balven spoke of the inevitable.

Daylon said, "You two review what's already been done, but I want you"—he pointed at Declan—"on your way to that point above the Narrows as the sun rises tomorrow. Take remounts so you don't kill your horses rushing there. Take four days, five if you must. The Church may not be moving against us anytime soon, but they will eventually, and I want our defenses in place. When you get there, make an assessment with the engineers already working on the defenses, and send a messenger detailing what more needs to be sent."

Balven added, "We need to be able to stop and search ships from the east, to ferret out spies as well as contraband."

"Do we care about contraband?" asked Declan seriously.

"No," Balven answered. "The more goods to trade here the better, for soldiers need to spend their gold, but it gives us a grand excuse to search for spies."

Declan gave him a pained smile. "So much to learn," he muttered.

Balven put his hand on his younger brother's shoulder. "You'll learn, and your instincts are good. You didn't need to study with our father to understand where we need to fortify."

Daylon nodded agreement. "Better that you puzzled it out yourself than we showed you, and you were entirely correct."

"Now, come along and let us see what sort of disaster of a mission we've contrived for you," Balven said. "Before you know it, it will be tomorrow."

As they left, Daylon turned and gazed out of the window of his conference room, overlooking the marshaling yard behind the keep. Horses were grazing in a corralled pasture, and new recruits were being instructed in the fundamentals of riding and caring for a mount. He sighed. He understood Declan's love of the forge, for he would give anything to be down there with the horses and young riders rather than being tasked with reviewing reports of food shortages, bandit raids, and every other hazard a king faced daily.

DECLAN SIGNALED A HALT. SIXTO turned and regarded the twenty riders in their company, who were coming to rest in orderly fashion. He gave them an approving glance and turned back to see what Declan was looking at.

Ahead lay their destination, an encampment of soldiers protecting a company of surveyors. As the king had instructed, Declan had taken a full five days to reach the site, and the mounts were all fresh. He knew that a galloper with remounts in tow could make the trip in just under three days if the need arose. He signaled for them to move forward.

As Declan came into sight, the lookout shouted and instantly the camp was abuzz with activity as twenty soldiers fell into line to salute the Prince of Marquensas. This was the part that Declan swore he would never get used to, but he understood the necessity of keeping up the leadership role that Balven had almost had to beat into him with a club. At least there were no drummers or trumpeters tooting a fanfare, he thought thankfully.

Still, Daylon put up with court foolery as a necessary part of the show, a point which Balven reminded him of constantly, so Declan waited until he reached the end of the line before dismounting. Looking at the men, he shouted, "Back to work!"

From behind he heard Sixto's laugh, and that triggered a laugh in return from Declan. Looking back toward his companion, now captain of his personal guard, he shook his head, and they exchanged a silent look of shared ironic humor.

"Let's get to this," said Declan as a soldier approached to take his mount. The newly minted Prince of Marquensas had finally gotten used to others tending his horses, even a company farrier tending their hooves, which was difficult for a skilled blacksmith, so he handed over the reins as his guards led their mounts away.

With a wave to Sixto, he communicated that he would consult with those building the emplacements, while his captain would oversee the unloading of fresh supplies and billeting the newly arrived company.

Reaching the top of the trail, Declan regarded the vista. The new fortification commanded the Narrow Strait below, and the road from the east equally. A garrison barracks was marked out to be constructed downhill toward the road, while a small plateau atop the peninsula, slightly below this hillock, would be a perfect site for ballistas capable of disabling a ship trying to sail past.

Declan was greeted by the king's master engineer, a man named Kendrick. He was old enough to be Declan's grandfather but had an echo of young power still in him, strength earned from years of masonry, carpentry, digging trenches, every task involved in building fortifications. Kendrick's face was like lined, tanned leather, starkly contrasting with hair, brows, and beard that were almost silver-white. In many ways, Declan thought he was much like Edvalt, and that earned him a great deal of instant respect from the prince.

"Got a good location, highness," said Kendrick.

Declan ignored the honorific and said, "Show me."

Kendrick pointed down to the area where other engineers were driving stakes into the ground and pulling rolls of heavy twine from post to post. "That spot is a ledge of hard stone. I think it goes back to there," he said as he turned and indicated where Sixto and the men were tending the horses.

Declan knew little about fortifications, but his time with Bogartis had gained him a military way of looking at things. That perspective was now part of him, and after a moment's study he asked, "How much digging?"

"With a hundred able men, a month, maybe less, but we have a lot of hill to clear away."

Declan knelt to get a different view and then turned slowly to study the approach from all angles. After another thoughtful moment, he asked, "Where do we put all that earth?"

Quickly, the discussion turned to repurposing the earth to build up breastworks in a semi-circle along which other defensive features would be possible, providing protection against assault from the road. In less than an hour Kendrick created a picture in Declan's imagination of a stout battlement featuring a sheltered emplacement of stone, topped by a platform large enough to mount three large ballistas. He pointed out the lines of rope indicating the barracks. He planned a kitchen and storage, and whatever else he could wedge into the space.

"So, if someone brought in siege equipment along the road, the sloping ground here would protect the emplacements?"

"Good eye," said Kendrick in an approving tone. "Ballista shafts would bury themselves in ten, twelve feet of soil, perhaps more, and it will be a solid embankment once we sod it to hold the earth firm. Get some tall grass, which will make climbing the slope that much more difficult. It's slippery stuff but has a deep root structure, so it binds the ground hard, so most catapult stones will bounce back or over into the Narrows. Stays wet in this climate, too, so no one can fire it to burn us out."

"Good design," said Declan and he stood and looked down at a large table before a tent, where two younger engineers worked on paper. "What are they about?"

"Mathematics," said Kendrick. "They will give us numbers on where we need to build things, and how far we can throw boulders and the rest. When I was their age we did this by guesswork, but the king learned from the King of Ithrace that guessing is not good enough. Give those boys enough time and they could put a boulder into an ale mug half a mile away."

"Impressive," said Declan. "I'll see to my men then we'll get to what you need to do the work."

"I have a list of things I'll go over with you later, highness."

Declan nodded and started walking toward his men. Reaching Sixto's side, he saw the horses were now picketed with nosebags and men were fetching water from a creek they had crossed a quarter mile down the road. A few were grooming their mounts, and all the saddles and blankets were spread in the late day's sun to dry out.

"Everything looks in order," Declan said.

"What now?" asked Sixto.

"Set up a camp. The masons are coming up with plans, and as soon as they know what we need here, they'll give me a list, and we'll send a rider back to the king, and . . ."

"Wait?" said Sixto with a smile.

"Well, we all could use a bit of rest, but in a day or two we should have some deliveries, the basic equipment, so there will be ample work for us all."

Sixto kept a straight face and asked, "Even the prince?"

Declan threw a playful blow at his friend's shoulder. "Especially this prince. I can't sit around doing nothing. I almost went mad recovering from that injury I had when we first met."

"Almost?" Sixto asked, and then quickly dodged back to avoid another punch on the arm.

Declan laughed. "I'd better get my tent up."

Sixto turned to walk with him as they moved down the narrow road to where the men were setting up camp. Declan paused for a moment when he saw that his own tent had been erected first, and that it was about four times the size of the others, which had mats for two men per tent. He looked at Sixto and blurted out, "What?"

"Balven," said Sixto. "I'm instructed to let the men do things for you, because, well, you are the prince."

Declan was silent for a long moment then said, "I may never get used to this." With an exhalation that was almost a snort of derision, he resumed walking to his tent. "What's next," he muttered, "a private mess kitchen?"

Sixto laughed. "No, just a camp kit, and two of the lads will cook, but Balven did say that you might start dining in private."

"Dining?" Declan echoed with eyes wide and eyebrows raised. "We've eaten monkey stew with our fingers, remember?"

Sixto slowly shook his head. "How could I ever forget?"

Reaching what Declan could only think of as a pavilion, rather than a mere tent, Sixto went ahead and pulled aside a large flap, allowing Declan to step through first. A sturdy wooden pallet with a thick mattress and blankets rested against the far wall, with a compact brazier near it, should the night turn cold. Next to it sat a small writing table with paper, quill, and ink pot. A pair of lanterns hung from hooks at opposite corners.

Declan regarded the bed with a skeptical look. He was used to sleeping on the ground or, over the years, a bed fashioned from a narrow wooden cot, a thin mattress, and whatever blankets might be about.

"Want me to light those?" asked Sixto.

"No, but what is all this?" Declan pointed to the table.

"I think this means Lord Balven expects you to send him reports."

"My writing is a dog's breakfast," said Declan.

"I can see if one of the lads has skills, or we can send to the city for a scribe."

Declan shook his head and said, "Nothing learned if not practiced, right?"

"Right," said Sixto as Declan sat behind the desk on a small camp chair.

"I'll send a note telling Balven we've arrived without trouble."

Sixto smiled. "Eat after?"

"Yes," said Declan. "Whatever's in the pot will do." Before Sixto could ask, Declan said, "I'll come to the mess tent, not here."

Sixto said, "I'll meet you there." As he pushed aside the tent flap, he turned and said, "Smart, sending that note to Balven."

"Why?" Declan asked.

"If he can't read it, he'll send a scribe without you asking." He laughed and ducked out quickly before Declan could throw something at him.

Declan sat back with a slight grunt, which quickly turned into a chuckle as he realized Sixto was correct.

HALF AN HOUR LATER, DECLAN entered the mess tent, which was almost twice the size of his pavilion, with two long tables with enough space between the ends for a man to walk between, and long benches on each side. Sixto was at the end of the farthest table and Declan moved to sit across from him. A boy no older than ten or eleven years of age, known to the soldiers as a "lick fingers" and to the sailors as a "galley swab," approached and said, "Highness?"

Declan forced himself not to wince, as he knew he had to get used to formal address from all but his closest friends. "What's for the late meal?" he asked.

"A fish stew, highness. It should be ready soon."

"Bring me an ale," he said, glancing at Sixto's mug, and added, "And him another."

"Finish the report?" asked Sixto.

"Yes, so what now?"

"We have messengers, ready at any time, so send it."

"Then what?"

"You're the prince, so be in command," said Sixto. Then in a dry tone he added, "Highness."

Declan closed his eyes. "Is there any reason I can't have you flogged?"

"None that I can think of," said Sixto as the boy returned with the two filled mugs.

"Stew will be ready soon, highness. We have some fresh bread, too."

"Bring some," said Declan suddenly aware he hadn't had decent food since leaving Marquenet.

"Butter?" asked the boy.

Declan's eyes widened. "We have butter?"

"A fresh tub. A dairy farmer came by yesterday on the way to the city and Master Kendrick bought it from him."

"By all means, bring us a pot."

Quickly, the boy returned with a wooden platter bearing a hot loaf of bread and a small pot of butter, along with a couple of knives. Declan ripped off a hunk of bread and picked up a knife, slathered the bread, and bit off a mouthful; he chewed for a moment and swallowed.

"Slowly," said Sixto with a chuckle. "I don't want to have to write to your brother and tell him you choked to death in the mess."

Declan pointed the knife at Sixto and said, "Tell me you wouldn't have killed for this loaf when we were trapped down in the Wound?"

Sixto finished his first bite then said, "Well, Oscar maybe."

Declan laughed. Of the men who had escaped from Garn's Wound with Declan and Sixto, Oscar was always complaining about something, no matter what. "I actually got used to the drone of his grumbles."

"Perhaps," conceded Sixto. "We did leave some good men behind us."

"That we did," agreed Declan, tearing off another hunk of bread. As he chewed, he found himself thinking of when he had returned to North Tembria and discovered his brother had assumed the title of king, and the preparations for the attack on the Pride Lords.

Sixto said, "You must have butter at the king's table."

Declan nodded, his mouth full. He swallowed and said, "Honey as well for the morning meal, but eating at the king's table sours me, so this tastes like the first real butter I've had since we got back."

Sixto's chuckle was a mix of humor and concern. "Like it or not, one day that's where you'll always be eating."

Declan rolled his eyes. He thought about all the changes in his life since he had left Oncon, and what rebuilding Marquensas entailed, and of the people still alive after the war. His expression became wistful.

"What?" asked Sixto, noting the change.

"Just remembering things, then Hava crossed my mind. She and Hatu changed greatly from when I first knew them."

"The innkeeper and his wife?" said Sixto.

"I think that's an act," said Declan. "From what I've learned of them since we got back, before they left, I think they're far more than they seemed. When I first met them, they were, as you said, an inn-keeper and his wife. She became the best raider captain on the ocean by all reports, and he . . ." He paused. ". . . I'm not sure, but there are times I could feel Hatu, even when he was not around. It's a mystery. But they are definitely more than they seem."

"That friend of theirs, Donte. He was quite the joker," Sixto said. "All very odd, them leaving with those strangers through that glowing thing."

"The rift," supplied Declan.

"A breach into another world," said Sixto. "If I hadn't seen them vanish through it, I'd count the tale a fable."

Declan was silent for a moment as the boy returned with two bowls of fish chowder and large spoons. After the boy set them down and departed, Declan said, "I wonder what that other world is like. I wonder how they are doing there."

CHAPTER 2

UNEXPECTED

Pug tapped Magnus on the shoulder.

They had been enjoying another sunrise together. It was becoming a habit when they wished to discuss something alone. Magnus turned and saw the three newcomers were approaching from the bottom of the bluff, accompanied by Ruffio.

Pug said, "They seem to be dealing with this change well."

Magnus smiled ruefully. "We'll see. They were a bit overwhelmed: it was late when they arrived, and they were exhausted after our chat, and that Donte fellow was obviously intoxicated. For the last few days they've been dealing with the real shock to their view of how things are."

Pug nodded. "That must have been amusing."

"Not," said Magnus with a hint of disapproval. "This world is different enough from theirs that we had no idea of how they'd react. There are no other natural sentient beings on Garn, just humans, for one example. For another, there's never been a single verified interaction with a god or other celestial being, demon, or any other being from another realm. I know you've been busy since they arrived, but you should spend time with them. They are remarkable young people, especially Hatushaly. He's why they're here; the one thing both worlds have in common is the thing in the pit."

Pug turned to look at his former teacher. Magnus was tall, a dignified-looking man with white hair flowing to his shoulders. The years had left little evidence of their passing. Pug knew Magnus to be centuries old, yet he appeared to be a man of early middle years, perhaps forty or so. Pug had learned years before that the powers they shared also prolonged life. Pug had been Magnus's pupil for more than fifty years, yet he did not even look fifty years old.

Over that half-century, Pug had come to think of Magnus as more than his master. There was a bond between them Pug didn't fully understand, a level of trust colored by a sense of the familiar that had existed from the first moment they met. Pug had been gathering shellfish on the rock-strewn beach near the town of Crydee when he was a boy. Magnus had been a passing stranger, yet in an instant, Pug had known implicitly that he was someone to trust.

Pug shrugged off that moment of reverie and turned his attention to the matter at hand.

Hava, Hatushaly, Donte, and Ruffio reached the top of the knoll. Hava wore a blue tunic long enough to serve as a dress and simple sandals. Pug decided the color suited her.

Hatushaly and Donte wore tunics, trousers, and boots. They all smiled in greeting.

"You are rested, I trust?" asked Magnus.

"Nice bed," said Hava, smiling at Hatushaly.

Donte laughed. "These buildings are unfamiliar to me, but very nice. Ruffio has been a good . . . minder?" The last was said with a hint of irony. "He gave us some history and explained how you rebuilt all this." He gestured back toward the villa.

Magnus said, "They fell on hard times years ago, and . . ." He paused, then added, "That story can wait for another time. Suffice it to say one of our goals is to rebuild everything that was once lost and add more."

"You leave a lot of very nice things lying around," Donte opined.

Hatu shot him a dark glance, knowing Donte's proclivities toward appropriating whatever took his fancy. He then looked at Magnus and Pug. "I'm a little confused. Nathan—" Hatu stopped. He was still trying to absorb how Nathan, his previous teacher, had simply turned into glowing particles and vanished before his eyes. He began again: "Nathan said I needed to come here to master my powers, and I'm obviously willing or I wouldn't be here. But while the villa seems like a nice enough place . . ."

"You expected more," finished Magnus.

"As dilapidated as the library at the Sanctuary was before we started cleaning it up, it was a massive library compared with that little room of books you have at the villa."

Pug laughed. "We have other buildings." With a slight lift of his chin, he said, "You haven't seen them all. On the other side of the big hill behind the villa, we have a library, too, and a few other . . . buildings."

Donte said, "I saw them. I took a stroll the second night we were here, before I went to sleep, over that rise and past the other buildings. I enjoyed it, so I did it again last night and went farther. On the other side of the island, I saw that castle up on the point, with those weird blue lights. What is that?"

Again, Pug laughed. "I'll show you soon. It's abandoned now, but the blue lights keep raiders, pirates, and treasure-seekers away. There's a long story about that."

"Speaking of pirates," said Hava. "I told Ruffio and Zaakara I need a ship if I'm going to hunt pirates down. Your people have been kind and we've talked about a lot, but nothing about ships. Do I have to steal one?"

This time Magnus laughed. "No, I think not. We have many resources. Perhaps after supper tonight we can discuss what sailing the Bitter Sea is like, and what sort of business you might consider." He looked from face to face. "All in good time, my friends."

"For the time being, consider this your home."

To Hatu he added, "Now that you've acclimatized yourselves, we can start serious work. This is where you will be studying, training, and even teaching. For how long we shall see. The short of it is we have never encountered anyone with your abilities. Trust me when I say, after many years of meeting magic-users of every description, you are unique."

Hatushaly said, "I don't understand."

Magnus took a breath and said, "We want the same thing, Hatu." He put his hand on Hatu's shoulder. "We want to understand what you're capable of, how to help you master your skills, and keep you from harming yourself or others."

Hatu looked puzzled. "That's what Nathan kept saying."

Pug moved to stand next to Magnus. "From one of Nathan's tales, you burned a ship down to the waterline without meaning to?"

"Something like that," Hatu admitted. "It was the event that . . . changed my mind about a lot of things. I can tell you the story."

"Later," said Magnus. "First there is something we must show you." He looked at Hava and Donte. "Alone, I'm sorry to say."

Donte's expression was a mask of indifference, but Hava's brow furrowed.

"I don't keep secrets from my wife," Hatu said.

"Very well," Magnus said. "If you wanted to share what we'll show you next, we have no way of stopping it." He glanced at Donte, then asked Hatu, "How about your friend?"

Hatu laughed. "Him? I need to keep a lot of secrets from him!"

Donte looked caught halfway between amusement and annoyance, then finally just shrugged broadly and grinned. "Ya, probably a good idea."

Ruffio said, "I'll show Donte the castle then."

Donte smiled, looking amenable to that.

"Follow us, please," said Magnus, turning and walking farther down the hill. Pug fell into step with him, and Hava and Hatu followed.

They turned off the path leading back to the villa and, after a short walk, approached a lovely lake. Magnus led Hava and Hatu along the right-hand shore toward a rising bluff. When they reached the face of the bluff, they saw a cave was hidden by a twist of the rock face, making it difficult to see the concealing crease in the rocks.

Magnus took a large torch out of an iron sconce bolted to the stone wall at the entrance. As Pug began to incant, Hatu flicked a finger at the torch and flames began to dance along the surface, causing Magnus to flinch as he thrust the torch away. Pug's eyes widened and he laughed.

Magnus also began to chuckle and said, "Surprising, but thank you."

"Sorry," said Hatu. "I didn't mean to startle you."

"Show off," said Hava, playfully elbowing Hatu in the ribs.

They entered a short tunnel which then widened into a cave. Benches had been carved out of the stone walls in a circle with a second and third ring above. A good two dozen people could sit easily here without crowding, Hatushaly judged.

"We rarely fill the seats, but events happened long ago that made us enlarge this meeting place. And what caused that meeting bears upon why you are here today," said Magnus. With a wave of his hand, he indicated they should sit.

Hava and Hatu sat down, Pug taking a seat next to Hatu. Magnus faced them and said, "We are more than willing, eager even, to help you explore your abilities, and learn to control them, Hatushaly. In turn, we hope by aiding your mastery of your talents to learn more about the arts we practice. So, consider our willingness and hospitality as somewhat self-serving, so you don't mistakenly credit us with too much altruism. You learn from us, and we learn from you."

Hatu smiled and Hava's expression held a slight hint of humor and a bit of doubt.

"I've been meaning to ask you something," Hava said.

"Yes?" replied Magnus.

"How is it we understand each other?" she asked. "On Garn there's a trading tongue, but each nation has its own language."

Hatu said, "They used a trick."

Pug laughed. "I had a friend once who said, 'There is no magic, only tricks.'"

Magnus cast a sharp look at his former apprentice, then said, "It's as your husband said. We have what we call a spell that allows us to understand one another. More, it also teaches you the language you're hearing so that eventually you will be able to understand without any 'tricks.'"

Hava inclined her head. "Very useful."

"We think so," offered Pug. "We have a common trading language from the Far Coast to the distant Kingdom of Roldem, which we call the Common Tongue, or simply Common, but even after centuries, there are a lot of local languages from—"

Magnus held up his hand, cutting him off. "History lessons can wait."

Pug's brow furrowed, and he fell silent, but his expression darkened.

"What I have to say is relatively simple at first, but it requires some thought," Magnus said.

"Which is?" asked Hatu.

"We will do what we can to help you master your powers and skills, but there will be a point, a point you can anticipate from what you saw on your home world in—" He glanced at Pug.

"In Garn's Wound," supplied Pug.

"Your training will go to a certain point, but beyond that point you must either agree to certain conditions or end your training."

"What are those conditions?" Hava asked before Hatu could speak.

"This island is many things," said Magnus. "From what I've heard in some ways it's a bit like your Sanctuary back on Garn. We have a community here which is small but productive, as over the years we've had to become more self-reliant. There's a small cluster of houses on the northwest shore where a group of fishing families provide catches for the island regularly, and an area on the northeast hills given over to terraced vegetable farming. There's a small grove of fruit trees, as well as berry bushes scattered around. Near the fishing village we have a small harbor—well hidden by our arts from passersby—where our traders arrive with goods we buy from various neighbors, mostly with the Free Cities and then the Kingdom."

"What kingdom?" asked Hatu.

Pug laughed.

"The Kingdom of the Isles," said Magnus. "Most people just call it the Kingdom." Hava seemed on the verge of a question, but Magnus held up his hand. "As I said, history can wait, and you'll have ample time to ask more questions and learn. I need to focus on one thing and then you'll be free to roam the island, ask questions, and discuss what I am about to tell you."

Hava and Hatu exchanged a quick glance, then nodded.

With a wave of his hand, Magnus said, "We who meet here are called the Conclave of Shadows. How we came to be is another part of history that can wait, but what we do is fundamental to the choice that awaits you soon.

"Ruffio and Zaakara have spoken to me about your ability for far-seeing thought, and you witnessing an . . . entity, let's say, in a pit on your world, and your ability to manipulate the strands of time that confine it." He paused, and then added, "A prodigious feat by any measure."

Pug smiled. "That is an understatement. I doubt there's anyone on Midkemia capable of such an act."

Hatu threw Pug a questioning look but said nothing.

Hava began to look impatient, but before she could speak, Magnus continued, "There will be a point in your training when we will be exploring issues that bear upon the work of the Conclave. At which point you are free to leave, but should you remain you have to join us, to serve—"

"He'll join," interrupted Hava.

Both Hatu and Magnus looked at her in surprise, while Pug seemed delighted by her.

"What?" asked Hatu. "Why—"

Before he could continue, she glanced at Magnus, then at her husband, and said, "You know how you are. You become impossible if you know there is something out there you need to know but can't. You were horrible as a child when the masters or preceptors wouldn't answer your questions." She looked at Magnus. "You have no idea. The tantrums, the fights—just ridiculous. He'll do it as long as there are things he wants to learn."

Hatu was rendered speechless by Hava's interruption, but after a silent moment he looked at Magnus and said, "She's right."

Pug looked amused.

"Well, let's agree to give you tonight to talk it over and if you feel ready to commit to the Conclave tomorrow, we'll accept that as a . . . provisional agreement." Magnus's expression turned a bit more serious. "Your potential is unprecedented, Hatu. You will be welcomed into our ranks. As the name suggests, this is more a meeting place than a true organization, but we are like-minded and committed to saving the world."

"Two worlds," Pug added quietly.

"Who's in charge?" asked Hava.

Pug began to laugh, but a dark glance from Magnus cut that short, though it looked as if he was struggling to keep his hilarity under control.

"In charge?" asked Magnus.

Hava shook her head as if she was talking to an idiot. "Every time something has to be decided, you don't get everyone in this conclave together and argue, right?"

Magnus could only nod.

"So, who is in charge of the everyday things?"

At last, Magnus said, "When you put it that way, I guess I am."

"Good," said Hava. "Now we're getting somewhere. So, if Hatu says he's going to stay, and you agree, then it's decided."

Magnus looked at Hatu, whose eyes widened. He held up his hands in a gesture of surrender.

Ruffio reached the meeting area and paused for a moment.

Magnus looked at him and said, "Lose your guest?"

"He's in the kitchen," Ruffio answered. "He said the trek up to the castle and back made him hungry."

"He's always hungry," said Hatu.

"Why he's not fat is anyone's guess," said Hava.

Magnus slowly shook his head, as if conceding this meeting was at an end. "I'll give you two tonight to talk it over more, then if tomorrow you still feel the same way . . ." He left that hanging. After taking a breath, he said, "Look, you might do well to go exploring a little. Pug, start with the library, and if you lose Hatushaly there, escort Hava down to the landing and talk ships."

Pug nodded with a broad smile and motioned for them to follow. When he neared the cave mouth, he said, "Excuse me for a moment, I forgot something."

Pug returned to where Magnus and Ruffio were still talking and finally couldn't restrain himself and burst out laughing. Both men looked at him, and Magnus said, "What?"

"I'm sorry," said Pug, "but I have to say, she reminds me so much of your mother it's painfully funny." He took a moment to let his mirth subside, then turned and departed.

Magnus stood silently, his face an expressionless mask.

Finally, Ruffio said, "Your mother—"

"Died before Phillip was born," said Magnus quietly.

"How . . . ?"

"He's starting to remember."

HAVA LOOKED DOWN UPON THE village from a bluff. Hatu was en-sconced in the massive library with Magnus, while Pug was escorting her around the island. She studied the buildings below and asked Pug, "How many families?"

"About thirty, maybe a few more," answered the magician. He indicated a series of net-drying racks and a long quay, with a large field of stones for the backfill.

"You built that for the fishermen?" she said, indicating the long structure.

"Not personally," said Pug. "It started before I was born. There was a very big . . . war, I guess you could say. Anyway, the conflict changed just about everything in this part of the world and a lot beyond, so this island had to become more self-sufficient and less dependent on trade."

Hava said, "Where are the ships?"

"On the other side of this bluff," Pug replied, pointing to a head-land to their right. He led her across the small promontory, stopping above a narrow pathway to another cove. There was a small set of buildings overlooking a bay. A long pier jutted straight out of a large dock for smaller boats.

Hava recognized what the configuration meant. "You don't get a lot of trade here." It wasn't a question.

Pug regarded her for a moment and said, "You're right. When I first arrived here, I was told that ships were kept away on purpose, to keep our existence secret from the outside world, from long before I was born, in fact."

Hava nodded, thinking of her home nation, Coaltachin, the King-dom of the Night, and how an elaborate fantasy had been concocted to keep the true location and identity of the Council of Masters shrouded. "I understand completely."

Pug said, "No doubt you do. Can I ask one thing? Were you serious about being a pirate?"

She chuckled. "In a way. It's probably more correct to say I was a raider." As they walked slowly across the broad meadow atop the cliff, she explained briefly about the war with the Pride Lords, how she had freed herself and the other captives. "When I got the *Queen of Storms*, I started hitting the Pride Lords' shipping to free other slaves and to get back as much stolen booty as I could. So, to the Pride Lords I was a pirate."

"Are you are looking to be a pirate-hunter now?"

Hava stopped, crossed her arms, and stared out at the ocean. "I love two things: my husband and captaining a ship. Coming here has made me wonder if I must give up one for the other. I would prefer to keep both."

Pug considered a moment, then smiled. "I think that is something we can arrange. We may not need a pirate, but someone who can knock them back a little would be welcome. So, pirate-hunter it is.

"There's an undeclared war of sorts going on with different powers in the Bitter Sea, and while we try to stay out of those struggles, Sorcerer's Isle does a lot of trade with the Free Cities and the Kingdom of the Isles. We need certain things we can't grow or build here. So, we do lose ships to raiders from Queg, Durbin, and elsewhere. Our magic can protect our shipments, but if we are to remain undiscovered we hesitate to intervene anywhere not close to our shore. So, having an agent who can fend off the raiders and protect our shipping would be welcome."

Hava smiled, looking a bit more reassured.

"Come," said Pug, "and we'll go down to see about ships. So when you chat with Magnus you'll have a better notion of what we can do for you." He indicated a track that arched around the bluff. As they walked, he continued, "Others can describe how it was before the cataclysm that changed everything, but the population of this island was smaller and the influence of those who lived here further reaching. After the cataclysm—"

"What was that cataclysm?" interrupted Hava.

Pug was silent for a few moments, then said, "I think you'll need to speak with Ruffio, Magnus, or one of the older magicians who lived through it to fully appreciate what a history-changing event it was. What I know is there was an evil so powerful that defeating it changed the face of this world. An unprecedented alliance of warriors from all nations, as well as most magicians and priests, came together to fight that battle. Half the magic-users on Midkemia, magicians of every type—sorcerers, powerful priests of every order—half of them perished in the fight, and of those remaining, half were rendered power-less, crippled for life, or mad. Countless warriors met a bloody end."

"Sounds horrible beyond belief. Our war with the Pride Lords left us devastated, but what you describe . . ." Hava let the thought fall away.

"I've heard stories all my life," said Pug, "and occasionally I've even imagined what it was like—vivid images almost as if I was there—but still . . ." He also let his thought go unfinished, then added, "An entire range of mountains sank into the ground, creating a vast valley, rivers changed their courses, a massive forest sprang into existence between the Kingdom and the Empire of Great Kesh . . . and more."

Hava said, "I lived through the ravaging of a large town, and city, but the scale you describe . . . ? I can't imagine it."

"History lessons," said Pug, his smile returning. "Time for that later."

Hava said, "Yes, I will have to hear more, but for the time being, I need to find a ship." She smiled and pointed to where the trail ended at the far end of the bluff above the cove and a long trail started down toward the beach below. "And that looks like a long hike."

Pug stopped and said, "I know a quicker way down."

Hava halted, turned, and, half-laughing, said, "What? Jump?"

Pug smiled and said, "Not quite." He reached out to put his hand on Hava's arm, and suddenly they stood upon the sand facing the build-ings on warehouses behind the long quay.

Hava blinked, her eyes widening. "What?" she exclaimed.

"It's a trick I learned a while ago," he said. Releasing her arm, he added, "I can transport myself to any place I can see or remember clearly."

Taking a deep breath and composing herself, Hava asked, "Can all you magicians do that?"

"Some can, and some can't," he replied. "It's something we've studied."

Hava appeared to do a bit of self-inventory, shifting her weight slightly between her left foot and her right, and after another second, she looked around, took a breath, and said, "Next time, no surprise, please."

Pug laughed. "Easier to show you than try to explain."

"As we are both undamaged, I concede you are correct, but again, next time a brief warning."

"Come along," he said, "let's see about ships."

Hava fell in beside him, still slightly shaken. Hearing about magic and experiencing it were two different things.

Moving between two warehouses, she discovered a relatively quiet waterfront. Used as she was to the thriving ports in the islands surrounding Coaltachin, as well as the bigger ports in North Tembria, this small landing site was positively comatose. Two workers carried a couple of bags from a warehouse to a waiting cart pulled by a single mule, but otherwise it was a still tableau.

"The boatyard is down there," said Pug, pointing to the northern edge of the cove.

As they walked, Hava surveyed the docks and asked, "Are there any other ports on this island?"

"None suitable for a ship with a deep keel, if that's what you need," he replied.

"Not cargo-carrier deep, but a swift-below-the-waterline craft needs a fairly deep keel, as she'll carry a lot of sail. So, not shallow draft either."

Pug nodded that he understood. "There are a couple of relatively shallow coves not too far from here, where small boats can beach, but this is where we offload cargo. The southern coast is mostly cliffs and rocks, with only a single anchorage near the old castle."

She caught sight of a boat cradle in the distance, with a couple of men apparently working on a longboat held within it. "Why don't you just magic up what you need?"

Pug laughed. "Transporting you or a crate of equal weight is something some of us can manage easily, but we'd rather spend our time on other matters. We keep this small port hidden from passing ships. To a strange vessel, this place looks like a rock cliff. And we liked to keep those who sell to us in the dark about who is buying."

Hava gave him a questioning look.

"Someone got the idea ages ago that magicians all have mountains of gold secreted away," he said, half-joking.

Hava laughed. "I have a few stories from when I was a girl about thieves who came to a messy end looking for treasure troves."

"Tried to rob a dragon?" said Pug with a chuckle.

"Not quite, given there are no such things as dragons. I'm talking about rich merchants—"

Pug interrupted. "Ah, here, dragons are real."

Hava stopped. Wide-eyed, she grabbed Pug's arm and said, "You're joking, right?"

"Not joking," he replied. "Magnus mentioned there were some important differences between this world and yours."

"I'll say," she said quietly. "Dragons . . ." She left the word hanging.

"You'll have many questions, and we'll attempt to answer them as best we can, but for now, let's see what we can do about a ship for you."

Hava was still trying to grasp the significance of dragons being real here when they reached the northwest end of the dock and found four men working on a new longboat. Hava instantly recognized this was a fine example of the boatbuilder's craft and nodded in appreciation.

"Zoilus!" Pug said loudly enough to be heard above the hammering.

The oldest man of the four turned and smiled. He had very dark skin, which caused his smile at seeing Pug to look brighter than most. His face was lined by years of hard work, and his dark hair was cropped close to his head and spotted with grey. Otherwise, he was a powerful-looking individual who moved with the fluidity of a much younger man.

"Pug," he said as he came to stand before the magician and Hava. "I haven't seen you for a while."

"Off doing this and that," said Pug cheerfully. "I want you to meet Hava."

"Ah," said Zoilus, extending his hand.

Hava took it and endured a strong grip that pumped her arm vigor-ously for a moment.

"Another otherworlder. At least you fetched the pretty one."

Pug laughed.

Hava ignored the flattery and stepped past the boatbuilder to inspect the vessel. The three workers halted hammering and Zoilus shouted, "Did anyone tell you to stop?"

The three men immediately got back to tapping hard on the wood with big wooden mallets.

Hava leaned over and inspected the inside of the boat. "Tongue-and-groove frame?" she asked.

"Yes, lapstrake hull planks," Zoilus replied, his expression reveal-ing a little surprise. "Nails get rusty. You know boats?"

"As well as some; better than most," she responded.

Zoilus grinned broadly. "Cuts down the time to swell the wood for fitting. Once the wood swells, you need a sledge to dislocate the fittings. It's almost like a single frame, and that cuts down on the time needed to make more adjustments."

Hava looked at Pug and said, "He's building this to last."

"Need a boat?" asked the master builder.

"A ship. I need a ship," she replied.

"I'm no shipbuilder," Zoilus said, "but I knew a few before landing here."

"Who's the best?" asked Hava.

Without hesitation, he said, "Samuel Benoit, in Port Vykor. When he's not overseeing ships for the Kingdom, he's building the best rough-water freighters on the Bitter Sea." He studied Hava's reaction, then said, "But his ships cost a fortune. What type do you need?"

"My last ship was a nimble raider. Two masts, jib and spanker, tight-est turns for length I've ever seen. Faster than any other in a following wind, and able to sail close to a headwind. I'll want something like her."

Zoilus laughed without restraint. "A raider?" he finally said, ignor-ing Hava's scowl. "What for, piracy?"

"That used to be my trade," Hava said flatly, and Zoilus's laughter faded. She turned to Pug. "Your friend Zaakara said something before I came here, that you have too damned many pirates around here."

"That's the truth," said Zoilus before Pug could reply. "I had to wait almost two years for the timber for this one boat and two others like it, just because my first two shipments got taken by raiders. We have Quegan privateers from that miserable little 'empire' of an island, some freebooters working for various trading companies out of the Free Cities with 'letters of marque' signed by this or that magistrate, and nests of the worst sort sailing out of Durbin, Ranom, and Limeth down along the coast south of here."

She looked at Pug. "He waited two years? Yes, you need a pirate-hunter. Who better to catch pirates than a pirate?" she asked seriously. She glanced at Zoilus.

Zoilus was silent a long moment, and then said, "I'm too old and seen too many things to doubt that, so I'll simply say, you'll need a good ship, and Samuel builds the best, but the prices will be dear."

She glanced at Pug, who gave a slight shrug as if saying that wasn't an issue.

"So, I need to get to this Port Vykor." She looked again at Pug, this time with a questioning expression.

"I can get you there."

"But it will take a year or more to build a swift ship," said Zoilus.

Hava considered that, then said, "I can keep busy while I wait. So, where is the best place to go steal a pirate's ship?" Her expression was only half serious.

Pug suggested they return to the villa. After they were out of the workers' hearing, he said, "It's clear that Hatushaly is vitally needed to help us understand many things. His magic is unique, and he has experiences with things that are alarmingly familiar to us on Midkemia. But you are just as important to him and to us, so if you really need a ship, we will arrange to get you one."

She continued walking in silence for a few minutes as she considered this. Finally, she said, "I can wait a year if I must, but I may have to borrow a boat just to get out on the water. As I said, my husband *and* the sea, not my husband *or* the sea."

"I think I understand," Pug replied. He appeared lost in reflection for a moment.

"Good," she replied. "If we can somehow keep things in balance, that benefits everyone. Now, again I want to know, where's the best place to steal a pirate ship?"

Pug broke stride and stumbled, then looked at her and saw that she was grinning broadly. He laughed.

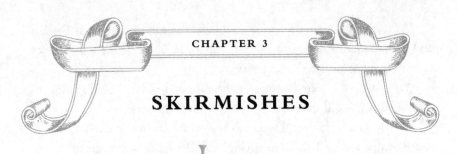

CHAPTER 3

SKIRMISHES

The soldier shouted.

Declan turned around and peered up the road toward where the lookout pointed. In a few moments the smudge in the distance resolved itself into a wagon lumbering toward them.

Sixto came to stand next to Declan, then glanced back at the encampment and saw the company was already turning out, adjusting armor and weapons, some saddling horses.

"Let's go down and see what the fuss is about," said Declan, glad his guards were well trained and hoping being battle-ready was unnecessary.

As the wagons drew near, Declan saw it was a five-wagon caravan, with half a dozen guards. Dust-covered and riding horses close to exhaustion, they slowed as they approached the first squad of Marquensas soldiers.

After a moment, Declan shouted, "Stand down!" He turned to Sixto. "It's Ratigan and Roz."

Sixto smiled. He had met the pair briefly while Declan was recovering from his near death after the sacking of Beran's Hill, and from some gossip had gleaned that Declan and Roz had once been lovers.

As the first two wagons began to slow, Ratigan holding one arm aloft as a signal to those behind, Sixto turned his attention to the second wagon. Roz was covered in road dust, her hair mostly grey instead of the flaming red of her youth, but she was still an impressive-looking woman. Sixto could understand why Declan had been hers for a time.

As the wagons finally came to a halt, the guards between Declan and the first set of horses relaxed. Ratigan, Rozalee, and their crew of teamsters were familiar faces to them.

"Declan!" shouted Ratigan as he climbed down. As he came to stand before his old friend he said, "Or is it 'highness'?"

"Only in court," said Declan as the two men shook hands.

Rozalee reached them and laughed. "I suppose giving you a hug and grabbing your arse is out of the question."

Declan laughed and stepped forward, throwing his arms around his former lover. "Hugs, never, but the other, maybe later?" The last was clearly a jest, and both chuckled. Rozalee had shared his bed every time she'd passed through the village of Oncon for a few years. While sex might be a thing of the past between them, the deep affection remained.

"What are you hearing from the east?" Declan asked.

Ratigan shrugged. "Lots of things. None of them good. We've had to quit Ilcomen. No king, no king's men. Thieves, bandits, and raiders abound, so we can't run a proper business there." He shook his head slowly. "Far worse to the east. People fleeing the Church. Bloody work all around. They're killing more savagely than those Pride Lords, slaughtering anyone who doesn't surrender and some who do anyway. I heard tales I can scarcely believe, Declan. Mothers and babies left bleeding in the streets, old men clubbed to death for just not moving along quickly enough. Public executions, beheadings, burning at the stake, flaying alive . . ." He let out a sigh. "I've seen a lot, especially during the last war, but from what people say, I'm glad I saw none of what the Church is doing."

He pointed to Roz. "We'll expand our business in Marquenet, and if Roz and I ever head back east it'll be behind your army, I think." He paused, then said, "I need to rest the teams, so is there a drink around here?"

Declan looked at Sixto. "The pavilion?"

"I believe *your highness* will find a selection of wine in a cabinet."

Declan made a backhanded slap at his shoulder which Sixto deftly avoided, to the amusement of Roz and Ratigan. Narrowing his gaze, he said, "Tell you what. Have your teamsters unhitch and care for the horses, clean up, and take a meal at the mess tent. The day is more than half gone. Spend the night and leave at sunrise."

Roz laughed and said, "Not that I'm shy, but where can I clean up?"

"I've got a bath in that pavilion, haven't I?" Declan asked Sixto.

Sixto nodded.

Declan waved a guard over. "Heat up some water for a bath and fill the tub in my pavilion." The guard saluted and hurried off.

"That will take a bit of time," Declan said to Roz. "So, there's a wash bowl in the mess tent, and we can grab a drink and gossip, and when the tub is filled, you can bathe."

"A real bath," Rozalee said. "It's been a while since I've had that pleasure. I could kiss you—" Then she said, "Wait, I already have!"

Color rose in Declan's cheeks as Ratigan and Sixto chuckled.

Roz slipped her arm through Declan's and squeezed. "Prince or not, I can still embarrass you."

That got Ratigan and Sixto openly laughing.

Suddenly, Roz's eyes widened, and her mood changed. She said, "I'm sorry, Declan. I forgot. Your wife—"

Declan interrupted her. "It's all right. The pain's still there, but it's no longer sharp."

He said nothing more for a moment, but Roz knew him well enough to see his pain was hidden behind a wall. He was silent for another moment, then announced, "Drinks!"

Everyone uttered noises of agreement and they walked toward the mess tent, which was empty except for the commissary staff readying for the evening meal. Seeing Declan enter, they all turned to face him and bowed, a greeting he waved off. "Get on with it," he said.

Roz quipped, "You really don't like the attention, do you?"

Declan just shook his head.

Sixto said, "Not for a moment. But Balven is training him."

Declan threw him a dark look, and Ratigan laughed as they reached a table and sat down. Ratigan said, "I've only met him a few times, arranging freight for the bar—I mean king. He's a shrewd bargainer."

"More than you know," said Declan in agreement.

A commissary porter hurried over and said, "Your highness?"

"Run over to my pavilion and fetch over here whatever wine or whisky we have to drink."

After the porter left, Declan said, "The east?"

"Little that makes sense," replied Ratigan. "As you would expect, Marquensas is the only place still intact at all. Ithrace was already a bone-picker's yard, and now Sandura is under the thumb of the Church of the One. They hanged King Lodavico—"

"I heard burned at the stake," Sixto interrupted.

"Well, neither of us was there," replied Ratigan, "but either way he's still dead. Their nobles have fled, or gone to ground, the ones not killed. It was butchery, and few were spared. The streets ran red with blood from the slaughter, I hear.

"Ilcomen was sacked. Zindaros and Metros had ports raided— nothing like up at Beran's Hill or Port Calos, but enough to visit chaos down there as well. They hit the South Tembria ports hard enough to keep their navies close to home and savaged any merchant fleet they encountered.

"On the whole, no one, not even the Church of the One, knows what's going on between here and Sandura. Lots of rumors, but nothing reliable. Villages burned, towns raided, and people claiming it's the Church as often as bandits causing all the misery and bloodshed. All I know is that east of Marquensas there are no safe places."

Declan considered what he had discussed so far with his brothers. "What is likely, I've been told, is we'll see roving companies, not just mercenaries, but bandits and murderers, and maybe the Church. Hence this new fortification." He sat back as several bottles were brought to the table along with drinking cups. Corks were quickly removed by the servants, and they turned to Declan.

With a wave of his hand, he said, "Bring them whatever they wish. I'll have one glass of that damned whisky, then back to work."

He waited until everyone was served, then took a sip of the bracing drink. "I thought I'd choke to death the first time Gwen's da gave me a drink of this, but after a while you learn to love it."

"Not too much," added Sixto, "unless you want to suffer the next day."

"Absolutely," said Declan. "That's a lesson hard learned."

"Painfully learned," said Sixto.

"More is not always the right choice." He laughed.

The wine and whisky flowed, and after an hour the teamsters began to drift in, and Declan said, "This has been wonderful, but I have some unfinished duties to attend to. Roz, the bath should be ready by the time you get to the pavilion. Sixto, host the drivers and Ratigan, and keep them from getting drunk enough to start a brawl. Find them quarters in the empty tents, and feed everyone so they don't wake up sick."

Sixto acknowledged the instructions and Declan trudged back to the promontory where the engineers continued preparing for the construction of defenses that would prevent any further attacks from the Narrows.

NEAR SUNSET, DECLAN ORDERED THE engineering crew to stand down and eat. He waited until the last plans and calculations were gathered up and put away in the big drawer in the table atop the bluff, then followed the last man down.

As he expected, Ratigan and the teamsters were halfway drunk. Declan sat next to Sixto, who was relatively sober, and nodded in approval. "Roz bathing?"

"She left a while ago," Sixto replied. "I think she's enjoying his highness's bathtub."

"A bath does sound nice, but I think I'll wait. There's going to be a lot more dirt flying around here before we head back to the city." He motioned for Sixto to follow him as he walked to a wash table and rolled up his sleeves. Sixto took a large pitcher of water and poured it into the wash bowl, and Declan picked up a bar of soap. He quickly scrubbed up, then asked, "What's to eat?"

Sixto laughed. "What else? Fish."

Declan shrugged. "That will do."

They returned to a table apart from the teamsters, and Declan shot a narrow gaze at Ratigan, silently asking him not to let things get too rowdy. He found himself hungrier than he had imagined after one bite of fish. He had lived his entire youth in a fishing village yet had no idea what it was he was eating. There were spices and herbs that masked the taste, which Declan assumed was probably strong, given the red color of the flesh. White fish were more delicate, but some of the darker red fish were almost inedible. He also was surprised at how good the fresh bread was, and the ample supply of vegetables. One large flagon of ale on top of a long day's work and he felt tired to his bones.

He glanced out of the entrance to the tent and saw that dusk was upon them. He stood and looked at Sixto. "I'm bedding down early. Keep an eye on that lot, will you?"

"They'll follow soon, I think," Sixto replied. "They have an early morning tending their horses before heading out."

Declan nodded and left. He made his way past a few of his men who were still savoring the evening breeze, a familiar experience to Declan, who would watch the sunset after a hard day at Edvalt's forge where he apprenticed. The cool, salt-tinged air was almost restorative.

He entered the pavilion and saw that the tub still dominated the large tent, and in the darker room almost didn't notice Roz sleeping on his bed until he stood next to it.

He reached down and gently touched her shoulder. She jerked awake and put up her hands defensively as Declan stepped back. "It's just me," he said.

Blinking awake, she moved back on the cot and drew her knees up to her chest, wrapping her arms around them. She let out a long breath and said, "Too many rough nights on the road, Declan. After what happened—"

"I know," he interrupted.

When the first sign of trouble in the Covenant had occurred, Roz had almost died at the hands of bandits working for the King of Sandura, who had raped her and left her for dead. It had been Declan and Ratigan who had found her. Following her long recovery, she had once again taken control of her shipping company. After her husband died and she merged her company with Ratigan's, she had appeared to the casual eye much the same as before. But Declan had seen the difference. The brutality had changed her, and he knew that false bravado had replaced her previous true fearlessness.

Now, she gave a slight shrug, almost girlish in the dim light, despite her years. Declan felt a fondness returning he hadn't felt in a long time, replacing the bitter emptiness that had lingered since Gwen died. Roz had been his lover for a while, and he had come to appreciate what a strong, resilient woman she was, qualities he had recognized in his wife, Gwen, too, when they first met.

"Stay where you are," he said. "I should probably bed down with my men, anyway. This prince business—"

She interrupted. "No, I'll go." She rose and put her hand on his shoulder. "It's not just foolishness, but a reminder to your soldiers you're more than a mere captain. Someday you will be king, and even when you're with them, you are always apart. Get used to it, Declan. Besides," she added, "if we're alone here too much longer, Ratigan will come looking for me, unless he's already too drunk to walk. Which will make for an interesting drive tomorrow, yes?"

Declan's brow furrowed and his head moved slightly back as he said, "Why?" Then his eyes opened wide. "Jealousy?"

She nodded.

"You and Ratigan?"

She patted his cheek. "Prince or not, you've always been a little simple at times." She nodded. "Ratigan's rough around the edges, but each of us lost a lot, people and property, in that bloody war. I've grown used to him, and he is surprisingly gentle with me. It doesn't heal the losses, Declan, but it eases the pain, and pain fades with time. That's something you need to think on." She gazed at him for a moment, then said, "Good night."

She left his pavilion and Declan sat on the still-warm cot, wrestling with what she had just said.

"PATROL COMING IN!"

It took Declan only a moment to realize something significant was upon them. The dust from the road revealed the riders were galloping, and by the time Declan had his sword belted around him he could clearly see the patrol riding hard toward the checkpoint on the road.

He glanced at the sun and realized it was almost noon, so this would be the morning patrol coming in fast. Whoever was chasing them must have been camped less than ten or fifteen miles to the east. He hurried down toward the horses.

Passing where the troops were garrisoned, he was pleased to see Sixto already had the horses being saddled, men donning armor, and a squad hurrying down the hillside to reinforce the checkpoint. He felt a moment of satisfaction that these former mercenaries and militia were acting exactly as trained. He had a good company of soldiers, not a gang of fighters.

By the time he reached the checkpoint, the riders had reined in, and he found himself confronting four dusty, exhausted scouts sitting on mounts that were lathered and blowing so hard that their nostrils were flaring. As a former blacksmith, Declan realized these horses had run miles.

"How far out?" was his first question.

"Ten miles, maybe less, my prince," answered the rider in front, a very young corporal. "They were camped, so we got away before they could start chasing us."

"Who and how many?"

"Can't say who, highness, but a lot. We didn't stay around to count, but from the dust I think at least fifty, maybe a lot more."

Before Declan could answer, Sixto shouted, "Positions!"

The soldiers of Marquensas had been moving briskly, but Declan could see a sudden quickening of pace, and before he and Sixto could reach their own mounts, the entire company had taken up defensive positions.

If fifty or more riders were approaching, Declan knew the forty men under his command—not counting any engineer who might be able to fight—should be able to fend them off. The proposed fortress would make that a certainty, but until then, his forces still commanded a very defensible position. He had twenty riders and twenty on foot, deployed to resist any first assault and then counterattack swiftly.

Sixto came and stood next to Declan. "Everyone's in position."

Declan kept his eyes on a now-visible cloud of dust. "Good. That was timely done. And these fellows are in a hurry."

Sixto said, "No advance scout means they don't care who might be here."

"They're coming hard," said Declan as he moved closer to where the archers waited behind a barrier of sandbags and piles of rocks. He surveyed the deployment. To Sixto he said, "Get four riders on the north side of the road; make them our four best bowmen and pull them back out of sight. If whoever's coming tries to skirt us to the north, I want the bowmen to harass them so we can close. If not, they can hit from behind."

Sixto immediately hurried off, shouting to four archers to accompany him to where the horses waited.

Declan reckoned they were as prepared as was possible. At least, he considered, if some spy had seen the work crew days ago and reported back, whoever was coming would find twice as many soldiers ready to fight than anticipated. Forty soldiers instead of twenty would be a surprise. For a moment he wished Ratigan and his teamsters and guards hadn't left at first light, as that would have meant more than fifty experienced fighters. Still, as Edvalt would often say, "That's like wishing for dry clothing in a storm."

To the soldiers crouching behind the barricades, he said, "When we stop them and it gets dusty, drop your bows, draw your swords, and hit them from the side!"

"Highness!" the nearest soldier replied.

The riders came into view, moving at an easy canter down the road from Ithrace. Either they'd ridden a long way through treacherous country, then wended their way through the southernmost passes of the mountains dividing the continent, or they'd disembarked from a ship in the Narrows to the east. However they got there was beside the point, Declan conceded silently.

The riders comprised a good-sized company of men in black, and Declan immediately recognized them as being from the order Bernardo had named the Church Adamant, the military order of the Church of the One. He saw the lead rider raise his right arm, fist balled, then gesture to the right, then left, finally ahead. Riders behind him fanned out on either side, and by the time the distance between the opposing forces had been halved, Declan estimated fifty or more trained cavalry were getting ready to attack.

"Archers, ready!" Declan shouted and the bowmen crouching behind the barricade stood, drew arrows from hip quivers, nocked them and raised their bows, ready to shoot. "Wait until they close, then loose!"

He half-ran, half-slid down the pathway to where a horse waited, held by an obviously nervous young groom. "If you can fight, grab a sword," Declan told him. "If you can't, hide!"

He settled into the saddle the moment the attackers hit the defenders and turned to see arrows from both sides taking a pair of soldiers off their mounts.

Declan circled around as the path from the construction site intercepted the road, dug his heels into the horse's flank, and felt the animal leap forward. He felt his perception changing as it had before. Things around him seemed to slow and he was better able to see where the most danger lay and how to avoid it. He hadn't experienced this since the battle that had taken Bogartis's life and left him in command of a company of mercenaries. He felt his own tension fade as he surveyed the struggle.

Sword out, he headed for a knot of fighters to his left, where Sixto and the archers were riding and shooting, confronted by a larger group. Declan directed his horse toward the melee and came up behind an enemy rider.

The attackers were, as he had suspected, clearly Church Adamant: all wore black tunics, trousers, gloves, and boots, and black cuirasses with a white circle embossed on them. Their helms were uniform, close-fitting, open-faced with a nose-guard and a fine-chain neck-guard.

The Church horseman sensed another attack and was turning toward Declan when the prince cut downward and almost severed the rider's leg above the knee. They might be fully armored from the waist up, but these fighters had elected to wear heavy cloth trousers, better for a long ride, but offering little protection in battle. For this one at least it was a fatal error. He shouted in pain as blood fountained and he fell out of the saddle.

Declan wheeled his horse to engage another, to the relief of a rider who was being attacked. Sixto and his archers dropped their bows and pulled swords, and with Declan's aid, that side of the battle began to steady.

Still, it was a close struggle. Declan's archers and defensive position had halted the advance, but the Church forces had the advantage in numbers. Declan had no time to count, he just knew there were more black-clad riders than his company. He could see his men holding their own, but he realized the Church riders were the best, most disciplined soldiers he had ever faced. Before he had encountered mercenaries, bandits, and savages, but this was the very type of soldier Daylon was trying to train, like those in the king's personal guard.

The midday heat was now upon them, and if the fight dragged on too long men were more likely to die from fatigue slowing them than from the enemy's skills. It might come down to staying power. Declan's men were rested and fed, and the Church forces had been on the trail for days, perhaps weeks, so he silently hoped that would tip the balance.

Declan struck out at a rider, turned his horse, and came in close to the man, getting a sword point inside his shield. His sword slid along the man's steel cuirass, but caught a leather strap on the shield arm and sliced through it. As the shield moved unexpectedly, the Church swordsman was caught off-guard for an instant, but that was all Declan needed to yank his blade upward and slice into his shoulder joint. The quality of Declan's blade was now demonstrated in battle, as the rider cried out in agony and blood spurted from a severed artery. Declan leaned over and used his leg to move his horse to the right, barely avoiding a wild swing of the dying man's blade. Declan again circled his mount.

He sensed more than saw that this was a close struggle. The few archers on the hillside had been rendered largely ineffective owing to the dust and confusion below them. They risked hitting their own men if they were careless. The arrows stopped flying, and Declan realized that his ability to slow things in battle had misled him. Mere moments had passed, and his soldiers were following his orders, dropping their bows and attacking the invaders' flank on foot.

Declan laid about him, striking here and there, occasionally wounding a fighter but mainly distracting attention from one of his own men for a moment, which often meant the difference between life or death.

Then out of the corner of his eye he saw another group of riders—six horsemen in the colors of Marquensas—and they were riding hard to help. One held a banner bearing the king's emblem, which he tossed aside as he drew his own sword.

The six horsemen swept in and suddenly the balance of the fight shifted, and Church riders were taken from their saddles, their blood spattering everyone nearby.

Declan spun his exhausted horse, expecting to see the enemy turning to run, but instead they were throwing themselves at Declan's forces.

He managed to catch Sixto's attention with a quick wave of his sword. Sixto dodged a blow from a Church rider and nodded that he understood. He moved his mount away from the attacking rider, who pursued him. Looping around toward Declan, other men of Marquensas fell into place, and within a few moments, the remaining Church riders were being surrounded.

Declan tried to shout an offer of quarter, but before he could speak, a rider slammed his horse into Declan's mount, almost tossing him from the saddle. Declan held on to the reins and his horse's mane, twisting to avoid another blow and keep from losing his stirrups. Sixto struck the attacker's shield, and he turned away.

Declan recovered and got his sword up to intercept another rider. He blocked a downward strike, slid his blade along his opponent's, then cut across his throat. Spinning his horse, he saw that not one Church rider was surrendering, even though the now higher numbers of Marquensas soldiers had finally encircled the Church horsemen and were cutting them down, as the soldiers on foot were swarming the riders and pulling them from their horses.

Then it was over.

Sixto rode over, perspiring profusely. "Not a single one surrendered."

"Fanatics," Declan replied. "Delnocio said as much." He signaled over one of his men, jumped down from the saddle, and threw the reins of his mount to the soldier.

Inspecting the dead Church horsemen, he turned to Sixto and said, "Look at that armor."

"Lacquered?"

Declan picked up a helm and nodded. "This is fine work. I know what Edvalt would have charged to make a helm like this for a vain noble, and this is designed for warriors, not for fat men on parade." He looked around at the fallen Church soldiers. "Sixty such, and matching cuirasses. Fine tunics."

He tossed the helm to Sixto, who looked closely at it. Without waiting for word from Declan, he shouted, "Strip all the armor and weapons!" He pointed to a hillock on the far side of the road from the hill where the construction was underway and shouted, "Build a pyre and burn these bodies!"

The exhausted soldiers hesitated, then began to obey Sixto's command. Declan nodded approval.

He turned to the newly arrived soldiers and asked, "Who's in charge?"

A soldier with the mark of a sergeant on his tunic stepped forward and said, "I am, highness!"

Declan looked around, numbering his dead and wounded. At least twenty-five soldiers from Marquensas lay dead. He then returned his attention to the sergeant, and said, "You arrived in timely fashion."

The sergeant could only nod. "I was sent by the king's first adviser with a message for his highness."

Trying not to wince at the honorific, Declan said, "What message?"

The sergeant reached inside his tunic and pulled out a rolled parchment, wrapped with a ribbon and a wax seal.

Declan broke the seal as Sixto came to stand at his shoulder. He read the message, then closed his eyes and shook his head slightly for a moment.

Sixto said, "What is it?"

"From Balven," said Declan. "The Church is attacking."

Sixto glanced around at the dead and wounded, then said, "I noticed."

An exhausted Declan sat heavily in his chair in the king's meeting chamber. He had ridden hard for days, with two remounts in tow, and caught short naps, but after two and a half days, he'd reached Marquenet.

Balven said, "You going to live?"

"Unfortunately," Declan responded as a servant placed a steaming mug of coffee before him. He blew across the top and took a sip, placing it down to let it cool a bit more. "I set off as soon as I got the message."

King Daylon said, "You left two days ago? Two nights?"

"A little longer. I got the message after we were hit by sixty or so Church cavalry. I left immediately."

Daylon glanced at Delnocio with a questioning expression.

The former prelate of the Church nodded. "Given the distances, both companies must have left Sandura about the same time. It was as close to a coordinated attack as possible."

"Both?" asked Declan.

"We got word two days ago that another column of riders struck Beran's Hill. Luckily, most of the work on the fortifications was finished and besides the hundred soldiers deployed there, we also had almost a hundred workers, many of them more than willing to pick up an axe or hammer and start swinging," said Balven.

Daylon asked Delnocio, "What's next?"

"These are patrols in force," answered the former episkopos. "Their mission is to probe, take a position if possible, then send for larger forces to advance. If no one returns after a certain time, they send a following patrol to see where the last one fell."

"It's a bloody way to get information," said Declan. "Not one of them surrendered."

"They won't," said Delnocio. "As I have said before, there are nothing but the faithful in the Church Adamant, to the point of fanaticism.

The Church may use mercenary forces when it suits them, but people like myself leave the army only by dying or joining the priesthood."

His voice hoarse with fatigue, Declan said, "A waste of some of the best fighters I've seen."

Delnocio nodded. "I think you still haven't fully grasped the point, my prince. The Church has soldiers to waste. They completely control an entire continent. They conscript thousands of youngsters every year, weeding out those unfit for their purposes, and have convinced the population of Enast that serving the Church is the highest calling possible. They pacified the whole of Enast when your grandfather was a boy." He tilted his head and, in a more sardonic tone, added, "And that also serves to uphold their status in the eyes of the people. So even if only one boy out of a hundred grows up to be a mindless believer, that means a vast army of those willing to kill and die without question."

Declan took a long drink of coffee, savoring the pungency, and said, "I thought we had our fill of fanatics with those Azhante on Nytanny."

King Daylon nodded. "We all wish that. But as Hava said, the Pride Lords were lavishly dressed criminals, not a true ruling nobility. They used that myth of monsters who ate people, claiming to have bested them to keep the population under their control."

Balven nodded. "Be that as it may, what do we expect next from the Church?" he asked Delnocio.

"They'll attempt to create a foothold somewhere between your north and south fortifications." Delnocio stood and moved to the map Daylon had pinned to the wall. Pointing to what had been northern Ilcomen, he said, "With no Ilcomen patrols, somewhere between here and the southern Wildlands, I suspect." He moved his finger westward. "Or in that big forest to the east of here, majesty. They could move in an engineering company and have a garrison camp built in a week or two. Once they have a staging point, they'll build up an invasion force, then hit the heart of your new kingdom, coming straight here. If Marquenet falls, Marquensas falls."

"I've already ordered Beran's Hill and the southern fortification reinforced, so let's get more scouts between," said the king.

"We've already been scouting," Balven reminded his brother, "but we'll send a few more out there." He looked at the map and said, "The eastern forest has long been ignored except for foresters around the edges and a few charcoal burners who glean branches and fell small trunks. We don't know what's in there."

"Time to find out," said Declan, rising. "I need sleep." He looked at the king, who nodded. "Tomorrow, if it pleases you, I'll ride to Beran's Hill and talk to whoever's settling in. While I trust our friend's estimation of things"—he nodded at Delnocio—"I think we're also vulnerable to a thrust between there and Copper Hills."

"Possible," said Bernardo, also standing. "But unlikely. A long battle is not the way of the Church Adamant. They simply hit hard and fast and try to overwhelm. Even if they overran the area, to the point of taking Port Colos, they'll announce their presence and provide us with time to prepare for an attack from the north."

Declan glanced at Balven and the king, noting Delnocio's use of the word "us," and giving them both a slight nod. He said, "That does seem to be their style. It was a close-run thing down at the peninsula. Those six riders who came with your message gave us the day. It was tight. We had position, they were tired, and they didn't expect a stout defense. But as I said, it was close."

The king rose and said, "That will be all." He motioned for Declan to linger after Delnocio and the attendants left. When only the three brothers remained, the king said, "Do I even want to know how close it was?"

Declan slowly shook his head. "Probably not."

"You'll return with a company at your back as soon as possible."

Declan was too tired to argue, and he saw the wisdom of that. "Very well." Looking at Balven, he said, "When you can, send along more builders and laborers if you can spare them. That southern fortification needs to be finished as quickly as possible."

"Already done," replied Balven.

Declan sighed deeply, from fatigue and tension. "What Hava said," he began, "about the Pride Lords being nothing but criminals . . ."

"Yes?" asked the king.

"It makes me wish she was still here."

"Why?" asked Daylon.

"Because sooner or later the Church will be bringing a fleet across from Enast, either up the Narrows, or landing in Sandura, but either way it would be nice to have our own fleet out there sinking as many ships as possible before they made landfall."

"Indeed," said Balven. "She is an impressive young woman."

Declan departed for his quarters and rest, and after he left, Balven looked at his brother and said, "Another world. I wonder what she's up to over there?"

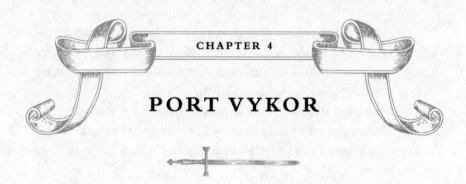

CHAPTER 4

PORT VYKOR

Donte's eyes widened.

He let out a "whoof" noise as the three of them—Donte, Hava, and Pug—appeared inside a large chamber.

Hava disentangled herself from Pug's grip around her waist as Donte spun in place trying to assess their new surroundings. A moment before they had been standing in a small garden between the buildings of the villa, and now they were in a large room illuminated by candle sconces.

A single door before them opened and a young woman in a black robe stepped through. "Pug!" The young woman appeared delighted to see him. She was slender with cropped brown hair and a deeply tanned complexion, which made her green eyes startling. "Who are your friends?"

"Delynn, this is Hava and Donte. Hava, Donte, this is Delynn, one of my more difficult students." Pug's tone was affectionate.

"Students?" said Hava as she took Delynn's outstretched hand and gave it a shake. Looking at Pug she said, "You're a preceptor?"

Donte's expression revealed he wasn't happy with that revelation.

"In a manner of speaking," Pug answered. "From what little I know of your education, nothing like you would expect. Here our methods are less severe, though perhaps as demanding."

"Where are we?" Donte asked.

"Come," said Delynn.

She turned and motioned for them to follow her through the door. They entered a long hall with torch sconces and doors alternating. Hava glanced at Donte, who was watching Delynn. Knowing her lifelong friend, Hava suppressed a chuckle: she was certain he was trying to decide if he found her attractive enough to make a fool out of himself. Usually that required a good supply of ale, wine, or spirits, but even when he was sober, attractive women made Donte act like an idiot.

The hallway ended and Delynn opened a door that revealed a long, curved balcony. Here, they found themselves overlooking a terrace and wide meadow that swept down to a distant beach, beyond which they could see water lazily rolling: dark waves, as the clouds above were hiding the sun. Hava shot a glance at Pug, silently echoing Donte's previous question, *Where are we?*

"Welcome to Stardock," said Delynn.

Pug smiled and said, "This is home to the Academy of Magicians. We need to stop here for a bit before moving on to Port Vykor."

"You have business in the Kingdom?" Delynn asked Pug.

With a broad smile, Pug said, "Always with the questions, Delynn?"

"None of my business, then," she replied, looking abashed.

Pug laughed. "No, it's a good quality, having questions; it's just that a time and a place should be considered." Before she could respond, he added, "No, my friend Hava has business in Port Vykor. She requires a ship."

"That's the place, then," said Delynn with a nod.

Pug looked at Hava and Donte and said, "There are a few things about visiting the Kingdom you need to master even to be able to approach a shipbuilder. We've enabled you to speak to anyone for a while, but many little things—"

Hava interrupted. "Donte and I were trained from childhood how to observe a strange place and quickly blend in. We come from a nation of thieves, spies, and assassins."

"Well and good," said Pug. "That will make what we do go quickly. And there are things we don't know, so I need to put out a few inquiries, such as how much is a fair price for the type of ship you seek."

"And how to dress so as not to attract undue attention," added Delynn.

Hava nodded and glanced at Donte, whose expression showed he also understood the logic. Their training was to fade into the background and not be noticed, but Hava was about to announce to strangers that she was a person with enough resources to commission a ship to be built.

Hava said to Pug, "I need to look like a woman of means. Someone with a story about why no one in . . ." She threw a questioning look at Pug.

"Port Vykor," he supplied.

"Why no one in Port Vykor has ever heard of me or anyone related to me. Being a mysterious woman only draws attention. If we were running a confidence game back home, Hatu or another would be the wealthy man, and I would be the wife or mistress."

"But she'll be in charge," added Donte.

Pug and Delynn exchanged glances and smiled. "Yes," said Pug. "You certainly understand what will be required. There is a lot of history involved—"

"But history can wait," said Hava with a chuckle.

"Very well," agreed Pug. "Suffice to say we have a lot of different people around the Bitter Sea and the Far Coast. It comes from there being a number of invasions, wars, empires, and kingdoms living cheek by jowl. So, for the moment, we'll have you two come from one of the trading consortiums in the Free Cities. We'll come up with some plausible stories."

"In my experience," supplied Hava, "gold makes most stories plausible. You said I wouldn't have to pirate a ship."

Pug's eyebrows raised and he looked a little bemused. "Magnus and I would rather not call attention to our island."

Donte said, "Don't worry. She's very good at getting people to blame others. Just tell us who you want blamed for stealing a ship and that's that."

Both Pug and Delynn laughed. "I don't think that will be necessary. Come now."

He and Delynn led them across the terrace into an alcove with a circular stairway. They went down a floor and out of a door to a small courtyard. "We have quarters for guests here," he said.

"How long do you think this will take?" asked Donte.

With a shake of her head, Hava said, "He gets restless if he's not doing something."

"We'll find ways to keep you busy," Delynn said to Donte.

"Before today I would have said a week or two, but now, perhaps two, three days and you two will pass for a rich trading couple from . . . Margrave's Port. It's one of the lesser communities in the Free Cities of Natal and you're far less likely to run into someone who has actually been there than one of the larger cities. The Free Cities have lots of merchants, and few shipbuilders, so they do a fair trade with the builders in Port Vykor."

"Sounds good," said Hava as she and Donte were shown to their quarters.

They were given adjacent rooms with separate doors that opened into tidy apartments. Each held a bed, a chest, and a dresser. Hava was impressed by a surprisingly clear mirror hanging over the wash basin. Delynn followed her inside and Hava said, "Where I come from this mirror would be very expensive."

Delynn smiled. "I think you'll find many things here in Stardock that are costly elsewhere. One of the benefits of having both Greater Path magicians and Lesser Path magic artificers living together."

"Greater Path? Lesser? I don't understand."

"That will be part of your training for the next few days," answered Delynn. "There are many things about Midkemia that will seem incomprehensible to you yet are taken for granted by people who live here."

"Like dragons?" said Hava, still doubting that claim.

Delynn nodded. "Few ever see them, but all know they exist."

Hava slowly looked around, then moved back though the door and saw that Donte was exiting his quarters. "Nice room," he said.

"You tired?" she asked.

"Not especially," he replied. "But I am hungry."

"You're always hungry," she replied with a slight chuckle.

"True." Turning to Pug, he said, "Is there anything to eat?"

"I was going to show you the dining hall later, but we can probably get you something now. Follow me and mark the way."

"We always mark the way," answered Hava. "Part of our training."

"I expected as much," replied Pug.

"I wonder what Hatu is up to?" said Donte as they fell in behind Delynn and Pug.

Hava smiled. "Knowing my husband, he's up to his backside in books somewhere."

HATU SAT ON A WELL-PADDED stool with a large volume opened on the table before him, his eyes scanning the page. Magnus sat to his right, watching in fascination as Hatu quickly turned each page gently, for the book was ancient. Late afternoon sunlight streamed in through a high window; Magnus had been with Hatushaly all day.

"I don't understand," said Hatu, after another moment.

"What don't you understand?" asked Magnus. He moved to an empty chair and sat down. "I thought you could read anything."

"So far. At least I've not found anything written in a language I couldn't grasp. Some take longer than others. No, what I meant was, I understand what is written here, but it just doesn't make sense."

"Can you explain?"

Hatu looked at Magnus as if grasping for words, then said, "This is a story. But I don't think it's real."

"Like a fiction?"

"Fiction?" Hatu echoed.

"A story made up to entertain, to perhaps make a point."

"Ah," said Hatu, nodding enthusiastically. "The tales spun by storytellers, singers, minstrels! Exactly, but why go to all the trouble of writing this down as if it's an important history? Vanity?"

"The author's vanity?"

"This is a great deal of work." He put his hand on the massive book. "The scribe work alone is . . . months at least, if there was more than one scribe. Years, if the author wrote it alone." He pushed himself back from the table and took a breath.

"What?" asked Magnus.

"But it doesn't read . . . like a tale. If it was something sung by a minstrel or told about in an inn on my world, the storyteller would be thrown out of the tavern."

Magnus chuckled. "That bad?"

Again, Hatu considered silently before answering. "Not bad in one way. It's as if the writer is . . . thinking? Suggesting? Anyway, it's about traveling through time, and no names or places are talked about, really."

Magnus laughed. "I think I know your problem."

"What?" said Hatushaly, his features darkening slightly as if he anticipated a rebuke.

Magnus held up a hand in a placating gesture. "I forget how different things must be where you come from, and whenever you speak of your 'school,' it's a training center for spies, assassins, and killers, not a place of education as we might know here.

"You're reading what is known as *theory*. That is, a work that makes suppositions, based on how much, or little in many cases, a writer knows on the subject.

"What does it say?" asked Magnus.

"It doesn't matter, really. This is all wrong."

Magnus's brow furrowed slightly. "What do you mean?"

"The writer of this massive book doesn't know what he's writing about—assuming Jashdahara Simborwack is a man, or even human. Time doesn't work the way he thinks."

"What do you mean by that?" asked Magnus eagerly.

"Just . . . he describes time like . . ." Hatu shrugged. "I don't know if I can describe this."

"Try. You can always change how you say things if you need to."

"I need to eat," said Hatu, sounding fatigued.

Magnus nodded as he stood up. "You've been at this all day. Come, let's go get some food and you can ponder what you wish to say at your leisure. My father used to say, 'Sleep on a thing,' as a rested mind often sees a solution to a problem that seemed insurmountable the day before."

"Sounds like a wise man, your father," Hatu responded, also rising.

"Very," said Magnus.

He led Hatushaly out of the massive library and class complex, which was cleverly hidden inside a hillside, outside to the path leading around the hill to the villa. The sun was low in the west and Magnus said, "We were there longer than I imagined. What's that old saying, 'Time flies when things are interesting'?"

Hatu laughed. "On Garn it was 'when things are entertaining.' Interesting and entertaining are often at cross purposes."

"That is true," Magnus agreed.

Then Hatu stopped, his eyes widening as he exclaimed, "Oh!"

"What?" asked Magnus, turning to face him.

"That . . . book, the one trying to explain time. I think . . . I'm almost . . ." He shook his head and said, "No, not quite yet, but I'm close to understanding why I think the writer is wrong."

"Tell me over a meal," said Magnus with a smile. "I've discovered I'm hungry, too. We forgot lunch."

Hatu liked the white-haired man's smile. His view of Magnus was based on a lifetime of training in the Kingdom of the Night: how to assess a person; judging the best way to take advantage of them. Now he saw a complicated man, apparently with several lifetimes' worth of experience, yet in some ways unsure of his relationships and whom he could trust. It was a wariness that most people would not note, and of those Hatu knew, perhaps only Master Bodai and Hava would also recognize it; Magnus kept it so well hidden.

Hatu considered he saw it only because of the close hours they had spent together in discovering what it was about Hatu's talents that made him unique in this strange land of magic and wonder.

Reaching the dining hall, they found there were still more than a dozen young men and women at the tables, while another group was hurriedly bringing food and clearing tables. Hatu had seen the routine enough times to feel familiar with it: students dividing up duties; different groups assuming different tasks. The way various groups within the population of Sorcerer's Isle were assigned tasks still perplexed him. There were no obvious servants or anyone of higher station. And the presence of several intelligent beings who were clearly not human still fascinated him.

He pulled his attention away from a particularly striking individual, who looked like a tall, thin human woman, but with deep blue skin and violet eyes with no white sclera, and black hair so fine it appeared to float around her head as she moved. She was engaged in a lively conversation with a young man who seemed oblivious to her alien appearance. "Don't stare," Hatu muttered to himself.

Magnus nodded thanks to the student who brought over a tray with two dishes full of stew, a loaf of bread, a pitcher brimming with ale and two mugs. Discovering he was hungrier than he had thought, Hatu grabbed a bowl, then the bread and started tearing off a hunk.

Magnus laughed as he filled both mugs. "We did ignore a midday meal, didn't we?"

Trying not to laugh with a mouthful of food, Hatu could only nod. Swallowing, he grabbed a mug and washed the food down with a slug of ale. Smacking his lips, he chuckled and said, "Yes, we did." After a moment, he added, "I never appreciated good beef stew until after the war at home."

"How's that?" asked Magnus.

"The raiders not only burned crops but slaughtered herds, so for the last year and more it's been mostly fish chowder and vegetable stew, and even that was hard to come by. Many days we had nothing but coarse bread and a thin gruel if there was grain left over from the bread making. We found some scattered livestock, and a few sheep and cattle were butchered, but the majority were left for breeding."

Magnus shrugged. "At least you had food. I've traveled to places savaged by war where there was nothing at all to eat."

Hatu inclined his head in agreement. "I've been hungry, but never starving. You make a good point."

"That book which troubles you—care to talk about it?"

Hatu shook his head. "I think I need to ponder further. There's something there I'm not seeing yet. Not in what was written, but rather in the belief it was built upon. I can't put it into words yet."

Magnus indicated that he understood. "Take your time."

Hatu tried hard not to laugh, since his mouth was half full. He swallowed and said, "It is all about time."

"In all my years of study and experience, time is perhaps the most elusive of all things to grasp, let alone master."

"Did you ever know anyone who mastered time?" Hatu was genuinely curious, his eyes fixed on Magnus over the brim of his mug.

"It's difficult for me to say. I've heard stories, from reliable sources, involving traveling through time, and visiting places where time doesn't seem to exist, but I've never seen such things for myself."

Hatu nodded. "One can't see events though the eyes of another. It's something we had drilled into us when evaluating information that we came across, and in relaying that information to our masters." He finished off his ale.

"Another?" Magnus asked, indicating the now-empty mug.

"Please," said Hatu, lifting his spoon to his mouth. He watched Magnus pour and abruptly the spoon stopped moving and his eyes widened.

Magnus noticed his change in expression. "What is it?"

"Stop pouring," said Hatu. He put down the spoon and reached out to take the mug. A quick series of swallows and he drained the half-filled mug. He held it out, belched a little, and said, "Fill it slowly, please."

He seemed fascinated as Magnus slowly poured out a trickle of ale. He fixed his gaze on the small stream of amber liquid falling into the mug. When it was full, Magnus stopped.

"Yes?" he asked Hatu.

"Not yet," he said, "but I think I'm closer to understanding what we were speaking of. Time."

Magnus looked at the now-full mug and said, "History teaches us that some discoveries start in stranger places than an ale cup, though I don't recall too many of them."

Hatu said, "I believe you. I just still need to ponder, but an idea is forming."

"Then let us finish and be off for a good rest. Perhaps tomorrow your idea will have formed."

"Perhaps," agreed Hatushaly. "Though my quarters are hardly inviting without Hava there. I do miss her."

Magnus inclined his head. "It's been a very long time since I felt that way about a woman, but I do remember. I expect Phillip will have her back here soon."

"I hope you are right," said Hatu, then he took another gulp of ale.

THE SUDDEN TRANSITION FROM ONE location to another still caused Hava and Donte a moment of disorientation, but both quickly surveyed their surroundings.

"Where are we?" asked Hava. She was wearing a simple but well-tailored dress that reached her ankles. Blue with a high collar edged with white stitching, fastened in the front with buttons that she had to fumble with until Delynn had assisted. She realized that the majority of her shirts were tunics, and that she preferred trousers and boots to dresses and shoes. Around her shoulders rested a light, pale-yellow shawl, purely decorative, as it offered scant warmth.

"We are in a small storage building that we use when we wish to travel here without attracting attention." Pug now wore garb appropriate to a general factotum employed by a trading house: a simple but well-made blue shirt with pleated sleeves, a wide black belt with a dagger—for fashion rather than for defense—and tan trousers tucked into the top of good black boots. On his head perched a black beret with a small red feather, set at a jaunty angle.

Hava looked impressed. It was a dramatic change from his usual black robe and sandals. "By us, you mean you and Magnus?"

Pug nodded. "And some others. Let me check outside to see if a coach we arranged is here."

He went out through the door and closed it behind him.

"Have I mentioned," she said, fussing with the dress's waist, "that I hate dresses?"

"Many times," Donte replied.

"I had to wear them constantly when I trained with the Perfumed Women."

"You never talk about your time there."

Hava shot Donte a sharp gaze. "Right."

Donte repressed a chuckle: it was clear that this topic was closed. He asked, "How do I look?"

He wore a black over-jacket with elbow-length sleeves, a pale-blue shirt, and plain grey trousers tucked into the top of mid-calf black boots, not very fancy, but obviously nicely made and well-polished. He held a walking stick with a lethal blade secreted inside the shaft. A fat purse of coins rested just inside the jacket, tied by a cord to his belt to foil any pickpockets he might encounter. Pug had explained the value of the coins, a very logical system in this Kingdom of the Isles. Ten copper coins equaled one silver, and ten of those was equal to a gold. The difference in size made it easy to tell just from touch which coin was being pulled out of the purse.

"Like a prosperous, but not noticeably wealthy, man of the Free Cities." Hava looked approving.

Pug returned to say, "The coach is here."

"Donald, of House Duran," said Donte, his accent changing slightly, raising the pitch of his voice. "We're in a trading consortium." Even his posture shifted enough to make his large frame appear less threatening as he moved toward Pug, extending his hand. "How are you, my fine fellow?"

Pug looked impressed. "You're both quick studies."

"When it suits him," said Hava.

Donte's tone turned serious. "I've never dropped a con by misplaying a role."

"That is true," she admitted. "Now that I think about it, I wondered why you weren't sent out on more confidence grifts."

"Because I find them tedious and went out of my way to avoid them. I'm a brawler, not a confidence trickster," he said. He looked at Pug. "The sooner we get on with this, the sooner we're done, right?"

"And the sooner you can run off looking for trouble, right?" said Hava.

Donte grinned. "You know me too well, m'dear," he replied in the character voice he'd developed.

Pug said, "Let us go, then."

Outside, there awaited a closed carriage with windows, more ornate than those Hava had seen when leaving the Perfumed Women, riding with Mistress Mulray, their leader. And less lavish, even, than King Daylon's. She looked at Pug and gave him a slight nod.

They boarded the carriage, Pug seating himself opposite Hava and Donte. The driver had been instructed on his destination and drove the team without Pug instructing him.

Hava pulled aside the window curtain and looked out. "A different world, yet it looks familiar. People look pretty much the same here."

Pug inclined his head as if agreeing. "So I've found traveling to other worlds. People are people. Different languages, customs, and beliefs, but for the most part they want safety, they love their children, and they just want to be able to survive." His expression darkened. "But the universe appears bent on denying many of those simple goals."

Thinking of the destruction of Beran's Hill, and the wholesale savagery visited on much of North Tembria, Hava said, "It does seem that way at times, doesn't it?"

Pug looked thoughtfully off into the distance through the window. Quietly he said, "Sometimes it can be overwhelming to consider the struggles that came before. Yet somehow, we're all still here . . . And look." His gaze dropped to the people in the streets, scurrying about their business, pushing carts, or peering into shop windows.

"Little bugger!" Donte exclaimed quietly.

Hava and Pug glanced to see him looking out of the window on the other side of their carriage.

He turned to them. "Got thieves here just like home."

Hava's eyes widened in a silent question.

"Four-boy team, I think," he said. "But I only saw two, the stall and the cutter." He shook his head slowly. "Not very good, though. If the mark hadn't been distracted already haggling with a merchant, he might have noticed the lad lifting his purse."

"He'll find out as soon as he tries to pay the merchant," Hava replied.

Pug's confusion prompted a quick explanation of the art of team pickpocketing by gangs of urchins. Hava finished by saying, "It's the first part of street training back where we come from. If you survive a year or two of petty thievery in the markets, you get moved up in the ranks in whichever crew you are assigned to."

Pug looked wryly amused. "I read a bit about your Kingdom of the Night from what Nathan told Magnus, and what Ruffio said after his time in the Sanctuary. It was transcribed for us to read. Not the details of your upbringings, apparently." He regarded his two companions with new appreciation. "It's easy to see why you two are so quick in adapting to changing circumstance and playing these roles."

"Adapt or die," Donte said as if repeating a mantra. "If I heard Master Bodai say that once, I heard it a thousand times."

"That, my friend," said Pug, "is true of all living things."

"Well, now we know this world is very much like ours," said Donte with a grin.

"I thought I might warn you Port Vykor can be a rough place to travel, but I see you're more than capable of judging the risks."

"No guards, constables, or watchmen?" asked Hava.

"Oh, this is a king's city. It's the most important Kingdom port on the Bitter Sea. Krondor, the capital, is two days' travel up the coast, and was once the biggest port, but it was nearly destroyed in a war centuries ago. This port was enlarged and used while Krondor was being rebuilt. That took almost a hundred years. By the time Krondor was re-established, this city had become the accustomed port for most shipping and trade.

"Then came that terrible struggle Magnus and I mentioned, and the entire region of the western Kingdom, the Free Cities, and the north of the Empire of Kesh was forever changed." He looked distracted for a moment, then said, "Sometimes the stories are . . . so real." He shook his head. "In any event, Port Vykor is now the second largest city on this coast and the largest trading hub. That trade is a shadow of what it was before the Great Upheaval, but it's still brisk.

"But it's a corrupt place. Merchants bribe gangs, gangs bribe watchmen and constables, and the military is too busy guarding against raids from the wilds to the south of the border."

Donte laughed. "Sounds like my kind of city."

Hava elbowed him in the ribs, and it wasn't a humorous jab. "Behave, fool!"

Pug's eyes widened: he looked to be caught halfway between surprise and laughter.

Turning to him, Hava said, "My idiot friend has an appetite for trouble."

At that point, Pug laughed. "I had a friend once—" He cut himself off. "I . . . I've heard stories of a friend of . . ." He winced as if in pain.

"Are you all right?" Hava asked.

Pug closed his eyes tightly for a moment, then took a deep breath. "I'm fine," he replied. "Just for a moment, there was a . . . memory." He chuckled. "No, it's just I've heard some stories so many times they're almost like memories. And a name popped into my head. Jimmy."

"Jimmy?"

"A legendary figure," said Pug. "According to all the lore, he was a street thief who befriended a prince, or rather the prince befriended him, and he rose to high rank, a duke."

"What's a duke?" asked Donte.

"It's a noble rank, just below that of king."

"Like our barons," said Hava.

Pug said, "We have barons, too, but dukes are higher."

Donte said, "Labels are nothing; we've seen a baron become a king. This Jimmy sounds like someone I'd like to meet."

Pug sat back against the cushions, "I think I would, too." After a while he said to Hava, "If you're to purchase a ship, I think it serves to let you know how things are in the Bitter Sea." He went on to detail something of the relationships as they existed now: the closing off of the Empire of Kesh to all foreigners, the revolt of Kesh's former client nations, and the abandonment of their cities along the edge of the Jal-Pur Desert. He finished by saying, "The Kingdom still trades with the Eastern Kingdoms and the Kingdom of Roldem, but that's the Eastern Realm. Sorcerer's Isle is concerned with the Western Realm, here and in Krondor, and up to Yabon. The island nation of Queg, the self-styled 'empire,' has always been something of a rogue nation of pirates, and the Free Cities, where you pretend to be from, they usually keep neutral on all but the direst of conflicts."

Hava smiled. "Sounds very rough and tumble."

"Indeed," said Pug. "As I said, we can keep ships away from Sorcerer's Isle, but getting them close can be a problem at times." The carriage rolled to a stop, and Pug glanced out of the window. "We're here."

They exited the carriage and entered a wooden building opposite the docks. Hava glanced around and saw that there were a half-dozen large dry docks in which ships were having barnacles scraped off their hulls, being repaired, or were under construction. One sat alone, and to Hava's eyes it looked finished. A heavy freighter from what she could tell.

At a small writing table by a door leading back to the rear of the building sat a clerk, a small man with a fringe of hair, pudgy features, and ink-stained fingers. He looked up and said, "Yes?"

Pug said, "We're here to see Samuel Benoit."

"He's busy," came the reply. The clerk seemed to puff up with self-importance and added, "What do you want?"

Before Pug could speak, Donte leaned forward to be eye level with the clerk, and said, "We're here to buy a ship, you worm. Now go get your master before I lose my temper and we take my business elsewhere!"

The clerk sat back, so fast he almost fell over, and scrambled to get off his stool. He blinked in confusion for a moment, then regained his composure. As he retreated toward the rear door, he said, "I'll see if Mr. Benoit can see you."

When the clerk had disappeared, Pug smiled and said, "Well done."

Donte grinned.

A few moments later, an older man with silver hair, broad shoulders, and a barrel chest came through the door. "You demanded to see me?"

Pug stepped forward and said, "Honorable sir, forgive my master's impatience. He seeks the finest shipbuilder in the Kingdom. He has specific needs and will not abide an inferior builder."

Samuel Benoit looked at them askance. "Flattery is lost on me. I'm busy and need to attend to my trade. What do you want?"

Before Pug could reply, Hava said quietly, "My husband needs a ship, somewhat bigger than a cutter, two masts, not one, but nimble. Fore and aft, with a square-rigged aft sail—a spanker—with a foredeck big enough for a ballista, cargo hold, and berths for thirty men."

"A warship? Not a freighter?" Benoit asked.

Improvising, Hava said, "My husband has freight carriers aplenty, good sir, but he is plagued by pirates and needs guardians. Used freighters are plentiful. Escort ships are not. Lost cargo is his concern."

Benoit was slightly taken aback that this woman was speaking and glanced at Donte, who feigned indifference and in his affected voice said, "I'm a merchant by birth and upbringing, but my lovely wife is the daughter of a sea captain, from a long line of the same. She was climbing in the rigging as a child and knows more about ships than I care to contemplate, so I always stand by her good judgment in such matters. If she says we need such a ship, we need such a ship. Cost is of no concern. Name a price."

Pug almost winced at the last.

Benoit was quiet for a moment. Then he said, "Let me show you something." He led them out of the front door, across the street, and down a short access road, to the dry docks they had spied earlier.

Up close, Hava took note that the work was proceeding at a slow, steady pace, and that more men would get the jobs done faster. She assumed that no one was paying extra for a quick refitting and reckoned that meant she had an advantage if she were to offer a premium for quick work. She admired the construction of the dry docks. Massive wooden cradles held the ships in berths that were emptied of water by a clever mechanism of water troughs, lifted and poured back into the bay, and when work was finished, the berth could be flooded by a simple lift gate in the larger barrier. Once floated, the ship could be towed out of the dock. Working this way was much faster than careening a ship on a beach or sending divers down while it was at anchor, both of which were time-consuming, and the latter dangerous.

The sun was out, and the breeze was fresh, and Hava decided she liked this city. If time permitted, she'd like to return and spend a little time exploring.

Turning to his right, Benoit led them to a work area at the end of the berths, a dry dock where a freshly laid keel waited, with the work on the hull timbers just underway. "She was going to be a coastal short-haul freighter. City runner up and down the coast from here to Yabon, but the buyer died. I was going to finish her at leisure in case a buyer for such a vessel wandered in."

Hava moved past him to take a look at the work done so far. She said, "Two lower decks, yes?"

Benoit nodded as she looked back at him. "Fore and aft orlop decks with room for ballast between, two freight decks, and a forecastle for a dozen men, and quarters for six officers."

"Galley?"

He shook his head. "She's a coaster, so it's open-deck cooking or camping ashore. I can take some space off the first lower deck and put in a galley and food storage, but she'll still need provisioning every few weeks. You're talking the Bitter Sea, then, not open oceans from here to Novindus or Wynet."

"Perfect," Hava said, "since we'll be shepherding freighters from the Free Cities to here. You said an eighteen-man crew?"

Benoit nodded.

"They planned on anchoring to shore most nights with a crew that small. Not in a hurry, were they?"

Benoit's expression as he turned to Pug and Donte made it clear how impressed he was with Hava's knowledge.

"Good," said Hava, her excitement growing. "Extend the forecastle to house twenty, and double the berths in the rear quarter, two bunks to a room, except for the captain's. Where are the masts going to be?"

Benoit took her down a few more steps and they began to discuss placing the masts back a few feet, allowing for a pair of ballistas on either side.

Donte said to Benoit, "As you can see, my good wife has a firm understanding of what I need. I shall leave this in her capable hands." He pulled Pug aside, and whispered, "Where's the nearest inn?"

Pug glanced back at Benoit and Hava, then looked at Donte. He whispered back, "It's barely past midday."

"I didn't ask what time it was, I wanted to know where the nearest inn is. It's been more than a year since I've been inside a proper inn and had a proper drink or a good brawl. I'll find my way back to your little building."

"You can find it?"

"I know how to mark my travels in a strange city."

Pug remembered Hava's earlier remark about that. "I believe the nearest inn is in that direction," he said, pointing up the street past Benoit's workplace. "Turn left at the first street, then right."

Donte smiled and said, "Thanks." He turned away and took a step.

A moment later Hava came up and said, "Where's Donte off to?"

"No good, no doubt," said Pug in dubious tones.

"You're learning," said Hava. "No worries. He'll find his way back, one way or another, and in his own time."

Benoit finished speaking to one of the workers and approached. "Your husband?" he asked.

"Off to shop, I expect," Hava said. "He's a clever man, but of ships he knows only the little he needs to. He'd rather be about other business."

"Well, we have some work ahead. We can make the changes you requested, and have it done in far less time than if we were starting from scratch. Now, let us discuss a price."

Hava smiled. "Yes, let's."

Benoit moved back toward the office and Pug and Hava fell in a step behind.

Hava glanced over and saw Pug looked strained. "Is everything all right?" she whispered.

Pug nodded. "Just an unexpected pain." He pointed to the side of his head. "It will pass."

"You get them often?"

"No," he replied, "they've only come on recently. If they persist, I shall visit a healer."

Hava reached over and touched his arm lightly. "Good. I think we're going to be friends and I don't have that many left to lose."

DONTE WAS DISAPPOINTED. THE STONE Street Tavern was quiet. He hadn't expected it to be rowdy, stuffed with workers and sailors at midday, but there were only three other customers there: two merchants by their appearances, and a man in the corner who appeared to be asleep.

The tavern keeper was a dour man, portly, with a florid face and rheumy blue eyes. His hair was a tangled thatch of grey with hints that it had once been ginger. Donte placed a silver coin on the bar. The tavern keeper said, "If you are only having one, do you have two coppers? If I break that silver down, I'll be short of change."

Donte swiped back the silver, dropped it into the purse, and fetched out three coppers. "For you," he said grandly.

As he turned away, Donte thought he heard the man mutter something like thanks, but he couldn't be sure. Tipping might not be a common practice here, he thought. It wasn't everywhere on Garn, and certainly not in any of the island inns of Coaltachin. Unless things were vastly different here, paying as you go would be the norm.

He moved to the end of the bar so that he could see the entire common room and took a long draft from the mug of ale. The two men in conversation looked enough alike that Donte assumed they were brothers, and the sleeping fellow in the corner had his chair tipped back, his hat pulled down over his eyes, and didn't move. As inns went, this was a very disappointing place. Still, he savored being in a common room, even if it was a poor one by his standards. But, he thought, there must be other inns and taverns, and the day was barely half over. He finished his ale and pushed aside the mug.

"Another?" asked the tavern keeper.

"Thanks, no. I have other places to be."

Donte sauntered out of the inn, pausing to see if the sleeping man had been feigning slumber and scouting for an easy mark. Donte's current fashion would have marked him as an easy target in any number of cities on Garn where Donte had worked.

He moved away from the docks, intuitively knowing that the landscape would change, not only physically, but also economically, in terms of who lived where, what sort of businesses and homes were nearby, and a hundred other details drilled into him since boyhood.

He rounded the first corner leading him away from the dockside and toward what he assumed would be some sort of merchants' district. He spied a boy idling on the corner, as if waiting for someone. The first merchant window he passed was not for display of goods, but to admit light, so Donte made a show of pausing and attempting to peer in, his hand shielding his eyes from light from above. He glanced behind him and saw the second boy.

Resisting the urge to laugh, he recognized that he was being stalked. Two or three other youngsters would be close at hand and a quick surveillance of the street ahead gave him a good notion of where these children would attempt to pick his pockets or, if especially bold, rob him at knifepoint. An alley ahead seemed like the most likely spot, and Donte forced himself to maintain his leisurely gait. He really wanted to pick up his pace and get to the next bit. He smiled. This was going to be fun.

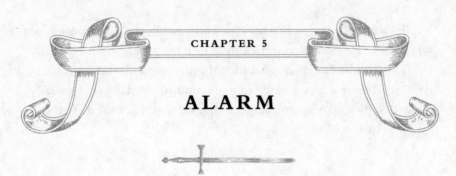

CHAPTER 5

ALARM

Declan squinted.

Against the setting sun he could barely make out the signal flag from the southwest. But the flashing light made it clear that a ship was approaching, and it was not one of Marquensas's burgeoning navy.

Turning to a soldier standing behind him, he said, "Send word to my brothers we have an unknown ship coming in."

The soldier turned and hurried away.

Glancing at Sixto, who had summoned Declan to the wall, he said, "I don't think one ship warrants turning out the garrison."

"You're probably right, but it could be a very big ship," Sixto replied in a mock-serious tone.

"It'll be after sundown before it reaches us," replied Declan, ignoring Sixto's humor. "I'll be with my brothers if it's anything we should hear about."

"I'll wait," said Sixto.

Declan smiled. "Yes, you will."

Hurrying down from his vantage point atop a castle tower, Declan quickly left the waning sunlight and found himself deep in shadow. The sun was almost set, and the garrison was shifting from the hustle of day to the relative quiet of night. Troops that had been on duty or in training were now heading for the barracks and then off to the soldiers' mess. Grooms were tending to the horses, and the only major activity was in the kitchens, where they were making ready the evening meal.

In the city below the tempo was changing. Work gangs were leaving the canal project which would connect the city to the sea, and the other improvements made by the king. Tradesmen were shuttering shops, and men would be stopping in their local taverns on their way home, or to eat a meal after drinking.

Declan left the stairs from the wall and crossed an open yard to a side entrance to the castle, where he was saluted by a guard stationed there. He returned the salute, knowing another guard would replace the man soon to stand the night watch.

Declan hurried to his quarters, where a page had readied his wash basin and fresh clothes. A proper bath would have to wait, but Declan had come to appreciate sponging himself off and putting on clean clothes before a meal. Balven's lessons were taking hold, he conceded to himself.

He finished a quick cleanup, then made his way to the king's private dining room, a small space set aside for King Daylon's more intimate dining with his brothers, an occasional lady companion, or an important visitor. A much larger dining hall—the King's Hall—had now been completed, with a long head table, and smaller tables so that as many as a hundred guests could be entertained for state celebrations and festivals.

It had been completed, but not fully decorated, for Daylon's coronation, and then only about thirty guests had attended. Now it was bedecked with historical tapestries, shields of long-dead ancestors, trophies, and many banners, most prominent among which was the recently created kingdom banner: a crossed sword and branch laden with orange blossoms in gold and white on a field of light blue.

Balven was already in the private dining room. Declan greeted him, adding, "This day has gone quickly."

"It goes by in a hurry when you're busy, and you've been at it since before sunup."

They remained standing behind their chairs, waiting for the arrival of the king. Daylon appeared annoyed when only the three brothers were eating that they waited for him to sit first, but it was part of Balven's insistence that they all started to observe protocol at all times, against a time when a social gaffe might undermine Daylon's authority. As Balven had said to Declan more than once—and probably to anyone else who needed to hear it—it was theater, but it was important theater.

King Daylon entered and all three sat down as servants bustled around the table with food and wine. The king looked at his youngest brother and said, "I haven't seen much of you, Declan. How did your day go?"

Declan laughed. "I know Balven keeps you informed of everything."

Both men chuckled. "Still," said the king. "Your report, then?"

"A messenger from the south says the fortification at the Narrows is now defensible and the ballistas are in place. The barracks are next, and there's still no sign of further encroachment by the Church.

"Training is going well, though we're getting a little short of food again, and probably need to attend to that sooner rather than later."

Balven nodded. "I sent a ship down to the Sanctuary to see if we can find some grain and livestock in Nytanny. And I've got scouts up in the northern mountains looking to see if any flocks or herds are still roaming in those narrow valleys—there are a lot of them to the east of the Copper Hills."

"Oh, and we should hear more about that approaching ship in a bit," Declan added.

"We also need to discuss a coming visit," said Balven.

Declan put his fork down and looked at Balven. "Visit?"

"A minor cousin to the late King of Ilcomen, Baron . . ." Daylon looked to Balven.

"Baron Gustaf of Mill Haven."

"Mill Haven?" asked Declan. "I've been to Mill Haven, delivering farm equipment when I was apprenticed to Edvalt. The whole town would fit inside the walls of this castle. They have a baron?"

"Apparently," said Balven. "Our records of other kingdoms' nobles were hardly up to date, but there was a baron of Mill Haven listed— Gunther."

"Probably his father," suggested the king.

"Or grandfather," replied Balven with a shrug.

"And let me guess," said Declan. "He has a daughter."

"Actually, two of them," replied Balven. "Baron Gustaf probably doesn't have enough gold to get a proper suit tailored, let alone provide a dowry, but a marriage to any relative of the late King of Ilcomen will stem some criticism of our annexing a large portion of that former kingdom. More importantly, it will blunt the claims of any pretenders to that throne."

"Stem some criticism, and blunt claims, not prevent them," said Declan, clearly unhappy at the idea of shopping for a wife. His tone was cold, but his anger was poorly hidden. Both brothers knew Declan was still haunted by the death of his wife, as was the king by his own loss. But unlike the king, Declan was the future of the Dumarch line of kings. Daylon might be able to sire another son, but he had made it clear he had no intention of remarrying. Daylon could mourn as long as he needed, but Declan did not have that luxury. Declan thought Balven would be a far better choice of ruler, but as he was publicly known to be illegitimate, his mother being a commoner, he could not inherit. Declan also knew Balven didn't want the title—he preferred what he currently did, be the key advisor, what he called "the last voice." He looked at Balven with a question in his expression.

"Politics is the art of the possible," said Balven. "All we can do is lessen the possibility of stupid people making things more difficult for us than they already are. We can never prevent it."

Daylon slowly nodded and sighed. "I'm the damned king, and I can't stop it."

Declan looked displeased but kept further remarks to himself. He'd had this fight with his brothers before and knew that it was futile.

A few minutes later a knock came from the door and King Daylon said, "Enter!"

A page peered into the room and said, "Captain Sixto and another man request to see you at once, Majesty."

"So much for a quiet supper," said Declan as the king waved for the men to be admitted, though he knew Sixto wouldn't be here unless it was urgent.

Sixto entered, followed a step behind by Bodai, once a false master of Coaltachin, the Kingdom of the Night. He was Hatushaly's mentor, and now the leader of the Flame Guard, the once secret society dedicated to protecting the legendary Firemane line of kings.

Without a word, Sixto motioned for Bodai to address the king.

"Majesty," he began, "I fear something . . . un—impossible . . ." He took a breath and started again. "It appears there is no magic on Garn anymore."

All three brothers put down knives and forks and turned their full attention to Bodai, their expressions revealing utter confusion.

"Explain," said the king.

"I can't," said Bodai, then quickly added, "Your Majesty." He took a breath and said, "If you remember Zaakara, one of the two magicians from the world of Midkemia—he returned though one of those rift gates they use to travel between worlds." He said this in a matter-of-fact tone, though it was still almost unbelievable to Declan and his brothers, despite all three of them having seen a rift.

"He is that world's most knowledgeable person about the place atop the center of Nytanny, that stone . . . city or whatever it is containing those frozen creatures. I believe 'Void Children,' or something like that, was the term. From what I've learned, they are a terrible threat to this world and to his own.

"In any event, he appeared, closed the rift behind him, spoke for a while with me and a few others in the Flame Guard, and wished to investigate that location and see with his own eyes what had been reported."

The king pointed to a pair of chairs against the wall and motioned for Sixto to bring them to the table. He did so, and when he and Bodai were seated, Daylon gestured to Bodai to continue.

The stout man took a deep breath and paused for a moment to organize his thoughts. "Let me see if I can make a bit of sense of this."

"Please," said the king, sounding impatient. "That would be welcomed."

"Since Hatushaly, Hava, and their friend Donte went through the rift to the world of Midkemia," Bodai began, "we of the Flame Guard have been reordering our order's purpose. We trusted the magic-users from Midkemia to explore further into Hatu's unique talents and powers, since it is far beyond our ability to help him to gain control of them.

"We went about our business rebuilding the Sanctuary, following the chaos that visited Nytanny with the destruction of the Pride

Lords, and helping where we could. Almost a month ago, a rift opened where it had before, on the island where you staged your assault on the Pride Lords—it seems there's likelihood of rifts re-forming where they were before—and we still have a small community there. A boat was dispatched with the visitor, the man Zaakara who came to gather more information on those alien creatures frozen atop the mountains on Nytanny. Apparently, that and the creature you found"—he indicated Declan—"in Garn's Wound, are linked with a similar creature on Midkemia." He stopped, almost out of breath.

Balven stood, went to a sideboard, grabbed a mug, and filled it with wine. He handed it to Bodai and said, "You look like you could use this."

"Thank you," said Bodai, and he took a long swallow. "What you may not know is how unique Hatu is." He went on to give a brief description of what had been known before Hatushaly's birth, that only women could employ magic of any sort, as oracles, seers, healers, or to inflict harm with curses or disease, but that men were somehow the sources of magic. It had been an agent of the Flame Guard who had secreted Hatushaly as a baby in the then–Baron Daylon's tent, the night after the King of Ithrace had been killed and his family murdered. As the only surviving child of the Firemane line, Hatushaly was considered to have a powerful link to all magic on Garn, a supposition which had been confirmed by many subsequent events.

"It's a balance," Bodai continued, "and until we encountered Hatu, we really had little understanding of how any of this truly worked. There was the legend of a Curse of the Firemanes, that should the line end, terrible consequences would occur. There were stories, fables if you will, that all magic flowed through that bloodline, which was marked by their copper hair, the long, healthy lives they lived, and their ease in creating beauty where they lived."

Both Daylon and Balven knew bits and pieces of that lore but remained silent as Bodai continued.

"What seems to have happened—without our knowing it—is that when Hatushaly went to Midkemia, he took all of the magic on Garn with him."

Declan, Daylon, and Balven sat speechless, just staring at Bodai.

After a long moment, King Daylon said, "I'm not sure I fully understand how that can be possible."

"Zaakara is a powerful user of magic on his world and expected to be able to do as he had before, to open a rift, visit me to prepare for an investigation of the creatures frozen in the center of Nytanny, then open another rift home, and leave.

"All went well, and we discussed what would be necessary to make that trek. I'll spare you those details, but when Zaakara felt ready to return home, he could not conjure up a rift. He tried other magics, things he said would be easy, usually almost without thought for him to accomplish, but nothing worked. *Nothing.*"

"Can you be certain that Hatushaly's departure is the cause?" asked Balven.

"And where is this Zaakara?" asked the king.

Bodai looked at Daylon, and said, "He quickly returned to the site of the first rift opened on the island, where you marshaled your forces against the Pride Lords. He said it was the most likely place for a rift to form should others seek him. He needed to be there to ensure they didn't close the rift and strand themselves here as well. He said he was desperate that if it was what he called a 'both ways' passage, they could safely return home, find Hatushaly, and return here."

To Balven, he said, "We could be wrong, but the inability of that magician to duplicate something he had previously been able to do easily, with the only obviously different thing being Hatushaly's absence, leads to the only logical conclusion."

"Does that mean Hatushaly, his wife, and his friend are now stranded on Midkemia?" asked the king.

"I don't think so," Bodai replied. "If the rift is reopened, Zaakara believes there's a safe way between the two worlds. It's just that we have no way to send word to Midkemia and must depend on them to eventually send someone to look for Zaakara."

"With all else that we face . . ." The king let the thought go unfinished. "Still, no matter what horrors may sit atop the plateau in Nytanny, we must prepare for what we know for certain is coming for us. The wake of carnage the Church Adamant is leaving behind clearly shows they are merciless and will not negotiate or respect sovereignty." His jaw tightened and his mood was clearly one of suppressed anger. "I was an accomplice in serving these butchers, when we betrayed King Steveren Langene—no man I admired more—and I'll not betray my honor again. We will be ready when they get here!"

Declan was still learning about his brothers, but at this moment he knew without uncertainty his eldest brother was resolved in his position. He would die before bending a knee to this evil Church.

Daylon pushed back his chair and stood up. Declan and Balven stood as well because someone not in the family was there. This was becoming the way of life for the three brothers. Informality was allowed only when they were alone.

"Obviously nothing can be done tonight," said the king. He motioned toward Balven and said, "Find Bodai a room."

Balven nodded and said to Bodai, "We should talk more tomorrow." He bowed to his brother and led Bodai and Sixto outside.

Once they were gone, Daylon said, "What do you think of that?"

"I don't know," Declan said slowly. "I wasn't thinking much about anything except getting ready for whenever the Church of the One attacks." He looked thoughtful for a moment, then added, "Still, if they have magic-users somewhere among their forces, that might work to our advantage."

"Wishful thinking," replied the king as he moved toward the door to his private quarters. When he got there, he turned and said, "We have never had word of them having anyone with supernatural powers. So far all we see is brute force and a core of highly trained soldiers. I'd prefer to focus on what we know, not something only remotely possible. Now, get some sleep and tomorrow we'll discuss the coming visit of Baron Gustaf of Mill Haven."

Declan's expression revealed that he was not happy with this prospect, but he said nothing, bowed, and as the king exited through one door, he left through the other.

As he made his way to his quarters, Declan weighed which disturbed him most: Hatushaly's apparent impact on magic, along with the slew of unanswered questions that created, the coming promise of war with the Church, or meeting potential wives. He came to the conclusion that worrying about any of it was not a good way to gain a restful night's sleep.

ZAAKARA SAT AS PATIENTLY AS was possible despite his anxiety. He wore brown leather trousers tucked into mid-calf black boots and a homespun grey shirt. He had a jacket folded next to him on the grass, for the days here were warm. Never since late childhood had he been without his magic abilities. He could barely remember his childhood before his powers had begun to manifest, so he found himself constantly fighting against an almost juvenile feeling of vulnerability. He kept glancing at the spot where he had come through from Midkemia. The shadows were lengthening and when he glanced westward, he could see the day was fading.

A small campsite had been arranged nearby, and a firepit was ready to be ignited with the coming night. He had been provided with two camp stools, and an open, waterproof canvas square was rigged up over a small table bearing his food, minimizing the risk of insect pests getting to it before he did. Though he had scant appetite since finding himself stranded on this world.

Across from him sat Sabella, an adept of the Flame Guard who was now the head librarian at the Sanctuary. She wore a sleeveless blue dress with a bronze-buckled black belt. She had seemed to Bodai and Zaakara the most likely of Garn's magic-users to be of aid in this vigil.

Zaakara had come to realize after three days that Sabella understood how vitally important this apparent loss of magic might be, beyond the simple loss of communication with Midkemia. She also clearly recognized his personal sense of alienation and loss, and fully grasped his distress.

She would relieve him at sundown so that he could eat and rest inside the tent. Another adept would take the watch sometime in the night, and Zaakara would resume his vigil in the morning.

He was thankful for her company. She came early and they would talk. She was eager to learn about Midkemia and, while most of her life had been cloistered, her skills had provided her with a surprising knowledge of Garn.

From Zaakara's perspective, she possessed an odd but impressive talent: the ability to sense magic in others from a distance. She was also curious about his abilities, as the manifestation of magic on this world was profoundly different to that on Midkemia. She had mentioned that she knew the instant he returned from Midkemia because his magic generated something like a specific mark, a signature as it were, that she recognized from his first visit to the Sanctuary.

He welcomed such new knowledge and things to ponder beyond being stranded on an alien planet—it might be a long vigil, waiting for someone to come looking for him. He had said he'd be gone only a day, but he also knew that the others on Sorcerer's Isle might assume he'd become distracted by something of interest and had lingered here of his own free will. They would probably not become concerned about him for many days.

It was a tedious and uneasy wait, so he found Sabella's presence a comfort. She had politely asked if he minded sharing information about his magic, and he had told her of his life.

His father, Amirantha, he had told her, had monitored his maturation closely, and his mother, Sandreena, had had enough experience with magic to have been greatly instructive about what should and shouldn't be allowed. Dealing with demons was always a tricky proposition which was beyond the ability of most, and those who had this ability were often people of dubious character.

"My father was a man . . . of . . . evolving character," said Zaakara to Sabella. "He found his way to our sanctuary, Sorcerer's Isle, because he was being hunted by one of my uncles." Sabella smiled a slightly lopsided expression of inquiry. He liked her eager expression and her manner and wit, and thought her dark hair and eyes striking.

"Hunted?" she asked.

Zaakara returned the smile and nodded. "To say my father and brothers were bad men is too simple. My father was a confidence trickster as well as a user of magic. Early on, he discovered this ability, the talent that earned him the title of warlock among his people, which also turned him into an outcast.

"My uncle Sidi was a practitioner of very dark magic, which I was told drove him mad. My eldest uncle, Belasco, was a profoundly evil man, serving a dark power, and he and my father were always at odds." He looked caught between amusement and sadness. "From what I was told, my father's family was . . . a mess." His smile hinted regret. "My uncle Sidi murdered his mother for a powerful amulet. No one is sure what happened to him. My father avoided his brothers until Belasco found him and used his magic to try to kill my father." His smile broadened. "I'm pleased to say he didn't, else I wouldn't be here chatting with you. Like my father and Uncle Belasco, I'm a warlock, a demon-summoner."

"Demons?" asked Sabella. "You've mentioned them before, but I'm still unclear as to what they are."

"They are creatures from a lower realm of existence, all chaotic and evil by our measure, though a few are relatively harmless, but none are benevolent. You probably have legends about such creatures with other names, but the difference between our worlds is there they are real, not myths."

Sabella hugged herself for a moment, then said, "Most of my life I was raised and trained for one purpose, to find the Firemane heir, and when that was over, all the girls of my calling were left without a purpose. I discovered mine in the library at the Sanctuary and found I had a desire to learn new things." She smiled broadly. "Even if many of the new things are difficult to understand or believe."

"Tell me more about your magic, or whatever you call your ability."

She lifted her shoulders slightly. "It's just there. On this world only women can access powers, or at least that was the belief until Hatushaly was born. But we were unable to use our powers unless we were somehow connected to a man who . . . I guess you could say was a vessel of power." Her expression changed to a wistful memory of a younger purpose. "We were taught to meditate, to remain still for hours. In that state, we let our minds . . . wander, you might say, seeking a strong source of that power. We were trained to . . . see is the wrong word . . . to sense, envision where that source was. For a very long time it was a punishing task, and over the years several girls succumbed to . . ." She shrugged. "I don't know how to explain it, but it was as if all their abilities just burned out like a candle reaching the end of the wick."

Zaakara nodded. "I understand. At Sorcerer's Isle I've seen students reach their limit. To push further invites a heavy price."

"You were talking about your uncles," she prompted.

Zaakara took a small breath. "Well, as I was saying, the men in my family had the knack for dark magic. My father and uncles all hated each other, and to this day I'm still a little vague about why, save that my father said it had a lot to do with how they were raised. He doesn't like to talk about it.

"My father used to conjure fairly harmless demons, though they were daunting in appearance and frightened local populations for a day or so. Then he'd appear and vanquish them for a fee."

"He was a criminal," Sabella said flatly.

"More or less," agreed Zaakara. "But compared to his brothers, he was a petty amateur. They were monsters, by all accounts. Sidi trafficked with evil, turned good men bad, and tried to seize power though manipulation. He was a necromancer, employing death magic. It cost him his life. Belasco was a warlock, like my father and me, but he employed demons as murderous servants. It was only with the help of others from Sorcerer's Isle that my father survived and finally defeated him."

"Is that why you serve those on the isle you speak of?"

"I was born there," Zaakara said. "My parents were a very strange couple and had crossed paths several times before they wed. My mother, unlike my father, was a holy warrior of one of our temples—the temple of the Goddess Dala, Shield of the Weak—and was by temperament and training as opposite to my father as one can imagine. Her name was Sandreena, and she's the reason I am the first warlock of my people not to summon demons for evil purposes, and when I find them, I hunt them down to banish or destroy them."

"That's quite a story," she said, obviously impressed. "Is your mother still with your father?"

Zaakara's expression turned reflective, and he gently shook his head. "No, unlike my father and me, she was not long-lived. Temple magic is different to the powers most magic-users employ on my world. She died many years ago. It took a toll on my father, and he is slowly fading away." His tone turned sorrowful. "I fear he may just choose to die."

She raised her eyebrows in a silent question.

He held his hands out, palms up, in a gesture of surrender. "It's difficult to explain, but every person has to have a will to live. Most do, but some people just give up that will and they . . . fade. My mother died before my father, long ago, as he knew she would. She looked more like his mother than his wife, though he never stopped loving her or caring for her." He let out a long sigh. "You expect to outlive your parents, but losing a lifetime partner is very painful. Especially when you outlive them by decades."

"That long ago?"

Zaakara laughed ruefully. "I'm old enough to be your grandfather, Sabella." He tilted his head and closed one eye in a playful expression. "Great-grandfather, probably," he added in a joking tone.

Her eyes opened very wide. "Really?"

"And unless Garn magic somehow makes you long-lived, I may be here to meet your grandchildren."

She blushed. Softly, she said, "Until Hatushaly was found, we all assumed we'd live our lives in service to the Flame Guard. The idea of being wed, having children or grandchildren was never considered." She took a breath. "This is part of that unexpected change we who serve the Flame Guard now face."

Zaakara was about to speak when a rift manifested a few yards away. The magic-user was on his feet a moment later and had just reached the edge of the rift when Ruffio stomped through.

Zaakara shouted, "Don't close the rift!"

A stunned-looking Ruffio half-turned to look back as he was about to close the rift, when Zaakara ran up and grabbed him around the waist, spinning him around and almost knocking him over. As Zaakara held Ruffio upright, the magician from Midkemia shouted, "What?"

"Don't close the rift!"

Ruffio took a small step backward with his hands up and said, "All right, why?"

"Because I couldn't open one when I finished speaking with Bodai."

"Huh?" Ruffio looked confused.

Zaakara quickly explained the problem he'd encountered, then asked, "One way?"

Ruffio nodded.

"Damn," said Zaakara. He looked at Ruffio. "Apparently when Hatu left, he took all of Garn's magic with him."

Ruffio's eyes widened. "What?"

"The magic here is just gone." Zaakara looked over at the rift. "Maybe some magic is coming through there. Let me see something."

The warlock muttered a chant and another rift appeared beside the one Ruffio had passed through, but smaller, about a third the size of the first.

"Odd," said Ruffio, still looking confused.

"That should have been a full rift home," said Zaakara.

Sabella said, "It's big enough to fit through."

Ruffio suddenly noticed her and gave a slight wave of greeting.

Zaakara said, "The problem is, if it failed to reach Midkemia, we have no idea where it terminates."

Ruffio said, "It could be inside a mountain, or out in empty space."

"Or in another world entirely," added Zaakara.

"So, you can't return though that one?" Sabella asked, pointing at the larger rift.

"I'll spare you a long explanation," said Zaakara. "Most rifts, like that one, only allow travel in one direction, from where it's cast to where it ends. You travel somewhere, you close the rift after you. Two-way rifts are more difficult and require more energy and art. We only use them if we're traveling somewhere to pick something up or to escort someone without magic ability to where we started."

"I think I understand."

"What do you propose?" asked Ruffio.

"We keep the big one open," Zaakara answered. "We see if we can contrive a way to turn it into a two-way rift."

"Has that ever been done?" asked Ruffio.

"I don't know," said Zaakara. "Magnus never mentioned it when he trained me, and truthfully, I wasn't his best student with rifts. I think I only got the knack because the spells are a little like the gates I use to bring in demons."

Ruffio nodded as if this made sense. "There's the risk," he said.

Zaakara let out a low moan of frustration. "I know."

"What risk?" asked Sabella.

"I'm not entirely sure," said Ruffio.

"Neither am I," added Zaakara. "Only when we were trained it was made clear that a long-standing rift though the Void tends to be a magnet of sorts for some very powerful and nasty things no one wants finding them."

"Oh!" she said, eyes wide.

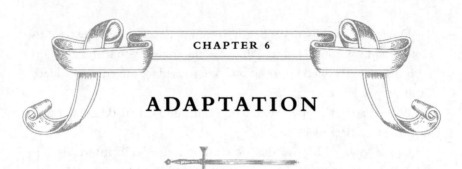

CHAPTER 6

ADAPTATION

Donte stood motionless.

With his back flat against the wall, inches from the corner, he waited for the boy to turn after him. The intersection was in shadow owing to the afternoon sun being blocked by a tall building to the west. It was not dark, but just enough in shade for eyes to take a moment to adjust.

If the pair had been trained well, the boy who had followed him on the other side of the street would loop around across to the far corner diagonal from Donte, while the lad trailing him from behind would wait for a signal that Donte had continued on his way.

As soon as the boy rounded the corner, Donte grabbed him by the back of the neck and swung him around, face into the wall, just hard enough to shock him, but not do serious damage. The boy instantly tried to duck down, and Donte lifted him so that he had to stand on his toes. A small knife fell out of his hand, clattering on the stones.

"Let me go!" the lad shouted.

Donte regarded his captive. He was a thin child, perhaps nine or ten years of age, with an unruly thatch of dirty sandy-brown hair and, under the street dirt, a fair skin. Green eyes glared at Donte.

"Maybe," answered Donte. "Where's your pal?"

"I don't got no pal," came the reply, a hint of defiance undercut by a clearly fearful tone.

From the way he turned his head, scanning as far as he was able, Donte assumed he was trying to see if his companion was near.

"I expect your pal's run off," said Donte.

"I got no pal, I told ya!"

Donte saw the boy's eyes begin to well up, even though he tried to keep up a brave front. "Listen, I'm not going to hurt you if you don't do anything stupid. I need information." He paused for effect, then added, "And I'll pay for it."

Immediately, the boy ceased struggling and a calculating look came over his face. "Pay me?"

Donte lowered him so that he could stand more comfortably but didn't let go of the knot of shirt he had wedged between the boy's neck and his hand. To emphasize still being in control, he squeezed slightly.

"Ouch!" the boy cried theatrically.

"You are a really bad alley rat." Whatever the magic used on Donte to enable him to speak and understand the King's Tongue, it seemed to work perfectly with Coaltachin slang.

"I ain't no mugger!" he cried loudly.

"Wall-climber?"

"No," the boy said, his volume lowering. He shook his head. "Too risky."

Donte said, "Cutter, then."

The boy slumped, then nodded.

"So, you were going to stall and cut, with your friend?"

"What's a stall? I cut, toss it to him, you chase after the purse, and I run the other way."

Donte laughed. He pulled out his purse and drew out two coppers. He held them up but didn't give them to the boy. "Now, two of these for each true answer. If you lie, I'll know, and you'll get nothing."

The boy nodded and Donte gave him the first two coins. "So, your friend ran away. He going to find some bullies to come get you loose of me?"

"Bullies?" The boy's eyes widened. "You mean bashers. Ya, they're bully lads!" He shook his head. "We don't have any bashers."

Donte handed him another two coins. "No bashers? What sort of crew are you? And what do I call you?"

"Tommy. And we're no crew, if you mean a gang. It's just me and a couple of mates." He held out his hand, and when Donte put two more coppers in his palm, he said, "That was two questions."

Donte chuckled. "You may not be a good pickpocket, but you've got smarts." He gave over another two coins. "So, who runs the gangs in this city?"

"Stranger, is it?"

"Yes," said Donte, snatching back two coppers.

"Hey!" said Tommy, his eyes narrowing.

"I answered your question honestly." Donte grinned.

"No one runs Port Vykor yet," said Tommy. "We got two rival gangs trying to take over and it's deadly out there at night. Me and me mates try to scramble for what we can during the day, but it's rough."

Donte nodded. He took a silver coin out of his purse, and Tommy's eyes widened. "Enough of this one question at a time. Tell me about who is trying to take over the gangs here."

Tommy could barely contain his avarice, and Donte could see his fingers flexing as he considered trying to grab the coin and run.

"Stifle your greed for a moment, and the coin is yours." Donte put it back in his purse and released Tommy. He wiggled his fingers a moment. "You're a tough lad to hang on to." He glanced around to see if they were being watched, but it seemed that if anyone had passed them, they had simply ignored Donte and Tommy.

"Okay, so there's a big city to the north, Krondor. They got a lot of gangs, but they all answer to this one guy: the Upright Man, he's called. The biggest gang is his, the Mockers. Some smaller gangs like the Over the Wall Raiders and the Harborsiders are working with smugglers and the Mockers, but this Upright Man keeps things in order. They been there as long as anyone remembers. They say this Upright Man lives forever."

Donte smiled and nodded. The masters of Coaltachin had spent more than a century crafting legends and myths that worked to their advantage. "Go on."

"So, the Mockers are trying to move down here. Seems they've tried a couple of times. I don't know, but Healer might."

"Who's that?"

"Old man, lived in the Bottoms a long time. We can't go to a proper chirurgeon or healing priest, no money and no temple offering." He shrugged. "So, Healer patches up and we do him favors."

Donte slowly nodded. "Favors, like nicking stuff he needs?"

"That, and he's a big one for gossip and news."

"I think we should go and talk to this Healer."

Tommy's eyes drifted to Donte's belt purse.

Donte reached in and pulled out the silver coin. He handed it over to Tommy and said, "You take me to meet Healer and there's another one for you."

"Done," said Tommy almost gleefully. Donte had no idea how long a boy like this would take to make a silver's worth of copper coins with his petty thievery, but it obviously was a long time.

Donte motioned and Tommy took off at a quick pace, and Donte took two steps and grabbed him by the scruff again.

"Ow!" shouted the boy.

"First rule," said Donte into the boy's ear, almost but not quite pulling him off balance. "Don't call attention to yourself by running. Walk. Beside me. Tell me if we need to turn a corner. Understood?"

Tommy nodded and fell in beside Donte. "Right at the next corner," he said.

They made the turn and Donte saw they were moving uphill, toward an open market, then a left at the edge of the market and down a steep hill that gave Donte a view of the city below.

Port Vykor was like many cities Donte had visited on his home world of Garn. The wealthy lived up the hill, with the view of the bay, and upwind from the places that stank. He saw that a small river emptied into a low series of coastal pools before spilling into the bay. A pair of simple piers jutted out far enough for shallow-draft boats to offload from, mostly fishing boats and the occasional smuggler, he reckoned.

A quick glance skyward oriented him. He saw that the shore swooped northwest but could see no headland or lighthouse. This bay was open-mouthed, he decided. He was no expert at seamanship like Hava, but he'd visited enough ports to have an idea how things worked. He chuckled to himself. It was part of his training to know how best to get out of a place.

Moving down the hill, he saw the quality of buildings change along with the quality of the air. Like other cities, this was where the working

poor, the very poor, and a lot of criminals would be dwelling. Tanners, slaughterhouse-workers, sausage-makers, tenders of chickens and
pigpens, all manner of noxious-smelling industries were shunted off
where the stench wouldn't offend the sensibilities of those with wealth,
all the way down to the wharf where the fishmongers would ready the
morning catch to take to market.

There was a lateral canal that drained from the docks to the west
side of the bay, and once they crossed over it, they stood in what was
clearly the most wretched quarter in Port Vykor.

Donte asked, "What do you call this place?"

"The Bottoms."

Donte looked around. Makeshift hovels, a few remaining walls
from empty buildings, and impromptu business stalls announced pov-
erty and desperation everywhere he looked. It was the lowest parcel of
dry land in Port Vykor, and it reeked of dead fish, sewage, and wet sand.

"Aptly named," he said. By the time he had turned twelve years
old, Donte had become acclimatized to such places. Still, the desperation that lingered was hard to ignore.

Tommy said, "If you got nowhere else, here's a place you can get
by. Most people leave you alone."

"I understand," Donte replied. He put his hand on Tommy's shoulder for a moment, then said, "Lead on."

Reaching an improvised street between two lines of tents and jury-
rigged hovels, Tommy said, "Right."

Donte let the boy move ahead and followed him as they entered
the narrow byway. It was wide enough for two to walk side by side, or
a small cart might be pulled by a goat or small donkey, but no wagon
would ever pass this way. Donte understood that this would be a handy
place to dodge into if one were pursued, especially by mounted city
watch, if such existed here. The horses would have to follow in single
file and enough of these buildings had overhangs and exposed but-
tresses that a rider would have to almost lie across the horse's neck. He
committed this place to memory.

About a dozen buildings down, several with rear doors emptying
into the alley, they reached another alley heading off to the left toward
the first big street. Tommy waved for Donte to follow and led him to

an odd-looking jumble of random trash, until Donte spied the entrance masked by it.

Tommy pushed some rubbish aside and stepped down to a small opening covered by a hanging curtain. It was an outside entrance to a basement. The stone stairs descended four more steps after the curtain, and there was a makeshift wooden door before them. Tommy knocked.

"Enter," came a soft voice from inside, and Tommy pushed open the door, which creaked noticeably.

Donte smiled. The entrance was haphazard in appearance, but at least that door wouldn't be opened quietly. He wagered there would be an escape hole somewhere on the other side of a second curtain, dividing the room.

It was dark, with just enough light coming through the open door to give Donte a moment to take in the surroundings. A pile of rubbish on one edge of the curtain hid what he was certain was a sword, as he was sure he could see a hilt poking out near the top. The ceiling was masked by a tapestry, probably to cut the chill from the stones above, though Donte suspected that if it were released, it would engulf an attacker, or perhaps even deposit something nasty on them.

The curtain was pulled aside, and an old man stepped through. He was slight of frame, his body hidden by loose clothing: an oft-patched grey tunic and brown trousers. His hair was raggedly cut, almost universally silver in color, with a tuft here and there revealing it had once been dark. His face was lined with age, but his brown eyes were bright, and he glanced from the boy to Donte, then said, "Tommy, my boy! Who's your friend?" Using a walking stick, he moved to sit on a stool.

"My name is Donte. The lad says you're the man to talk to."

The old man regarded Donte for a long moment, then said, "Sir, my young friend often exaggerates, so I fear whatever it is you wish to talk of, I am unlikely to be the man, whoever that may be."

Donte remained silent, as he surveyed the part of this hovel he could clearly see. There indeed was an art to the chaos of odd items.

Then he knelt, so that he could be at eye level with Healer. "I like the codger dodge, and the hovel is convincing." He smiled. "I reckon behind that drape there, we'd find another cluttered crib, but some-where I bet there's another room, hard to find, that's posh."

Healer's eyes narrowed. "I don't follow you, sir."

"Forget the 'sir,' and don't let this rig fool you. I'm on a bit of a con myself."

Healer glanced at Tommy, who nodded and said, "He's got silver." He held out his coin as proof.

Instantly, Healer's posture shifted. He sat up straighter and lost the rounded shoulders of an elderly man. When he spoke his voice was lower, without the quavering note it had had before. "All right, what is it?"

"You run the local boys, then?"

"I don't 'run' anything. I tend their wounds and ills occasionally and every so often they do me a favor. What do you need?"

"Information. Tommy said this and that, but he mentioned you love gossip and rumors, and to me, that's a tell. You're a rumormonger?"

"No," said Healer. "I deal in many things, but I listen to rumors. I don't spread them."

Donte nodded. "Not a snitch, I guess, else you'd have fallen out with someone already and be floating in the bay." He smiled. "I have a gold coin here that says you can explain everything about the two gangs trying to take over Port Vykor."

"Everything?" said Healer with a smile.

"As much as you know. Hold anything back and it won't go well, but be straight with me, and I'll see you're compensated. And there's more to come down the road."

"To what end?" asked Healer, now clearly amused.

Donte laughed. "A gang war means chaos." He emitted a short, barking laugh, and without thought quoted a maxim taught by the Coaltachin masters: "Chaos breeds opportunity."

Healer's eyes widened and his mouth started to open, then he quickly closed it so as not to gape.

HAVA SMILED.

Pug asked, "You're pleased with the transaction?"

They were walking from the docks to where the carriage waited to take them to the small building where they could transport themselves back to Sorcerer's Isle.

Hava nodded and said, "Not ideal, but close. What I've lost in the design I had in mind, I've gained in the speed of construction. If I understand your calendar, we should see this ship finished in less than half a year."

"A practical woman, maybe unique," Pug said. "Calendars are odd. Magnus and the older magicians have shared stories, and I've traveled to a few other worlds. It seems that for humanity to live on a world, it has to have certain similar conditions, but the oddest thing is calendars. With some exceptions, most humans divide a year into twelve months, which is mathematically elegant as there are by common calculation thirty times that many degrees in—"

Hava held up her hand and said, "You must meet Bodai someday. You two would get along famously."

Pug chuckled. "Sorry, I tend to the pedantic when I find something interesting."

"As Bodai began as a pedagogue, what we call a preceptor on my world, you two would have a wonderful time chatting."

They reached the carriage, and it was a brief journey back to the nameless building. On the way, Hava asked questions and Pug answered them, trying to improve her knowledge of Midkemia.

"So, if I'm to be hunting down pirates, tell me more about those who are sailing the Bitter Sea," she said.

Pug paused, then said, "It's complicated, as relations between neighboring states often are. I'll spare you the ancient history, but suffice it to say that compared to today, those times seem positively tranquil, even with the wars, intrigue, plots, and all the other usual doings between nations.

"Today we live in the dark shadow of what was a massive struggle against the Void, which literally changed the face of Midkemia."

He took a breath. "Still, pretty much all of them are one step away from being pirates and some of them are unabashedly raiding one another. Your task will simply be to protect Sorcerer's Isle, which may involve a great deal of conflict at sea. We most certainly could use someone who can shoo pirates away from our shipments."

She smiled, and said, "I think I can do that."

"Hatushaly will continue to study. He's unique and I feel he hasn't begun to grasp what he's capable of becoming."

Hava said nothing but nodded. She had a feeling that if these people could give Hatushaly what he needed, she would be staying here with her husband a long time. She ignored a nagging little itch at the corner of her soul that said she wanted to return to Garn. What she really wanted to do was to helm the *Queen of Storms*, no matter how much the prospect of a new ship and new sea to plunder appealed to her. She fought against the desire to return to the brief days of satisfaction and happiness in Beran's Hill and the Sanctuary, where she had felt closest to Hatu.

The carriage pulled up and they stepped out, finding a small boy with light brown hair and filthy clothing standing by the door to the building courtyard. He looked at them and said, "You Hava?"

She glanced at Pug with a roll of her eyes, then looked at the boy and said, "What's Donte's message?"

As the carriage pulled away, the boy smiled. "He said you'd know what's what. Don't wait for him. He's found something to do, and if he needs to get back, he'll find a way."

Then the boy ran off, leaving Pug staring at Hava. "He'll find a way back? To Sorcerer's Isle?" he said softly.

Hava chuckled ruefully. "Donte plays the buffoon artfully, so well and so often that even Hatu and I occasionally forget that deep inside is as cunning a mind as one is likely to encounter. Determined as well. If he wants to return, he'll find a way."

Pug considered for a moment, then opened the door to the small court between the street and the building. Once inside the otherwise empty building, he said, "I think I'll see about keeping an eye on Donte."

Hava smiled and said, "That may prove difficult, even for you magicians. Still, if you can somehow find a way to do so, it might be wise."

"I'll also set a ward here, so if he returns, someone at Sorcerer's Isle will be able to come quickly to fetch him back."

Hava shook her head, and her expression was one of resignation. "Donte," she muttered with a sigh.

HATUSHALY ALMOST LEAPT OFF THE chair when he saw Hava enter the room. He threw his arms around her and squeezed until she shouted, "Break a rib and I'll gut you!"

They both laughed, then kissed as if it had been ages since they had been together, rather than days.

"I admit to being caught up in all that is to learn here, but getting back to an empty room is unsettling," Hatu said.

She grabbed his cheek and gave it a playful squeeze. "Can't live without me?"

He kissed her again. "Absolutely."

"Good," she replied, smiling.

He looked around and said, "Where's Donte?"

"Off being Donte." Looking over at Pug, she said, "Thank you for everything. I am in your debt."

"No debt," said Pug quickly. "If you're happy, he's happy, which is important. So, having you here is to our benefit more than yours." He laughed a little, and said, "Were I wed, I'm not sure I'd care to have a wife who sought out danger and took risks . . ." Then his eyes lost focus as if he were staring off into the distance.

For a moment it looked as if he might fall. Hatu took a step toward Pug, but the magician gave a shake of his head and took a breath and was apparently fine. He smiled and said, "That was odd. For an instant I felt like I was somewhere else. Perhaps too much jumping about." He smiled at Hava. "Please, enjoy some rest." He gave a bow and left.

Hatu and Hava exchanged glances. A moment of silence was followed by a long kiss, and then Hatu said, "So, a ship?"

"Yes," she replied with a smile. "Not the *Queen of Storms*, but a good design. If the builder is what they say he is, she will serve well."

"Got a name?"

"Not yet. Something will come to me."

"Hungry?" he asked.

"Yes." She put her arm around his waist and gave a squeeze, then released him and said, "While we eat, tell me what wonders you've discovered here."

He laughed. "Too much for one meal. But I'll try."

Arm in arm, they left their quarters and headed for the dining hall.

DONTE LOOKED AROUND THE DISUSED warehouse. He'd arranged for Tommy to round up as many urchins as he could: those known to him and Healer. Donte had spent a few hours in conversation with Healer while Tommy had spread the word of this meeting.

The children ranged from barely able to feed themselves, five or six years old, to perhaps thirteen or fourteen years of age. The eldest were just young enough to avoid being pressured into joining the gangs from Krondor or Kesh or coerced into joining the Kingdom military. None of them would ever be apprenticed to an honest trade, so their future was bleak by any measure.

"My name is Donte. I've seen a little of what you can do. I'm here to set you right and get you in a better place."

There was silence.

"He's got an idea," said Healer.

Immediately the room came alive with the children all asking questions. Donte put up his hands, palms out, and said, "I'll give answers, but first let me ask you questions. I'll start with you." He pointed at the tallest boy, a youngster with very dark skin and large brown eyes, his head covered with a dark blue kerchief. "You," he said. "Tell me of the gangs from Krondor and Kesh."

The boy looked slightly surprised at being singled out, but he shrugged and in a surprisingly deep voice said, "Mockers is from Krondor. They've been around long as people can recall, but they never got in good, dug in, you know? They came and went, did some dust-ups with this gang or that, sometimes the king's crushers, thief-catchers, you know? The Kesh gang's got no name, not one we know, but we call them Ferrets, because they slink in and out of tight places, quick-like, you know?"

Donte smiled. "Ya, I know."

Some of the children laughed, and the tall boy looked confused.

"What's your name?" asked Donte.

"David," he answered.

Donte nodded, fixing the name to the face. He rarely used the tools taught him by the masters and preceptors, mostly out of petty recalcitrance, but he remembered. He knew now he needed to learn the name of every child here.

"Before we go further," Donte said, "from now on, what we say here stays here. Got it?"

Most of the children looked at Healer, who nodded. In turn the children said yes or nodded agreement. It was David who said, "We pretty much don't have anyone else to talk to, anyway."

Donte gave a single nod of understanding then said, "All right. None of you have any training, so we'll see to that, but first you all look like you're starving to death." He pointed to a gangly boy with an unruly mop of dirty blond hair and asked, "Name?"

"Mark," he said. His face was a mask of grime, but startling blue eyes returned Donte's gaze.

A girl a year or two younger stood close to him, and Donte said, "You?"

She said, "Perri."

Donte nodded. He turned to Healer. "I'm a stranger here, so what things cost is new to me. What's it take to feed this lot?"

"That silver piece you bandied about should cover a banquet."

Donte fetched a silver coin from his purse and tossed it to David. He pointed to Mark, David, and Tommy. "You three get out of here and go get bread, cheese, whatever passes for some fruit around here and whatever else will start putting some meat on these scrawny bones. We have a lot to do, and starving people are useless."

Donte saw David do a quick head count and nodded his approval. "Good, but not rich-people food," he said.

David grinned and led Mark and Tommy out of the door to the alley. After a moment, Donte said to Perri, "Now go tail them and see if they get it right." She smiled and jumped up to follow.

Donte said to Healer, "This place should serve for a bit, but it's too easy to find. We need a better hideout. Got an idea?"

"One place," Healer answered. "Needs work, and it's tricky to get to, but that's a good thing."

"Yes," said Donte. "A very good thing. Now, we also need a couple or more bullies."

Healer looked confused.

"Bruisers . . . Ah," Donte said, remembering his earlier discussion with Tommy, "you call them bashers."

Healer nodded. "Protection."

"Yes. Got to keep these boys and girls out of harm's way best we can. Are there any to be had?"

"All the good protection is either working for the Mockers or the Ferrets, the Keshians." Healer was thoughtful for a moment, then said, "I'll poke around. There may be one or two."

"Until you find them, we'd best be very cagey and keep out of the way."

Healer said, "Agreed."

One of the older boys with a tanned face under a mop of brown hair, said, "Mister?"

"Yes?" replied Donte.

"What are we doing this for?"

"Good question." Donte stood and walked over to the boy, towering over him. Remembering how he had felt as a child in his training, he went to one knee, put his hand lightly on the boy's shoulder, and said, "We are going to turn this scruffy lot into a first-rate crew. We are going to put food in your bellies and find you a warm place to sleep, get you cleaned up so you're only filthy because it's part of a dodge, and then . . ." He paused. "Then we're going to train you up and put you to work."

"Work?" said another boy. "Honest work?"

Donte laughed, loudly and with genuine humor. "Honest? Who said anything about honest?" He stood and returned to Healer. "I'm going to train you up to be the best crew in Port Vykor."

"What about the Mockers and the Ferrets?" asked another child as voices in the room began to rise.

Donte held up his hands for silence, then when the babble died down, he said, "Well, they want to fight each other, so we're going to help them out." He grinned.

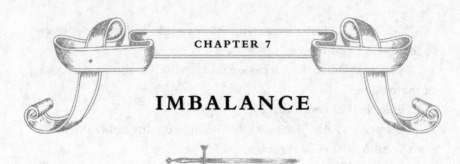

CHAPTER 7

IMBALANCE

R uffio shouted.

It was a sound of pure aggravation and exhaustion. All night and into the morning he and Zaakara had labored to adjust the rift to Midkemia, energizing it enough to reach the other world. A subtle pulsing had manifested, but after a few hours both magic-users determined the rift had indeed not reached its intended target.

Sabella had remained and had been joined by two soldiers drawn to the site out of curiosity. Both were waiting for orders to be somewhere else, but until then the novelty of watching the two men muttering, waving their hands in the air, and stopping to discuss things completely beyond the soldiers' understanding, broke the monotony. A full company remained, and the rumor was that the king had plans for this island, but for the moment there was little for the soldiers here to do beside eat, sleep, and train.

Sabella had been sitting quietly, saying nothing for a few hours. At last, she stood up and said, "Can I try something?"

The men exchanged glances, and Zaakara said, "Please do."

They stepped aside so she could get closer to the rift Ruffio had used to travel from Midkemia.

One of the soldiers motioned to his companion, who carried a water skin. He moved to offer it to Zaakara, who took a long drink then handed it to Ruffio. They both thanked the soldier and sank to the ground, obviously exhausted.

All watched as Sabella moved as close to the rift as she could without touching it. She stood motionless, arms slightly out to the sides, legs spread, and her head tilted back.

Zaakara saw that she had her eyes closed. He glanced at Ruffio, who returned a questioning expression, and Zaakara shrugged to signal he had little idea of what was happening. A short time later a sergeant approached and shooed the two guards off to some duty and was about to speak when Zaakara held up his hand for silence.

The sergeant nodded, pointed at himself, then at the tent used by the soldiers to indicate that was where he'd be if they needed him. Zaakara indicated he understood.

Hours passed and the sun began its descent toward the western horizon.

Abruptly, Sabella took a faltering step back, slightly shaking her head as if trying to retain her balance. Zaakara and Ruffio were both on their feet immediately, steadying her against a fall. After a second she took a deep breath, then looked from one to the other. "I think I may know how to fix this," she said.

DECLAN WAS ON THE VERGE of awakening when a pounding sounded on his door. Half asleep, he said, "I'm coming."

He rolled out of bed and quickly pulled on his tunic, trousers, and boots. He opened the door and was a full step past a court page who said, "The king—"

Declan cut him off. "I know."

He rubbed his eyes and shook his head to force himself fully awake. Glancing out of a window, he saw that the sky outside was just starting to lighten. It was less than an hour before sunrise, and he would have been up soon anyway.

As he reached the king's private conference room, a guard was already pulling open the door for him. Once inside, he saw his brothers sitting and a large pot of coffee between them. Balven took the pot and poured a mug out, sliding it across the table as Daylon motioned for Declan to sit down.

"One of our scouts just reported in," said the king. "There are signs of Church forces moving through the Wildlands, into abandoned lands in Ilcomen, apparently coming this way."

Declan wiped coffee from his mouth with the back of his hand, bringing a disapproving look from Balven, who glanced at the cloth on the table before Declan, folded nicely. Declan resisted rolling his eyes, and asked, "Where?"

"Somewhere in the center, but close to our border," Balven replied, then added, "Or inside our border if we claim the north of Ilcomen."

The Wildlands were well named, a stretch of forests, scrub, open grassland, and rocky hills between the former Kingdom of Loment and the Dividing Range, a largely impassable line of mountains that stretched from the Narrows in the south to the north coast of North Tembria. Only through the Dangerous Passage could a caravan or army move.

Declan considered. "They're moving to the Darkwood."

Balven glanced at the map on the wall and said, "I've never been there."

King Daylon said, "I have. Father took me there when I started training." He shook his head slowly. "It's a nasty place. The trees are so thick; if you don't know the game trails you can find yourself completely blocked and are forced to retrace your steps to find another way through. Father thought of it as a natural barricade, since no force of any size could get through there. There was a small spring we watered the horses at, and I don't think we ever got more than three miles deep within it before we had to camp and turn around the next day. The trees are tall and it's dark in there, even at noon." Daylon looked at Declan and asked, "Why do you think there?"

"Because if they can get a company of engineers and laborers in, they can start felling trees and clearing land. Then they build a redoubt. Small bands can trickle in, and stores can be stockpiled. They wait until they have that position secured, then start felling trees to make a road out—"

"—to attack," finished the king. "That would put them due east of us, so with a quick strike they could be at the city walls before we could summon the troops we have down at the Narrows or up at Beran's Hill."

"And strewn around a dozen other locations," added Balven.

"What are we going to do about this?" said the king in a rhetorical tone, drumming his fingers on the table. He looked at Declan and said, "What would you do?"

Not looking pleased at being asked the question, because he knew the answer, Declan let out a sigh. "I'd send me, with Sixto and the best company I could put together, to grind our way through that forest to find where the Church staging post is. I'd kill or capture as many of those engineers and workers as possible—we know the soldiers will fight to the death—then leave enough men there to welcome every Church squad that turns up."

Balven added, "We could certainly use any stores they bring." Both Daylon and Declan looked to see if he was joking. "I mean it," he responded. "Right now, I'd trade a dozen of those special swords we're making for a flock of sheep. Bring us a score of beef cattle and I'll throw in a catapult."

Daylon nodded his agreement. "It's going to be another two or three years before we're back to farming and herding enough to return to where we were before the Pride Lord invasion. The only reason we're not all starving is there are a lot fewer mouths to feed than there were before."

The mood was somber. "Well, then," said Declan, standing up. "I'll gather the lads, we'll grab something to eat as we ride, and head to where I think those Church murderers slipped into the Darkwood." He studied the map for a moment. "There is no easy way in, but the east side of the forest is a bit thinner. To ride around and find a way in will take up to a week." He tapped the map. "If we had a way in on the west side, it's only a two-day ride. Did the scout speculate on the size of the party?"

King Daylon picked up a roll of parchment, pulled it open, and said, "Tracks of maybe twenty mounted men, a donkey cart or perhaps two, and an unknown number of footmen, as the trail became muddy." He put down the roll. "What are you thinking?"

Declan was silent for a moment, then he said, "Thirty men. The riders may be escorts, as they'll not get those horses far into the Darkwood. So, we find where they entered, follow them . . . and end them." He sounded weary of spirit.

Balven said, "Why you? We can send your man Sixto. He's competent enough."

"Because I've been there, and Sixto hasn't. Bogartis's company of mercenaries probably never got within a ten-day ride of that forest." He looked at his brother the king. "Three days in? I've been there four days, cutting timber for the forge and for sale as a journeyman smith to make bandsaws, heavy axes, and the rest." Remembering his early life, he took a breath to cleanse himself of rising anger. "I have to go."

The king's expression revealed an unhappy acceptance of that statement. "Don't die" was all he said, waving his hand in dismissal.

Declan headed down to the main barracks and past them to where Sixto and the special unit, as he thought of them, resided. Several men from his escape from the raid on Abala and those he'd found in Garn's Wound were among that company, supplemented by men Sixto had singled out during training. They were considered the primary core of the king's army. Declan felt kinship to these men and that they were his own. And he realized that someday, when he became king, they would indeed be his own.

He entered the barracks to find Sixto fully dressed and turning the men out. "You heard?" Declan asked.

"I heard scouts came in, horses all in a lather, so I assumed we'd likely be riding out today."

Declan put a hand on Sixto's shoulder. "Could be a nasty one. Get food to eat on the road, then tack the horses up to ride. We need two packhorses, and two engineers. I want young, big lads who know their way around axes and, speaking of axes, a dozen on the packhorses."

"So, we're cutting our way through woodlands, then."

Declan let go of his shoulder and nodded, then raised his voice. "Lewis!"

"Sir!" came the response as a man moved through the press of soldiers dressing and came to stand before Declan. He was a hard-looking, broad-shouldered fellow, with shoulder-length black hair, a narrow jaw, and dark eyes. He was the best scout in Declan's company. "Highness?"

Declan saw men starting to don tabards, and said, "No tabards!

This is no dress parade, and those light blue and gold beauties make for easy targets."

"So, it's a fight then?" asked Sixto.

"Almost certainly," Declan replied. To Lewis he said, "Scouts came in last night. As soon as you eat, ask them what they know and have them mark the map where we need to go."

"Yes, highness." Lewis saluted and left the barracks.

"Sebastian!" Declan shouted.

The man who responded quickly was one of those he'd met down in Abala, a member of the band of local mercenaries that had joined his company and survived the escape from Garn's Wound. He was Declan's best tracker and horse archer. "I'm going to have you and Lewis breaking trail on this. When Lewis gets back with the map, we'll head out."

"Sir," said the older fighter. His hair had gone completely grey, but he still had the look of a dangerous man Declan would rather have on his side than on the enemy's.

Declan said, "I'm going back to get into something a little less dainty." He tugged at the light cotton tunic he wore. "As soon as we're ready, we head out."

Sixto gave a casual salute, and said, "Yes, highness."

There was no levity in his tone. It was likely they were riding straight toward a vicious enemy.

ZAAKARA WALKED UP FROM THE beach below the large tent left behind by King Daylon after launching his attack against the Pride Lords from this island, now referred to as Marshaling Island or King's Island. With him came four young women, all former seers who had once worked like Sabella in the search for the Firemane baby, Hatushaly.

Sabella waited at the entrance to the pavilion and greeted the others. Then she said, "Let's head up that hill."

As they walked, Sabella said to Zaakara, "Ruffio seemed almost desperate that someone be by those rifts but was unclear as to what I should do if something happened."

Zaakara inhaled a long breath, then said, "Probably because no one knows exactly what might happen." As they reached the rift, he said, "Ruffio, these are Zara, Daria, Eefa, and Beryl." The four young women stepped forward and Ruffio nodded a greeting.

Ruffio said, "We who were trained in rift-magic were warned not to leave rifts open. The obvious risk is someone blundering into one and discovering they were far from where they wished to be. But . . ."

Zaakara continued, "There were other reasons given, but most of us came away with the feeling there was something far more potentially dire than what we were told. So, the solution is to fix this problem, get word back to Sorcerer's Isle, and close the damned rift before whatever terrible thing that might happen, happens."

Sabella stepped forward. "This is what I think we can do." She waved for the other young women to come and stand beside her and told them, "Get close to that big shining silver oval in the air, but don't touch it."

"What happens if we do?" asked Beryl, a dark-skinned girl with black hair and big, expressive eyes.

"Nothing dangerous," answered Ruffio. "It will tingle but not harm you."

"It's that tingle which had me step away . . ." Sabella stopped. "It's that feeling we get when . . . the magic works?" She held out upraised hands in a questioning gesture. "Please," she said to the other Flame Guard adepts.

The adepts stepped closer and stood still. They all closed their eyes and their heads tilted back slightly, as they stood there motionless, shoulders back, chins slightly forward, arms down and fingers spread. They stayed like this for long minutes.

Then Daria, a short, stocky woman with light brown hair, stumbled a half-step backward and turned wide-eyed toward Sabella with an expression of excitement. "I see it!" she exclaimed.

"Yes?" asked Sabella.

"Yes," echoed Zara. "I see it, too."

"What do they see?" Ruffio asked.

He and Zaakara stared at the shimmering oval of silver that they'd seen so many times that they took it for granted.

Sabella turned to him. "We see a . . . pulse of . . . light? Something in that wavy pattern that we recognize."

"What?" asked Zaakara.

"I think we can actually see shreds of magic along the edges of the waves rippling across that rift. I first felt it, and now . . ."

Standing up, Zaakara came to stand before the slight woman and asked, "What does it mean?"

"As I told you, here men somehow hold the magic, and we women use it." With a gesture to the rift behind her, she continued, "That's what we feel when we use magic. That's what we fed on when we searched for Hatushaly. It's flowing gently from your world to ours."

"Are you saying you can channel the magic from the rift as you did before Hatushaly left?" asked Ruffio.

"We can try," she answered.

"What then?" asked Zaakara.

"Something we have never done before." Sabella smiled. "We will see if there's a way we can help you repair that rift to Midkemia."

The Midkemian magic-users looked at one another and each saw their own expression of surprise mirrored on the other's face.

"YOU KNOW THERE IS ONE good thing about this rain," Sixto almost shouted.

The sound of rain was so heavy it almost deafened Declan to normal conversation.

"What is that?" asked Declan, water streaming down his face and soaking through the oil-treated travel cloaks he and his men wore. The cloaks had kept everyone relatively dry for the first hour after the rain began, but now it was driving, and the wind was picking up.

"They won't hear us coming until we ride over them," Sixto said.

Declan failed to see the humor in this.

Sebastian and Lewis had alternated as trailbreakers. Each morning one left at first light, then stopped where the horses would be rested. Then the other man rode the freshest mount again to the next break, both camping with Declan's forces at night. For three days Declan's company of forty men had made good time over relatively easy land.

Closer to the city were vegetable farms and fruit orchards, the almost legendary orange groves of Marquensas, but a day's ride brought them to the large grain farms and livestock meadows. Once busy enterprises feeding not only Marquenet but exporting grain and meat to the five kingdoms were now mostly fields gone to tall grass and weeds. The groves had been picked clean the year before and though the newly budding tree branches promised a harvest in a few months, even they looked forlorn as rain had washed away the early blossoms.

"Is there anywhere near here we can shelter?" Declan asked Lewis.

Lewis pointed off to the left. "There's an old farm less than an hour's ride in that direction, highness."

Declan glanced back west. "Unless this gloom has me completely bewildered, we've got less than three hours of light left."

"About right," Sixto said.

Declan turned in the saddle and surveyed the column of soldiers behind. They rode without complaint, but he could see they were cold and miserable.

"If we have a fight ahead, and we likely do," began Declan, "it wouldn't help if half the men were down with ague."

Sixto said, "The coughing alone would let the Church soldiers know we were coming."

To Lewis, Declan said, "Ride up to Sebastian, then the two of you join us at that farm. If there's any kindness in fate today, there will be at least a leaky barn we can hole up in and dry out a little."

Lewis's face brightened. "Yes, highness!" He urged his horse forward at a canter.

Sixto signaled and the column followed as he and Declan moved off.

After an hour's miserable ride through rain getting colder as the day faded, they reached the abandoned farm Lewis had described. Sixto quickly signaled for a group of men to search the farmhouses and another barn, with a third riding a sweeping patrol around the perimeter to investigate the outbuildings or anywhere an enemy scout might secrete himself.

From the size of the open meadow and limited fencing near the barn, Declan judged this was more properly a cattle farm rather than one for crops. The barn was small, with room for perhaps four horses, and the house was tidy. Declan suspected the building to the rear was for workers who tended the herd and drove it to Marquenet's market.

He rode to the barn door and dismounted as two of his men came out and indicated it was empty. A quick survey of the interior showed there were a few tools for shoeing and saddle repair, but nothing significant. The tools had most likely been abandoned during the raid from the Pride Lords, and left rusting to uselessness.

A few minutes later Declan stepped into a tidy family room with an open kitchen. Some old furniture had been broken up and a fire had been started in the fireplace which doubled as an oven, for it had a metal box instead of a stone hearth.

"Get a picket line up for the horses to be tethered," said Declan. "No corrals here: get the packhorses and the saddles and blankets into that barn so maybe we can keep them a bit dry. I hope this rain will be gone by tomorrow."

"So do we all," replied Sixto. He motioned to one of the soldiers who had started the fire and said, "Pass the word." The soldier ran off.

Declan looked around and saw nothing else to sit on, so he squatted before the fireplace and looked at Sixto. "Set up watches, but have the men eat and rest, and pray for dry weather tomorrow."

Sixto nodded and said, "I've been praying for that all day."

A SMALL TABLE HAD BEEN put up in the pavilion, surrounded by several chairs so that the magicians and the former adepts from the Sanctuary could rotate in their attempts to gain power from the rift and find a solution.

Zaakara sat with Sabella while Ruffio was observing the women who were absorbing the energy coming through the rift. Sabella looked fatigued. Yet she still had a happy expression and a wide smile.

He was also exhausted from short sleep and concerns over the consequences of keeping the rift open so long. He said, "Do you feel more confident about finding a solution?"

"I have no idea. I just know I'm on the verge of something . . ."

She took a deep breath, as if she was expelling something she wanted out of her. "All my life since I left my family, I've sat still, listening." She waved her hands in a way that Zaakara interpreted as meaning she had no other way to explain her search for Hatushaly. "And the rest was eating bad food, bathing in cold water, having a few minutes here and there to talk to them." She pointed to the other adepts, who were now standing rigid before the rift. "It was not a life!" There was anger in the tone.

Zaakara reached over and put his hand on hers.

She took a deep breath and added, "Something here is . . . new, and I must know what it is."

"I understand the feeling," said Zaakara, patting her hand reassuringly. "But curiosity sometimes comes at a nasty price. Be cautious."

She nodded. "It occurs to me there may be two possible ways to fix that small rift. If we can take the energy we're drawing through it and give it to you."

Zaakara held up his hand. "How?"

"I don't quite know," she said, her voiced edged in frustration. "It's just an idea. The other idea would be for you to tell us how we can make the rift work."

His mouth dropped open. "I have no idea how to do that," he admitted at last. "Maybe . . ." He let the thought go. "Come with me," he said, standing up. His staff was leaning against the table, and he grabbed it out of habit.

She followed him, and when he was closer to the rifts, Zaakara shouted, "Ruffio!"

The magician turned and walked a few yards downhill to meet them.

"Sabella has an idea, actually two, and I need to know what you think."

She repeated her two thoughts, and Ruffio's expression was less astonished than Zaakara's had been, but still he looked dubious. "Transferring that energy to one of us, maybe. Teaching the four of you to finish the second rift . . ." He shook his head. "Unlikely. Those of us who studied rift-magic with Magnus were already somewhat well practiced in certain arts, and even then, it was a long and difficult process. It's why we still keep those golden orbs around and working. There are many magic-users who simply can never master rifts."

As the three stood silently contemplating what to do next, a sudden explosion of air almost knocked the adepts off their feet.

Zaakara looked at the source of the noise and shouted, "Run!"

It took no prompting for the adepts to race down the hillside toward the pavilion. A curious soldier saw them coming and what was behind, and shouted, "To arms!"

Zaakara looked at the thing that had emerged from the rift, recognizing it for what it was. Dark to the point of seeming to suck light out of the air, it shambled like a lumbering hound, but had a long snout ending in tusks. It was waist-high to a tall man, and as broad across the shoulders as a large boar. Puffs of green hair grew seemingly at random on a mottled hide of grey and purple. Its forefeet featured long black claws, which it raised as it sat back on its haunches.

Zaakara didn't hesitate. He wielded his staff like a battle club, striking the creature as hard as he could. He knocked it backward and it rolled and came upright, shaking its head as if dazed.

The first soldier reached Zaakara's side, and the warlock shouted, "Don't let it get a claw on you! There is no healing magic here that will save you from death. It hates cold steel so use your sword to fend it off."

The soldier shrugged off his horror at the sight of the creature and extended his sword. The thing advanced slowly.

Two more soldiers arrived, with another half-dozen leaving the pavilion below. One unslung a bow and quickly fired an arrow at the creature. It stuck hard into its shoulder, and instantly the creature whirled in a frenzy, like a dog chasing its tail, trying to dislodge the steel-headed shaft. The wailing sound it emitted was painful and those not holding weapons covered their ears. Eefa and a soldier both fell to their knees.

The archer maintained his concentration despite the ear-splitting howl and shot another arrow into the creature. This time it flipped over on its back, flopping like a fish on a boat's deck. A third arrow took it in the gullet and after a few more moments of thrashing, the beast lay motionless.

With silence those nearby regained their senses, and Zaakara put out an arm barring the soldier next to him from approaching the monster. "Do not touch it!" he shouted to everyone nearby.

"What do we do with it then?" asked a soldier.

"Get tent poles, or oars from one of the boats, whatever you can use, pick it up without touching it, then dump it somewhere away from here. It will be gone in a day or two. It will dissolve, I guess you could say. And the local scavengers, birds or insects, will not touch it."

A sergeant who had been hovering behind started barking out orders and soldiers set quickly about doing what Zaakara said.

"What is that thing?" asked Sabella.

"That's a demon, and why we were trained that leaving rifts open was a bad idea."

Ruffio said, "Had we our magic, we would have made short work of it."

"At least we had the king's soldiers here," said Sabella.

"They risk death at the touch of that creature," said Zaakara. "It has a malignant touch that can kill. Only healing magic can stop it."

"Frightening," said Beryl, her dark hair all tangled. "I thought my head would split."

Zaakara said, "Let's get back to working out how to repair that small rift. I think we should close the big one altogether."

Ruffio said, "We risk losing all contact with home."

"I know," answered the warlock, "but Magnus and Pug both are adept enough to find their way here, and when we close it, they'll know something's amiss. It's best to close it."

Ruffio nodded his agreement; then, since he had opened the rift, he sought to close it. After a moment, he turned and said, "I can't close it. I lack the power." His laugh was bitter. "No magic, remember?"

"We are stuck then," said Zaakara. He motioned for the sergeant who had been quietly listening. "Are you in command?" he asked.

The sergeant said, "All the officers have left."

"You'd best station men here and, as I said, let no man touch any creature that may emerge. Not all are death to the touch, but none of you can tell the difference." To the gathering soldiers he said, "Set up guards now, and be ready for something like this. Whatever comes through, if it's anything like that, kill it as quickly as you can."

The sergeant said, "I understand, and those who saw this thing come through will pass along word to the others around the island that this is not a jest."

"Most certainly not," said Zaakara. Pointing to where the dead creature lay as soldiers moved up the hill with poles to move it, he added, "That was a little one."

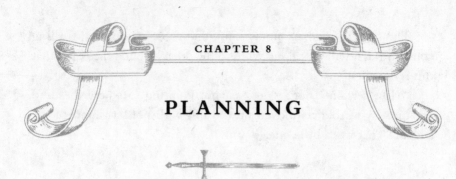

CHAPTER 8

PLANNING

Hatushaly yawned.

He and Hava had finished supper and returned to their quarters. Hava was detailing her expedition to Port Vykor. They had eaten well and drunk some exceptionally good wine from somewhere called Yabon and were now both feeling its effects.

"You'd better not be getting bored with my company," Hava said in mock-scolding tones.

"Never," he replied with a chuckle. "I've just been at my studies all day and could use a good night's sleep."

Hava laughed. "You're the only person I know who can get tired sitting all day."

He feigned hurt. "Concentration is hard!" He grinned. "And I drank too much wine."

Hava smiled. "So did I." They were lying side by side on the bed. After a pause, she said, "I hope you're not too tired—"

A knock at the door interrupted their banter. "Well, there goes that," said Hatu, getting off the bed and moving to the door.

Magnus stood there. "Sorry to intrude on your evening but I need to ask a question, if I may."

Hatu motioned for him to enter. Hava sat on the edge of the bed as Hatu pulled a chair from a small table next to the bed, then moved to sit next to his wife.

Once seated, Magnus asked, "Is there anything you can think of on that Marshaling Island with the rift that might pose a serious danger to Zaakara and Ruffio?"

Hatu straightened up a little, his expression turning serious. "No, nothing immediately springs to mind. Why?"

"Zaakara opened a rift to Garn to confer with your Master Bodai and was scheduled to be back in a couple of days. Mostly to see if there was any new intelligence as to those creatures you found in the center of Nytanny. After four days we began to be concerned. We thought perhaps he had been delayed or diverted, as that can happen with any of us on such a mission.

"But after a week, we sent Ruffio to see if anything was amiss, and now he has not returned as expected. I'm holding off sending anyone else until I'm sure they won't be emerging into some sort of battle or into the arms of hostile agents. We don't know if Zaakara popped into a battle on the King's Island or bumped into something worse. If the Children of the Void you spied atop that plateau have awakened, that is a threat to your entire world and to this one as well."

"That's very odd," said Hatu. "I see why you're worried. From what I've seen and heard, both are capable of dealing with common threats, even without the small garrison King Daylon left there. So, if something forced them to go . . . silent, it must be something bad."

"I'm left with a conundrum. Ruffio left the rift open, so anyone here can just step through."

"Why is that a problem?" Hava asked.

"Open rifts tend to attract denizens of the Void—"

"Wait," interrupted Hatushaly. "I thought the Void was . . . a thing, like a creature . . ." He paused, then said, "Pug and you have both told me bits about the war between the Void and . . . everything else. The Void wanting to go back to some perfect moment that never changes."

Magnus's expression turned even more concerned. "Trying to explain the inexplicable sums up what you've been told. We are limited in our perceptions and what we know is probably only a fraction of what we should know. The problem is we are dealing with things we can hardly understand, let alone explain. Those things you saw atop the plateau in Nytanny, the Dread, they are beings of sorts, but we do not grasp precisely what they are.

"I wish I could more clearly explain but suffice it to say there are places within the Void, that grey nothingness outside all the universes and realities, where we can venture and some where we cannot. Some of us have traveled into the Void and returned. Not many . . ." He took a deep breath. "Perhaps to clarify, we should return to calling the . . . place between worlds rift-space? That was also the term we used. The Void, the inexplicable force we confront . . . think of it as a being, for simplicity's sake."

Hatu sat silently for a long moment, then said, "I think I understand a little. It's like me trying to describe what I 'see' when I send my mind to deal with the energy lines from what Nathan called 'the furies,' and Pug called 'nodes.' It's impossible to describe, really." Then he brightened a little. "But at least I can show people."

Magnus said, "So I have been told. Zaakara especially was impressed with the display you shared. Multicolored lines like threads on a loom, he said."

"I can show you sometime," Hatu offered.

"Some other time. Right now, I need to weigh the risk of sending someone else through that rift."

Hatu stood up. "I might be able to . . ." He looked at Hava and then said, "Something I did with the aid of Nathan, back on Garn. I was able to find people I knew well . . . by sensing them—their unique energy, you could say. I don't know if I could manage that across . . . however far it is to Garn from here."

"That's a problem, as we have no way to measure the difference between Midkemia and Garn." Magnus paused, as if weighing his words. "Travel between worlds has been going on for a long time. Even longer than before the first incursion from Kelewan to Midkemia, the first Riftwar." He glanced at Hava and then said, "More history that can wait until later.

"The point is that the universe is vast—more properly, all the universes—distances beyond measure, states of existence we cannot even imagine. But we do have connections."

"What connections?" asked Hatu.

"Rifts, to begin with," said Magnus. "There have always been myths and legends. The first rift between worlds we know of came about by accident. The Tsurani magicians from the world of Kelewan had discovered how to create rifts to move from place to place on their own world. A Tsurani Great One, what they called their Greater Path magicians, was on a ship carrying something precious to the Warlord of the Empire—exactly what we do not know—and to save the ship from a terrible storm, he attempted to create a rift big enough to sail it to safe waters, some location known to him. But instead, by some fluke we cannot understand, he opened a rift to this world, on the Far Coast, near the town of Crydee."

Hatu could see this recounting was affecting Magnus, for his manner changed, as if the memory had personal meaning to him. He glanced at Hava, and she nodded slightly, indicating that she had noticed it as well.

Magnus continued, "My father was a prisoner on Kelewan, but they prized magic above all else and as soon as my father's powers were discovered, he was elevated to the ranks of their Assembly of Great Ones. While there he devoted himself to the study of rifts and was the most adept magic-user on two worlds in their use and control." He shifted his weight forward, looking directly into Hatu's eyes. "He also came to understand their risks. I'll give you the full story some other time, but a rift acts like a lodestone, a magnet, for the very thing we seek to keep as far away from us as possible: the creatures of the Void.

"He taught me everything he knew. It was decades of study, and I may have built on what he taught me a little. But as much as I know of rifts, there is much more that I don't know."

Hatu said, "I understand. In the short time I've been here I've learned there is so much to learn."

"The first and perhaps most important lesson," said Magnus. "I have had reasons over the years to stay away from studying rifts. The major reason is that risk I spoke of, which manifested most profoundly in what others often call the Great Upheaval, or the Cataclysm, or the Chaos War. Again, more history for another time, but what you need to know is that we faced the worst threat to this world, to the universe perhaps, as a consequence of a rift in what is now known as the Sunken Lands.

"There, wild magic twisted the very fabric of time and space, altering reality in ways no mortal could have imagined. What lingers there is a small world of wonders and horrors."

Magnus got to his feet. "In any event, I've taught Phillip as much as I could of rifts. He's proven a remarkably adept student, as I knew he would be. He knows perhaps more than I ever did at this point." The last pronouncement had a hint of irony to it. "If you would meet him tomorrow at the opening to the rift, perhaps the two of you may arrive at a solution that has so far eluded us. Are you willing?"

"Certainly. Where is the rift located?"

"After you eat, Phillip will find you and take you there." Looking at Hava, Magnus said, "Again, sorry to interrupt your evening. Good night." He let himself out.

Hava said, "What do you think?"

After a second, Hava laughed. "I know that expression. You're going back to the library, aren't you?"

Hatu's expression had gone somewhat distant. "There's something I read a few days ago . . ."

"Go," she said with a resigned laugh. As he moved off the bed, she said, "You know what's odd?"

He stopped and looked at her. "What?"

"He always calls him Phillip. Everyone else calls him Pug. Why is that, do you think?"

Hatu said, "I never noticed." He shrugged. "I expect there's a story there." He smiled at her. "I'll be back soon."

As the door closed behind him, she said, "No you won't." She started to fluff up a pillow, then just put it down and punched it.

THE CHILDREN WERE RESTLESS. DONTE shouted, "Quiet!" Instantly they fell silent. "I've had time to get to know something about what's going on here in Port Vykor and Healer has let me know something about you lot.

"So, here's the deal. You do what I say, and you'll be fed. You don't do what I say, and it's out on the street with no friends." He let that sink in.

"Here's your first lesson," he went on. "Most adults don't notice kids until the kids act up. Same with servants, but we'll save that for

the older kids later. So, if you're in the street doing something that calls
attention to yourself, you're failing. Got that?"

Blank looks were all he got. He turned to Healer and said, "I forgot."

"Forgot what?"

"I'm not at home. Where I was born, the youngest of these would
have been a year in training already. And all would have shown potential."

Healer shrugged as if he didn't quite understand either.

Donte took a deep breath and exhaled. "All right," he began, "we'll
take it slow. You"—he pointed at a little girl no older than seven—
"what's your name?"

"Sarah," she replied, looking a little intimidated by being singled
out. She had a tiny frame, suntanned skin with freckles, and a mop of
brown hair. She stared at Donte with big blue eyes.

"When you're out in the streets, what do you do?"

She looked at Healer as if seeking guidance on an answer.

He waved his hand slightly, in a "go on" gesture, indicating that
she should answer.

"I hide a lot," she answered. "But most of the time I pick."

Donte looked at Healer and asked, "Pick?"

"She's a gleaner," answered Healer. "She picks through rubbish,
trash piles, anywhere she might stumble across something worth keeping. She brings whatever she finds to me. A loose coin, an old metal
pot, anything that can be sold, traded, melted down, whatever might
be useful."

Donte nodded his understanding. He looked at Sarah and said,
"From now on, we have a different task for you. You're going to keep
picking, but you're not there to find things. If you do, fine. Bring what
you find to Healer and me." He waved his hand, indicating the empty
building they occupied. "We'll do this place up, so it's warm and dry
and you'll have food when you come here. Now," he said, pointing at
Sarah again, "what will you be doing while you're pretending to pick?"

"I don't know," she said, her eyes wide.

"You will listen. Healer and I will tell you where to go, maybe to a particular market, or down by the docks, and we'll tell you what to listen for. Think you can do that?"

She nodded dubiously. Donte tried not to show dissatisfaction with her reaction. He remembered all too well the beatings he used to get when he gave a wrong answer to his grandfather.

He sat down on an empty crate and let out a long sigh. "Lots of work to be done here."

"Depends on what you want," said Healer.

"I think right now I want a place I can start to train these little ones, away from nosy bystanders. Can you think of somewhere?"

"Not yet, but I can check around. How close to the city?"

"Close enough I can go from there to here and back in a day."

Healer nodded. "One of the upland villages, I think. Find a little farm. Out of the way." He stood up and asked, "I'll meet you here?"

Donte nodded. "I'm not going anywhere. Not yet anyway."

HAVA ENTERED THE MASSIVE LIBRARY and saw Hatu alone at a large table, with a half-dozen volumes, some open, before him. He was staring intently at a book in his left hand, while turning the page with his right. She stopped as she had never seen him this focused on anything before.

His head moved slightly up and down, as if he was scanning the pages, and he turned them at a remarkable rate. She stared at him silently, while he quickly read through the entire volume. As he closed it and put it on the table, he caught sight of her and said, "Hey, what are you doing out of bed?"

She looked at him with a rueful expression. "It's morning, time for breakfast. You've been reading all night."

He looked genuinely surprised. "I have?"

"Did you learn anything useful?"

"I learned a great deal. How useful remains to be seen."

"Get up," she ordered. "You need to eat."

He complied and as he stood up gave a slight groan. "I think I sat in one position too long." He moved his arms a little, twisted his torso to the right, then left, and exhaled loudly. "I just got lost in what I was reading."

"Apparently," she said, motioning him to come with her. "I've never seen you read that fast before."

Outside, they walked toward the dining hall next to the villa. Hatu saw the sun was still behind the hill that sheltered the library and judged it almost half an hour past sunrise. "I never have before," he replied. "I was in a hurry to see if I could learn something that might help with the problem Magnus shared last night . . ." He looked a bit lost for a moment, then said, "So I kept reading faster and faster, until I was able to scan many pages in the time it used to take me to read one."

"Can you remember any of it at that speed?" she asked.

He smiled a little lopsidedly. "That's the thing. I am now able to recall any written page I look at. If I read it, I understand it. If I understand it, I remember it, all of it."

"A new ability?"

He said, "Maybe I've had it all along since my training began with Bodai and Nathan. I just never felt the need to hurry before."

She gave out a soft chuckle, put her arm through his, and said, "You're a constant source of wonder."

He pulled her a little closer, leaned over to kiss her cheek, and said, "So are you."

They entered the hall and found Pug waiting for them, eating from a large bowl containing a boiled grain of some sort, and some bread with cheese. He gestured that they should join him after they fetched their own breakfast.

Hava pushed Hatu toward Pug and said, "I'll bring you yours. Go sit and talk."

"Magnus said you might be able to help with our problem," Pug said to Hatu as he sat down.

"I think I can sort out a few things," Hatu replied.

"Good." Pug continued to eat.

While he waited for Hava, Hatu said, "I did some reading last night and I think I understand most of the main properties of how rifts function."

Pug's spoon stopped halfway between the bowl and his mouth. "You do?"

"If I understand what I read last night, a rift bends . . . the universe, I suppose you'd say, so that two places impossible distances apart now 'touch' each other and create a doorway from one side to the other."

"The doorway part is widely known, but the bending the universe part is . . . a new way to look at it."

Hatu's expression became animated. "My first instinct was to think of it as a passage, perhaps a magic tunnel, but repeatedly I read that the transfer was instantaneous, like stepping though a doorway. I pondered how that could be if there was any distance between the two points. Even with a little distance, there would be some sense of time passing, wouldn't there?"

Pug sat back and regarded the much younger man. "That's a reasonable assumption."

"So, I considered how one would achieve that bending of . . . everything. That led me to consider some things Nathan said back on Garn, and what I read last night in the library on rifts."

"What did you read?" asked Pug.

"Everything I could find."

Pug's eyes widened, "Everything? There must be thirty different volumes and scrolls."

"Thirty-seven, actually," Hatu responded.

"I've read all of them over the years. You read them all in one night?"

Hava arrived with a tray and set it down between her chair and Hatu's. "He explained that to me. Seems he can read a page in seconds now." Her tone was matter-of-fact.

Pug glanced back and forth between the two of them, and then said, "Some of those are in alien languages."

"I discovered I could read anything back when I was studying with Bodai at the Sanctuary." Hatu gobbled a big spoon of the warm cereal.

"I am amazed," said Pug. "It's been a long time since I've experienced that."

Hatu shrugged off the remark. "I just did it."

Hava slowly shook her head side to side, then looked at Pug with an expression that communicated her own astonishment.

"I also found a couple of works that touched on rifts but were mostly regarding time."

Pug blinked and sat back. "Such as?"

"It's from a discussion I had with Magnus, and I think I'll wait until you both can hear my theory."

"That can be quickly arranged," said Pug. It was obvious he had finished eating, but he remained seated to wait for Hava and Hatu.

When they were done, Hatu quickly loaded the tray with their dishes and Pug's, then carried it over to where whoever had kitchen duty that day would take the dishes to be washed. He turned to Pug and said, "Show me that rift."

Pug led them out of the dining hall and across an open court to the old villa. He went through a larger open court, then up the pathway that led to the cave where Hava and Hatu were first introduced to the Conclave of Shadows. Instead of continuing past the villa, Pug halted before the last door in the northernmost building and opened it.

He waved them inside, then followed. Instantly, Hatu sensed a powerful energy swirling throughout the room. He saw what at first he took to be a large oval mirror, then saw it wasn't reflecting light, but emitting it. Silver swirls in a big oval, large enough for a person to step through, were contained in a frame of either metal or painted wood—he couldn't tell which at this distance.

A young adept sat on a chair reading. He looked up as Pug shut the door. The only other illumination in the room was a large wax candle on a small table to his left, providing reading light. He put the book down and stood up. "Pug," he said in greeting. He was slender with dark hair and deeply tanned skin.

"Jaroly, this is Hava and Hatushaly."

The adept stepped forward and extended his hand. "I've heard much about you already," he said as Hava first, then Hatu shook hands.

"Jaroly is here in case something happens to that rift," said Pug, pointing at the silver oval.

Hatu nodded, and stepped past Jaroly, getting as close as he could to the rift without touching it. He could feel energies dancing across the undulating face of the silver light in a pattern.

Pug started to speak, but Hatu held up his hand, signaling silence.

Hatu stood motionless for a long time, while the other three watched quietly. After a while the door opened, and Magnus entered. Pug held a finger to his lips, indicating silence. Magnus nodded.

More time passed as Hatu stared into the seemingly random pattern of shimmering ripples across the rift. Then he turned, and took a step toward them, almost stumbling. He shook his head to clear it as Hava moved to catch him if he fell.

Hatu held up his hand in a reassuring gesture. "I'm all right. That was . . . unique."

"What did you see?" Magnus asked.

"See is perhaps the wrong way of putting it," Hatu replied. "If you don't mind," he said, walking over to the chair and sitting down. "That took a lot of energy, and I didn't get any sleep last night."

Pug said to Magnus, "He read thirty-seven books last night."

Magnus responded with raised eyebrows but said nothing.

Hatu sat back and said, "When I first learned of the energy that stretches between what Nathan called positive and negative furies, in my mind I saw them as lines like threads in a loom. Different colors that I just knew represented different states of energy, like living things, fire, water moving . . ." He waved his hand in the air. "I don't know how I knew; I just did." He looked at Magnus. "I think I understand what you meant about explaining the inexplicable. I experienced things by delving into that rift . . . I don't know if I can find the words . . . to properly express . . ."

Hava scowled and said, "Just try. You never seem to be at a loss for words most of the time."

Hatu laughed with a touch of exhaustion and gave her a look of surrender. "What I saw was . . . a space between." He looked at Pug. "Remember how I said I thought rifts bent space so two distant locations touched each other?"

Pug glanced at Magnus and said, "Over breakfast this morning." To Hatu he said, "Yes."

"Well, I was wrong. Not by much. The two ends of the rift almost are in contact, but there is a tiny space, almost impossible to notice if you just step through like we did when we came here from Garn, but I saw it, or rather felt it. A tiny crack, and I think I sensed what you call the Void—or rift-space—in that crack."

Magnus looked impressed. "That would clearly explain how things like the Dread, and demons, can find their way into the rifts and come out into our realm."

"And the Dragon Lords," said Pug. "How could any of us forget that battle at Sethanon . . . ?" Suddenly he closed his eyes and dropped his ever-present staff. It clattered to the floor, and he reached up with both hands to grab his temples. A moment later he fell to his knees with a groan that rapidly rose to a scream of pain.

Hava and Magnus barely caught Pug as he keeled over and lay on the stone floor, writhing. His eyes rolled up and he started to tremble.

Magnus looked at Jaroly and shouted, "Go get a healer!"

Hatu jumped up out of his chair and came to stand over the trembling figure on the floor. "Is he having a seizure?"

Magnus said, "I don't know. My knowledge of healing is slight, even after all these years. We have others here who are far better than I. Still, I will try to help."

He closed his eyes and rested his hand on Pug's trembling chest, and after a moment the trembling subsided, but it was clear that Pug was unconscious and in distress. His complexion was now pallid and his breathing shallow.

A few minutes later the door opened and a man in a brown robe and matching flat cloth cap entered, and without a word knelt next to Pug. "How long?" he asked.

"He keeled over in pain a few minutes ago," answered Hava.

Hatu could see deep concern etched into Magnus's features. Jaroly looked at the most senior magician on the island with a silent question on his face. Hatu saw that Magnus's attention was fixed on Pug, and said to the younger adept, "I think you can go now."

With a look of relief, Jaroly quickly left the room.

Hatu looked at the man in brown as his lips moved in a silent incantation and he put both hands on Pug's temples.

Hatu watched intently, then after a few minutes, he whispered, "I see."

Hava came to stand next to him. "See what?"

"I see what he's doing. The spell—it's . . . different."

Magnus stood up and told Hatu, "This is Father Athanasios. He's a priest of Silban, the Earth Mother. We are fortunate that he is studying with us, as he is among the greatest healers on Midkemia."

Hatu's expression was one of wonder. Softly he said to Hava, "I've seen nothing like this."

Hava looked worried. "Since we came here, you've said that almost every day."

Minutes dragged by and Hatu watched as the healer worked his magic on Pug. Finally, Father Athanasios rocked back on his heels and said, "I've done all I can. I've calmed his heart and made sure he can easily breathe, but there is more going on that is beyond my understanding."

Abruptly, Hatu looked at Pug and softly said, "Damn!"

"What?" asked Hava.

"I see it."

"See what?" asked Magnus.

"I see in him . . ." Hatu stood back. "Do you remember me telling you how I might be able to find Ruffio and Zaakara by their . . . energy? How each person's energy is different from everyone else's, and I can recognize people that way?"

Magnus nodded.

"Pug's energy is changing."

Hatu saw Magnus go pale. "Go on," Magnus said.

"He's different to how he was this morning. Let me see if I can see . . ." Hatu closed his eyes and stood still. After a moment, his eyes opened wide. "I don't know . . . there are two . . . two different . . ."

"Two different what?" asked Magnus.

Hatu slowly shook his head as if clearing it. "It's as if there are two different Pugs, both struggling within for control."

Magnus almost stumbled as he stepped back and gripped his staff for support.

Hatu looked at Father Athanasios and asked, "Can you keep him alive?"

"At least for a while," answered the cleric. "I do not fully understand what you say, but whatever conflict resides within Pug is exacting a toll and he cannot withstand that struggle for long."

Hatu nodded and said, "I think I can help. But I need rest and food." Suddenly he seemed to go weak, and Hava reflexively reached out to put an arm around her husband's waist to keep him steady. "I can come back as soon as I am able, and I may be able to help with this."

"What can you do?" asked Magnus.

Hatu took a deep breath and said, "I think I need to enter his mind and observe the battle between the two . . . minds. Perhaps I can even somehow . . . calm it."

Hava could see tears beginning to well up in Magnus's eyes.

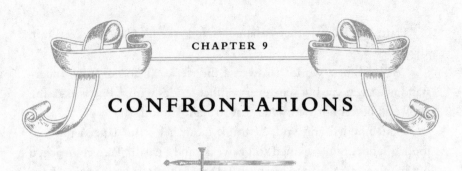

CHAPTER 9

CONFRONTATIONS

Declan held up his hand.

The company came to a halt and waited. He turned to Sixto and spoke softly. "Dismount and use hand signals only."

Sixto turned in his saddle, and with a gesture signaled to dismount. Every member of that company knew the enemy might be within hearing range.

It was less than two hours after sunrise, and the sky was still dark with clouds as the storm moved away. The night had been cold and wet, despite Declan bedding down closest to the hearth because of his rank, and the tack and saddles in the barn were still damp.

Yet, the day held promise as they were within minutes of reaching their destination, and Declan was eager to finish up this business and get back to Marquenet, a hot bath, and dry clothing. Since the destruction of the Pride Lords in Nytanny, after so much bloodshed and death, his appetite for revenge had been waning, despite his lingering sorrow over Gwen's death. He saw this conflict with the Church as absolutely necessary. They were the authors of much of the carnage he'd experienced, and their ambitions made this coming war a clear act of survival—but even so, it was not a fight he welcomed.

Declan signaled with an upraised fist, then one finger, then three, and every third man took the reins of three mounts and led them away, to be picketed in a pasture where they could crop grass.

Sebastian had returned. He waited for them to secure the horses, then moved to stand before Declan. In a voice barely more than a whisper he said, "Four guards, a dozen horses. I don't know what sort of trail we'll find in all this mud, but at least we know where they entered the forest."

Declan nodded. "Good work." He glanced skyward and added softly, "The clouds are thinning. This will be clear by noon. We'd best take the advantage while it's there. Church soldiers?"

Sebastian nodded. "Church Adamant, from their tabards, so it's a fight."

"What's our best attack?" Declan asked.

Sebastian motioned off to the left. "That way to a copse just outside trees so close they form a wall, then follow the edge, and we'll be less than thirty yards from the pickets." He glanced up at the sky and added, "They'll be awake, but with the time of day, dark weather, and boredom, we may be able to hit them before they realize what's happening."

"Good." Declan turned and motioned for his men to form up behind him and Sixto, and once the column was in line, he indicated for Sebastian to lead.

Quickly the squad moved out, each man following the one in front, all of them hurting from long hours in the saddle but ignoring the aches and attending to stealth. With ten men remaining behind to tend the horses, Declan still had a massive advantage of thirty men to take down the Church guards.

Declan realized a few seconds after moving out that his ragtag group of mercenaries, men who had accompanied him escaping Garn's Wound, had become a highly disciplined unit. He found an unexpected satisfaction in that moment.

They moved briskly past the copse to the main forest, then skirted the edge as they circled toward the Church encampment. Declan heard a horse nicker and held up his hand. Everyone froze in place. The sentries might not hear his company approaching but they'd start to be wary if the horses acted up.

Declan judged that the wind was not in their favor or the Church guards', as it was blowing across them both. He waited and heard the horses settle, then motioned for the men to follow.

As they rounded the edge of the forest, Declan took a glance into the thick trees and, just as he remembered, twenty feet in was complete darkness. He hunched over and peered around a tree bole; Sebastian turned to face him, then pointed out a tiny clearing. Declan gave one brief nod. From that clearing led a narrow path that would get them to the enemy camp. He motioned for Sixto and the others to follow. It was a large enough pathway that the men could walk in single file yet alternate a bit so that each could see over the shoulder of the man in front. Declan prayed nobody stepped on anything that would trip them or make a loud noise.

As he neared the exit of the pathway, Declan smelled smoke from a campfire and looked around the edge of the trees. A dozen horses were picketed to a line, while four men sat eating near the campfire. Declan calculated that by the time he and his men reached these four they would be on their feet and ready. Still, he had the advantage in numbers and every one of his men knew these Church soldiers would not yield, so it was a fight to the death.

Declan slowly drew his sword and turned to see if those behind were ready. Sixto nodded, and Declan turned and ran out of the cover of the woods, keeping silent.

The lack of a battle cry seemed to gain him a few seconds, as the Church guards were slow to react to the sight of men racing out of the woods at them. They dropped their bowls and spoons, stood tossing their heavy cloaks over one shoulder, and started to draw their weapons.

The first guard was barely ready when Declan fell upon him, Sixto one step behind. The Church soldier parried a high blow from the prince, but Sixto came in under and stabbed at the man. His blade slid off a chain shirt, but the blow knocked the man backward.

Declan moved with the falling man and took him in the throat with the point of his blade. He turned quickly and found that the other three were surrounded. In moments they lay dead on the ground.

His men stood looking down at the dead Church soldiers.

"That was quick," said Sixto with a note of satisfaction.

"Anyone wounded?" Declan asked.

A new recruit to the company named Jax said, "Got a nick to my arm, but it's nothing."

Declan saw blood flowing from a gash and shook his head. That "nothing" could fester and cost Jax his arm or even kill him if not treated. He said, "Stay here with the horses, and get to sewing and salting that wound."

At the mention of salt, Jax visibly winced, but he simply said, "Yes, highness."

Glancing skyward, Declan saw the overcast was clearing. "Do you think the noise carried?" he asked Sixto.

"I doubt it. Not through that many trees."

Declan regarded the Darkwood and knew it was likely that the engineers and guards were far away. He looked at the horses. They had tried to pull away from the violence but were still firmly tied. "How many riders did that report say?" he asked Lewis as he came forward.

"A dozen."

"So, eight left," Declan said. "They're likely on their way back to wherever the Church has men ready to come here once things are underway with the redoubt."

"Send men after them?" asked Sixto.

Declan shook his head. "If no one returns, the Church officers might get suspicious and send someone to see what's wrong."

Sixto nodded agreement. "That reconnaissance force would not be welcome. What hit us at the south border? Forty men?"

"Yes," said Declan. "So, we let them go and report everything is going well." He considered, then said, "So, that leaves eight riders on foot, but we don't know how many foot soldiers as well. Let's say a squad of twenty."

"If they're dug in when we find them, that could get tricky."

Declan said, "Make camp. We'll go at first light, and hope they're not dug in like ticks on a dog."

"And I hope it stays dry." Sixto glanced skyward as more blue appeared between the clouds.

"No joy there," Declan answered. "As thick as those woods are, those paths will stay muddy for a few days."

"Well," answered Sixto, "at least the worst of the dripping from the trees will be over."

Declan couldn't help but laugh. It was a welcome release of tension. "You do find the bright side of things, don't you?"

"I try," said Sixto wryly.

"Send for our horses," Declan said. He saw that his men were already dragging the dead Church soldiers away after stripping their weapons. "We can use those twelve for remounts when we leave."

"How many men do we leave here?" asked Sixto.

"We need as many in the forest as we can have. The horses are not going anywhere, but they need to be moved so they have grass to crop. Leave Jax and seven others. The rest of us will see what's in that forest."

"Nothing good, I'll wager," Sixto offered.

Saying nothing, Declan nodded his agreement.

SABELLA LOOKED READY TO FALL over from exhaustion. The other four young adepts had been resting, but she had insisted on staying with Zaakara and Ruffio to discuss the possibilities of fixing the "broken" rift, as she called it.

The three had spent the entire night discussing the possible ways she and the other women could somehow transfer their power to the men. It was as alien a concept to the women as it was to Zaakara and Ruffio.

"You look all out on your feet," said Zaakara to the young woman. "Get some sleep and Ruffio and I will trade off watching the rift with the soldiers." He glanced out of the opening of the pavilion and added, "It's a few hours to dawn, and maybe we'd all do well with some rest."

She nodded and stood up, accidentally slipping a little. As she grabbed at the table, she put her fist into a half-full pitcher of water. The stumble caused her to laugh, and she took her wet hand out and dried it on a cloth on the table. As she regarded her hand, her eyes widened.

"What?" asked Ruffio.

"That rift you tried to create back to your world. Why does it have to be so large?" she asked the warlock.

"So that I can step through," said Zaakara.

"We don't need a person to go through it," Sabella said. "If I understand what you said, your home world is just on the 'other side' of that rift, correct?"

"It's like stepping through a doorway, across a threshold," said Ruffio.

Her mood brightened. "You don't have to go. Just write a message and drop it through for your friends to read."

Zaakara and Ruffio exchanged looks, and it was Ruffio who said, "But the rift doesn't reach Midkemia."

Zaakara said, "If these acolytes of the Flame Guard can somehow give me their power, I don't need to do more than have an opening that's just big enough to put my hand through—"

"And that might lengthen it enough to reach home!" said Ruffio, now excited at the possibility. He looked at Sabella and said, "You are a wonder. If we get this done and can get home, you must come and visit. I think you have the makings of a magic-user."

She blushed. "I have simple gifts."

Zaakara said, "Here. There, perhaps a great deal more. I'll spare you a lecture. You get them enough from Bodai."

She laughed at that.

Zaakara said, "Simply put, the amount of energy, what many people call *anima, orenda, tangata, doko, mana,* or other words, some in languages no human can pronounce, is a force. This energy that Hatushaly can see, wield—"

"And take with him, apparently," added Ruffio darkly.

"—it varies from world to world. Sometime, when you're in the mood for a long talk, I can tell you about the Hall of Worlds, which I suspect was how Nathan got here in the first place. There are worlds out there with no mana, no force to speak of, just the natural energy of all living things, but there are worlds like Midkemia where the energy is so strong it manifests in ways that can only be legends here.

"But if I can get enough energy from you and your companions, just enough so I can manipulate the energy already trapped in that rift, then perhaps we can get a message home."

Sabella seemed eager, despite her fatigue.

"Get some rest," he said. "We all need to be at our best to try this."

"I still need to talk to the others about how we get the power to you. There are tales, from ancient times to now, about natural magics:

dance-magic, singing-magic, sex-magic, blood-magic, elemental magics that are dangerous, even deadly, so we have to contrive a way to do this without doing harm."

"That would be welcome," said Ruffio. "Magic by its very nature is dangerous to the unpracticed."

"Sometime even to the well-practiced," Zaakara added with a wry smile. "Now, go and get some rest."

"I shall. You as well." She retired to a corner of the big pavilion that had been curtained off for the women's privacy.

"Do you think we can do this?" asked Ruffio.

"I have no idea," replied Zaakara. "But it's the first intelligent idea I've heard since we started looking at this problem."

Ruffio nodded. "Leave it to a woman to see what we don't."

Zaakara laughed. "My father would have said the exact same thing about my mother." He rose and said, "I'll take the first watch. Get some sleep."

"I will not argue," said the magician, rising and moving to another corner of the pavilion where there was bedding on the ground.

Zaakara walked slowly to where two guards sat by the two rifts. As they heard him approach, they came to their feet and he said, "Sit down. You may not see anything for a very long time." He thought it would not matter if they were on their feet should the wrong kind of demon come through.

SIXTO DETAILED THOSE WHO WERE to remain while Declan spoke with Sebastian and Lewis. "I've only been in this forest a short way—just to load timber. But I've heard the stories."

Lewis said, "As have I, highness. I've been around the edges like some who live near here. There are stories of evil spirits, ghosts, and the like. Men wandering lost until they starve to death."

"Probably just to scare children into behaving," said Sebastian.

"Whatever the truth, we'll soon be meeting death face on—at the hands of creatures, spirits, or soldiers of the Church—so you two need to be most on your guard. You're the trailbreakers."

Sebastian clapped his hand on Lewis's shoulder and said, "Then we best get to it." To Declan he said, "We'll start along this path and see if it takes us to a stream bed or game trail. Whatever we find, one of us will return with word."

"Get started," said Declan.

Sebastian gave a casual salute, and the two scouts turned and walked into the forest. Declan was surprised at how quickly they vanished from sight.

The rest of the soldiers were organizing their gear. Enough food and water for a week's march. Given the density of these trees, Declan thought they'd be lucky to get half that progress.

He and Sixto inspected the soldiers' kit. Cloth wraps were tied around sword hilts, and small buckler shields were slung over each man's back to prevent noise as they moved through the forest. Each archer carried his bow, with a hip quiver, while the other soldiers carried easy-to-drop hip-packs of food, and water skins.

As they were ready to enter the woods, Lewis returned at a quick half-run. He hurried to Declan and said, "Sebastian's holding a position, and we may be in luck."

"Go on."

"The Church trailbreakers were heading as we are, for at a fork just half a mile ahead, where we found a charred tree."

Sixto nodded slowly. "They marked the way for the soldiers and engineers to follow." He laughed softly. "By my ancestors, they may be evil bastards, but they're not stupid. They did what we planned on doing."

"Let's move," said Declan. With a wave of his hand, he set Lewis off ahead and motioned for the column to fall in behind Sixto and him.

Entering the forest, Declan was as surprised as the first time he had come into the Darkwood, years ago, with foresters to stock up on wood for Edvalt's furnace, forge, and hearth. Within a hundred yards, the light from the sky was shaded by thousands of branches. It was a canopy so dense it might as well have been a roof. The gloom was close to the first light of dawn. Stepping ahead was not the problem, but a look to either side and within half a dozen yards there was nothing to see but tree trunks and darkness.

The other change Declan noticed was the smell. The open fields had held a scent of grass, and occasionally flowers that were still in bloom. He had noticed that on first leaving Marquenet, the hint of spring orange blossoms and sea salt had faded, to be replaced with dust and grass.

Now it was wet earth beneath the men's boots, and a musty tang of moss and lichen. The rain had cleared the air, but the odors of the deep forest were quickly returning. To Declan, it added to his sense that they were not welcome here.

Lewis was easy to see, but not much ahead beyond him was clear. Suddenly, Sebastian was ahead holding up his hand.

Declan signaled and the men behind him came to a halt. "What have you found?" Declan asked.

"I've scouted ahead, and the way is clear for a few hundred yards. I think they were blind to the possibility someone could get past their sentries at the forest's edge and follow them in."

"Well, we might as well be blind to anything off this path, so did you hear anything?" asked Declan.

"No, highness," answered the old scout. "No sounds of felling trees or hammers, so they must still be miles ahead."

Sixto stood at Declan's side and asked, "How far do you think sounds like that might carry?"

Lewis held up his hand, one finger pointing upward. "Do you hear anything?"

Both men listened and after a moment, Declan said, "Nothing."

Sebastian nodded emphatically. "Yes, no bird or animal sounds. Everything with fur or feathers knows we're here. So, the question we must ask is: will the Church have guards on the perimeter or just assume they're safe? If they're felling trees immediately, the birds have already fled. So no flocks rising to give us away."

Sixto almost laughed. "If the Church engineers are sawing and hammering, they won't hear us coming."

Declan smiled. "I think you're right." He turned to look at the men behind him and said, "Try to keep silent, but we are going to a forced march." He motioned to the two trailbreakers, and they set off at a loping jog.

Declan signaled and started after them. They would find the enemy sooner rather than later, and Declan was pleased about that. He was not pleased about the bloodshed yet to come.

SABELLA SAID, "I THINK WE found a way."

Zaakara rolled over from the mat upon which he had been sleeping and blinked as he came awake. "What . . . ?"

"I said I think we found a way to get the power to you to fix that rift." She squatted and looked him in the eye. "You need to wake up."

"Where's Ruffio?" he replied, coming to his feet.

"He's at the rifts. Something came through, but it was little, and the guards killed it without issue."

"I need coffee," he said, still blinking.

"Over there," she replied.

He half-stumbled toward the part of the pavilion set up for eating and found a tray with mugs and a large pot of coffee there. He poured himself a mug, tested it with a sip, then drank half of it down. "It's not cold, but it's on its way."

Sabella motioned to one of the soldiers standing duty as a steward, and said, "More hot coffee, please."

He nodded, took the pot, and headed back to where the kitchen had been set up.

Zaakara shook himself out of his half-awake stage and asked, "How long?"

"You've been asleep for five hours."

"Not nearly enough," he complained.

"Come on, old man," she said in a teasing voice. "We need to do this now."

By the time he reached the rift, he was fully alert. He saw the other four young women were there with Ruffio, who was slowly shaking his head as if he wasn't believing what he was hearing.

"What?" asked Zaakara.

"If you are willing, they think there's a way for you to adjust that rift."

"Willing to do what?"

Ruffio flipped his hand over and pointed at Sabella, who said,

"We've considered all the lore we know about how power flows from men to women here. The best possible way to reverse that is to reverse our assumed roles. You must become . . . passive, accepting. We will be the . . . repositories of energy."

"I have no idea what you mean." He looked at his empty mug and said, "I need more."

Sabella turned to a soldier and said, "There's someone with a pitcher of hot coffee down there. Please go and tell him to bring it here."

The soldier seemed amused by the request but nodded and ran off.

Zaakara said, "Do we have a message?"

Ruffio said, "I penned one earlier."

"Let me see."

Zaakara accepted a piece of heavy parchment with Ruffio's writing on it. It read, "We're trapped. No magic. Send Hatushaly now. Keep rift open both ways."

"That's to the point," Zaakara said, handing it back to Ruffio.

Ruffio put up his hands and said, "You keep it. You're the better rift expert here, so if anyone can get it home, it's you."

Zaakara took the parchment and said, "What next?"

"More coffee," said Sabella as a soldier appeared with a full pot.

Zaakara took his empty mug and held it out so the soldier could fill it. He tested the heat, blew across the mug, and when he was ready took a long swallow of the black, pungent drink. He blinked twice and handed the mug to Ruffio. "I'm as ready as I'll ever be."

"Stand still," said Sabella. "Do not move until we tell you."

Zaakara said nothing but stood as motionless as he could.

The five women surrounded him and moved as close as they could without touching him. Sabella said, "Close your eyes and just be willing to take what comes to you."

Zaakara said nothing, but let out a slow breath, took in a long one, and stood ready.

The five women linked arms, forming a circle around him, and began to chant. He felt a chill come over him, as if a sudden cold breeze had struck him, and his skin reacted with raised gooseflesh. A raw energy ran up from his shoulders, causing his neck to tighten. Throughout his body, muscles tensed, and he felt strange ripples of power course through it.

He felt his toes try to curl, almost cramping, and flexed them. Then a wave of pleasure ran from his toes to his scalp, a tingling that caused him to suck in his breath and gasp in wonderment as his hair rose.

He felt his entire body shudder, and then his flesh get rigid, as he rose up on his toes. His muscles were taut, even his groin aroused, and suddenly he was floating a foot above the ground. His mind was open and with eyes closed he saw the skies above. Beyond the clouds and flocking birds, his vision raced upward to a darkened dome dotted with stars.

Suddenly, he was in pain and sucking in air to fight for his life. And then he saw the rift.

He reached out with his mind and commanded the rift to contract and lengthen. He felt the circumference contract, and the energy that produced sped away from him. A vibration—silent yet reverberating in his mind like a gong—ran through him, and for a moment his senses were almost overwhelmed. Sights of familiar places sped through his mind, familiar scents teased him, fleeing at the moment of recognition, followed by a soft caress of sea breeze tinged with salt: a smell he recognized; one he had known since his birth. He was home.

His feet touched the ground, and he stumbled forward. Before the others could grab him to hold him upright, he thrust the message though the smaller opening and let it go.

He collapsed as they caught him before he struck the ground and saw a circle of faces above him. "Did we do it?" he asked. Then the light fled, and he lost consciousness.

CHAPTER 10

RECOVERY

Hatushaly sat motionless.

Pug lay upon a sleeping pallet that had been brought into the chamber, so as not to move him other than lifting him off the floor. Father Athanasios had been joined by two other masters of healing magic. One was Father Jacob of the Order of Sung the Pure. He wore similar garb to the other cleric, but of white cloth rather than brown. The third healer was an elven Spellweaver, Nitlanta. She struck Hatu as very humanlike, except for an exaggeratedly lithe frame and upswept, lobeless ears. Her hair was a light red-blond, and her eyes were closed as she incited her spell to heal the fallen magician.

Hatu sat back and looked at the circle of concerned faces around him and said, "I will need time. How long can he remain like this?"

Father Athanasios looked for a moment at the other two healers, then said, "It's difficult to say. He is suffering and while he may be young in appearance, he . . ." He stopped. "I cannot say."

Magnus said, "My father once spoke of the time a princess of the royal family was poisoned, and he encased her in a . . . time bubble, slowing things down to a moment inside the bubble taking a day to pass while others sought a cure."

"Can you do that?" asked Hatu.

"I think so. I have my father's notes and remember enough that it should take me only a short time to erect such a bubble." He shook his head in a way that Hatu interpreted as a mix of hopelessness and futility, then went on, "But even if I could, you or whoever else was in that bubble would also be slowed, hence no good would come of it. It would be useful if we could contrive a cure away from Phillip, outside such a bubble. Or if we could find a way to slow him without harm."

Hatushaly shook his head. "No, that . . . Wait."

"What?" asked Magnus.

"I think I might have a way."

Hatu closed his eyes and let his mind move away from the chaotic energies he saw in Pug's mind, where it was as if there were two warring sets of furies. He turned his mind instead to Pug's body, his pumping heart and laboring lungs. He felt the stress and tension in Pug's muscles, and in internal organs that seemed to be struggling to answer conflicting demands. He discerned the healing energies of Father Athanasios, and the investigating magic of Father Jacob and Nitlanta. He probed at every aspect and eventually found an element he had seen once before.

Hatu rocked back on to his heels. He said to Magnus, "When I saw that thing in the pit in Garn's Wound, surrounded by those twisted people, the time bonds that held it frozen were weakening. They seemed to be moving faster. I'm not sure that's a good explanation, but I saw those bonds moving, a tiny fraction, but definitely moving. So, I touched them and slowed down their . . . change. I don't understand why, but I know how to slow things down."

He closed his eyes again and turned his attention to Pug's still body, and suddenly he saw the link to time within the framework of his being. At the very center of each thread, he perceived an even tinier filament of time. For a moment he felt doubt and wondered if what he was about to try could be fatal. The old and familiar anger from his childhood threatened to rise, and he knew it was doubt that had to be shunted aside. But berating himself for his hesitancy was pointless and danger-ous, for the magician would die if something wasn't done quickly.

Hatushaly took a slow, deep breath and saw which way time moved in the fibers of Pug's being. He reached out gently with his mind and touched that filament of time, willing it to slow. It resisted and he felt a tug in his mind, a sense that he was not supposed to perceive it like this. Yet he understood this was just a perception, and that time itself was a thing barely understood. He stroked it, as if he had a hand on a line and was slowing how it played out, preventing too fast an unreeling.

He imagined he was a brake on a fishing reel and applied the slightest pressure.

Abruptly, his own heart started to beat faster, perspiration formed on his skin, and he felt his body tingle. There was something new there and he felt pulled in two directions; one side of his mind wanted to investigate the new sensation, and the other half demanded he attend to the matter at hand. Pug's life hung in the balance.

Energies flowed in patterns wholly new to Hatushaly. He'd seen complex weaves of energy tugging between positive and negative furies enough to recognize this was the most challenging display he'd ever encountered.

His uncertainty returned. To pick the wrong thread, pull in the wrong direction, was to invite disaster, even death. A sudden wave of fear washed over him, and he opened his eyes and saw those around him depending on him to act. He sat back, his eyes welling with tears, and he turned to Hava.

"What?" she asked.

Wiping away tears of fatigue and worry, he said, "I need you to come behind me, and hold me tight."

She moved instantly to comply and grabbed her husband from behind, wrapping her arms around his waist and holding him close. "Why?" she whispered.

"Because you are my anchor," he whispered back. Then he closed his eyes and returned to the struggle.

In his mind's eye, Hatu saw as complex a display of forces as he had ever beheld. He scanned and judged, then realized the threads of energy were not a jumble of lines, not a skein of tangled yarn as he had first perceived, but two sets moving in opposite directions, tangling as they tried to move past one another, each blocking the other's way. He reached out gently to untangle the first two threads from the countless lines of Pug's life.

DONTE MOTIONED FOR DAVID TO come to him. The children had been running back and forth across a cleared patch of grass, which had once been a garden of some sort, Donte assumed.

The youngsters were laughing and shouting as if this running was a type of play. Donte was feeling at a loss, for he realized he had begun this scheme of starting his own crew, and building from there, with absolutely no idea how children not in a Coaltachin school were going to act. His father and grandfather had raised him from infancy to assume the mantle of clan-master one day. He didn't even have the childhood memories of life before the school that some children like Hava had. Moreover, he had pretty much ignored children whenever he encountered them on his travels. The ones he interacted with were crew urchins, all trained before they were sent to work for the crews.

David said, "Yes?"

"Were you born here?"

"No. A village to the south, near the Green Reaches. Why?"

Donte made an exasperated sound. "What did I say about questions?"

"I forgot."

With an audible sigh, Donte repeated, "What did I say?"

"Not to ask questions until you ask us if there are questions." David seemed unsure about this, but when Donte slowly nodded, he brightened a little.

"What are the Green Reaches?" asked Donte.

"Big forest, sort of, or a jungle, between here and Kesh. Used to be tough to get through, just because it was really thick with trees and stuff, but now people say you can't. Lots of weird plants that are poisonous, and creatures, they say. Everything in there tries to kill you, they say."

Donte resisted the urge to ask who "they" were. "Was that an important route?"

"Once," David answered. "Healer would know. Besides, Kesh doesn't trade with the Kingdom anymore, so nobody tries to get through there."

Donte held up his hand. "That's enough for now. You could have just said, 'A big forest to the south of here.'"

David lost his bright expression.

Donte said, "So, is that where you were born?"

"Yes, just to this side of the Reaches. Where my folks were, too.

A lot of our grandparents with Keshian blood got stranded there when the weird magic hit."

Donte decided that was a topic to talk to Healer about. "So, your folks are from the other side originally?"

"Ya, dark as me, the people from Kesh are."

Donte nodded. "Mainly, what I'm trying to work out is who will get noticed where in Port Vykor. Like, if you walked into a shop, would they look at you different than the others?"

David seemed a bit confused by the question and said, "Of course they would. I'm a rag-picker and they know I've got no coin, so they'll toss me out on my arse. Any one of us goes into a shop anywhere but the Poor Quarter, and we're dusted out of the door."

Donte nodded. "So, it's not who your parents were, but if you can spend?"

David nodded.

Donte took a slow, deep breath. He stood up and entered the former farmhouse and looked around. Rough pallets lay everywhere on the floor, and blankets were tossed about randomly. He looked at the dirty hearth and filthy wash basin and realized that to these children grime was a way of life.

Dirt was a costume in Coaltachin. If you needed to play the role it was easier to rub dirt on a clean face than to wash a dirty face. He'd played street boys since he was five years old, but at home, in school, he and the other children were expected to stay clean. Washing in a cold stream was preferable to being punished by a preceptor or master. Besides, Master Bodai had lectured that it kept illness away.

Donte had examined this hovel before taking possession, but still wandered around, poking at this and that piece of refuse as if he might discover something he'd previously missed. He knew, without doubt, that he was completely unprepared for the task at hand.

At the rear of this tiny house there was a single window, without glass but with an outside shutter that prevented rain and cold from entering. He stared out at a long, rolling pasture overgrown with weeds and bordered by a small creek across the back. "What could we do with that?" he wondered.

Donte had worked with enough livestock in his time running different dodges, spying, or simply training with the Kingdom of the Night to know that of all the animals that could turn a profit, sheep were the least bothersome. They were a nuisance when it came to shearing, but for the most part, they were stupid, didn't wander off if there was ample grass, and they weren't spooked. They were work, but less work than cattle and smelled less than pigs. Perhaps chickens were even less bothersome, but they also stank, and everyone had a few, so they were not a serious market.

Sheep it would be.

He walked back to the front of the house where the children were now playing some sort of ball game, kicking a ball of rags at an overturned barrel.

He waved David over again, and said, "So, where do I buy some sheep?"

IN HIS MIND'S EYE, HATUSHALY saw lines of energy slowly disentangle themselves, and a sense of order revealed itself. At first, it had been one strand up and another down, unweaving and reweaving, as if his own mind were fingers on a loom.

He lost any sense of time passing while he focused on the task, and as he moved through countless threads, his ability to unweave became more assured. He recognized the patterns and moved threads in a way that somehow made sense. There was a rightness to his choices, and he felt his fear of failure diminish and his sense of purpose intensify.

Then a darkness began to manifest at the periphery of his mind's eye, and began to close in, making it harder to "see" what he was doing as the center of his awareness became smaller.

A sudden pull and he lay on the floor, his vision swimming, while he heard his name being called.

Crippling fatigue washed over Hatu. He felt Hava fall away from him. Magnus and the elf Spellweaver hovered over him.

"Are you all right?" Magnus asked from behind Nitlanta.

Hatu moved and suddenly everything hurt. Joints creaked and muscles unclenched painfully, and he found his vision slowly clearing and his own voice sounded far away. "I'm alive," he croaked.

Nitlanta spoke softly. "Your wife hung on until she fell down from exhaustion, and then you collapsed on top of her. You both need rest."

Hatu could barely sit up, but he managed it and nodded. "Pug?" he asked.

"His body is calm," came another voice.

Hatu was too tired to see who spoke.

Father Jacob stepped into Hatu's field of vision and said, "Whatever you did calmed Pug's body and now he seems far more at peace, though his heartbeat is very slow and his breathing even slower. Yet I detect no injury to him. What you've done is amazing."

"I've not finished," Hatu said as he took a drink from the water skin the elf healer held out for him. He nodded his thanks and added, "I have no idea how much more there is to do, but I've begun untangling a rat's nest of energies unlike anything I've encountered, a snarl that makes me wonder how he's survived these many years."

"That takes some explaining," said Magnus, obviously exhausted as well. "Rest now." He looked at Father Jacob and got an approving nod.

"What?" said Hava in groggy tones as she regained consciousness.

"You fainted," said the elf.

Hava gave her a sour expression and said, "I may have momentarily lost consciousness, but I've never fainted."

Hatu shook his head slowly in wonder. Some lessons from childhood linger, no matter what. He suspected the difference in the terminology had something to do with not being considered a weak woman. Changing the topic, he said, "You may have saved Pug."

"Me?" she said, coming more alert. "You were the one inside his head."

"Yes, but I think I would have gotten lost in there if you hadn't stayed with me. As I said, my anchor."

"Come on, then," Hava said, rising unsteadily with the cleric's help.

Hatu waved a hand. "Give me a few moments to catch my breath."

Magnus asked, "Do you need help getting back to your quarters?"

"A few moments more," said Hatu, "and we should be fine."

Hava agreed. "I think we can manage."

"Good," Magnus said. "If you can save Phillip, there's one more thing you need to do."

"What?" Hatu asked, still a little woozy.

Magnus held out a parchment, and said, "Apparently you need to return to Garn as soon as possible. I surmise from this message that when you came here, you brought all of Garn's magic with you and now Ruffio and Zaakara are stuck there."

Hava and Hatu both stared at him, and Hatu said, "Yes, of course." He started to stand up, and felt his knees begin to buckle and sat down again. "Maybe I could do with some help getting to our bed. If I'm going to be able to help, I must rest."

"Of course. They've waited for a few days, so another day shouldn't matter."

Magnus opened the door to the chamber and motioned for two young students to attend to Hava and Hatushaly. As they left the room, Hatu said, "I'll return as soon as I can. There's so much more to be done."

When they were gone, Nitlanta said to Magnus, "I've seen many things, but this is remarkable beyond my imagining."

Magnus nodded. "If he can save Phillip, I will forever be in his debt."

"I know your former student is dear to you," said the elven Spell-weaver.

"Former student?" Magnus clutched his ever-present staff and said, "He's so much more."

DONTE STROLLED THE STREETS OF Port Vykor. He'd arranged for livestock to be sent to the farm he had appropriated.

Abandoned farms were scarce in the islands of Coaltachin. Arable land was rare on an atoll that was mostly sand and rock, and the masters of the Kingdom of Night were in control of pretty much everything in their region. No usable land was allowed to lie untended.

But here it seemed that if a farmer died and the rest of the family left, or if market forces drove them away, there were not as many opportunists as he would expect back on Garn. Healer had found one such abandoned, but workable, farm just at the limit of Donte's desired distance from the city.

Donte had found a sheep farm fairly close to the city and had brokered a deal for half the flock. He estimated they should be arriving tomorrow.

Donte was of the opinion most of the differences between here and Garn stemmed from the big disaster that everyone else seemed to know about, though they spoke of it as if it was history. He made a note to himself to ask Healer what that disaster was all about. He suspected there had been a lot more people living in this part of the world before that catastrophe than there were after. Even the pace of daily life here seemed sluggish compared to what he knew on Garn.

He assumed the demand for mutton and wool in Port Vykor and the other cities to the north was low and there was no market to the south because of what David had told him about the impenetrable Green Reaches. Still, even a slow market gave him cover for a farm where he'd secretly be training up a crew of youngsters.

Trade talk had always put him to sleep at school, but now he wished he'd paid a bit more attention. He often wondered what his life would be like today back on Garn. He had no wish ever to see his grandfather again, and his grandmother had never been kind, just less demanding than her husband. Still, the familiarity of everything in Coaltachin was a little reassuring.

He reckoned he had an hour or two before sundown and was again walking through parts of Port Vykor he hadn't visited before. He'd purchased simpler clothing than the fancy outfit the magicians at Stardock had provided for him—which were nicely folded and tucked into a haversack he had slung over his left shoulder. His grey shirt and trousers were accompanied by black boots and a dark grey over-jacket. He topped off his ensemble with what he thought was a jaunty-looking black hat, which the merchant had called a peaky cap. He looked like a simple traveler, with perhaps enough means to be welcomed at most merchants.

As cities went, Port Vykor was big enough, though it didn't compare to the former Kingdom capitals on Garn. Sandura, Ithrace, and Ilcomen were much larger. He had been told the capital to the north, Krondor, was a larger city, and he'd like to get up there someday and poke around. Perhaps meet this Upright Man and his Mockers who ran all the grifts and cons.

He had looped through the farthest part of the merchants' quarters, lingering for a few minutes around the stalls of a small open market. To the north were homes he assumed were occupied by people of means, given the location away from the stench of the Poor Quarter and a lovely view over the bay.

To the northwest was a fortress of some sort, in itself not terribly impressive, so he judged it to be a garrison, occupied by guards, port and government officials, but no nobles, or at least none with a taste for the ostentatious. On balance, he thought Port Vykor a pleasant little town, but hardly a major trading center by Garn standards.

Geography was another subject he needed to discuss with Healer. He saw the welcoming door of an inn and decided to stop there and see if there was a room for the night. He'd ride to the farm in the morning. The warehouse he'd originally chosen as a base would only be used for the older children to sleep when in town, for it was cold, dirty, and had the usual population of fleas and ticks. This inn looked promising. They might even have clean bedding.

He paused for a moment and wondered how Hava and Hatushaly were getting on. Sorcerer's Isle seemed a nice little place, but Stardock was just too odd for his liking. Port Vykor might be a small city, but it was a city and that was where he felt most at home. Idly, he wondered if he was missed. By now his family would assume he was dead, and Hava and Hatu would probably be caught up in those things they got caught up in. Besides, he'd vanished from their sight for longer periods than this one. He glanced up at the sign.

On it was depicted a simple red rose, so he assumed that was the name of the inn. He pushed open the door and instantly was struck by the strong aroma of a beef haunch roasting over a spit before a large hearth to the right. Tables were half full of drinkers, and there was a standing bar. He walked over and put his haversack on the floor next to a small man dressed in fancier clothing than those he wore, but not by much. Some sort of merchant, Donte assumed.

Donte sensed more than saw someone come up to stand behind

him, and moved his foot against his haversack, so he'd feel anyone touch it.

The barman asked, "What will it be?"

"Tall ale," he replied, having learned that here beer, ale, and stout came in two sizes, a short or tall mug.

The large mug appeared a moment later, and Donte slipped a silver coin from his waistband and said, "Let me know when I use that up."

The barman looked a bit surprised at the silver but took the coin and said, "Will do."

Donte picked up the mug and slowly turned to see who was standing behind him. The man remained motionless as Donte looked him up and down. A basher if ever he had seen one, dressed in clothing that wouldn't hamper him in a tussle. He was almost as tall as Donte, and while running a little toward fat, was well muscled underneath. He had a blue knitted cap pulled over dirty blond hair that came down over his neck, and Donte suspected he had a few weapons hidden under his shirt.

After a long pull on a very good light ale, Donte said, "Something you want?"

The man looked Donte in the eye and said, "Stranger, ain't ya?"

Donte nodded. "Never sailed here before," he answered. "Thought I'd look around. Clean bed would be welcome."

"You're far from the docks," said the man, stepping close. Donte didn't take his eyes off the man, but he'd already scanned the room before reaching the bar. Out of his peripheral vision he saw the short man next to him move away.

"I just said I like to look around."

"Well, we have a rule in this part of the city. Visitors who come uninvited have to pay a fee."

Donte mustered all his self-control not to laugh. Smiling, he said, "Shakedown, is it?"

"Local merchants like us to make sure those who come here can afford to be here."

"Barman," Donte said, raising his voice slightly.

From behind the bar Donte heard, "Ya?"

"Have a room?"

"Yes."

"Is it clean?"

"Changed the bedding last week. Only been used twice since then."

"That'll do," Donte replied. He looked at the man before him and asked, "What's your name?"

The bruiser said, "I'm called Scully, why?"

"Just like to know names," said Donte, putting down his empty mug. "So, you're not dark enough to be a mook from Kesh, so that means . . . what? You're one of those Mockers from Krondor?"

"I'm just a Port Vykor man, looking to keep the locals—"

Before he finished the sentence, Donte kicked up between Scully's legs. The man's eyes almost crossed as he let out a groan, gripped his groin, and collapsed.

Before Scully hit the floor, Donte had turned to stare at two men starting to rise from a table near the door. "Don't," he said menacingly as he took out a knife he'd secreted under his jacket. "I'll put up with one man's nonsense, but three of you? Then it gets serious."

His manner was persuasive: the two men exchanged glances and then bolted for the door.

The barman had come up behind Donte, who spoke without looking back. "You can put away the billy. I'm not shedding blood today."

Donte turned and saw the barman held an impressive head-knocker ready to club troublemakers if the violence escalated. "Now," he said. "About that room?"

The barman put down the billy club and said, "I'll see it's swept, and have the blankets shaken out." Without Donte asking, he refilled his mug, then left the bar to see to Donte's room.

Donte knelt before the still-prone Scully, who was curled up, groaning. "You'll live," he said. "Now, get up and let's have a polite conversation."

HATU ATE AS IF HE was starving.

"Slow down," said Hava. "You'll make yourself sick, then what good will you be?"

Hatu had slept from the moment he'd reached their bed until more than an hour after sunrise and awoke rested but noticeably thinner. Hava had said he looked as if he'd spent a month at sea on half-rations.

He nodded and put down his spoon. Taking a deep breath, he said, "I had no idea how tired and hungry doing what I tried with Pug would leave me. I can't remember anything I've done before that left me like that, not even when we were running for our lives for that town where we met Bodai . . ."

"Pashtar," Hatu reminded her.

"Yes . . . We were little more than children then."

Hatu nodded slowly. "Sometimes I feel as if we still are. I think it's because so few of the choices before us have been ours to make. It's as if some god or fate just makes us go where we need to go."

She nodded and as he took another spoonful of hot grain and vegetable soup and put it in his mouth, she asked, "What would you do, had we a choice?"

He stopped, leaned back in his chair, and said, "At times I wish we were back at Beran's Hill, before the raid, running our little inn. Other times I think staying at the Sanctuary, doing as much as I can for the Flame Guard in rebuilding is where I'd rather be. Whatever mood strikes me, I guess; things change, but in all those musings, you are at my side."

She smiled. "I love hearing that. As much as the sea calls me and as much as I relish the challenges commanding a ship brings, I always want to return to you."

Lightening the mood, he said, "Good. Now that we've settled that question, I should return to trying to save Pug. The sooner that's accomplished, the sooner we can return to Garn and save the other magicians." He found this slightly humorous and smiled broadly.

"Eaten enough?"

"No," he said, standing up. "But if I eat more, I'll be back to sleeping like a bear in winter."

"Well considered," she replied, standing also.

They moved quickly from the dining hall to the room where Pug lay. Entering, they saw that it looked as if Magnus had been at Pug's side all night. His expression was haggard, but he still stood over the unconscious magician as if he were standing guard. Father Athanasios had returned to attend to Pug's needs.

Magnus remained silent as Father Athanasios rose from his chair and said, "He's resting. I do not know what you did, but you accomplished much. He is still in conflict, but he is less at risk."

Magnus said softly, "Thank you. Are you willing to continue?"

"That's why I'm here." Hatu resumed his position, sitting next to Pug. He looked at Magnus for a moment and said, "I know I can save his life, but now I'm trying to save his mind."

Hava said, "Do you wish me to hold you?"

In a light tone, Hatu replied, "Often, but today I think just having you near will suffice. No need for both of us to become exhausted by day's end."

She smiled and knew he was making light of it because he was worried. "I'm here" was all she said.

Hatu closed his eyes and rested his hands on Pug's chest. Then he reentered the magician's mind.

CHAPTER 11

ESCALATION

Declan raised his fist.

Everyone froze as they waited for the prince's next signal. Lewis returned from his exchange of trail breaking with Sebastian and said, "Something you should see, highness."

Declan turned to Sixto. "Wait here."

He followed Lewis for about a hundred yards and the young soldier pointed at the side of the trail. There was blood on a clump of bushes, which Lewis pulled aside. A soldier lay where he'd been covered up, his throat cut, eyes staring vacantly at the trees above. He wore uniform trousers and shirt, but his tabard and cloak were gone.

Softly, Lewis said, "Either he said something that angered his commander, or there's someone else in these woods besides us and the Church."

"No signs of a fight," said Declan, looking around. "Looks like he was garrotted from behind. Look at the red line across his throat. A wire did that." Checking the other side of the trail, he added, "Must have been a rearguard, and maybe not missed until they reached their destination."

Lewis said, "Especially if whoever took him put on his tabard and cloak. Anyone looking back would see what they expected."

"Where's Sebastian?"

"A way ahead. He said he'd hold until I came back, then he'll lead on. I'll wait until you catch up."

"No need. If there's someone else here playing fast and loose with men's lives, I don't want you traveling alone. Let's go and find Sebastian."

"Sir," said Lewis, and he waited until Declan signaled for Sixto and the others to follow.

A short while later they could hear distant sounds of men working. Declan signaled to slow the pace and they advanced at a moderate walk. Now that they could hear the enemy, every man in Declan's company was fully alert, ready for combat.

As the woods rang with the sound of axes and saws, Declan knew Sebastian must have gotten close enough to see the camp. He sent Lewis to fetch Sebastian back, while Sixto and the men quietly readied their weapons.

Lewis returned with Sebastian, who came to Declan and spoke softly. "They've done some clearing and are felling trees. From what I can tell, they have a dozen engineers, about the same number of foot soldiers, and eight cavalrymen on foot."

Declan said, "Thirty-two swords against our thirty-six. Do the engineers look like fighters?"

"Hard to tell. They're not soft men, from the way they're swinging those axes and pulling those saws, but none are armed or wearing armor, so maybe a few might wield an axe, or maybe they'll just run."

Declan motioned Lewis over. "Do you think you can find a way to skirt this clearing without being seen?"

Lewis looked to his left, then to his right. Pointing to the right he said, "Looks a little thinner that way. Most likely I can find a way, but the question is how long it will take."

Sebastian nodded. Declan waved Sixto over to join them and said, "We risk being discovered if we linger. I thought we might hit them from two sides but setting that up might take too long. Besides, if there's someone else in these woods, I'd rather not split the company."

Sixto said, "Understood. If we hit them fast and hard, we can gain advantage. I'd say when they're getting ready for evening meal, but as murky as these woods are already, a fight in the dark is to no one's advantage."

Declan asked Sebastian for a quick description of the clearing, and he and Sixto listened closely. "It's a jungle. Pass word to watch where you step: they've got branches and trunks scattered. Some stumps to get around. There's a little clearing in the center, maybe big enough for a good-sized campfire without burning the whole damn forest down."

Declan returned to the head of the column and motioned a few of the men forward. "Put down your packs and double check your weapons. We go in single file. Once we get to the clearing, break opposite the man before you. If he goes right, you go left. Don't stop or you'll trip up those behind. Last, watch for stumps, logs, and branches. If you fall, good chance you'll die. If an engineer asks for quarter give it, but those soldiers will fight until the end. Now, pass the word and get ready."

The three men who had come forward turned and carried the orders back. Declan could see packs being dropped on the trail and he hoped enough men would return to retrieve them all.

He motioned for those behind to come closer and turned to Sebastian and said, "I want you and Lewis to stay to the rear. If it all falls apart, one of you needs to get back to the king."

Sebastian nodded.

Declan removed his buckler shield from his back harness, put it on his left arm, and drew his sword. He signaled for them to advance, and slowly moved the column out. He crept to the verge of the clearing and waited a moment—then one of the engineers saw him. Before the man could raise an alarm, Declan jumped forward and had his sword unleashed at a guard just as he turned. He took the man in the neck and kept running forward. As before, Declan felt his perception slow, and suddenly he was in another place, where he could see every possible opponent, and each avenue of attack. This knack for seeing an enemy's move almost before he made it had first manifested itself when slavers had tried to raid the village of Oncon, where Declan had been raised. Several times it had saved his life and that of his companions.

The engineers scattered, and Declan noticed how one grabbed his axe, holding it in a defensive posture. He was not an immediate threat. Guards on the other side of the small clearing sought to pick their way around fallen trunks, tangles of branches, and stumps. A guard came at Declan with a shout and the prince barely got his buckler up in time to deflect a fatal blow.

This was a skilled fighter, wearing a black lacquered chest-piece emblazoned with the white circle of the Church Adamant. Declan moved back one step, as more of his own men raced into the clearing and his archers unleashed arrows at their targets.

Declan's opponent staggered slightly when an arrow struck his breastplate and bounced off, which gave the prince the opening he needed. He charged the man, striking him in the chest with his buckler, throwing him further off balance. The Church soldier caught his heel on a large branch, and Declan leapt forward before he could bring his sword up to defend himself. With a quick thrust, Declan cut the man above the top of his armor, and blood fountained from the wound. Dead or not, he was not getting back up to fight.

Declan saw two engineers on their knees, hands raised, and ignored them. He had cautioned his men not to kill them needlessly and felt no need to remind them.

The Church Adamant soldiers were as well trained and determined as Declan remembered, but his men had the advantage of surprise and archers to take down opponents before they could close. It would take a lucky shot to bring down a man wearing chest-armor and a helm, but a few arrows slowed or disabled Church soldiers enough that the balance quickly swung in Declan's favor.

Still, it was bloody, exhausting work, and despite Declan's almost preternatural ability in battle, it was never easy. He found one particular soldier almost too much, as skilled a swordsman as Declan had ever faced. Fresh, Declan would have had the advantage, but after a long ride and little rest, he was barely able to hold his own. After a few minutes of struggle, chance found Sixto behind the man. Just as he killed one soldier, he turned and saw Declan hard-pressed. Sixto struck the man from behind, slicing the back of his neck.

Declan nodded and moved past the dead man to come to the aid of one of his men about to be overwhelmed by two Church soldiers. Declan took the direct approach of simply running at the man on the left and slamming into him, shield to shield, throwing him off balance enough to cause the other soldier to hesitate. That gave Declan's man, Billy Jay, enough time to find his own balance and unleash a wicked slash that clanged off his opponent's shield.

Two more Church soldiers had moved back-to-back, and four of

Declan's men circled them warily. Declan could feel fatigue seeping into his arms and legs and knew this fight must end soon—not because they would lose, for victory was assured, but to prevent men dying.

He sped at the pair of Church warriors and again hurled himself into them, risking serious injury, but enabling his men to quickly finish them.

Sixto gave Declan a hand up. "May I be forgiven for pointing out what you did was very stupid? I will tell you now, my friend, though I love you like a brother, if you get yourself killed, I will not be the one to return to tell your brother the heir to the throne is dead. I will sneak away, don monk's robes or whatever disguise works, and find a way to flee from Marquensas as quickly as possible. So, if you care for me at all, *don't* get yourself killed."

Declan took a breath, gave Sixto a half-smile, then hurried to where his men had a trio of Church soldiers cornered. Rather than turn and attempt to flee through the dark woods, they stood at bay, ready to die for their masters. Faced with the prospect of a tightly knit group determined to fight, Declan's soldiers ran the risk of obstructing one another.

Declan yelled, "Hold!"

His men retreated a half-step, and he pushed his way to the fore. Looking at the three Church warriors, he said, "There is no shame in throwing down your arms. There is no dishonor."

The two soldiers in the front were crouched, ready to respond to an attack, but the one behind threw off his cloak, and ripped off his tabard. Two daggers appeared in his hands, and he took a step forward and stabbed each man before him in the backs of their necks. They fell to the ground as he dropped his daggers and shouted, "I yield!"

Declan stared at the last man standing, and it took him a long moment to understand what he had just witnessed. Then comprehension dawned. He said, "Marco Belli."

"I have never been more pleased to be recognized before, highness," Episkopos Bernardo's man said.

"There's a story here, but it will have to wait." Declan gave out a long breath. Turning to Sixto he said, "How many did we lose?"

"Four," replied the captain of Declan's guard. "Trevor, William Butler, Horace, and Jack Sawyer."

Declan winced at the last name. The Sawyer brothers, Mick and Jack, were members of Declan's original company, which he had inherited from Bogartis: men who had survived the attack on Abala, crossing the Burning Lands, and escaping the massive canyon of Garn's Wound. He grieved the loss of any of his men, but the handful who had shared that with him and Sixto from the beginning were like brothers. "See to their burials" was all he could say.

Sixto understood his pain as he acknowledged the order.

"How many engineers are left?"

"Some fled; a few died." Sixto indicated some bodies a short distance away who were not wearing fighting gear. "At the hands of these Church murderers."

"They wanted you to take no prisoners," said Belli. "Those that ran into the forest may as well be lost, but those three over there"—he pointed to three engineers—"should provide all the information you desire. And I have vital information for my master."

"Your master?" asked Declan. "Bernardo is now a guest of my brother's, and he needs to share everything you've learned with the king. You might as well share that now, so we can be certain the news reaches King Daylon."

"That may well be, but my duty is to my master, and should he share what I know with your king, that is his choice. I am bound by a pledge."

Declan glanced at Sixto, whose hurt expression communicated much. Declan looked back at Belli. "So, staking you out over an anthill or putting hot coals in your trousers will avail us nothing?"

Belli laughed. "I don't see any skilled torturers among this company, and I've been trained to withstand the worst. So, let's head back to Marquenet as fast as we can, and allow my master to decide what to share with your brother."

Sixto clapped a hand on Declan's shoulder and said, "Seems reasonable to me."

Declan surveyed the carnage in the clearing. He glanced at the sky above through the trees, and said, "Clean up this mess, and get a fire started. Send Lewis back to those guarding the horses and tell them we'll be with them tomorrow." He let out a long breath of exhaustion, then added, "We'll make camp here, rest until morning, then start back." He looked first at Belli, then toward the engineer prisoners. "We will leave this all to my brothers to decide. I am not the king."

With a slightly scoffing tone, Sixto said, "Not yet."

SABELLA LOOKED OVER HER SHOULDER and saw Zaakara moving up the knoll to where she stood. She smiled and asked, "How are you faring?"

He held a big mug of coffee. "As well as can be expected, I believe is the appropriate answer." He sipped and said, "I must endeavor to locate whoever invented coffee and thank that worthy person." He let out a long sigh. "I have done many things in my youth I regret, and I have fought in battles that have made me wish I had been far away, and there are any number of foolish things I've blundered into over my life, but I've never been so left on the doorstep of total exhaustion as from that task you set me to. It's the worst hangover I've ever experienced, yet I haven't had a sip of wine or ale for days."

"I'm sorry," she said.

He laughed, and despite his haggard appearance, delight animated his face. "Never be sorry. You found something remarkable! Ruffio and I would still be puzzling out what to do next had you not seen something we missed." He took a deep breath, then a drink of coffee, and continued, "I've known a lot of very intelligent people, and many who are better at certain things than I am, but there are very few who see things in a whole new way. You, my friend, are a person with vision."

She blushed.

"If we solve our current problems, and your duties permit, I think a visit to Sorcerer's Isle would be the thing. There are people there you and your friends might do well to meet, and I'm certain they would be eager to meet you."

Sabella looked down shyly. "I think I would like that. I've never seen much of this world, let alone another."

"Well, let us hope that day will come," Zaakara replied. "If the message got through, we should be receiving help soon."

Sabella's eyes widened suddenly just as Zaakara felt a familiar wash of energy that caused his hair to rise: a tickle of rift-energy.

Both turned toward the open rifts and saw a scroll come through the larger one, which suddenly winked out of existence.

Ruffio hurried up from the pavilion. "I felt that!"

Zaakara picked up the scroll and opened it. He read it, then took a half-step back, his expression one of surprise. He read, "Hatushaly is busy trying to save Pug. Close the other rift, and we will be there as soon as possible." He rolled it back up and said, "It's signed Jaroly for Magnus."

"Save Pug from what?" Ruffio asked.

"Something dire," said Zaakara, "or they'd be on their way. And closing the rifts makes sense if they assume they will return for us."

Dryly Ruffio said, "Well, if they don't, we can contemplate a much simpler life here on Garn. With no magic there are only a few things I'm capable of to earn a living."

"Chilling thought," said Zaakara.

Sabella tried to sound reassuring. "I am sure this will all work out."

"I hope you are as right about that as you were about sending that message," said Ruffio. "As much as I admire your work here and what you've accomplished after that war you had, I'd rather get back home."

"I understand," said Sabella.

"Well, as the note said, let's close this little rift."

With a wave of his hands, Zaakara watched for a moment, then the small silver opening hanging in the air winked out of existence.

"Now we leave it to others," he said.

DECLAN HAD LEFT SIXTO IN charge of the company at the clearing, with instructions to clear away as much as possible and set up a defensive position should more Church soldiers appear up the same route Declan's men had followed. Lewis, Jax, who had been wounded first, and two other soldiers had ridden with Declan and Marco Belli for Marquenet. The journey straight east from the redoubt had taken hours by foot, then days of hard riding, three circling the forest, then straight on to the city. Declan had pushed the horses to the edge: anymore and they would have been ruined. As it was, they would need a month's easy pasture to regain full health. But once the west side of the forest was cleared, opening a passage, a fast rider would be able to reach the redoubt from the castle in less than two days.

Grooms ran up to take charge of the tired horses, and Declan said to a guard, "Carry word to the king that I am back and ask him to have Episkopos Bernardo join us."

The guard ran off and Declan told the soldiers to clean up, eat, and rest. Then he said to Lewis, "You especially get a good night's rest, for tomorrow you're leading a company to reinforce Captain Sixto." Lewis did not look pleased at the prospect of turning around and heading out immediately, but it was his duty, so he merely said, "Highness," and turned toward the barracks for the king's guard.

Declan motioned for Marco Belli to follow him, and they entered the rear door from the marshaling yard into the castle.

Once inside, he stripped off his armor and handed it to a porter who would carry it to the armorer, to be cleaned and repaired if needed. Belli remained silent while the prince gratefully washed his face, neck, and hands in a wash basin.

Upon reaching the king's private room, they found Daylon, Balven, and Delnocio, along with Master-at-Arms Collin, waiting for them.

"Glad to see you back in one piece," said the king.

"Pleased to be back in one piece. We surprised them, but it was close for a while." Declan sat down and detailed the journey and the surprise on the Church forces, ending with: "And that's where we discovered your man," he said to Delnocio, "secreted among the Church army."

Episkopos Bernardo looked at Belli expectantly.

The man known as Piccolo said, "I bring word, master."

"Which he wouldn't tell me," interjected Declan.

"I swore an oath," Belli replied.

"He takes these things very seriously," Bernardo offered. "You may speak here," he said to Belli. "Whatever you have of importance to say, I would share with his majesty anyway."

Nodding, Marco Belli said, "I reached the Dangerous Passage with Samuel and Rudolph. We lost Rudolph getting past a gang of raiders. Once into the Sea of Grass we lost them. Samuel and I reached Passage Town and our safe house there. Gilberto was there, but with little hope any other of our agents would join us. Word from Fondrak is that the city of Brojues was locked down one night by the Church Adamant and only a few of our allies got out safely. The message warning you of the betrayal is by quirk of fate why we are still alive."

"No one?"

"Just Gilberto, who remains in Passage Town and will endeavor to send word of any note," replied Belli. "It is dire, master, for what I heard were rumors and speculation. A few who fled Sandura before the Church Adamant seized that city claim that every man in the King of Sandura's army was forced to bend a knee and pledge fealty or lose his life. All swore to join the Church."

He paused, then added, "Those who hesitated were killed instantly. The Church butchered everyone they doubted. The women were forced to watch as their children were skewered on spears. Then they had their hands cut off and were forced to run until they bled out." Belli's urbane mask cracked as he recounted the horrors. "As to the men, some were stripped and nailed to doors, their manhood cut off. Others were beheaded, their corpses left to rot where they fell.

"At the end those who swore loyalty were soiling themselves and battle-hardened men were crying like children. I've seen the Church's butchery before, but it has risen to a new level of carnage." He took a breath. "Somehow it's more than brutal, for the Church was always savage in achieving its ends, but this is beyond that. This is evil."

Daylon's expression showed revulsion. He said, "Lodavico was not a ruler to inspire loyalty. He was a terrible man who wronged too many with his plots and conspiracies. Those who served him were craven." He shook his head in disgust. "It's hard to believe that being in his service was a better choice. Without the Church and those men from Nytanny—" He looked at Balven questioningly.

"Azhante," Balven supplied.

"Azhante," Daylon repeated. "Without them, he never would have contrived to destroy Ithrace, or bully the lesser barons into aiding him."

With rising anger, he said, "And I include myself in that cursed company." He looked at Belli. "You came with that company of murderers: what did you learn of their intent?"

Belli was silent for a moment, then said, "All I saw says that what you feared the most is inevitable. The Church is coming, and in numbers." He paused, then added, "Destroying their advance camp will set them back, and they might even wait for next spring if your men defend that position well, but eventually they will come here to finish off the last independent ruler in North Tembria."

Delnocio sat back, looking grave. "The Church Adamant began as a core of true believers, centuries ago, to anchor the army and ensure the goals of the Church were attained. They grew in power over time. While I was in their ranks, I saw other members of the clergy form alliances with key members of the martial order. Others blindly ignored their rising power within the Church.

"Long before I served, the Church Adamant was a martial arm of the Church, servants not masters. By the time I elected to leave the military to become a cleric, I could see the appetite for control manifesting itself in their ranks."

He looked regretful, then continued, "We, the clergy, in our arrogance, assumed we could control them. We were so focused on our own internal struggles for power and dominance over the abundant wealth coming to the Church that we ignored the simple fact we had raised a generation of fanatics.

"From the reports I read while serving in Sandura, the Church Adamant has a rabid, mindless adherence to the dogma of the Church. Its followers think nothing of butchering innocents and scorching the land so that generations will starve. They have no humanity left. These fanatics rival those of the hard-core Azhante you stamped out in Nytanny.

"But there are a lot more Church followers in Enast and here than all the Azhante in Nytanny. They believe that each murder is a sacrament to the faith and, having come to view the ruling council of episkopos as corrupt—which to some extent was true—simply took matters into their own hands. Now they are imposing a council of their generals and a few episkopos who cultivated relationships with them early on.

"In short, you are not facing a cabal of petty criminals, but an army many times larger. They are, to a man, willing to die for their beliefs, and are eager to take as many of us with them as they can."

Daylon's face drained of color. Shaking his head, he asked softly, "What do we do?"

Declan said slowly, "We get a bigger army."

Balven smiled at the remark, but his tone was dubious. "We can hardly feed the one we have, and even though we're paying them on time, they are not all men who will die for a noble cause. I wager a great number of them will throw down their swords or run if the battle turns against us."

Declan closed his eyes for a moment, as if in pain. His fatigue was clear, but his voice was strong. "We get a bigger army, and we train them *not* to run away."

Daylon laughed. "I applaud your vision, little brother. But while that is a simple solution, you must remember, simple doesn't always mean easy."

Declan rose and said, "Understood, sire. But we need to start now. Is Bodai still here?"

"Yes," answered Balven.

"Then we need see what he can tell us about this Kingdom of the Night, this Invisible Army that has plagued us for longer than I've been alive."

"To what end?" asked the king.

"The Church may overrun North Tembria, but does anyone here think they will for a moment tolerate assassin, spies, and thieves in the islands? From what Bernardo says, the Church Adamant seems willing to spend lifetimes conquering, and they will go from island to island beyond the Clearing until they find the heart of Coaltachin, and stamp out their masters, root and branch.

"Then on to Nytanny and the chaos there. Eventually, they want the world, and we haven't even contemplated what that might mean when they reach that nest of evil in the center of that continent, those Children of the Void. They might unleash that horror on the world, thinking to control them or to destroy them, but either way . . . it surely leads to catastrophe."

Daylon leaned forward and looked around the table. First he spoke to Master-at-Arms Collin. "Step up the production of armor and arms, and training. Find the best men you can and add them to . . . whatever we call that core force Declan has built."

Collin stood up and said, "I think we call them the 'King's Own,' and I will train them up to die if need be, though killing the enemy is better." Without another word, he bowed, and departed.

To Declan, Daylon said, "Go find Bodai. Share what we've found with him and bind him to this service: he must help us form a defense. He is the only man on this world who understands both the Flame Guard and the Kingdom of the Night. He can speak to both leaderships if necessary, and I think before all this is done, it will be necessary."

The king stood up and the others followed his example.

"Spend the rest of this day conferring with those you must speak with, but in confidence, sharing only what is necessary. Trust me, if word of this spreads, we'll have desertions by the hundreds, in the hope they can hunker down till danger passes. We have a great deal to do." Daylon glanced out of the window, then added, "We have three hours until darkness, and all of you will have supper with me here. We will continue this discussion and continue to plan. I will not have this king-dom fall before it is fully formed." He turned and left the room.

Declan watched as Delnocio and Belli also departed, leaving him alone with Balven. "What now?" he asked his older half-brother.

"I've got to tally up resources, to see what we have and what we need. You go and seek out Bodai as the king commanded." He shared a resigned expression and a half-smile with Declan. "And if Bodai balks, remind him it's only the fate of this entire world that hangs in the balance."

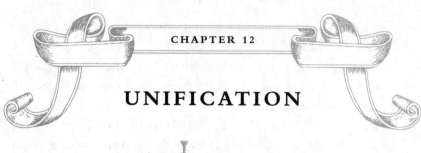

CHAPTER 12

UNIFICATION

Magnus stirred.

He blinked and for a moment he was unsure of his whereabouts, then he sat up straight in the chair and looked around the chamber. Exhaustion had overtaken him despite his desire to stay with Hatushaly and Pug. He felt as if he had only drifted off for a moment. He disabused himself of that idea, realizing he must have been asleep for hours.

Hatushaly and Hava both lay on the floor, sleeping. Alarm gripped Magnus as he saw the pallet upon which Pug had lain was now empty.

He quickly rose from the chair, grabbed his staff from the floor, and went to open the door. Jaroly stood outside. Closing the door behind him, Magnus asked, "Pug?"

The young magician looked at Magnus with an expression of wonder. He pointed toward the western rise and said, "He went there, an hour ago."

Magnus hurried to the western meadow, past a small stand of blossoming trees, and even in the low light of the Small Moon, he could make out Pug standing at the top of the low ridge that marked the boundary of cultivated land.

Pug was gazing out over the sea. Magnus saw him standing there motionless, breathing deeply as if he was savoring the moisture and salt tang on the air.

"Hello, Magnus," he said without looking back.

Magnus halted, unable to move for a moment. There was something different in Phillip's voice: there was a slight shift in how those two simple words had been pronounced that was both unexpected yet at the same time completely understandable.

Magnus came up to stand next to him. "You're finally . . . whole?"

Pug nodded and let out an amused sigh. "I always was, I believe, but for whatever reason, my memories were . . . curtained off. My life as Phillip is . . . it's still my life, but all that came before has suddenly returned." He held up his arms and let the sleeves of his robes dangle. "I can sense a strange mixture of the feel of cloth upon my skin, the taste in my own mouth from swallowing, dozens of scents on the night air, sea, and flowers, grass, and moss—all are both very familiar and barely remembered."

Magnus looked at Pug with an expression of wonder. "I can imagine it might be difficult. For most of our time together after finding you in Crydee, I suspected who you might be, but after almost a hundred years I . . . I guess I forgot. Or at least pretended to forget. When I remembered it might possibly be you returned, I thought perhaps it was another cruel prank by Kalkin."

"The Trickster, yes," said Pug, nodding slowly. "But only Lims-Kragma has dominion over the dead. Only she assigns what position one takes on the Wheel of Life." He let out a long sigh. "Perhaps my happy childhood was her way of saying thank you." He smiled at Magnus. "You were asleep when I awoke," he said. "You were collapsed in a chair, and I could see your exhaustion, so I thought I'd let you slumber."

Magnus's voice was barely above a whisper. "When I awoke and saw you gone, and Hatushaly and Hava asleep on the floor, I feared—" He stopped.

Pug smiled. "I am all right. Hatushaly worked magic that I can barely understand, but it made things . . . as they should be. I remember . . . everything."

Magnus looked as if he was unable to speak.

Pug glanced toward the east and saw a few torches illuminating the villa and the dim light from the Small Moon above. "I'm pleased you didn't do as I did. I let the villa decay out of petty anger and resentment. Losing your mother, your brother Caleb, and . . . everyone . . . it made me bitter. You lived a life of redemption and reclamation." He looked directly at Magnus and said, "You did very well, son."

Magnus took a step forward and embraced the man who had been both his apprentice and his teacher, who—with his memories fully restored—was again Pug of Crydee.

"I guess I should no longer call you Phillip," Magnus said with a fatigued smile on his face.

"Call me what you wish." Pug laughed softly. "It would be strange to many here if you suddenly started calling me 'Father,' though."

Magnus laughed. "You still look like Phillip," he conceded.

"That's because I am Phillip," Pug said. "I've lived two separate lives, had two families as a child, my own and Tomas's mother and father, Magya and Megar, who treated me as much a son as they did Tomas. He was a brother to me." Pug gazed out into the darkness. "I now mourn him afresh; for Phillip, he was someone I only heard about, but to Pug, he was lost mere moments before my death."

"You have always been one of the most indomitable people I've ever known."

"Second perhaps to your mother," Pug said.

Magnus chuckled. "Indeed."

Pug put his hand on Magnus's shoulder. "Remember the time you berated me about how much I was willing to sacrifice to 'do the right thing'?"

"Vividly," Magnus replied. "It was the first time you and I had a violent disagreement as adults."

"Disagreement?" said Pug with a wry note. "It was a fight. But you were right."

Magnus moved slightly back, an expression of surprise on his face. "Right?"

"Right that the question is necessary: for me it was about my sacrifice, and I ignored what the cost was to others. I was so lost in my own pain about your mother and Caleb dying that I ignored your pain at losing a mother and brother. I went blindly forward without regard to the price others paid." Pug sighed. "There's a lot I've learned being Phillip for over a century, but I still don't grasp many things."

Magnus said, "I understand."

"It's like seeing things through different windows, one clear, the other cloudy. I may be able to explain better someday, but for now, just assume I'm the man you called Father, because that lifetime was far more defining of who I am than my time being Phillip."

Magnus looked into Pug's eyes and said, "That may be difficult."

"We've faced agencies of chaos that wished to see an end to life as we understand it. We've battled armies. That was difficult. This is just coming to grips with a situation that is unique and inexplicable."

Magnus sighed. "I've missed you."

Pug looked at his only surviving son and said, "At least I had the pleasure of being with you all these years."

They hugged each other again.

Finally, Magnus stepped back with a dry laugh and said, "But you understand this will take some getting used to."

"Fair point. Now, would you be put off if I were to say that I'm starving?"

Magnus grinned. "Not in the least."

"Good." Pug glanced over Magnus's shoulder to the east and said, "Sunrise soon."

Magnus turned and saw the sky was lightening over the hills, the false dawn heralding a new day.

"We can talk about what I've missed," said Pug. "The years between the battle at what is now called Magician's End—and we need to talk about that name—and when I became your student, the period I've been told about, but did not witness. I have some questions."

Magnus laughed, a full-throated sound that caused him to stop moving and just let it out. "You always have questions!" He wiped tears from his eyes and added, "Oh, how I have missed that mind of yours."

Pug said, "Come, let us eat together and catch up."

Magnus said, "Let's."

DONTE SAT BEFORE THE CHILDREN as the sun rose just above the eastern hills. He'd arrived late the night before. Scully stood to his right, with two other men, both of whom had fled when Donte had bested Scully. Robertson was a thick-necked, broad-shouldered, dark-haired man with a scruffy beard shadow, and Lyndon was a slender, dark-skinned man with a bald spot surrounded by tightly curled black hair. All three looked positively uncomfortable confronting a room full of children.

"Here's the deal," said Donte.

The children looked at him silently.

"These three lads are 'bashers,' or bullies, enforcers, or whatever name suits you. Their task is to ensure you stay safe. Now, some of you little ones are going to stay here with Healer, and some of you will train a bit with me. Those I send on errands into the city will have one of these three nearby. If anyone tries to harm you, their job is to break a face and get you away safely. So, that's who they are."

The children were apparently not entirely sure what had just been said, but a boy named Milton asked, "What errands?"

Donte sighed. "I don't know what errands. Maybe carry a message, maybe deliver a package, maybe just shut up and listen!"

The boy drew back, fear on his face.

Donte waved a hand. "Don't be frightened. I won't send you out to do anything you're not ready for."

He vividly recalled many times he had seen children beaten by preceptors or their assistants for not knowing a task perfectly, even if the instruction had been poor. In that moment, he realized he had touched on a memory regarding his own training that had formed his rebellious nature. He looked at the children and added, "I know you are finding all this strange, but if we can do what I see is possible, there will be good food, a warm place to sleep, safety, and people around you who will care about you." He hiked his thumb at the three men behind him. "So, remember, these men are there to make sure you're safe."

The children reminded him of feral kittens. Everywhere he looked small faces regarded him with a mix of curiosity and fright. There was going to be a lot of work ahead of them.

Turning to Healer, Donte said, "Have you tumbled to any rumors about the Mockers or the Keshians?"

"Someone's been hinting that a cargo of something rare is due in soon, but I don't know who's running this smuggle."

Donte smiled. "Then I think it's time for me to head down to the docks and start poking around." He stood up and said to the children, "Healer will be in charge while I'm gone, and David is bringing back food. So, Healer will decide who does what in the kitchen and please don't burn the building down." He looked at Robertson and Lyndon and asked, "Either one of you farm boys?"

Both shook their heads.

Donte muttered, "I guess that was too much to hope for," then said, "Well, don't eat everything when David gets here. That flock I bought should turn up today, so make sure the sheep are in that fenced-off meadow and that the gate stays closed. I don't think the shepherd is likely to try to con you, but they're already paid for." To Scully, he said, "You're with me."

The big man followed Donte outside and asked, "Where are we going?"

"Port Vykor." Donte glanced skyward. It was barely an hour after dawn. "We should be there in time to grab a bite of supper. What's the best inn for dependable gossip?"

"What kind of gossip?" Scully asked as they reached a small run-in shed for the horses.

Grabbing a blanket and saddle, Donte said, "The sort of gossip an enterprising fellow who's well known, such as yourself, is likely to find of interest when it comes to who's doing what and where. The sort of information a rival gang might pay for."

"Who's planning a job?"

"Something like that," said Donte.

"Inn of the Four Ravens," Scully answered. "There's always a snitch or rumormonger about, and some are reliable."

As they finished tacking up the horses, Donte said, "So, to answer your question, we're going to Port Vykor to stir up some trouble."

THE INN OF THE FOUR RAVENS was crowded, noisy, and as choked with smoke as any inn Donte had ever seen, for the air was filled with the product of a boar being roasted on a spit before a fire, as well as a dozen or more men smoking what he had been told was tabac. Donte knew of several types of plant smoked back on Garn and assumed from the smell that it was probably what was called shagleaf in Coaltachin.

Scully moved to a corner of the room where a single man occupied a table and sat without asking permission. The big man leaned on one arm and moved so he was directly in front of the man's face, glaring.

Donte kept a straight face but found the entire act amusing enough to want to laugh. After almost a minute, the man stood up, tossed back his mug of ale, and said, "I was just leaving."

Donte clapped Scully on his shoulder and said, "Well done. Now, do we wait or go looking?"

"We wait," said Scully, indicating Donte should sit down.

"So, I'll go to the bar and grab us two ales," said Donte.

"We may be a while," Scully replied.

"So, I'll go to the bar and grab us a pitcher of ale."

Scully nodded and smiled.

Donte edged his way to the bar and waited until the man serving others turned to him and said, "What'll it be?"

"Pitcher of ale and two mugs."

"Let's see some coin," replied the barman, before Donte could even reach for his coin purse. The man had a sour expression on a narrow face framed by unkempt grey-shot brown hair. Donte decided that this inn was too disreputable even for him. He fished out five copper coins and put them on the bar. The bar keeper nodded and was back after a minute with the pitcher and two mugs.

Donte managed to reach the table and sit down without spilling anything. After pouring out the ale, he sat back in his chair and said, "I've been in some poor excuses for inns—shacks on a beach, once in a cave with a board on two barrels for a bar, and even a four-wall hovel with no roof—but this may be the most disgusting one so far. Why is it so crowded?"

"For the reason you wanted, because this is where the worst of the worst in Port Vykor come to do business."

Donte took a drink of ale and almost spat it out. "And this is the worst ale I've tasted in my life!"

"The wine is worse," said Scully. "But it is cheap."

"That it is," agreed Donte, taking another drink. "It's terrible, but it's still ale."

Scully laughed. "I'm starting to like you, boss."

"Good, because when it gets nasty, I need to know you're not running."

Scully shook his head. "You pay, I stay."

Donte laughed. "I enjoy a self-aware man. We understand each other."

"For a young man, you're pretty cagey," Scully offered.

"Where I'm from, you grow up fast or you don't grow up."

"Where is that?" asked Scully.

"Far enough away from here you've never heard of it."

"One of those cities down in Novindus, then," Scully said.

Donte let the comment pass. He was surveying the room, identifying what looked familiar and what didn't, attempting to filter out distractions so he could evaluate potential threats and targets. Even as a boy he had been taught to look before he acted, though his predilection for impulsive, even rash acts often earned him the masters' and preceptors' ire, and more than one black eye or bloody nose. As he got older, he become more adept at identifying situations that could bring him into real danger, but still his impulse had almost gotten him killed more than once. On this alien world, he finally accepted the wisdom of caution. He also wished Hatushaly and Hava were here. He missed their company and their appraisal of things, which was better than his own. He pushed this thought aside and said softly to himself, "I might as well start learning not to be stupid."

After a few minutes, Scully reached over and tapped Donte's arm with the back of his hand. "The three that just walked in," he said just loud enough for Donte to hear.

Donte scanned the room, spotted the three men, then looked past them so he wouldn't be seen staring. All were dark-skinned and dressed as common workers, but he could tell from how they carried themselves this was a trained crew. The first of the three looked directly at someone he recognized, while the other two scanned the room, one to each side, to see who might be watching them. Softly to Scully, Donte said, "Rough boys."

"Widow-makers, all of them," Scully replied. "They're best given a wide berth."

"I've seen worse," Donte whispered. While the three men were clearly brawlers, he knew that a single Coaltachin assassin would have no problem taking out all three, and the average crew boss in any city of the Kingdom of the Night had agents who would have seen these three gone as soon as they turned up. The masters of Coaltachin controlled every aspect of crime in any city they claimed.

Scully said nothing.

After a moment, Donte asked, "Who are they talking to?"

"Robbie's the name. He's one of those rumormonger types you were asking about. He would know if something was going down anywhere in Port Vykor and around. If he doesn't know himself, he knows who to ask."

"Just the gent I want to talk to." Donte sat back. "After those charmers who walked in leave, obviously." He glanced over to Scully. "Keshians?"

"Maybe. Lots of folks whose people came from Kesh live around here."

"Still, what's your gut tell you?"

"Might be that Keshian gang trying to move in."

"They call themselves anything?"

"What do you mean?"

"Gang name, crew name, like the Mockers from Krondor."

Scully said, "Not that I know but I call them the Ferrets, those skinny little, you know, ratcatchers? They can slip into the damnedest places, and if they're not trained, they can be mean bastards. They're a tricky lot, those Ferrets, got muscle and eyes everywhere, so they don't need to be down low. They just turn up and throw a lot of pain at people. Heard stories, back in the day, about this thief and that smuggler, but here they just barge around."

"Makes them easy to see coming," Donte said.

"Too right. But the boys from Kesh . . ." Scully shrugged.

"Not obvious," said Donte.

"Well, you see them around, like we did, and if it was just one, you'd think him a local, but the way those three came, casing the layout, on the lookout, well, that's dodgy right there, so something's up."

"Which is why, in a little bit, you and I will wander over and talk to Robbie."

"Better be now. Looks like he's finished his business and is about to leave."

Donte saw Robbie put down his mug, wipe his mouth with his coat sleeve, then say something to the barman and move toward the door.

"Better," said Donte. "Now we can talk to him in private." He stood up, expecting Scully to watch to see if anyone followed him without being told.

Outside, Donte saw Robbie moving at a leisurely pace down the road away from the harborside. Glancing back at Scully, who had caught up with him, he said, "Here we go."

Donte set out at a quick pace but quietly enough not to alarm the man he followed. Despite sunset having passed, there was just enough city noise to mask his approach. He matched pace with Robbie and just as they passed an alley to the right, Donte took a quick step ahead, grabbed Robbie's left wrist and elbow, moving him as if he was steering a cart around the corner.

Robbie reached into his jacket with his right hand but found Donte's left hand now clamped around that wrist, while continuing to hold his elbow. Donte's size and strength prevented the smaller man from using the knife he had pulled from inside his coat.

"Now," said Donte, "no need to be rash. I just want to have a word."

Robbie looked past Donte and his eyes widened. "Scully, what are you doing?"

"No harm," said Scully and Donte released Robbie's left elbow but hung onto the wrist of the knife hand.

"What do you want?"

Donte said, "I saw you talking to three Keshian charmers. You and I have similar interests, I suspect, so I'd like to reward you handsomely for sharing with me what you shared with them."

"What?"

"Information," Donte said. "What did you tell them?"

"Scully," Robbie began. "What is—"

Donte picked him up so that he had to stand on his toes. "Talk to me!" he said sharply, without raising his voice.

"Just there's a ship from Queg anchoring off the harbor tonight and they've got some spices from the Free Cities, silk from Kesh, other luxuries they're paying to get past the governor's customs. Cargo will land tonight at half-watch, between midnight and dawn. Somebody's being paid to look the other way."

"If the Keshians aren't the ones smuggling, they must plan on stealing the loot," Donte mused.

Robbie said, "Only reason they'd pay for that information, right?"

Donte let the informant go. Stepping away, he said, "This happen often?"

It was Scully who said, "Not that bad so far."

"Then I think I wandered in here at just the right time." To Robbie, he said, "I think you and I are going to be good friends, Robbie. Now, here's what I need you to do." He reached into his belt pouch and pulled out a gold coin. "This is for what you just told me."

Despite the dim light, Robbie could tell it was gold just from the weight in his hand. He said, "What else?"

"You have to be sly about this one, but it would be useful for me should those Mockers get word the Keshians plan on hitting their hand-off tonight, and you're telling them for free just because you want to stay on their good side. Can you do that?"

"If I betray those Keshian cutthroats, I'll have a death mark on me."

"Given your line of work, someone always wants you dead, am I right?" asked Donte.

Robbie grudgingly said, "Often."

"Well, as you don't want to be dead, don't be. Scully and I will be back at the Four Ravens until they throw us out—"

Scully said, "If you're spending, he won't throw us out."

"How's the food?"

"Terrible."

Donte shrugged, palms up. "I've lived on terrible before. Let's get this done then get back to . . ." He saw Robbie's expression grow keen, and said, ". . . back."

Scully said, "Fair enough."

"See you back at the Ravens," Donte said to Robbie, and they left him in the alley.

As they neared the inn, Scully said, "You're probably going to get that greedy little bastard killed, you know?"

"Probably," Donte replied. "Just not tonight, I hope."

PUG LOOKED UP AS HAVA and Hatu entered the dining hall. He stood up and walked around the table and without a word grabbed Hatu and hugged him closely. "Thank you."

Hava and Magnus both looked on in surprise, but Hatu simply returned the embrace and said, "It was necessary." His voice was quiet, his manner a little shaken. He looked into Pug's eyes and softly said, "I saw so much."

Hava waited for a moment, then said, "If you've finished, can we eat? I'm famished." There was a twinkle in her eye that revealed her pride in Hatu's accomplishment.

"Of course," said Hatu, disengaging himself. He recognized Hava's expression and smiled, even though he was fighting to overcome the cost of saving Pug. His youth and health had been sorely tested.

Pug returned to the table and said to his son, "A remarkable young man."

"I think that's an understatement. He's capable of things I can only imagine."

"There's a lot of work to be done."

Magnus could only nod in agreement.

Hava and Hatu returned to the table with a tray of food and a pot of coffee.

"What time is it?" Pug asked.

"Two hours after sunrise," Hava answered. She sat down. "We are wrecks. I hope you're worth it," she said to Pug.

Magnus laughed and for the first time since meeting him, Hava and Hatu could see absolute relief on his face.

Pug smiled and said, "Time will tell."

Magnus said, "He is. I could regale you with stories, but you'll discover in the end that my father is as fine a man as you'll ever meet."

Hava blinked and dropped her spoon into the bowl of hot meal she was eating. "Father?" She looked between the two black-robed magicians, confused, since Pug looked years younger than Magnus.

"It's a long story," said Hatu.

"Obviously," said Hava, fishing her spoon out of the porridge.

"You know the story?" Pug asked Hatu.

"I was in your mind for . . ." He looked at Magnus. "How long?"

"Almost three full days."

"I don't know everything, but I saw a lot. I probably know you as well as any man, or at least almost as well as you know yourself."

Pug said, "As I do you."

Hatu stopped chewing and put his spoon down. "I'm sorry?"

"You were in my mind. I was in yours. I understand you almost as well as anyone I've known for years." With a tilt of his head, he indicated Magnus.

"You were unconscious," Hatu said.

"Yes, but you learn even when unconscious: the mind is still working."

"Tell me something you learned," Hatu said.

Pug pointed a finger at Hava and said, "Stay on her good side."

Hatu laughed. "Certainly true, but you've known her long enough not to need my mind to tell you that."

Pug nodded. "Reza walked you across a lovely stone arched bridge to meet his father, Zusara, who in turn had you meet a seer, whom you suspect was also his lover."

Hatu sat speechless for a moment, and looked over at Hava, who said, "You never told me that!"

Hatu took a deep breath and said, "I told you."

"You told me you met Zusara, and that Reza took you to Coaltachin, and even about the seer, but you never mentioned a stone bridge."

"True," admitted Hatushaly.

"We can follow that up later, but for now there are other issues to discuss," Pug said.

Hava sat back in her chair and said to Pug, "You're changing."

Pug nodded. "Apparently."

"No, I mean you look different. We're trained since childhood to notice how people behave."

Magnus regarded him and said, "You carry yourself differently now than when you were Phillip. Your speech has changed a little."

"More," said Hava. "Who are you?"

"I am a man who lived long ago and died. The gods have decided I needed to return, in the flesh of someone else."

Hava's expression showed that she wasn't comprehending.

Magnus said, "On your world, the gods are apparently abstractions prayed to out of duty, or blind devotion. Here, celestial beings are real. And they meddle."

"I think I'd rather not be here," she said.

"I understand," Pug replied. "After I died, I was reborn as Phillip, and knew nothing of my past. I met Magnus, who took me on as an apprentice and tutored me in all things magical. About the time you two"—he indicated Hava and Hatushaly—"appeared here, I began to have memories of my previous life. The short of it is, your husband was essential to my surviving the integration of my two lives."

"Why?" she asked.

"Only the gods know," Magnus said. "We can merely speculate."

"Well, if I may say," Hava began, "this entire gods-mucking-about-in-people's-lives thing is not good."

Magnus and Pug both laughed. "Welcome to Midkemia," said Magnus.

Hatu finished eating his meal and asked, "What's the reason for all of this?"

Magnus was about to speak, but Pug held up his hand to cut him off. "Midkemia and Garn are linked. As Midkemia and Kelewan once were linked." He slowly looked from face to face. "You are here because you need to be." He pointed at Hatu and said, "You had to be here to save me." Then he pointed at Hava. "You are here because he is not complete without you."

Hava and Hatu looked at each other and silently nodded their agreement.

With an unexpected chuckle, Pug added, "And why Donte is here is anyone's guess."

Hara and Hatu both looked a little taken aback by this unexpected humor.

Pug said to Hatu, "You've seen the battle with the Void, and the price countless people have paid in service to that struggle."

Hatu said, "Yes. In your mind." He was slowly regaining his usual demeanor.

"We need to speak of many things about the struggle yet to come, for the Enemy is unrelenting and just because it's been quiet for a while doesn't mean it's not returning. There was a Darkness that attacked first in the city of Sethanon, and while we won that struggle, the war continues."

"Why here?" asked Hatu.

Magnus said, "The war has a center somewhere. Why not here?"

Pug said, "It's not here."

Magnus looked at Pug with an unspoken question on his face.

"Where, then?" asked Hava.

"From what I saw in Hatu's mind of the unspeakable horror in Garn's Wound and the frozen stone city in the center of Nytanny, I can say with certainty that this war is no longer here.

"The final conflict will be on Garn."

CHAPTER 13

AWARENESS

Pug watched closely.

After a day's rest and catching up as much as possible, he and Hatu began preparing for his return to Garn. To help Pug understand Hatu's powers as much as possible, Hatu was showing Pug his ability to link minds and share what he could see of fury energies.

Hatu had chosen a simple demonstration, picking a spot in the garden in front of Magnus's quarters, where a cluster of flowering plants flourished. Insects were scurrying around, pollinating, foraging for food, or otherwise behaving normally.

Hatu and Pug were sitting on a polished marble bench that rested beside a small pool in the garden. Both men were motionless, their eyes closed.

Pug could see through Hatu's mind a vision of energy flowing through each living thing, both plants and insects. "Fascinating," he said quietly. Hatushaly had organized the energies into different colors—deep greens bordering on dark grey, through pale blues close to white—and Pug was captivated by the display.

"It's amazing," he said, opening his eyes.

Hatu opened his as well and nodded. "One of the things I learned from Nathan."

Pug nodded slowly. "Nathan." With a sigh, he said, "I suspect Nathan was, or is, an avatar of an old friend of mine."

"Really?" Hatu asked.

"It's a very long story and is almost certainly related to why you are here and why I was given a second life."

Hatu's expression was curious.

"You have no divinities or celestial beings on Garn, from what I've learned," Pug began.

Hatu nodded. "We have many gods, stories of spirits, legends, and people of deep faith, but the truth is that my nation of Coaltachin teaches us that our faith lies in our duty to our masters and nation. No one I know of has ever seen any supernatural being. As for magic . . ." His expression was one of wonder. "What you have here . . . to me it's impossible to believe, yet I've seen things with my own eyes, and I've done things I can scarcely believe, so I must learn many new things."

"As must we all," said Pug. "I've lived a very long time but still know so very little of what there is to know."

Hatu smiled. "Yet you hunger to know more."

Pug smiled back. "Perhaps that is part of the reason I now have my second life. To revive my curiosity, to make me eager again to discover new things.

"At the end of my first life I was tired. I had been battling against the Void in its many manifestations for lifetimes. People I loved died, and friends were left in the wake of my life as if I were a ship passing islands in a vast sea."

"I can't imagine that."

"Because you are very young."

"There is a saying among the people of Coaltachin who served the masters. 'You grow up quickly or you don't grow up.'"

"Sounds ominous."

"It's a warning. At a certain point in a student's life, failure is death. You know too much to be allowed to just leave and seek out another life. You are either an agent of the Kingdom of the Night, or you are killed."

"Brutal," said Pug. "If time permits, remind me to tell you about Magnus and my journey into the realm of the Dasati. That was a brutality that was unimaginable until we actually witnessed it.

"Now," he continued, "as I see it, we were brought together for a purpose that hasn't yet been revealed to us but is out there waiting for us to discover."

"Tell me why you think the Void will attack Garn," Hatu asked.

Pug took a breath, then said, "Magnus has told you about the different levels of energy on Garn, yes?"

"Yes."

"Apparently Garn is a much lower-energy world than Midkemia. In my travels, I'll say the highest level of energy was here or on the world of Kelewan. I've visited some low-energy worlds with just enough energy that I could leave. I can't imagine how Ruffio and Zaakara are feeling with no power left to use. I endured two boyhoods without magic ability, but that was due to lack of training. The ability was there from birth, as it was with you."

"Which is how I was able to burn that ship simply because of fear?"

Pug nodded. "My first use of power was much the same. I was with the daughter of the Duke of Crydee, Lord Borric, and we were attacked by three lowland trolls—more bestial than intelligent beings— and had I been without my power they would have killed us both. In my panic, I shocked them with something like lightning, and they drowned in a creek.

"Over the years I've studied many different aspects of magic use, and it's clear to me there must be a strong feeling involved, like fear or anger, to make magic work. Even Magnus, who always appears outwardly calm, is a man of very strong emotions."

Hatu laughed. "I had ample anger as a child. I got furious when I couldn't understand something, and it cost me a lot of punishment when I behaved badly."

"I gleaned some of that history when you were in my mind," Pug said. "Not experiencing it, or even 'seeing' it, but rather your memory of it, an impression. I was fortunate, for in both of my early existences, I was gifted with people who cared deeply for me." He smiled with a hint of regret. "I see you with Hava and know how lucky you are. I was wed twice, and both women were remarkable. My first wife, Katala, bore my first son, and we took in an orphan and made her our own daughter. Katala died from an illness we could not cure. Years went by and I realized I would have lost her, eventually, after I saw others age much faster than I." He spoke matter-of-factly, but there was a hint of sadness in his eyes.

Hatu said, "Do you think that will happen with Hava and me?" He sounded concerned.

"Let's face one problem at a time," Pug said. He stood up. "I think Magnus is ready for us to do a bit of experimenting."

Hatu followed Pug to the chamber where the rifts were generated. Magnus and Hava were waiting there, with Jaroly standing nearby.

"We've arrived at a plan," said Magnus.

Pug nodded. "That's why you're in charge here."

Magnus laughed. "I've been in charge here a very long time."

Pug winced slightly, and said, "I'll get used to this . . . eventually."

"As will I," Magnus replied.

"What's the plan?" Pug asked.

"Simple. The next rift to Garn is a two-way rift."

Pug nodded his agreement. "If there are no problems, we can shut it down, but if we have to return for some reason, that way is open."

Magnus looked at the person who was both his father and his student, and said, "You always were quick to learn."

Hatu said, "Shall we do this?"

Hava came to stand by him, put her arm around his waist, and looked at Magnus expectantly.

"Nothing to add?" asked Magnus.

"You boys have done enough talking. Open the damned rift," she said calmly.

Pug held up his hands, palms out, in a gesture of surrender, and glanced at Magnus. "I've never been there before."

"Neither have I," replied the white-haired magic-user. "But I stood with Ruffio and Zaakara when they opened their rifts to Garn more than once. I think this should be fairly straightforward."

"Remind me to tell you the story of when we were facing the demons who chased the Saaur from their world to here, and opened a rift in the wrong place," said Pug.

"I've heard that story," answered Magnus. He closed his eyes, concentrating as he muttered words so faint they were unintelligible to the others. After a long minute, a whoosh of air accompanied the appearance of a large silver oval of energy.

Pug looked at Hava and Hatu and said, "We used to have to employ devices, but now . . ."

"Enough," said Hava, taking Hatushaly by the hand and stepping forward, into the rift.

"Wait—!" Magnus shouted, but they were gone before he could finish.

"Best not tarry," said Pug, stepping after them.

Magnus turned to Jaroly. "I was going to tell them I would stay here in case . . ." He looked at the young apprentice, who now stood in mute uncertainty, then said, "Don't let anything bad come through." He then stepped through after Pug.

Jaroly stood alone in the chamber, looking around in confusion. "Anything bad? Me?"

DONTE AND SCULLY WAITED IN a now near-empty taproom. The last two other residents were Shad and a snoring man in the opposite corner of the room. As Donte pondered ordering another pitcher of ale to keep Shad happy, Robbie slipped through the entrance.

Donte sat back down and waited until Robbie came to the table, sat, and said, "It's done."

"Took a while," said Scully.

"Those bashers from Krondor were not entirely trusting. They kept on about why I was telling them about the smuggler drop without cadging a bit of a price. I told 'em what he"—he hiked his thumb at Donte—"said to say: that I was doing it to get on their good side. It took me hours to finally set it right when I said I wanted in on whatever they took tonight, just a little taste, as it were."

"Well done," said Donte. He drew out a gold coin and put it on the table. As Robbie reached to snatch it, Donte grabbed his wrist and squeezed enough to ensure the snitch knew he wasn't getting away that quickly. "Now, before you get that, when and where?"

"Like I said, between midnight and dawn, so maybe an hour from now. The where? Sandy Wash Bottom."

Scully said, "The Sandy Wash is the mouth of Vykor River. Not much as rivers go, more like a big creek. But the bottom is a beach to the west of the harbor docks, and it's a good place to land cargo in a shallow boat. Get a crew of lads there and you're in and out in a short time."

"Somewhere we can watch?"

"There's a roof or two at the end of the docks that will give us a fair perch."

"Good," said Donte, rising. "Let's go." He neglected to release Robbie's wrist, so the slender informant had to follow whether he wanted to or not.

Once outside, Scully indicated the direction with a tilt of his head.

"Let go of my wrist!" Robbie demanded.

"And have you run off?"

"Run off? Without the gold?"

Donte laughed quietly. "Now I know who I'm dealing with." As they hurried along, following Scully, he added, "Just so you understand who *you're* dealing with."

"If you're trying to wrangle with both the Keshians and the Mockers, you're a madman," Robbie said. Then: "But you're a madman with gold."

Donte released Robbie's wrist, and as they started to turn a corner, the little man said, "Not that way!"

Scully turned around and said, "Why?"

"Them Mockers have hunkered down in Sad Landing, and they'll be coming down that road"—he pointed at the next street down from where they stood—"anytime now. This way." He motioned for them to follow him and went straight up another street, then pointed at a building. "There's a way up." Again he led them, and after turning a corner, they found a sturdy ladder bolted to the side of a building Donte took to be a warehouse.

Scully didn't hesitate and climbed the ladder.

Donte looked at Robbie and with a wave of his hand said, "After you."

Robbie scurried up the ladder and Donte followed. On the roof, he saw that the buildings between where they stood and the edge of the docks were descending, so they had a clear view of the edge of the harbor, the west end of the docks, and a stretch of beach beyond.

Donte was still amazed by the existence of three moons on this world. The large moon had risen earlier that night and was now overhead. The view was like twilight on Garn, not brilliant but enough to see boats in the water bobbing with the swells in the bay.

Robbie said, "This is as close as we dare get unless you have a death wish."

They sat, and Donte said, "Pretty bright tonight."

Scully said, "We should be fine if we're not showing lights. At least it's not three-moons bright."

Donte just nodded. He remembered the first night he had arrived in Midkemia and how two moons were close to setting while the little moon was rising in the east. He assumed "three-moons bright" meant all three were overhead and wondered how close to daylight that might be.

After a while they could see a large longboat, crewed by twelve rowers with a flat barge in tow, approaching the beach. With lapping water at the shore, it was an easy move to swing around and let the barge beach. The cargo was secured with a large tarp over it, tied down to deck cleats.

As the boat and barge neared the shore, a line of torches appeared from the streets a few buildings southeast of where Donte, Scully, and Robbie sat.

"That will be the Ferrets, I expect," said Donte.

Scully said, "Torches for sure mean they bribed the city watch to be elsewhere. Those Keshians don't feel the need to come skulking about."

The boat swerved off to their left, circled around, and then the rowers backwatered the oars to slow it to a stop. The barge beached gently, and Donte said, "Now that's a thing of beauty. It's a pleasure to watch men who take pride in their craft."

Within minutes the Keshians had established an efficient routine of unloading the cargo and stacking it in an orderly fashion, and Donte and his companions could hear a nearby wagon and team moving down the street toward the docks.

"If I were a betting man, and I am," said Donte, "I'd wager a coin or two that the Mockers are now quietly creeping into place, waiting for the Keshians to unload the barge and load the wagon. Why do the heavy lifting when someone else can do it for you?"

Scully nodded. "Sounds likely."

"So," Donte asked Robbie, "these Mockers, how do they roll?"

"How do you mean?"

"Are they proper outlaws, with archers waiting in the shadows to pick off Keshians, or ordinary street toughs, who are just going to swarm out and hope the Kesh lads are too tired to put up much of a struggle?"

"Not outlaws," Robbie replied. "Least I never heard of them being soldiers like with bows and such. Clubs, knives, maybe a short sword, but it's all pretty much street scuffling and head busting." He paused. "If the Keshians run off, the Mockers won't chase them. They'll just grab the wagon and head back to their hideout."

"You know where that hideout is?"

"Just somewhere in Sad Landing, not the exact place."

"It's a short way from here, though," said Scully.

Donte looked at Robbie and asked, "Can you find out where without getting yourself killed?"

"After tipping them tonight, maybe, but it'll be risky."

"There's more gold in it if you can."

Robbie's eyes widened just enough for Donte to know that was the right thing to say. "How much more?" he asked, barely controlling an open display of greed.

"What do you think it's worth?"

Robbie's expression turned calculating. "If I don't get my throat cut by those murderers, five gold coins!"

"I was going to offer you one," said Donte in a lighter tone. "But tell you what, get me the exact location by the end of the week, I'll make it two, and I won't beat you senseless for trying to rob me on the price."

"Three," said Robbie, nodding, though his tone was less demanding.

"Three, but you take the beating," Donte replied.

Robbie paused for a moment to see if this was a jest, but Donte's expression was unreadable. "Fine, two," he said.

"Just one last thing," Donte added. "Get clever and sell me out, I will gut you like a fresh-caught fish. Understand?"

"Yes," said Robbie, standing up.

"Where are you going?" Donte asked.

"If I'm poking around looking for the Mockers' lair, best to do it when they're elsewhere."

"Fair point," Donte conceded.

Robbie scurried off.

Donte asked Scully, "You think he'll try to sell me out?"

"Absolutely."

Donte nodded. "Need to scare him more, I guess. Oh, make sure you say nothing about the farm and the kids to Robbie, or anyone for that matter. I'll tell the others when I get back there."

The barge was unloaded, the hawser was shifted from the beach-side cleat to the opposite side, and the longboat crew began pulling it back to the ship.

Just as the Keshians finished loading the big wagon, a shout sounded from a harborside building and dozens of men raced toward the wagon. The Keshians were slow in drawing their weapons and were quickly routed.

As Robbie had predicted, the Mockers didn't chase them, but quickly secured the wagon. As it drove off, the remaining men hurried back into the city to disappear.

After a few minutes of quiet, Donte stood up. "That's a lot of muscle. How big are the Mockers?"

Scully also stood up, and as they slowly walked back to the ladder to the street, he said, "No one's sure. But if they had that many bashers, they'd already be running Port Vykor." He turned and started down the ladder ahead of Donte. "Either they brought in some help from Krondor, which is unlikely, or they hired some local lads to put on a show."

"Find out if you can, then come to me at the farm." Donte started down the ladder. "If they're hiring local muscle, that means there's local muscle for hire."

Scully waited until Donte was on the ground, pointed to himself, and said, "Obviously."

"No," said Donte, lightly thumping Scully's chest. "For all I knew, you three jesters were the only locals around. Remember, I come from a long way away."

"There are a few of us still scraping by."

"Good, then the other thing I'd like to know, besides how many lads from Krondor are in residence, is how many bashers I could hire that I can trust."

Scully said, "Hire, no problem. Trust, that's a whole other problem."

"Go on," said Donte.

"Just saying it's going to take time to build a reliable gang."

"Time I have," said Donte. He glanced around, then said, "Find a play to lay low and start looking for trustworthy lads. I'll come find you in a few days." He turned and stepped away.

"Not going back to the Ravens?" Scully asked.

"I expect Shad closed it after we left, and besides, I need to steal a horse to get back to the farm."

"Why? What happened to the one you rode to get here?"

"Someone stole it," said Donte as he ambled off into the night.

HAVA AND HATU STEPPED INTO a late afternoon breeze off the ocean and were confronted by half a dozen Marquensas soldiers ready for a fight. Behind them stood Zaakara and Ruffio, and the five women from the Sanctuary.

On seeing Hava and Hatu they all looked visibly relieved. "Thank the gods," said Ruffio.

"I'm pretty sure the gods had nothing to do with this," said Hava.

Pug followed a moment later and greeted his companions from Sorcerer's Isle. Then Magnus appeared.

Pug looked over his shoulder and said, "Who stayed?"

"Jaroly," Magnus replied.

Pug's expression was dubious. "It's a good thing there are a few dozen other magic-users nearby. Jaroly has more ability than he realizes. It's his uncertainty I worry about."

Magnus nodded.

Pug looked around and said, "Lovely evening."

Zaakara moved aside to let Sabella pass. She walked up to Hatu and said, "Yes, I feel it."

The other women all voiced agreement.

"Feel what?" asked Hava, with an unsure expression.

Sabella closed her eyes a moment and said to Hatu, "I can sense you."

"So, the magic's back?" Hava asked.

Sabella nodded, and Ruffio held up his hand. A sharp light shot heavenward, bright enough to be seen in daylight, probably blinding in the dark. It pierced some small clouds above. He looked upward, then with a smile said, "A simple spell. Yes, we can now get home."

Magnus said to the two Midkemian magic-users who had been stranded, "It's two-way. You head back." He motioned to the rift. "Pug and I will arrange things here. If we need you, we'll send word."

Zaakara turned to Sabella and said, "Want to come?"

"May I?" She looked around as if seeking permission.

Zaakara said, "There's no reason not to, and no one here to say no."

She grinned and nodded enthusiastically.

With a nod to Magnus and Pug, Zaakara led her into the rift. Ruffio waved good-bye and stepped through after them.

The king's soldiers were moving away, and a captain approached and said to Hatushaly, "We are very glad to see you return."

Hatu looked confused. Hava gave him a prod in the ribs, and he said, "Thank you. How are things here on Garn?"

The captain said, "We have a ship moored, ready to get you to his majesty as swiftly as possible."

Hatu glanced at Pug. "As possible?"

Pug looked first at Magnus, who nodded slightly, then said, "That thing you showed me, with your vision. Can you show me where the king is?"

"Yes," Hatu answered.

To the captain, Pug said, "The ship won't be necessary. I can get us to . . ." He glanced at Hatu.

"Marquenet," Hatu supplied.

"Marquenet," Pug finished. "But first, I think, food and rest." Glancing skyward, he asked, "Is it east or west of here?"

"East," answered Hava.

"Then it's already night there. So, let's rest here, then we'll attempt to travel to Marquenet tomorrow."

All were in agreement. They made their way down to the pavilion. The captain indicated where they could sleep later, and ordered that food be prepared as a few soldiers who were off duty wandered in.

As they sat around the table, Pug noticed a dark expression on Hava's face. "Is something troubling you?" he asked her.

"I just ordered a ship!" she snapped. "I was supposed to be hunting down pirates, protecting your ships."

Hatu looked at his wife with wide eyes, then burst into laughter. He saw anger arising and grabbed her, pulling her close. "It's just a ship!"

Hava's posture grew rigid. She put a hand on her husband's chest and pushed him away. Then she looked into Hatu's face and suddenly started laughing with him. Hugging him, she said, "There's a ship around here I left behind."

He kissed her cheek and said, "There will always be a ship for you."

She ducked her head shyly for a moment, then regained her usual poise.

Hatu held her close and, with a lift of his chin, indicated to the others that everything was going to be fine. He asked the captain, "Is the *Queen of Storms* still anchored at Toranda?"

"It was when we left," the captain answered.

Hatu whispered in her ear, "We're home and if you want to go raiding, your ship is waiting for you."

She said, "Let's eat. Then to bed, and you better not fall asleep on me."

He laughed. "When have I ever fallen—"

She put her finger over his lips, turned, and said, "Where's the food?"

Pug and Magnus exchanged laughs, and as Hatu and Hava headed to the sideboard, Magnus said, "You were absolutely right. She is so much like Mother."

Now that they were alone, Pug said, "This is difficult, and it may take a long time. How long was I your student?"

"Almost a century."

"And your father so very much longer." He stood up. "It may take a *very* long time to come to understand our new relationship, but one thing you absolutely must know: I loved you without a second's doubt as your father, and I loved you as my teacher. However this turns out, know that."

Magnus stood up and said, "I always knew who you were. I think it's just going to take time to come to terms with the situation."

Pug smiled. "You always had a bit of your mother's pragmatism in you. Sleep well."

"Bed?"

"I think I'll take a walk but yes, soon."

As Pug left the pavilion, the sun was about to touch the western horizon, and he walked to the higher point on the island's north shore to look out over the sea. He held his staff and leaned on it slightly as he watched the sun of Garn lower to touch the surface of the ocean. Emotions rushed through him, and he felt a strong urge to cry or to laugh as memories ripped through him.

A deep breath cleared his mind and he silently reminded himself these were only memories, events long gone and occasionally ill-remembered, but attached to intense feelings.

As the sun lowered over the horizon, he saw a green flash of light for an instant and laughed aloud. He knew the conditions that were required to concoct that illusion of light and atmosphere, and felt a burden lifted from his heart.

"Life goes on, no matter what," he muttered to himself.

A voice from behind him said, "I once said to a man who was dear to me: 'There are sunsets above other oceans, Ghuda. Mighty sights and great wonders to behold.'"

Pug turned and saw a small man, almost wizened in age, with a scrawny frame and a skinny neck. His head was ringed with a fringe of grey hair, and he looked ancient, but his eyes were as alert and aware as any Pug had ever seen. He wore a ragged robe of orange, cut off at the knees, one shoulder left bare, and he carried a rucksack over the other shoulder and held a staff in his right hand.

Looking at a face he never imagined he'd ever behold again, Pug whispered, "Nakor?"

The little man held up his left hand, palm upward, shrugged dramatically and said, "Maybe. I'm not sure."

CHAPTER 14

UNFOLDING

Hatu asked, "Where's Pug?"

He and Hava had slept soundly in the portion of the pavilion set aside for them. Hatu had woken to find his wife already up and in the common area, but when he looked, he saw no sign of either Pug or Magnus.

Hava said, "He went outside a little while ago. Why?"

"I just have some questions, but they can wait."

She looked at her husband with a dubious smile and gave him a gentle push. "Go, find him. If you have questions, you won't sleep. Just get back and get some rest, all right?" Their lovemaking had been intense but brief, and he had fallen into a deep slumber almost immediately afterward. She knew all the magic he had employed on Midkemia had taxed his strength greatly.

"No one knows me better than you, my love." Hatu kissed her on the cheek and hurried out of the pavilion.

One of the soldiers stood guard at the entrance and Hatu asked, "A man in a black robe. The one with the dark hair. Did you see which way he went?"

The soldier said, "He went over toward that bluff over the sea." He pointed.

Hatu walked quickly, feeling a delicious familiarity with every breath. The air was just a bit different here, closer to the Sanctuary, than it had been on Sorcerer's Isle. It was also a lot darker at night on Garn compared to Midkemia, given how small Garn's single moon was. Still, it was just after twilight and the moon was up, so Hatu could easily make his way toward the bluffs.

As he neared the overlook, he saw two figures, Pug and a slight, even scrawny, little man, though his posture and something else about him communicated a hidden strength. As Hatu neared, Pug and the other man turned.

Hatu sensed a familiar energy about the little man. His eyes widened. "Nathan?"

The little man shrugged. "Maybe. I don't really know, Hatushaly."

"You called me by my name," Hatu said.

"Should I call you something else?" asked the little man in a whimsical tone.

Pug said, "This is Nakor."

"Maybe," Nakor said.

"But you have the same . . . energy as Nathan. How is that possible?"

"I don't know," said Nakor. "I've died at least once, maybe a couple of times. I have blank spots in my memory. Some of them years long. I'm pretty sure I'm not that demon Belog . . ."

"Then how do you know of him?" asked Pug.

Nakor shrugged and said, "I don't know!" He sounded irritated. "But I do know there's a demon running around with some of the same memories as me. Somebody must have told me." He paused. "Or maybe I am him." He looked at Hatushaly. "Tell me about this energy thing and 'Nathan,' but first I need something to drink." He pointed to the pavilion. "Wine? Ale?"

"Both, and some whisky," answered Hatu.

"Good," said Nakor, and he started to walk toward the pavilion without waiting to see if the others were following. "Haven't had a good whisky in . . . I don't know how long. I'm in more of an ale mood, anyway." Pug and Hatushaly caught up and Nakor said, "Energy?"

"After reaching Sorcerer's Isle my abilities grew . . . I don't know how to put it, but I can do things faster, more easily and I'm learning new things every day. Every person has an energy that's different from everyone else's. It's not something that I see all the time . . ." Hatu said.

"Ah," said Nakor, "you can see people's auras." He turned to Pug and said, "There's an order of monks on . . . I forget which world, but they study for years to learn how to read auras. A lot of what they claim is nonsense, but some of what they teach is useful."

They entered the large tent. A few soldiers were finishing a meal after their evening tour and Nakor looked around quickly. "Where's the ale?" he demanded.

A soldier turned to look at the funny little man, then returned to his companions. A servant hurried out of the field kitchen attached to the tent and surveyed them. He recognized Hatushaly and nodded at him. "Sir?"

"A pitcher of ale and three mugs . . ." Hatu spied Magnus pushing aside a curtain which had walled off the sleeping area and said, "Make that four mugs."

Magnus took two steps toward them and when his eyes fell on Nakor, stopped for a moment. Regaining his composure, he moved to the table that everyone else was sitting around.

Before Magnus could say anything, Nakor said, "Magnus! Good to see you're still alive. Your father neglected to mention that."

"Father," said Hatushaly, looking perplexed. "I'm still having trouble grasping all of it."

"It is a very complicated story," said Pug.

"Indeed," said Hatu. "All those memories I sorted out of your former life."

"They were my father's," added Magnus.

"I saw that part," Hatu said with a note of wonder. "I still just find it all confusing."

"Easy to do," suggested Nakor. "What was it, a few hundred years' worth of memories?"

"Something like that," Pug answered. "How did you—"

"You're different," said Nakor. "But familiar, and after a few moments, I saw who you once were, and are again."

Pug looked on with open amazement on his face. "You saw—?"

Nakor said, "I know a place where they once grew a hand back for a friend. If you want to go back to looking like you did before, they can do it. It'd take a while, but they're very good."

Pug, Magnus, and Hatu sat in silence. Finally, Pug said, "I think I'll keep this body. I've gotten used to it. Besides I'm taller than the last time."

"True," Nakor agreed as the servant brought out a tray with the pitcher of ale and mugs.

Hatu rose and said, "I better go see if Hava is still awake. If she is, I need to bring her to see this."

After he left, Nakor said, "Wise man. Keeping a woman waiting is a bad notion." He looked at Magnus. "That's why your grandmother left me and married Macros. I was always off doing things and I kept her waiting a lot."

"I thought it was because she wanted more power so she could conquer the world?" said Pug.

Nakor shrugged. "That too." He drank a long swallow of ale, wiped his mouth with the back of his hand, and said, "Now, why am I here on . . . ?" He cocked his head, then said, "Garn. Took me a moment. Yes, Garn?"

Pug said, "The Void."

Nakor looked genuinely surprised. "The Enemy, here?"

"I'm certain," said Pug, and when Nakor looked at Magnus, the white-haired magician nodded agreement.

"Damn," said Nakor. "We need more ale."

DECLAN HURRIED FROM THE FORGE toward the palace. He had stopped in to see how things were progressing, before he joined his brother's war council. As he had suspected, stopping in turned into a very long conversation with Edvalt and a few of the older smiths on how the production of arms and armor was progressing, and then how best to hasten the process. That turned into a short debate about what corners might be cut without losing too much quality, and before he knew it, Declan was late to the council meeting.

As expected, Declan was the last member to take his seat, and before he could apologize, the king waved him to silence, an expression of resignation struggling with one of anger.

"A report just arrived this morning from Captain Sixto," Balven said.

Master-at-Arms Collin and General Baldasar both turned to the king. General Baldasar asked, "What news?"

King Daylon said, "Apparently our reinforcements arrived in a timely fashion. Another company of Church engineers escorted by soldiers arrived just as our reinforcements were digging in with Sixto's men after you left," he said to Declan. "The Church forces had to leave their horses at the edge of the forest, as that access trail hasn't yet been widened—part of the Church's plans, it appears—so our forces were able to withstand an assault, though not without a price." He paused. "We lost a dozen soldiers." He motioned to Balven.

The king's first adviser said, "None of the Church soldiers surrendered." Both Baldasar and Collin nodded: this was expected. "But we gained another five engineers. Sixto reports they seemed relieved to no longer be working on behalf of the Church and were eager to give us needed information. They even provided us with a full set of plans for the redoubt. Apparently, it was designed simply to be a holding base while they cleared enough forest to build a huge fortification."

Episkopos Delnocio put his hand on the table. "The Church is not always hasty. No doubt they have agents here who have reported back that food is a problem, and that most of your army is mercenary, so desertions are likely. Assume that whatever is done which can be seen from the city, or even here in your palace, they will know about within a few weeks." He took a moment for thought, then said, "A fortification of the size in the Darkwood could cut your kingdom in half, isolating Beran's Hill, Copper Hills, and Port Colos from the south. They mean to grind you down, then strike when they think you're at your weakest."

"So, we need a plan to prevent that, obviously," said the king. He turned to a court page and said, "Send him in."

A moment later Master Bodai was ushered into the chamber and the king waved him to a seat. Bodai bowed, then sat down.

"How goes the farming and fishing in Nytanny?" Daylon asked.

Bodai said, "It goes well, Majesty. The farmers who've settled the islands are beginning to deliver ample food for themselves and the Sanctuary, as well as increasing our shipments to . . . well, here."

"We need more," the king said.

Bodai sighed. "We have no more to give, Majesty. We give what we can because you freed us from the Pride Lords, but we are still building. Our farmers and most of our fishermen are refugees from here, people who are starting again. They need to hold back seed grain for next year's planting, cuttings for new vines, and saplings to grow fruit. If you send more boats, we can provide more fish—"

"Fish we can find ourselves here," said the king. "The Pride Lords tried to cripple everything, but at least they couldn't destroy our fishing."

Declan said, "Can we get more from South Tembria?"

"We do not have enough men to spare for another expedition south. Your men who settled in Abala are barely self-sufficient as it is, and that's the only friendly port down there. Zindaros is in chaos, each port now a city state, and Materos is being harried by Church ships to keep us away."

Bodai said, "I have an idea, although it may seem—"

"Out with it," said Daylon, his temper rising.

"If Hatushaly and the men from Midkemia can open that portal between worlds again, perhaps we might trade with someone there?"

Daylon sat back, his expression changing from annoyance to thoughtfulness. "Not a totally mad idea," he said.

"We should hear very soon if Zaakara and Ruffio were able to get word that we needed Hatushaly back here," said Bodai.

"Thank you, Master Bodai," the king said. "Now, there is another matter for which I need your counsel."

Bodai's expression became more guarded. "Me returning to Coaltachin," he said.

Daylon nodded. "You understand why we need the Kingdom of the Night at our side against the Church?"

"Yes," Bodai said. "My concern is partially for my own safety. My sudden reappearance after this long an absence, especially considering all that's happened since then, will instantly rouse suspicion. And the truth very well might get me killed as a traitor to the Council." He gave a slight sigh. "It's not just death: as an agent for both the Flame Guard and a master of Coaltachin, I accept that we all must end someday, but I do no one any good, least of all your nation and people, if I'm dead very soon."

"Understood. I cannot force you to go," said the king. "I could toss you in a cell until you agreed, but that would be foolish. I need a willing partner in this, not someone who might be inclined to vanish, a skill I suspect you are well versed in."

"I am," said Bodai without a hint of boastfulness. "I'm also fairly adept at getting out of cells and dungeons."

"No doubt," said Balven.

"I am willing to travel to Coaltachin, Majesty," Bodai went on. "But I need time to plan my best approach. Some masters will be more amenable to discussions than others. One or two will almost certainly want to kill me the moment my true identity is revealed."

"Is that necessary?" asked Declan.

"Perhaps not," said Bodai. "The fact is, the truth of who the Azhante are, and the origin of our nation, will sway many now that an imagined threat is shown to be false. Replacing that with an even more dire threat is what requires a bit of art."

"I understand," said Daylon. "My brother's dealings with your previous brethren clearly demonstrated the ability of your Kingdom of the Night in playing roles to deceive, spying, and other feats of near-magic."

"That was the art of our illusion, Majesty. May I go?"

Daylon said, "Yes, Master Bodai."

Bodai quickly departed and the king said, "I'm not entirely happy to be dependent on him for two vital missions, but we have no other choice."

Declan said, "For the moment, can we return to fortifying Sixto's position?"

The king looked at Delnocio and asked, "How long before the Church sends more soldiers?"

"If what I was told is accurate, the first Church expedition sent word back that all was well just before Prince Declan and his men took out the base. So, whatever time it took before the first and second companies' arrivals then add perhaps another week, as those in command may assume some reasonable delay is preventing the arrival of a new message.

"When no message is forthcoming, they'll send a large force to that location. That's where the first battle will be fought and that's where you may set them back a year or more on their schedule. Take away that central fortress and they will have to come at the north via the old trade roads, against your fortress at Beran's Hill."

Daylon nodded. "They can't come straight here on the southern road, or through the Narrows, so they will have to come from the north." He shook his head, and his frustration was evident. "We could easily resupply Beran's Hill from Port Colos and here, if only we had supplies to spare!" He slapped his hand on the table.

"Let us hope those magic-users from another world can provide a source of supplies, otherwise we will all be tightening our belts by the coming of winter, let alone getting through the winter—and fighting a war? I'd rather we fight now in the forest.

"Declan, be ready to march to . . ." He paused. "We really need a name for a fortress if we're going to build one there."

The men around the table all nodded.

"I'll think of one," said the king. "For the moment, Declan, how many men can you house at that site now?"

Declan said, "That depends on how the logging is going. Cutting down the trees is the easy part. Hauling them away is the trick. The only path in is the one we used.

"If Sixto is smart, which he is, he's cutting a second path out to the west, to make it easier for us to support his position. But he still can't get horses or wagons in there, so it's going to be men dragging trees and branches until he gets out. He's seen the plans and has the engineers with him, so if he just turns the redoubt around, make it stronger facing east, we can hold it with another two hundred men. The Church would have to send a thousand or more men against it, and there's no room for an organized attack."

General Baldasar said, "Unless there are overwhelming numbers of attackers, the advantage is always to a stout defense. The plans they sent are sound, and if Captain Sixto's captured engineers remember them, or there's more than a single copy, he could be halfway finished by the time more soldiers reach him. If we get on quickly, we could end the Church's campaign for a year or more."

"Then organize the soldiers," the king said to Baldasar. To Collin he said, "Arrange wagons with arms, provisions, and bring extra mules and harnesses. I want a large crew cutting in from the west to join Sixto's men as quickly as possible."

Both men stood and bowed, and as they turned to leave, Collin put his hand on Declan's shoulder and said, "It's going to be a grand fight. We'll make sure you have everything you need."

Declan nodded and after the door to the room closed behind the two men, he turned and said, "Grand or not, it's one we must win."

The king nodded silently in agreement.

SABELLA GAWKED, MOUTH OPEN, AS she watched the students file into the dining hall at Sorcerer's Isle. They had left Garn at sunset but when they arrived at Sorcerer's Isle it was the middle of the night and Zaakara had arranged for Sabella to use the empty rooms previously used by Hatushaly and Hava. It had been a short night's sleep, but it had been restful being back home. Zaakara watched her for any sign of alarm, but to the contrary, Sabella seemed delighted by the nonhumans scattered throughout the hall.

"They're beautiful," she whispered.

"Who?" asked Zaakara.

"All of them," she said softly. "The patterns . . ."

"Patterns?"

"Can't you see the patterns?" she asked, a little confused.

"Do you mean the energy, the way you found Hatushaly?"

She moved to sit at a table with him and said, "Yes. I assumed with your many talents you could see . . ." She shrugged. "I don't know."

"What do you see?"

"It's *feel* more than see, though there are times it's like lights surrounding a person. It's how I found Hatushaly and could send Denbe to where Catharian had found him and bring him safely to the Sanctuary. But these others . . ." She looked around the hall. "They are so different, but . . . beautiful is the only word I can think of. It's like a kitten, puppy, or any other creature. They are all different, yet they are the same. Do you understand?"

"Not really," he admitted.

"All people have this fundamental quality, so they don't resemble . . . dogs, birds, fish, but each person within that group has a unique . . . look?" She blinked as if trying to see something. "From far away, I can say, 'This is a person, not a donkey.' But if I don't know you, I don't know which person it is. If I know you, I recognize you. Now do you see?"

Zaakara chuckled a little and said, "I think so. Hungry?"

"Not really." She turned with an eager expression and said, "Can you show me more?"

"Certainly," he said, rising from the chair.

He gave her a brief tour of the villa itself and she said the garden was wonderful. He then took her back around the dining hall and showed her the complex built into the side of the massive hill that occupied the center of the island.

Inside the first door, she looked around in amazement. As far as she could see, tall bookshelves rose on massive cases. Softly, she said, "How do you reach the high ones?"

"We have some ingenious ladders, with baskets to lower and raise books. In the rear we have narrow walkways every third of the way to the top, with a circular staircase in the corners, so you can get to any book there.

"We have people such as yourself, to catalog and organize every title here, and we have a number of people on this island who don't need ladders. Like your Hatushaly, who I understand can just put out his hand and have a book float off the shelf and down to him."

"Yes, he can," Sabella said eagerly. "I've seen him do it."

"My father, when he first came here, would summon an imp to fly up and fetch a book down for him."

"Imp?"

"A small, relatively harmless demon. Demon summoning became frowned upon after Magnus's mother and brother were killed by demons. Then there was some business with some demons who came . . ." He shook his head. "It's a very long story, but that's why I use my abilities only to ward against demons who attempt to harm those here."

Sabella nodded, though she was only half listening. "How do you keep track of all of this?"

"I don't. We have a librarian by the name of Wejuan, who can show you the system she uses, and she has several assistants. She's probably still eating, so we can return later."

"I'd like that." Sabella smiled. "This place is truly amazing."

"Just remember, we've had many more years to gather all this together than you have had at the Sanctuary. From what I was told, you've barely started to reclaim your library."

She smiled again. "True."

"Let me show you a little more of this island."

Outside again, the day was freshening, with a rising sun warming their faces, and a soft breeze carrying a sea-salt tang and floral hints.

"It's lovely here," said Sabella. "Is the weather always this nice?"

Zaakara laughed. "This is called the Bitter Sea for a reason. It's late summer, so the heat is hardly noticeable, but we can go from scorching hot to wicked cold in any month. A lot of it depends on the tides and the moons. The moons don't impact the seasons much, but they can make the tides terrible."

"Ah," she said, nodding. "I think I understand."

"The nice thing about living here is there are many people to share information with. We have new students, but for the most part we all teach what we know and learn what we don't know."

"That sounds wonderful," she said, her eyes beginning to glisten. Looking around, as if trying to absorb everything at once, she said, "Since I was a child I had one task, to find the last of the Firemanes. I trained with the few surviving members of the Flame Guard, and it was a harsh life. At times every one of us tasked with waiting for him to emerge felt hopelessness and despair. When I found Hatushaly, suddenly we were without purpose. I traveled with Bodai and Denbe to take him to safety, and it was the first time I had left the Sanctuary.

"I struggled every step of the way," she continued, seemingly eager to share this with Zaakara. "We arrived just before the destruction of most of North Tembria began, and barely got Hatushaly away as thousands were put to the sword. It was a terrible time.

"Once we returned to the Sanctuary, I was without purpose again until Bodai gave us the task of reviving the library there. But this? I could live in that library, I think." She wiped away glad tears and added, "If I didn't have so much responsibility at home, I would wish to be a student here." Then she laughed. "I sound ridiculous, I know."

"Not in the least," he reassured her. "With your ability to sense people's energy, there may be things you can come to learn. Speak with Bodai when you return."

She looked embarrassed. "What is beyond that rise?" With a tilt of her head, she pointed with her chin.

"Beyond that rise is a long path down to the fishing village, and a small boatyard on a harbor."

Sabella stood on tiptoes as if she could somehow peer over the rise. "I can almost see," she said playfully.

Zaakara started to speak, then stopped. She kept staring into the distance and finally he said, "Sabella."

"What?"

"Look down," he said softly.

She did and saw that she was now floating a foot above the grass. She gasped and fell.

Zaakara stepped forward and caught her by the waist, keeping her upright.

Softly he said, "I don't think you need to speak with Bodai. Sabella, you are a magician."

NAKOR SAID, "SO, THAT'S WHAT you know?"

Hatu nodded. "I showed Zaakara the 'stone city' as I think of it, in the middle of Nytanny, with those frozen 'Children of the Void,' he called them. My sense of them is close to what I found in that pit when I went looking for Declan."

Nakor looked at Pug. "Now I see why you think the battle will be here, and not on Midkemia. The Void is unknowable, but apparently not stupid. It picked this world because it's almost devoid of stuff."

"Stuff?" asked Hava, who was fascinated by the all-night conversation. Hours before, they had stopped drinking ale and now were on their third large pot of coffee.

Pug said, "Nakor insists there is no magic, that everything is 'tricks.' Stuff is energy, mana, juju, whatever people call it."

Nakor nodded. "Some people know how to do things with stuff, and those are tricks."

"I am too tired even to think about that," said Hatu.

"Anyone hungry?" Nakor asked.

"Famished," said Hava. Others nodded. "I'll fetch us some food," she volunteered.

"No oranges in your rucksack?" asked Pug.

Nakor laughed but looked annoyed. "That trick stopped working a long time ago. The fruit shop I bought burned down while I was dead. First time I realized something was not right was when I saw this isn't the same rucksack. It looks the same, but there's no hole in it."

"Hole?" asked Hatu.

"Not that kind of hole," said Magnus. "He created this tiny permanent rift to a fruit vendor—" He looked at Nakor. "Where was it?"

"I don't remember," Nakor said. "Somewhere in Kesh, I think, or maybe back home in Isalani. Anyway, now if I want oranges, I have to buy them." Then his expression turned serious. "To me, I just 'woke up' here, yesterday. How long is it exactly since the battle at Magician's End?"

"You were there," said Pug.

"No, I wasn't," said Nakor. "That was the demon Belog with my memories." His tone softened. "I don't know how I know some of what he did."

"Kalkin?" suggested Magnus.

"The god who breaks all the rules," added Pug.

Hatushaly yawned. "It's dawn." He looked past the others out of the pavilion opening as the curtains of night were pulled back and early morning light poured in.

Nakor looked at Hatu as daylight streamed in to where they sat, and with a smile, he pointed and said, "I like your hair!" In the dawn Hatu's hair was even more vividly red-gold than usual.

Hatu smiled. "Thanks. It's something I've had to hide most of my life."

Nakor rubbed his bald pate above the grey fringe, "Maybe I'll get my friends to make me a head of hair that color!" Then his expression darkened a little. "If I'm around long enough." He looked at Pug. "So, what do you think?"

Pug replied, "Lims-Kragma may have put me back on the wheel after I died, but your appearance here, this link between Hatushaly and me—all of it smacks of more than one power, working together."

"Seems logical," said Magnus.

Hatu leaned forward, elbows on the table, and said, "I must find out about these gods of yours."

Pug said, "Magnus is the man for that. He once compelled the goddess of death to come to him."

Hatu's eyebrows rose. "Truth?"

Nakor said, "People call them gods. Celestials. Divinities. Supernaturals. All sorts of names, and they're sometimes very powerful, but as often as not they're creations of the people who worship them." Then with a playful smile he said, "Magnus can explain it all."

Magnus did not look amused as Hava returned carrying a tray, followed by a pair of the kitchen service staff bringing two more. The aroma of fresh bread greeted them all.

"Now I'm starving," said Hatushaly.

"Coffee, some tea for anyone who wants it, juice."

"Orange?" asked Nakor brightly.

"Grape," answered Hava.

"That will do," said Nakor.

They began serving out the portions and eating, and Nakor said, "From everything you've said, we're looking at a battle unlike anything before."

"The Void seems to learn in its own way," Pug said.

"The final battle at Magician's End changed the face of Midkemia. Can Garn withstand a bigger conflict?"

"We have no choice," said Nakor.

"It's the fate of the world," said Hatu.

"More," said Pug. "It's the fate of countless worlds, not only this universe, but countless universes, realities beyond our abilities to contemplate."

Hava sat back and said, "In short, the fate of everything."

"My guess is," said Nakor, "if we lose, and the Void reclaims that—what did you call it?" he asked Pug.

"That one perfect instant of bliss."

"That," resumed the little man. "Not only will we lose, we will . . . never have existed."

"I can't fathom that," said Hava.

"Few can," said Pug. With a gesture he indicated himself, Magnus, and Nakor. "Even we barely can."

"If time returns to that original state," Nakor said, "then it never went all stringy, pulled out in a line, like we live it." Then his brow furrowed, and he added, "I think."

Hatushaly glanced at Magnus.

"What?" asked Magnus.

"Time," said Hatushaly.

"What about it?"

"I'm still not quite sure, but something in this situation is all about time."

"Well," said Nakor. "That question is interesting, but speaking of time, there is something we need to do soon."

"What?" asked Pug.

"I think we need to get the stuff in Midkemia that lets you do tricks and bring it here."

Magnus and Pug exchanged looks, and Pug said, "How?"

Nakor shrugged. "I don't know."

CHAPTER 15

DARKWOOD

Declan raised his left arm.

Then with a downward motion, he signaled for his column to veer off the road and start following Sebastian toward the Darkwood. A recently promoted captain, a broad-shouldered, dark-skinned man with vivid blue eyes named Joran, looked at the prince and said, "Sir?"

Declan said, "You have the column, Captain. You know where to start cutting into the forest. With good fortune, we'll meet you in the middle."

"Highness!" he said with a salute.

Declan turned and watched as Sebastian broke trail the same way they'd ridden twice before, and Declan spun his horse and rode back to the lead wagon.

"Ratigan!" he shouted.

The scrawny driver smiled ruefully. "I always knew you'd get me killed one day, Declan." His tone was half playful, half doubtful.

"If anyone from the Church gets to you, I'll already be dead, so you can take a little comfort from that."

Ratigan laughed.

"And it's 'highness' or 'prince.' You only get to call me Declan when we're drunk," he said with a smile.

"I look forward to that," said Ratigan, getting the joke. He was one of Declan's oldest friends since the first raid on the village of Oncon, when Declan had been a smith apprentice and Ratigan a simple teamster. They had survived despite the butchery and hardships they had witnessed.

Declan watched as Joran's company of wagons and guards moved slowly past, filled with equipment and men, a quartet of engineers, and twenty fit men with timber experience who would show the forty guards how to fell and haul trees. Expert timbermen, with more expected down from the mills in the mountains east of Copper Hills, were already heading south to join the effort, bringing mule teams and sleds for hauling. It was the king's desire to see a road into the heart of the Darkwood as quickly as possible.

Declan watched for a few minutes as the wagons continued north while his cavalry split off toward the northeast to loop around to Sixto's company. He battled rising doubt that all that was needed could be accomplished in time.

Shaking off dark musing, Declan turned his horse and, with heels to flanks, encouraged him into a rocking canter to overtake his column. Those in Marquensas who had been shown existing maps and descriptions of the heart of the forest gave estimates of how fast that road could be cleared. They were not promising. Declan knew that some of those massive oaks were hundreds of years old, with trunks measuring ten feet or more in diameter. Larch, beech, and ash stands were impenetrable for anything larger than a forest cat, squirrel, or rabbit. The one narrow path cleared by the Church that Declan had used was a widened game trail.

As a smith, Declan had fashioned many axes and two-man saws, and had learned a fair bit about the craft, so he knew there could be a serious fight with the Church before that supply caravan reached the clearing Sixto was enlarging. The Church could arrive in strength at any moment, so from this point forward, every member of Marquensas's army needed to be ready. Declan fervently hoped they were.

Lewis had ridden ahead to inform Sixto that relief and more supplies were on the way. Each of Declan's men carried extra provisions behind his saddle, enough for two men for two more weeks. Another resupply would be leaving Marquenet in a week.

Declan rode easily, but kept scanning to the northeast, for any Church advance would probably be from that direction. He had sent outriders to his right flank to warn of any sightings. They were to rendezvous at the small copse of trees just to the southeast of where the path into the Darkwood started.

Near sundown, Lewis came riding toward Declan at a good speed, his horse lathered and nostrils flaring. Pulling up before the prince, he saluted.

Declan asked, "What news?"

"Highness, Captain Sixto says work goes slowly but steadily, and he's pleased you have more provisions, as the men are eating too much." Lewis paused, and said, "I can't tell if that was a joke, sir."

Declan let out a low chuckle. "It was, and that means so far no contact with the Church." Glancing at the fading sun, he said, "Where shall we camp?"

Lewis turned in the saddle and pointed. "An hour more should get us to the small stream we've used before and leave us enough light to stake the horses. That will put us in the forest two hours after we rise, and at the captain's camp before noon. Or, if you wish, we can push to the forest edge and be there just after nightfall."

"No, let's camp at the creek." Declan looked around and said, "Take your horse to the rear and ride in a wagon. I know where we're going."

"Highness." Lewis saluted and rode slowly to the rear of the column.

PUG WATCHED THE SUN RISE and conflicting emotions rose up within him. As Phillip, he'd had many mornings when he'd pause for a moment to enjoy the dawn, then get about his tasks. But among Pug's first memories was watching the sun rise with his first wife, Katala, who had died when no magic healing art could save her. Their children had perished during the Emerald Queen's war. It was during that conflict that he'd met his second wife, Miranda, and later they had watched sunrises with Magnus and his little brother, Caleb, when they were boys. Then he had watched as Miranda and Caleb had been killed by demons when Sorcerer's Isle was attacked, and the villa had been destroyed. And he had outlived many people: Caleb's family, friends, and others he loved.

He felt fortunate that his years living as Phillip, that happy child-hood and his life before becoming Magnus's apprentice, all that had distanced the pain he felt so many times in his first life. The battle to master magic with Kulgan and Father Tully, the start of the Tsurani invasion. His capture and enslavement on Kelewan, his elevation to Great One, and his return to Midkemia: all were memories with both glorious triumphs and agonizing losses.

"Memories?" said Magnus from behind him.

"A different sunrise, but still, as glorious as the ones at home."

Magnus put his hand on Pug's shoulder and said, "I've lost count."

"I still prefer sunsets," Pug said lightly. "I think that's because both my boyhoods were in Crydee. Sunrise was blocked by mountains and forests, but sunsets were over the ocean."

"That was one of the things I loved about living on the island," said Magnus. "We got both sunrises and sunsets over the sea."

Pug laughed. "It's the reflection on the water that makes it different, right?"

Magnus gave Pug's shoulder a squeeze. "Right, as always."

Pug laughed again. "Always? We've had a few times when you didn't think that."

Magnus said, "Old wounds I would rather not reopen."

Pug nodded. "Just understand that you were right. I needed to be certain I could afford the price I demanded of you and others to protect our world."

Magnus was silent for a moment, then said, "I always sensed Phillip was you, but thought perhaps that fact could be ignored, as if you'd been given a new lease on life and we could put all the past behind us, but now . . ." He sighed audibly. "Very well, it's evident you were given a rest, a reprieve from the constant struggle, but now you're being asked to rise to the occasion and save . . . everything, again."

"The part of me that is Phillip thinks that's actually amusing." Pug watched the sun clear the horizon and said, "Let's get something to eat. I suspect we will be leaving here today."

"Finding Bodai, meeting the king, all of the serious things required don't leave much time for reminiscing. Breaking fast sounds good."

They walked back down the rise to the pavilion. Several guards were coming off duty and sitting down for their last meal before sleeping while others were eating before their shift.

"We'll need someone to guard the rift," said Magnus as they sat down.

"You mean a magic-user, not soldiers."

"Yes. With Ruffio and Zaakara both gone home, there's no one here that can close the rift if something comes through."

Magnus didn't look happy, but said, "I created the rift, so it's probably best that I close it. You are also better at magic transport than I, so I think I stay, and you go."

"We could ask for someone from Sorcerer's Isle to join us," Pug suggested.

"No," said Magnus with a smile. "Boring as it can be to sit here, it is necessary for word to be carried to the king. Plans must be made to deal with whatever it is the Void brings next."

Pug motioned a porter over, ordered a meal and coffee, and then said, "Whatever that may be. I wish we had some sense of what is coming out of the Void." He looked around.

Magnus asked, "What?"

"Nakor. Where is he?"

"That's anyone's guess," said Magnus. "Nakor or one of those doppelgängers the gods like to inflict on us, the odds are good that unpredictability will be a constant."

"There is that," agreed Pug.

"Still, I should seek him out, and Hatushaly, Hava, and I need to get to the King of Marquensas and warn him of the coming battle."

"I don't envy you that task," said Magnus.

Pug saw the four women come in whom he had been told were librarians here, and he stood up. "I'll be back in a moment," he said to Magnus.

Pug approached the table where the four women had just taken their seats and said, "May I ask you something?"

A dark-haired woman called Beryl said, "Certainly."

"Do you all possess the same ability as Sabella?"

"Do you mean our ability to sense where Hatushaly is?" asked Daria, a stocky woman with light brown hair.

Pug smiled. "No," he said, "I'm almost certain he's still sleeping over there." He pointed to the portion of the pavilion that was curtained off for sleeping quarters. "I mean finding someone in general."

The women looked at one another, then the blond one, Eefa, said, "If we have some idea of who we're looking for, yes."

"Do you remember that short fellow in the torn yellow-orange robe, with the staff and rucksack over his shoulder who was here yesterday?"

Eefa glanced around the table to the others, and Zara nodded, then pointed and said, "You mean him?"

Pug turned to see Nakor entering the pavilion and, with a resigned expression, said, "Never mind. Thank you."

"Out for a walk?" Pug asked Nakor as the little man sat down next to Magnus.

"Yes," said Nakor. "This is a nice island. I don't think I've been to this world before . . . at least I don't remember being here."

"Help yourself," said Pug, watching Nakor dig into Pug's breakfast. He motioned to a porter to bring another plate and mug. "We must get to see this king . . . Daylon. And find that other fellow."

"Bodai," said Nakor around a mouthful of food. "You'll like him." Then Nakor's eyes widened. "I have been here before. I remember him. I gave him oranges, too."

Magnus said, "Unless he's over a century old, how is that possible?"

Nakor shrugged, as was his habit, and said, "I don't know. I love questions I don't know the answers to; they keep me going. So, we find Bodai and maybe then I'll work it out." He stood up, looked at Pug as his plate and cup were placed in front of him, and said, "Hurry up. We need to go."

Pug's gaze narrowed. "Sit down," he said coldly. "That was my breakfast you ate, so now I'll eat yours."

Nakor sat again and with a laugh said, "Seems fair."

DECLAN WALKED INTO THE CLEARING and was greeted by Sixto. Declan laughed as he threw his arms around his friend, and said, "I haven't seen you this filthy since we climbed out of Garn's Wound."

Sixto wore heavy black gloves, which Declan assumed came from a dead Church soldier, and waved a hand toward the work in progress. "This is hardly the sort of work one undertakes if staying clean is an ambition."

"True," said Declan, surveying the site. The clearing was now surrounded by a large ring of tree stumps, and to the south stood a large pile of tree boles.

"Those plans we sent you call for things we don't have," Sixto said. "Stonework and iron fastenings. Those engineers we freed are contriving a wooden breastwork around some of the stumps."

"With luck, you won't need it," said Declan. "Tell your men to rest. Each of my men has brought extra rations."

"Welcome news," said Sixto, wiping perspiration from his forehead with his forearm. "We're low on rations, with the extra mouths here. Some of the engineers who fled found their way back here starving and miserable."

"How many?"

"Fourteen."

"Good," Declan replied as his men started unloading the saddlebags of food.

Declan and Sixto sat on a freshly cut stump large enough to accommodate both of them comfortably. "These stumps are beyond my knowledge," said Sixto. "I've seen a few so old they have an almost stonelike hardness, and I don't know what to do with them."

"I've got a supply caravan coming," Declan answered. "The king has decided to cut a road in from the west. Lumberjacks from the north should be meeting Captain Joran any time now. They're bringing mules, chains, harnesses, whatever they need to get these things pulled out."

"How?" Sixto asked.

"I've seen only a little of what they do, but I've helped Edvalt build big"—he held his hands widely apart—"wedges, and big hammers. They dig around, cut the roots they can see, cut a cross in the stump down to the soil, then drive the wedges in. It breaks the stump up and then they use iron bars and shovels to finish."

"So, mostly muscle," said Sixto. Looking at the now-crowded clearing, he added, "Muscle we have."

"The mules haul them out, and if we had a river nearby, we could build a timber yard."

"That would be handy," Sixto conceded. "Maybe if we survive this war with the Church, these engineers can do something with that creek we camp at. Excavate it a little, build some sort of dam."

"First, we survive the war," said Declan.

"That would be a good idea."

Declan stood up and stripped off his tunic and sword belt.

"Going to work?"

"I've been working since I was a boy. My brothers may find sitting all day reading reports 'work,' but I don't." He turned to look at the men eating and stood up, stepped up onto the stump where he had been sitting, and shouted, "All you who came with Captain Sixto, rest! All of you who came with me, strip off those tunics and grab axes and saws. If you don't know what to do with them, someone will show you."

He got off the stump and looked at Sixto. "You. Rest."

Sixto finished eating a large piece of salted pork, took a long drink from a water skin, then stood up and said, "Unlikely." He picked up the axe he'd used before Declan arrived and said, "Got a tree to cut down."

ROBBIE WAS WAITING AT THE Four Ravens when Donte returned from the farm. Donte had spent a few days there and left satisfied that things with the children were moving along. Once he'd understood these were not children of Coaltachin, he spoke to Healer about how best to train them. Without any discipline ever being instilled in them, these children had been driven by desperation and fear. Now that they were feeling safe and well fed, that drive was gone.

Donte had quickly understood that trying to bring back that desperation and fear would only drive the kids away. So, at Healer's suggestion, he adopted the position that he needed to convince them they wanted to learn, wanted to please him, and wanted to provide for themselves as a group. Donte wasn't entirely convinced this was the right choice, but he lacked any better idea, so he followed Healer's advice.

Donte had sent Lyndon ahead by a day to get word to Robbie he'd be back at the Ravens and wanted information on the Mockers' whereabouts. He went to the bar and ordered ale. He noticed Scully and Lyndon sitting at a nearby table, watching as others drifted in and out of the inn.

"What did you find?" Donte asked them.

Robbie said, "I found I'll likely get killed if I keep messing with these Mockers. I almost blundered into one and only didn't get my throat cut because he coughed just enough that I heard him. Cold, damp night it was." He picked up the mug put before him, took a drink, then pointed a finger at Donte. "This much I found out. Like I said, they're holed up somewhere in Sad Landing. And most of what I saw had them coming and going closer to the land side than the water side. But you need a monkey on a roof to follow them, and I bet they got a watch up there just in case you have a trained monkey."

"Trained monkey, no," said Donte. "But I know my way around rooftops. Just tell me how far you got, and I'll watch tonight."

"It's your throat then," said Robbie. "My gold?"

Donte looked at him with a twisted smile. "When I get back."

"What if you don't?" Robbie almost shouted.

Donte grabbed the front of the smaller man's shirt, and said, "Then I'll know as I'm bleeding that you sold me out to the Mockers. So, if that was your scheme, you'd better think about it. Now, where do I go and what awaits me?"

Robbie did not look remotely pleased but nodded. "Very well. You head down to where we watched the Mockers take the Keshians' loot, but don't turn toward the dock but away. Last street you reach, turn left. Go downhill to Sad Landing."

He continued to describe the short path after that and Donte formed a mental picture of the route, knowing that now he could trust Robbie's information. It was not in Robbie's self-interest to betray him. Just as he had been taught back home: only trust those you know, and not very much.

SABELLA SAT IN A KIND of rapture, eyes wide, as she listened to instruction from a creature from another world. Short, with a barrel chest and long arms that almost reached his knees, the instructor was from a world whose name she barely could make out, a trilling sound that resembled a bird call more than any noise a human could make. He was understandable to all through the magic Pug had mentioned to Hava and Hatu. She thought his name was Izcucu but wasn't sure. She was the newest student, but because of her previous reading in the library at the Sanctuary, she felt able to absorb this new knowledge. He was lecturing a class of six new students on the concept of magic power, what they knew and didn't know at Sorcerer's Isle.

She and the other students sat in a circle on a grassy lawn near a pleasant flower garden. It was a gentle, sunny day, and she felt more alive than she had in her life.

"Often," Izcucu said, "beings can traverse an entire cycle from birth to death unknowing of what is unknown. To be clear, I mean one can wonder about how deep an ocean is, but does a being consider the contours under the water, how many creatures live there? Does a being ponder the lights in the heavens, simply thinking they're sparkles just out of reach, or, as you know, distant suns with planets in orbit?

"The unseen power, what is known as magic, is variable from world to world. Most beings traverse their cycle unaware of this power's existence, but a few, such as yourselves, perceive it, and can even utilize it."

Sabella looked around and saw the other students appeared attentive, but she felt familiar with these concepts. Then she looked to her left, toward the open meadow, and saw Zaakara. She got up quickly and looped away from the other students. She hurried across the meadow, and when she reached Zaakara said, "Thank you again for bringing me here!" She gave him a hug.

"You are more than welcome," he replied. "You seem to be flourishing."

"So much to learn!" Her eyes were aglow, and he had never seen her this animated.

"If I'm not mistaken you have already started changing—only a little bit, but noticeably."

"What do you mean?" she asked, her tone suddenly more subdued.

He smiled. "Nothing to be concerned over, but you seem . . . You've got more color in your cheeks and your eyes are bright."

"The food here is wonderful," she said, and added shyly, "And I have been eating more than I could at the Sanctuary."

"Well, good food and rest can do wonders," he replied, "but I think it has more to do with you . . . opening up? Accepting the powers that lie hidden within you?"

She nodded. "That's it, I think. Everything here feels . . . so abundant! The air is charged with . . ."

"I understand," he said, his expression half wonder and half amusement. "My powers felt diminished on Garn. Not obviously so, because we were asked to do little other than come to meet and investigate Hatushaly. But when they vanished altogether, that was when the energy differences between our two worlds became starkly evident."

"I wish I could take this back to Garn," she said.

Zaakara chuckled. "That seems to be a topic of conversation," he said. "From what young Jaroly said, some confusion arose before Hatu, Pug, and Magnus appeared and Ruffio and I returned here. If we can find a way to increase the magic energy on Garn, we can see to more training there, but otherwise, the only way that happens is for Hatushaly to stay there. Now, what can you tell me about the so-called Firemane Curse?"

She glanced back to where Izcucu was lecturing and said, "I should probably get back."

Zaakara gently took her by the elbow and said, "I know that lecture well. I've given it myself. You already know what's being taught. It's what we're speaking of right now. Walk with me and tell me of this malediction."

"All right," she said.

He motioned for her to walk toward the southern coast and down a long, gentle slope that led to an overlook above a boulder-strewn shore.

She began, "I know only a little of the history of this lore, what Bodai taught others before I was born, before he left to assume the role of a master of Coaltachin. The simple story is that should the Firemane line end, a horrible curse would befall Garn."

"There seems to be a grain of truth in that, seeing as when Hatushaly departed, he took magic with him. Should he have died, I think that would have ended all magic on Garn."

She nodded vigorously. "On Garn, I could not do any of the things I already can do here." She stopped and for a moment levitated herself more than a foot off the ground, then gently returned. "I practiced alone last night," she said with a grin.

"Remarkable," said Zaakara. "We have students that can't do that after months of trying."

She beamed. "What I find a mystery," she said, "is why things are so different. Not just the amount of energy here and how little there is on Garn, but why men on Garn can't use magic at all—except for Hatushaly—and women need men who have some . . . access? Or they hold it inside somehow, for a woman to use later? When Hatu was at the Sanctuary, I felt better and could think more clearly. I began to notice his effect on me when I first met him in Marquensas. It's all very strange."

"Something new always seems strange at first," Zaakara replied. "We just don't understand the differences." He paused, then added, "But it is a mystery, and an intriguing one."

They reached the edge of the cliffs and Sabella looked out over the Bitter Sea. "I want to see it all," she said eagerly.

"All—the whole world?"

"Worlds," she said with a laugh.

Zaakara shared her humor. "You may someday. If the powers awakening in you are the same as what most of us here have, you'll live a very long life, with luck. If you avoid getting killed, that power will keep you relatively young for a long time. My father was probably two hundred years or so when he wed my mother, and she—a holy warrior of the Order of Sung—was also older than she looked. Most women are long past childbearing at sixty years of age, yet here I am."

"Your parents are not with us, I believe."

"Yes, servants of the churches live long lives, but nothing like me, Magnus, or others. From what I was told, Magnus's mother was older than Pug—"

She looked confused. "Pug?"

He said, "That is another story. Let's go find some food and I'll tell it to you."

She agreed and they started walking back to the dining hall.

HAVA WATCHED AS PUG, NAKOR, and Hatu stood ready to depart. She had decided to stay until the next supply ship from the Sanctuary arrived in two days and would inquire about things she wished to know: most importantly, to her, the status of her ship the *Queen of Storms*. If she was going to remain on Garn, she would have that ship back as soon as she could.

Pug turned to Hatushaly and said, "If you can show me clearly where we need to go, I can transport us there."

"I have a very clear memory of the king's palace in Marquenet," Hatu said. "Join with my vision and I'll show you."

Pug closed his eyes and found it very easy to rejoin with Hatu. The work the young man had done with Pug's memories had forged a link that made seeing what Hatu saw almost effortless.

Pug saw a modest castle surrounded by outbuildings and a wall. In his mind he heard Hatushaly say, "Word is they've built new structures so, before we go, I should look around."

Pug said silently, "It would not do for us to materialize inside a wall."

As if flying at great speed, like a sparrow on the wing, the vision of the king's castle sped around Pug at a dizzying rate. Abruptly the image halted, and Pug heard Hatu say, "This is where we need to be. We need to speak with that man."

Pug saw a man of middle years sitting at a large table with scrolls and books set before him and an inkpot, long pen, and a blotter close at hand. An unlit red candle for embossing a document rested near a big brass seal.

"Balven," said Hatushaly. "The king's brother and first adviser."

Pug opened his eyes and motioned for Hatu and Nakor to come close. He reached out and gripped each by their upper arm, and abruptly the three of them were standing before Balven.

Balven's eyes widened in shock. He was on the verge of shouting for the guards when Hatushaly said, "Balven, it's me, Hatu!"

It took a few seconds for that to register, but then Balven regained his composure. "How—?" He took a deep breath. "You startled me almost to death." He slowed down his breathing and said, "I knew you were rumored to have some sort of special power, but how—?" He again stopped, then said, "I'll listen."

"Something very bad is going to happen and these are my friends, Pug and Nakor. They're here to help."

Balven regarded the man in the black robe and the scrawny fellow in the faded and patched yellow-orange robe, and his expression was dubious. "Bad how? We've already got a war coming with the Church of the One. How much worse can things get?"

Nakor smiled and said, "Much worse."

Hatu said, "We need to speak with the king."

Balven stood up, pushing his chair back. "In that case, I think you do," he said. "Follow me. He's organizing more soldiers to ready them for the fight."

"We need to speak with Bodai, too," said Hatu.

"You just missed him. He left yesterday for Coaltachin."

Hatu winced. "Why?"

"Because we need the Kingdom of the Night to fight the Church."

They left Balven's offices and walked across the large hall toward a side door that led outside.

Nakor gawked a little and said, "Nice throne room."

"Thank you," said Balven, not quite sure what else to say.

"I've seen better," Nakor added.

Balven's face reflected several different reactions, and Pug said, "Nakor?"

"Well, the Empress's palace in Kesh all those years ago."

Pug waved his hand, indicating this wasn't the time or place. "That wasn't a palace. That was dozens of floors of a city atop a bigger city."

Nakor started to reply, but a harsh look from Pug stopped him.

They exited the castle and entered a side marshaling yard, where the king was conferring with several officers. Seeing his brother arriving with three others, Daylon dismissed the officers, and turned toward Balven. "What's this?" he asked as they approached.

Hatushaly bowed and was followed a moment later by Pug and Nakor. "Hatu!" said Daylon. He looked around, then asked, "Did Hava also come? The navy could use her."

Hatu said, "No, she's got business at the Sanctuary." He left out the explanation that she was waiting for word of her ship's whereabouts. He introduced Pug and Nakor and said, "We are here because there's danger on its way."

"The Church? We know about that," said the king, then saw Balven shaking his head. "What then?"

Nakor said, "There's this thing that wants to end all life on Garn."

Daylon was speechless.

Pug said, "I've faced it before, and . . ." He was about to say "survived," then thought better of it. ". . . prevailed. It can be stopped, but we have to prepare for it."

Looking at his brother, the king said in almost plaintive tones, "Can't we just have one war at a time?"

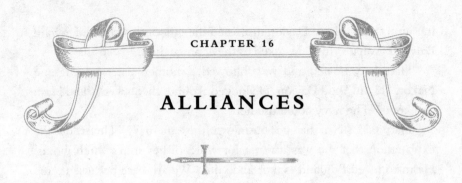

CHAPTER 16

ALLIANCES

Donte hunkered down.

He situated himself behind a short chimney, one he could tell hadn't vented smoke for a while. There was a difference between the stench of a stale furnace flute and an outlet for recent ash and soot. He couldn't put an exact word to it, but he just thought of the former as old and the latter as fresh.

Everything about this sector of what Robbie had called Sad Landing reeked of disuse and abandonment. Donte could see why an organized gang from a foreign city might choose this section to take over for a base. At one time it might have been a low-priority landing for lesser freight-haulers, because it was at the very edge of the old docks and was a more difficult location for unloading cargo and transporting it into the city and beyond. Time and circumstances had turned it into an abandoned quarter.

Donte played the buffoon as well as anyone and, truth be told, he often enjoyed the mayhem that caused, but he still listened. He might feign indifference to many things that others found interesting, but he always took note of information that might serve his ends.

He did not know the specifics of Kingdom history, the loss of Krondor as the major Bitter Sea port and the elevation of Port Vykor to preeminence, but he did remember that something terrible had happened and that trade had dwindled. So, he deduced that the requirements for shipping intake had fallen off, and here was the area of the city that had suffered the most from that decline.

All of this was in the back of his mind as he contemplated what to do about the sentry camped out at the other end of this roof. Both men squatted at opposite ends of an abandoned warehouse, and that alerted Donte to two things: first, he was in the right location and Robbie's information so far was accurate, and second, if he made a wrong move, he was likely to end up dead.

It was only by sheer luck he hadn't been spotted by the sentry. He had made a short leap from the neighboring building closer to the docks, landing behind the short chimney. The guard had heard the slight noise and had walked over to investigate, but he had stopped short of the chimney and peered over the side of the building. He lingered there, while Donte crouched low and was ready with a dagger to end him.

He heard footsteps approaching. Donte tensed, anticipating a fight. He knew the quickest way out of Sad Landing if he needed to flee. The sound of others getting into position stopped, then he heard the guard moving to the side opposite where he'd just been.

Donte imagined the guard was trying to see if something was amiss below. He kept his breathing slow and calm, preventing his heart from thumping out of his chest. He was by nature a quick-tempered brawler, so the patience of the assassin—the ability to stay motionless for hours without fatigue or muscle cramping—had been for him among the most difficult lessons he had endured as a child. He was certain that had his grandfather not been a master, Donte would have been relegated to a minor role in Coaltachin.

Now he was thankful for at least having had some of that training remain with him. After another long moment, the sound of lightly treading feet moved away, and Donte felt his body relax a little as tension began to fade.

Donte considered his predicament. He was safe so long as he didn't call attention to himself. He could easily go back the way he had come by keeping the low chimney between himself and the sentry. A slip over the eaves and drop to the ground below would have him out of sight before the guard could come and investigate any noise he might make. There were enough stray dogs, alley cats, and vermin swarming through this part of the city that the Mocker on duty might easily dismiss any slight sound.

That option frustrated Donte, as he was only a little closer to locating the Mockers' hideout. Still, he thought, there were other ways to discover where they had dug in.

"What would Hava do?" he wondered. She was easily the cleverest of his peers at spycraft. Then he realized he knew exactly what she'd do.

He slipped away and dropped to the ground with little noise and ducked across the empty street to shelter around a corner. He flattened himself against a wall and waited for any sign of torchlight or the sound of footfalls approaching. He counted slowly and when he reached a hundred, he reckoned he'd got away without detection.

Despite his often-erratic behavior and conflicts with authority when growing up, Donte had mastered much of the Coaltachin craft, and one thing he was very good at was building a map in his head. He needed only to know which direction he was facing—north, south, east, or west—and as he moved from point to point, he could memorize a detailed plan of key locations, cross streets and alleys, bridges, tunnels, and important buildings. So, he returned to where he had entered the Sad Landing area and decided to loop around the farthest building, then come back in from another direction.

Many hours later, as the sky to the east was beginning to lighten, Donte had constructed a mental map of Sad Landing, the location of half a dozen sentries circling one area, and a promising-looking tunnel entrance he was certain led to an underground lair of the Mockers. He might not have felt so certain except that tunnel was guarded by two sentries, and they had been the most alert of all those he had encountered. He was certain had he lingered any longer, they might have spotted him.

He sneaked out of Sad Landing and once in a part of Dockside, made his way back to the Four Ravens. He reached the inn as the eastern sky lightened with the dawn.

As Donte expected, it was open early, Shad behind the bar, and the smell of something cooking was in the air. Scully sat at a table, half awake, while Lyndon's chair was tipped backward, wedged into a corner, and he was snoring.

Scully pushed Lyndon, waking him, as Donte approached. Scully looked expectantly at Donte.

"Found them," Donte said as he sat down.

"Where?" asked Scully, while Lyndon shook his head slightly as he came fully awake.

"So, the Sad Landing quarter," Donte said, holding a hand up, palm out as if he were illustrating something in the air. "West side, halfway up, then six buildings in. A large street running more or less north to south, and a street from the west empties into a cross, but instead of continuing, it faces a big tunnel entrance. The tunnel is where they're holed up." He put his hand down.

Scully nodded slowly. "The old fish market. That makes sense."

"Why?"

"My father told me, when I was a boy, how Sad Landing came to be."

"I guessed at part of that story," said Donte, "about the big war or whatever it was that dried up trade, along with all the strange stuff, like that jungle to the south."

"Green Reaches," Scully said, nodding. "So, my father says his father was a boy when all that happened, the big crazy that changed everything. One thing stuck out, though: the last people to leave Sad Landing were fisherfolk, and before it was called Sad Landing it was Fisherman's Landing.

"That street from the tunnel? It used to go from there to a dock that fell apart before I was out of nappies, and the tunnel leads down to a deep stone-lined underground . . . warehouse, I guess you'd say. It gets bloody hot here some days during midsummer, and you know heat and fish."

Remembering the time after he had escaped from the Sisters of the Deep, living in a fishing village, Donte said, "All too well. Ice is hard to come by when it's hot."

"You have to have fast freight, which means lots of gold," said Scully, "and fisherfolk usually don't have any."

"Or a magician around," Lyndon added, now that he was completely awake and attentive.

"And they're harder to come by than gold," said Scully. "Anyway, it's cool in the hottest summer days down in that warehouse, and in the winter it's downright icy. But here's the thing: there are other, smaller tunnels leading up to the street from there, to where the old fish market stood."

"They most likely would be sealed off," said Donte. "Except maybe for a bolthole."

"Makes sense," said Scully. "You going to go looking for that bolt-hole?"

"No." Donte rubbed his chin. "Not for what I have in mind."

"What would that be?" asked Lyndon.

"Tell you later," said Donte. "Right now, I need you to go dig up Robbie, wherever he's holed up. Tell him to be here at sundown. I have another job for him."

Lyndon rose and said, "I know where to find him."

After the dark-haired thug was gone, Scully said, "What do you need Robbie for?"

Donte smiled. "To tell the Keshians where the Mockers are hiding their loot."

DECLAN HAD MOVED BACK, HIS hand halfway to his sword, when he abruptly recognized that it was Hatushaly who was standing before him. Next to him was a brown-haired man in a black robe, holding a staff.

"Where did you come from?" he shouted, as every other soldier within hearing turned and looked on in astonishment at the two men standing before the prince. They had not been there moments before.

"From your brother," said Hatushaly. "This is Pug, highness."

Pug bowed from the waist and said, "I forgot to ask what the for-mal address here was, highness."

Declan laughed, grabbed Hatu in a hug, and said, "Does any of this look formal?"

Pug smiled. "Industrious, yes. Formal, no."

"So, you're back from that other world," said Declan. "Seems your absence has caused a stir."

"That's why we're back," said Hatu. He motioned to Pug and said, "Pug is from Midkemia. He is here to help."

Declan studied the figure before him. "What can you do?"

Pug said, "What do you need doing?"

Declan moved his hand around in an arc, and said, "We're trying to clear this area and build a redoubt. But until we get the road cleared from the west, all we're accomplishing is making stumps and piling up timber. Can you chop down trees?"

Pug chuckled. "I think I can help. Where do you want that road to go? West?"

"West of here to the highway that connects Marquenet to the north. Right now, it's a five, even six-day journey to the city. With a straight west route, two days."

Pug motioned toward where men were sawing at a giant oak, and said, "Call them back, please."

Declan caught Sixto's attention and yelled, "Clear everyone out of that section!"

Sixto hurried around a pile of stumps and fallen branches, reached the team sawing at the oak, and ordered them away. When the area was clear, Pug moved to face the large oak.

He put out his hand and incanted a few phrases, then suddenly the tree began to shake. Vibrations ran through the ground. With an ear-splitting noise, the earth shrieked as Pug focused his power, and a massive oak lifted slowly out of the ground. Everyone could see leaves and small branches falling off as it continued to rise. Cracks appeared in the bark from forces ripping it from below, as if a pair of giant hands were gripping it and pulling upward.

Even Hatu, who had some idea of what magic could do, stood in open-mouthed amazement as the tree kept rising higher and higher, until dangling roots hovered a yard above the torn soil. Clods of earth and leaves rained down from the oak.

"Where do you want this?" Pug asked Declan.

The Prince of Marquensas could hardly speak as he said, "Somewhere away from here, please."

With a flick of his wrist, Pug caused the tree to soar up into the sky to the east, and a few moments later, everyone heard a distant crash loud enough to awaken half the forest. The squawks of birds as they took wing and the scurrying of animals fleeing the impact was a faint echo in the distance.

Pug turned to Declan and Hatu. Pointing at Hatu he said, "If he wasn't here, I'd be as helpless as any old man, but if I was at home, I could clear this road for you in a day." With an apologetic expression, he said, "As it is, I can help a little."

Declan gathered himself. "I wouldn't call that a little." He turned to Sixto. "Get this man whatever he needs. Give the workers a rest and let's see how fast this goes."

Pug glanced at Hatu and said, "Now I'm sorry we didn't bring Nakor along. He may be a problem at times, but he's a hard worker when he needs to be." He turned his efforts to a smaller tree behind the hole in the ground where the oak had stood, and it started to quiver. Soon, every soldier and engineer ceased working and watched as the strange man in the black robe waved his hands and trees ripped themselves out of the ground.

Clouds of dust and flying clumps of detritus spattered those closest to Pug, but he appeared indifferent. Each tree rose slowly from the soil, trembling at times as roots were torn lose from Garn's tight grip, only to be lifted and thrown in a high arc, as if a child tossed a ball into the sky. The distant crashes were evidence of just how large the trees he was removing were. Pug proceeded as if they were weeds plucked from a garden.

An hour went by, and a dozen trees had been removed. Pug turned to Hatu and Declan and said, "I think I need to rest a bit."

Declan bade him come and sit on a nearby stump and Hatu said, "That was astonishing."

Pug smiled and said, "I have no doubt by the time we're finished here, you will have puzzled out how to do it without my instruction." Pug tapped the side of his own head. "You were in here for a while, remember? I expect that particular 'trick,' as Nakor would call it, is somewhere in that head of yours, waiting for you to stumble across it."

Hatu looked at Pug with an uncertain smile. "That may be, but I think I won't try, given the last time I did anything without guidance, I managed to set fire to a ship." He looked around at the mess, dozens of trees and branches still cluttering the clearing, and added, "This is not the place to start a big fire."

"No, it isn't," Pug agreed. Looking at the area he had just cleared, he said, "A small start."

Declan said, "You may think it small, but you just saved my men half a day's clearing in one hour. If you can manage another hour before sundown, that saves us a day."

Pug motioned for a nearby soldier to approach and pointed at the water skin he held. He took it, drank deeply, then stood up and handed it back. "Then I'd best get to it." He said to Hatu, "Do you need to return to find your friend Bodai soon?"

"He's on a ship in the Narrows, so another day's sailing or so will still find him a good distance from where he's heading. I'll stay here for a while, watch what you do, and see if I can find that knowledge in here." He tapped his head. "Then, when things are better here, we can chase Bodai down."

"Very well," Pug said. He pulled back his sleeves, faced the now-empty section, and began to focus on another tree.

HAVA WAS DELIGHTED TO SEE the ship reach the mooring and drop sails. It was a freighter she had captured, the *Golden Rose*. She had been amused when she had quickly and quietly taken it from the Pride Lords, because it was a very ordinary, dull-looking ship with a glorious name. The *Rose* was a squat brig with two masts and a rough weather trysail that was currently furled as weather was calm. She was the perfect size to make small cargo runs if there was no hurry.

Once the ship was moored, the longboat was lowered and behind it came a barge. The longboat reached the shore as Hava hurried down to meet it and was happy to see a familiar face in the bow.

"Sabien!" she cried.

"Captain," he replied, jumping over the gunwale and wading the last few yards to where she stood. "You've been missed," he said.

She clapped him on one shoulder. "So, they made a captain out of you yet?"

He laughed, delighted to see her. "No, I'm still a mate, working under George."

"George is skipper of that barge?"

Sabien again laughed. "That barge suits his nature, truth to tell, and I like serving with him. So, here we are."

"Who has *Queen of Storms*?" she asked.

"Rigart, if you remember him. Why? You want her back?"

Hava took a deep breath and looked out over the water, then said, "I miss it, but times change."

He nodded understanding. "Rigart's a good enough captain and *Queen*'s got it quiet for the most part. We've chased away most of the raiders and as we don't care much what happens on Nytanny, don't bother with chasing smugglers. It's why I went with George to be first mate on the *Rose*. Hauling freight keeps us busy. Sitting and waiting for something to happen is no life for me."

"That I understand," said Hava.

"Where's Hatushaly?"

"That's another story. Tell George we should get a drink when you've finished offloading, and I'll tell it to you. I assume you're laying up for a day or two?"

"We need to take on water, but we're well provisioned. We're laying up for one night. I'll tell the captain, and I think he'll want to come ashore and have that drink."

"How are things at the Sanctuary?"

"Not much different to when you left. Farmers farming, fishers fishing—the usual. Rebuilding is slow but going along. You haven't been gone that long."

She chuckled ruefully. "It feels like ages."

"Big changes?" he asked, looking over to where the men were unloading the barge.

"Go," she said, seeing that he was anxious to make sure things were done properly. "I'll tell you and George the whole story later."

"Good. We have two more loads after this one, so we'll be done around sundown, I'm thinking."

"See you then."

"Till then," he replied, hurrying off.

Hava weighed staying until Hatushaly returned or riding back to the Sanctuary with George and Sabien but put off deciding which until after drinks and a meal after sunset.

She roamed for a bit, having nothing specific to do here except wait. She thought perhaps a nap would be in order, then decided she was too restless, and a good walk around the island would suit her better.

Hava got in some brisk exercise and felt good by the time she finished a walk along the beach. She enjoyed climbing over some rocks below cliffs and tossing a few stones into the sea. When she returned, she noticed something that had escaped her attention before. As what she took to be the last barge was halfway back to the *Golden Rose*, she spied a light-blue banner flying from the mainmast. Her eyes narrowed and she made a soft "Hmmmm" sound.

By the time Sabien and George entered the pavilion, Hava was sitting at a table with a pitcher of ale and three mugs. Hava and George embraced. George smiled and said, "You've been sorely missed, I can tell you."

Sabien nodded.

After taking a drink, Hava said, "I see you're flying a top banner."

"Flag of Marquensas," said George. He took a drink, wiped his mouth, then added, "It just sort of happened as we were running goods back and forth from South Tembria."

Hava said, "I like Declan, but his royal kin? I'm not sure about this. Spent enough time with this king to think him a good man, but when I left, we were still free. How did he convince you to join his navy?"

"Well," said Sabien, "he didn't really have a navy, just a few ships scattered about. Before the war with the Pride Lords, he'd use Zindaros ships if he needed a few. So, he needed a navy and, well, it was pretty easy when Declan brought those ships back with him from Zindaros to make a little fleet, but he was short of sailors, so—"

"He's paying everyone's wages," interrupted George. "No threats or bullying, just 'swear to be loyal and I'll pay the men monthly.'"

Hava laughed. "I guess that means everyone took the oath."

"Tripping over themselves," said Sabien. "But we don't have a great leader. Admiral Kean—"

"Admiral?" Hava exclaimed.

"Had to call him something besides captain," said George. "He's not very happy at that. He's a good enough seaman and happy to captain one ship, but that business with bringing ships here, then running down to Akena Bay to hit them Pride Lords, that was all you.

"I say this with respect, you may be a youngster, but you know how to get things done and, truth to tell, I've never seen someone so young naturally take charge of things the way you do, not even the noble children up in North Tembria. That's why the king really wants you back in Marquenet."

Hava sat back a moment, then said, "Well, I don't know if I'm going to be able—"

She saw both men look past her with expressions of surprise and turned to see her husband walking from the side of the pavilion that faced the rift on the hill.

Hava jumped up and threw her arms around his neck. "I was wondering if I was going to see you again!"

"I will always find you." Hatu kissed her, then said, "We have to leave."

She stepped back a little and looked around and said, "Where's Pug?"

"He's back in the Darkwood, helping Declan."

She moved a little farther away, wide-eyed. "If he's there, how did you get here?"

"Pug showed me a trick. I'll tell you about it later."

"Where are we going?"

"To see the king," Hatu said, slipping his arm around her waist.

"How are—"

Suddenly they vanished.

George and Sabien looked at the empty space for a moment, then at each other, and both reached for the pitcher of ale.

ROBBIE SAID, "NO, I WON'T do it."

"I just need you to carry the word," said Donte.

"Those Keshians almost cut my throat the last time I ran into them, and if they suspect for a second that I was the one who got word to them Mockers about their smuggling, I'm dead."

Donte resisted the impulse to bully Robbie, because his instincts said the man was genuinely terrified. Years of training had enabled him to judge this man would no longer be a valuable source, so he said, "I understand, but besides you, who else is a good rumormonger?"

"There's no one else in Port Vykor—"

Donte held up his hand, cutting Robbie off. "I don't need a sales pitch. If you want to . . ." Donte realized he'd been going about this all wrong. "Never mind. Forget about a rumormonger. I need a tipster."

"A snitch?" asked Robbie.

"I need a good one."

"If they're still alive, they're good," Robbie answered.

"Obviously," Donte agreed. "I need an informant . . ." His eyes widened as he realized he had an answer. "I don't need you to go to the Keshians," he said with increasing enthusiasm. "I need you to tip a snitch!"

"How's that?" asked Robbie.

"So, here's what you do," Donte began. "You find the least trust-worthy bastard you know, and just tell him you're more desperate than usual, and you're eager to find out where the Keshians are lying low."

"But I know where they are," Robbie whined.

Donte tried not to show his frustration. "I know that, but whoever you're talking to won't. Tell him you have valuable information and you're willing to share a few coins—don't get too generous or he'll suspect—and let him know that you know where those Mockers took the Keshian booty, but you're not sure how to reach the Keshians. You'll work out the rest of the story. Play stupid about where the Keshians are hiding." Donte slid a silver coin across the table. "Give him this and offer him another for getting word to the Keshians."

Robbie looked unconvinced, but Donte's willingness to pay well so far had him eager to keep getting paid. "I think I know a fellow, but he's a shrewd one, which is why he still has his neck about him. I'll see what I can do." He rose, snatched the silver coin off the table, and hurried out of the inn.

Donte looked at the corner table where Scully and Lyndon sat. With a tilt of his head, Donte had Lyndon leaving his chair and following Robbie.

Scully got up and came to Donte's table. He sat down and asked, "What now?"

Donte leaned back in his chair, and said, "We wait."

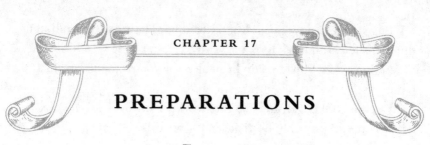

CHAPTER 17

PREPARATIONS

Declan waited.

Standing next to Pug, he could see the wagons and mules between trees, and when the first wagon halted, he said, "Let's go."

They made their way to where Captain Joran could see them. His soldiers tensed and were about to draw their weapons until they recognized the prince, and everyone relaxed.

Joran saluted, "Highness!"

"You can start here once Pug has removed this last stand of trees. Some stumps remain and a whole lot of branches need to be hauled out. Mainly you have a lot of big holes to fill up."

Looking around, Pug asked, "Where's Hatushaly?"

Despite his fatigue, Declan laughed. "I have no idea. I think he may be waiting for us back at the palace."

Pug's expression was openly quizzical.

"He watched you work for a while, just as impressed as the rest of us, then wandered over to a far corner and . . . jumped?"

"Jumped?"

"I don't know what you'd call it, but he stood in one place, then suddenly he was about ten feet away?"

"He transported himself!" Pug's expression was one of pure astonishment.

"If that's what you call it. Then he saw me watching, waved, and then he was standing right next to me." Declan took a breath and said, "Damn near scared the wits out of me. Then he said he was going to go and get Hava, and he'd see us back at the palace."

Pug said, "I know this is lost on you, but Hatushaly just did something in a few minutes it took me years to master." He went on, "I need to rest, but when you're ready I can also get you to the palace in a . . . jump."

Declan looked around at the workers unloading wagons and said, "I should probably do that, and leave this to Sixto and Joran to oversee. But—"

Pug interrupted. "You don't like leaving tasks unfinished. I know." He looked at Declan. "After a few hundred years you get good at sensing what a person's like after a short time."

Declan said, "You're right. I am not good at leaving tasks to others, as my brother Balven constantly has to remind me."

"Well," said Pug, "let's both rest, and when you're ready, we'll go back to Marquenet after you've reassured yourself you've left things here in good hands."

Declan tilted his head to indicate his agreement. He motioned Captain Joran over and said, "Once the other timbermen from the north arrive, start widening here and get those holes filled. The king will want a stone-paved road through here as soon as it can be built, to connect to the King's Highway."

"Understood, highness," the young captain answered.

As they started back, Pug said, "A stone road? That's a good idea. Given how close this is to the sea, you must get a lot of rain."

"Had you been here about a week ago you would have seen that firsthand," Declan replied.

"I lived near the sea for a very long time," Pug said, "so I know how unpredictable the weather can be. Sometime I should tell you the story of how an unexpected storm put my feet on the path I walk today."

"My wife's father owned an inn. I was there a lot when I was courting her and worked there after her father died until she sold it—to Hatushaly and Hava, as a matter of fact. I learned to enjoy good stories."

"Wife?" said Pug. "I would enjoy meeting her."

Declan's expression grew somber. "She was killed. And that set my feet on the path *I* walk." He turned and began making his way back toward the clearing.

Pug hesitated, weighing the obvious pain Declan still felt at the death of his wife, and decided now was a good time not to say anything. He understood better than most what losing a wife meant; he'd endured that hurt twice.

DONTE ENTERED THE RED STARFISH quietly and moved to the end of the bar. He had given up on Robbie carrying any more messages, even with the lure of more silver. The informant had found the man he sought, exchanged money for information, but when he returned Donte was hardly pleased with the result. He'd discovered the name of the inn the Keshian smugglers frequented, and a name, Albeck. But beyond that he had gained little knowledge.

Whatever other faults he might possess, Donte had a good instinct about just how far he could push someone to do something against their will. He often employed that skill to good effect, despite sometimes just starting a brawl when the mood struck him.

He scanned the room and saw his likely targets: four very dark-skinned men, some sporting prominent scars, wearing what he took to be some tribal fashion. They wore their hair down to their shoulders, save for one fellow whose hair was fashioned into braids that hung to just above his shoulders. Their clothing looked well made, if not richly adorned. And they had the look of men who knew which end of a blade to use and which to avoid.

Perhaps for the first time in his life, Donte waited and watched. Before he had been captured by the Sisters of the Deep and kept alive by their dark magic, he would probably have just walked up and started something that would have ended in a brawl and likely bloodshed. Since that experience, he had become more aware of his own mortality. His first impulse still tended toward rashness, but he was developing a knack for not always giving in to his first impulse. Life might be a harsh teacher, but he was not an entirely stupid student.

He waited, sipping very bad ale, and watched.

A dark, well-dressed man with very fancy clothing entered, with two obvious bodyguards one step behind. Immediately Donte was struck by the difference in his appearance. The men at the table were like the bodyguards, being broad-shouldered, narrow in the waist, obviously strong and probably quick: fighters to a man. The newcomer had a slightly lighter complexion, he had a narrower face, and while he was not fat, something about him told Donte "merchant," or perhaps a fence or broker. He was no warrior.

As soon as the newcomer reached the table, Donte changed his mind: this was the boss. The men around the table all shifted in their chairs and their posture changed. Whoever this man was, he was important.

Donte worked harder than usual to blend in, be just another worker at the bar. The two bodyguards were very alert, watching for anything that might be a threat.

After a minute, Donte turned to the bartender and indicated that he wanted another mug. He'd hardly drunk the first one, occasionally tipping his drink to spill here and there. Given the condition of the floor in a place this seedy, no one noticed.

When he looked back, the boss, as Donte thought of the man, was still speaking to the men at the table, and the guards were still being attentive to the room. He did notice that those moving through the taproom were giving that table a wide berth. That told Donte the locals had seen these men before and wanted no trouble.

Risking a little attention, Donte turned to a solitary drinker next to him, a burly fellow with a thatch of unkempt dark hair, a short beard, and the clothing of a worker. Probably a stevedore or warehouseman rather than any manner of thief, basher, or dishonest sort, he thought. In a light tone, Donte said, "Who's the fancy fellow with an audience?"

The man raised his eyebrows and said, "New around here?"

"First visit," said Donte. Feigning slightly drunken speech, he added, "Stands out a bit here, don't he?"

"He's someone you don't want any part of, stranger."

"Ah," said Donte. "A man of means."

The other man chuckled, and said, "If you're saying he has the means to see you floating in the bay, that's no lie."

Glancing at the man's now-empty mug, Donte motioned to the

barman and said, "Another for my friend here." He smiled. "My name's Peter."

"I'm Burt," said the big man.

"As I said, I'm new to Port Vykor and am looking around a little."

"Where you from?" Burt asked.

"An island so far from here you'll never have heard of it."

"Try me," Burt said jokingly. "I traveled when I was younger."

"Coaltachin," said Donte, knowing the fewer lies he told, the easier it was to keep track of them.

"You're right," said Burt. "Never heard of it." He drained his mug.

Donte waved for another round and said, "I'm looking for an opportunity here."

"What sort?"

"Any that I tumble to," Donte said. "I trade and broker, as long as it don't cross the line."

"What line?"

"Whatever line the local magistrate or men like our fancy-dressed fellow over there draw in the sand," said Donte with a chuckle. "I've got ambition, and the first is to keep breathing. So, a slight bit of this or that, but nothing that's going to bring down trouble, if you see what I mean."

"I take your meaning," said Burt. "You might have picked the wrong city, friend. That fancy-dressed man you noticed, he and the men at the table, and a few more like them, are new around here. Been here less than a year, trying to set up shop, so to speak." He lowered his voice. "Smuggling. Some goods up from Kesh, and that's always a big market. Comes by way of Durbin, I gather. They'd be a rough lot, as Kesh'll put their heads on spikes and the Kingdom will have them on a work gang until they drop.

"Then there's another group, down from Krondor, and they try to control everything else. What's that old Keshian saying? 'When the elephants fight, the mice run and hide.' Something like that."

Donte slapped Burt lightly on the shoulder and said, "Good advice. No one wants to be trampled."

He steered his questions to more benign topics: good housing, possible locations for a shop, and where the better brothels were. Burt departed, half drunk, and thanking Donte for the ale. Donte thanked Burt for the information.

He saw the fancily dressed Keshian and his bodyguards depart, and for a brief moment considered following them, but decided against it. Another time. His conversation with Burt urged him to caution. He hated that.

Donte put his almost-full mug of ale on the bar and slipped out of the Red Starfish unnoticed.

"ZAAKARA!"

The warlock turned and saw Sabella waving.

When she reached him she said, "Your library is truly incredible."

He laughed. "Well, it's not really mine, but they let me use it."

She laughed in turn. "You know what I mean."

"Wejuan has been showing you around?"

"She's amazing," said Sabella. "I haven't seen you in a few days, so I spent my free time between classes there. I'm looking for anything on . . ." She waved her hands in small circles. "Energy, enèji, mana, tenogo, juju . . ."

His laughter increased. "You certainly learned a lot of words for it."

She shook her head emphatically, as her humor faded. "You know what irks me? There are all these words, and facts about how that energy is used, but not one thing I can find that tells me what it is! We have a label for something we don't understand."

He nodded sympathetically. "I remember that frustration. When my father began to teach me the art of being a warlock, so many times I asked, 'How?' and his answer was, 'I don't know, that's just how things happen.'"

Sabella looked as if suddenly something made sense. For a few seconds, she stood motionless, then her expression changed, and with wide eyes she said, "You're brilliant!" She grabbed his head, pulled it down, and gave him a kiss on the cheek, then turned and ran back toward the library.

Zaakara watched her run off and realized, even though he was a century older, that she might be the most remarkable woman he had ever met.

SABELLA ALMOST RAN INTO WEJUAN as the older woman was carrying books around a corner. It was only by sheer luck that she pulled up in time to avoid knocking the librarian to the ground.

"What?" demanded the stout woman, her grey hair tied up in a knot and her face a map of fine wrinkles.

"Something I've wondered about since I arrived, and now I think I have an answer."

"Help me put these away and tell me what this is all about," said Wejuan.

Sabella took half the books and followed Wejuan to the end of a massive shelf. Next to it lay a spiral staircase that rose to a landing halfway up the wall. She followed the older woman up the stairs until they reached that landing and Wejuan said, "This task is pure drudgery."

Sabella said, "I can help if you'd like."

Wejuan found the first space she sought and put the topmost book in her stack with her right hand, while deftly balancing the others with the left, and said, "That's a lovely offer, but you're a student. You won't have the time and besides, it would take me a long time to train you."

Sabella laughed softly. "People always underestimate me."

Wejuan looked at her.

"I did this back where I come from, and I think I've already come to understand most of your system." Sabella looked at the shelf before them, and said, "These are all chronicles of some sort: diaries, journals, tales of travel and exploration." She pointed to the high case directly opposite, a free-standing but very tall construction with a ladder for reaching the top placed at the far end. "Those are catalogs and inventories. On the other side you have rows of books on potions, concoctions, how to mix things—"

Wejuan nodded approvingly. "Very well, you're indeed a quick learner. Now tell me what got you so excited." She turned and began walking to the next place to replace a book.

Sabella said, "It's a bit of a jumble in my head still, but something

Zaakara said got me thinking. A lot of what's written here is . . . records? In the spell books, I mean. How a user of magic tried one thing then another until they somehow came to understand how to make a spell work."

"It's called trial and error, and it often ends up disastrous for the one experimenting. That's why this island became what it is. It's a place to study what's come before and not turn yourself inside out or burst into flames." Wejuan put another book on the shelf.

"That's what I'm getting to," Sabella said as they moved to another place on the walkway. "You know of Hatushaly?"

"Everyone here knows of Hatushaly," Wejuan answered. "Especially me. When he's not with Magnus, or Pug, he's in here." She put away the last books and turned to look at Sabella. "I can hardly believe he reads so fast, but apparently he can. I've never seen anything like that."

Sabella nodded eagerly. "I've spent a great deal of time with him, back in the Sanctuary—you know about that?"

"Yes," Wejuan answered. "Now, come and let's get some tea over at the dining hall, and tell me what all of this has to do with me?"

"It's this," said Sabella as they walked out of the library. "Hatu had little training at first, but he has the knack for understanding things swiftly. As I understand it, he can actually see the lines of energies and knows how things work together."

Reaching the top of a slight rise that stood between the library and the dining hall, Wejuan said, "I'm not sure I follow."

"You have a system, right? For organizing all the books, tomes, and scrolls here."

Wejuan nodded.

"Hatushaly sees how things are organized, underneath all the spells and devices used, and he just uses that . . . energy?"

Again, Wejuan nodded. "Mana, juju, whatever it's called." Then she laughed. "'Stuff,' as Nakor calls it."

"He's a strange man, but I think he knows a lot."

"You're not the first person to make that observation. Even before he turned up with Pug, stories abounded about him. He's a walking invitation to chaos, but he was also a valuable source of knowledge when the great conflict ended." Wejuan smiled. "That was many years ago, long before I was born. I'm old, but not that old."

"I only met him briefly, here, and then he was off with Pug and Hatushaly," said Sabella, "and he said some very odd things about 'stuff' and 'tricks' that I didn't understand."

"You are hardly alone in not understanding Nakor," Wejuan replied with a wry smile.

"Anyway, it's still a jumble in my head, but so far, it's like this: what if we gather all the works on one thing: say a spell to start a fire or bring rain—anything. We look at the works and try to determine what they all have in common. What Zaakara said a while ago was that each of those spells was arrived at through trial and error. A lot of what they did was particular to each spell, but maybe that process is unnecessary?"

Wejuan's expression began to change from amusement to a keener interest. "Go on."

"Maybe some of those details are getting in the way of how people learn. I don't know how I learned to levitate: I just did. Something about the abundance of 'stuff' here maybe, but also maybe because in looking for Hatushaly I spent a great deal of time . . . sensing his mind, I suppose you could say.

"So, anyway, my idea is to strip away the unnecessary and leave only what is absolutely necessary to make the magic work. Maybe then each person will need to change a bit here or there, but it would be like building from the foundation up, not the top down.

"Whatever the reasons, the things I saw in Hatushaly's mind showed me a quick and easy way to float up in the air without having to unlearn the unnecessary bits. So, what do you think?"

Now with an expression of focused attention, Wejuan reached over and patted Sabella on the hand. "A lot of very smart people have lived and worked here for centuries, but you're the first person to think of this. I think there is far more to you than meets the eye, girl."

PUG AND DECLAN APPEARED IN the courtyard, startling the troops nearby. Seeing the prince, they eschewed drawing their weapons, but

the sight of his sudden appearance with the black-robed magician left
them shaken.

Declan ignored the confusion as he led Pug through the marshaling-
yard doorway into the palace. Ignoring those who bowed or saluted as
he passed, Declan headed straight for the king's private study, where he
was certain he'd find his brother and Balven. He signaled to the posted
guard to open the door before he reached it.

Inside, he was not surprised to find his brothers, Delnocio, Hava,
and Hatushaly seated. "Ah," said the king. "I was about to send for you.
Everything secure in the Darkwood?"

"So far," said Declan, sitting in the chair next to him.

Daylon waved to Pug to sit down. As Pug sat next to Hatu, he gave
him a questioning look.

"Later," Hatu said softly.

Nakor entered and looked around. Grinning, he said, "Am I late?"

"Where, might I ask, have you been hiding?" asked the king.

"Here and there, poking around." Without waiting for permission,
Nakor sat in the last empty chair.

Pug looked at the king, shrugged, and said, "He does that a lot."
Looking at Nakor, he said, "Were you back on Sorcerer's Isle?"

"For a while, then I went to some other places."

The king said, "Very well, if there is even more menace about to
threaten this kingdom, I need to know about it, but one thing at a
time." He looked at Declan and said, "First, I need to know exactly
how things stand with our current plans, so tell me, does the work go
apace?"

Pug opened his mouth to say something, then closed it again.

Daylon noticed Pug's expression change and before Declan could
answer, he held up his hand, saying, "Wait." To Pug he asked, "Something troubling you, magician?"

Pug felt a rising impatience but recognized it as Phillip's nature as-
serting itself. Patience had been hard learned during Pug's life as a slave
on Kelewan, and his training with the Great Ones of the Assembly of
Magicians had instilled patience in him down to his core. "There is a
matter of grave importance, Majesty," he replied, "but as you said, one
thing at a time."

The king looked at Declan, and said, "So, again, how goes the work?"

Declan indicated the magician. "Pug cleared more forest in a day than the men could in a week. A road to the highway has now begun and the construction of a redoubt is underway."

Balven had listened silently, then looked at his two brothers and said, "It might be wise to clear even more forest, and as soon as the redoubt is completed, start building a permanent garrison, a small fortress."

Daylon said, "Agreed. If we're going to press a claim to the western half of Ilcomen as now being part of Marquensas, and the rest as a vassal barony, we'll need more fortifications to the east. The new garrison in the Darkwood will serve as a staging point for that.

"Now, we will need to finish the road before next year's rains come, otherwise whatever we build there will effectively be cut off. Packhorses and mules will get there, but wagons will be hub-deep in mud if we don't get the stonework in."

Pug said, "If I may. On my world we have workers in stone— geomancers—magic-users who can create stone out of the soil already in place."

Daylon stared at him in amazement. "Truly? Can you bring them here?"

"A pair," said Pug. "It's an art practiced by a race of elves from . . ." He stopped. "It sounds far-fetched."

"Says a man who came here from another world," inserted Bernardo. "At this point everything I ever believed in has been proven to be more or less false, so I'm pretty open to anything right now." He looked to the king and said, "Sorry for interrupting, Majesty."

Daylon waved away the remark. "I fully agree."

"Two stone crafters are in residence on my home island. I can ask them to come. I fear their arts may be limited. When I aided Declan, I felt my strength to be only a fraction of what it is back home."

"Not as much stuff," said Nakor. "I knew that."

Hatu nodded.

"Even if they only help, it will still speed things along," said Balven. "Finishing that road means we can resupply through the winter.

It rarely snows much in the hills, and some years we get none below the mountains, but we can get drenching rain that makes travel all but impossible, and sometimes curtailed altogether because of flooding. A straight, stone road from here to that fortress could be the difference between defeating the Church or losing this throne."

"I'll see what I can do," said Pug.

Daylon looked at Hava and said, "I have a task for you if you're willing."

Hava's expression indicated she was ready for an argument. "I'm having a ship built on his world," she said, pointing at Pug, "So I can stay close to my husband, who wants to study . . . everything. I don't want to be—what is it, an admiral?—and command a fleet."

"I want you to command a fleet," said the king, "but not as an admiral."

"Whatever the title, I won't do it," said Hava.

Hatu was about to say something, but she held up her hand and her eyes held a warning. Hatu stopped before he started and sank back into his chair a little.

The king said, "I need the best captain this world has to offer, and if you can find a better one, I'll take him. But I don't need another warship, at least not yet: I need someone to sail food from his world"—he pointed at Pug—"to this one. We're on the verge of starvation and the Sanctuary has sent us all the food from Nytanny they can."

Pug didn't look pleased. "Sailing through a rift is tricky. The only time I remember someone attempting it, the ship ended up crashed on the rocks in Crydee.

"That's another long story. It can be done, and I think with enough preparations it can be a relatively short voyage, perhaps as short as a few hours, as the ends of the rift can be close to the docks here and there.

"Some time is required to ensure the best chance of success." Pug paused, then said, "I think it can be done."

Balven said, "I have no idea of the cost of food and livestock on your world, but we have gold in abundance, if your people value it."

"They do," said Nakor. "It often leads to mischief."

Pug said, "I'll send word to Sorcerer's Isle and have them begin arranging for grain—that will be easy. The other things—cattle, hogs, and vegetables—will take more time. We can manage to provide enough to feed your army for the near future, and the rest of your people until your own farms and herds begin producing more abundantly.

"I will stay here against any manifestation from the greater threat."

"Good," said the king. "We shall discuss that next." Looking at Hava he said, "Can you sail a ship through a hole between two worlds?"

Hava looked intrigued. "I'll need to know about different winds and tides, so I don't cause a disaster." She thought for a moment, then said, "You want a fleet then?"

"As much as that booty you took from the Pride Lords can buy to fill as many ships as you can muster."

Pug said, "We need to discuss details. We can try with a single ship first." He looked at Hava, who nodded her agreement. "There will be few sailing the Bitter Sea who cannot imagine a voyage to a distant world, let along sign on to man one."

"Let me see about that," said Hava. "I have an idea."

"No doubt," said Hatu, repressing a smile.

"Good," said the king. "So, fortifications are in progress and food being sought."

Daylon paused a moment, sitting back a little, and then looking at Pug he said, "Now, as loath as I am to ask this, Pug, tell us of this other menace to our kingdom."

"Not just your kingdom," said Nakor. "Everything."

"Everything?" asked Balven.

"He'll tell you," said Nakor, pointing at Pug.

The king looked displeased but said, "How much time do we have to prepare? And what sort of enemy is coming?"

Pug started to speak, but Nakor interrupted. "Nobody knows about time."

Hatushaly nodded. "Yes," he began, but Hava put her hand on his, stopping him.

"It will come when it comes," said Nakor.

"It?" The king looked confused. "Why it?"

"Because it's not an army, or it might be, but we don't know," said Nakor. He motioned to Pug.

Pug threw Nakor a dark look. He put aside his irritation, as that again echoed how Phillip saw things, and while his former persona was emerging more as days went by, Phillip would never be totally gone.

Composing himself, Pug took a breath, and began. "It's the Void, Majesty. To attempt to describe it will take a long time, but if you're willing to listen, I will try to share what we know of it. We've faced it many times before, in various guises and forms, agents working on its behalf, and still, we hardly understand it.

"It has some link to my world, going back perhaps to the creation of everything. We just don't know."

"If it's tied to your world, why would it come here?" asked Balven.

"Why not?" Nakor replied. "You don't have a lot of stuff here, what he calls 'magic,'" he said, pointing at Pug.

Pug said, "A host of magic-users on my world barely prevailed in our last conflict with the Void. Midkemia paid a terrible price but survived. Here, without that sort of power, this world would be consumed in days."

Nakor nodded. "Yes. Because if you got all the armies on this world to stop fighting and come together, you'd still lose."

The color drained from the king's face. Quietly he asked, "Can anything be done?"

"We need to work out how to take some stuff from Midkemia and bring it here. Then we can fight it."

"Is that possible?" asked Daylon.

"I don't know," said Pug, "but we'll try, somehow. Because here you need more magic to fight the Void than has ever been imagined in the history of this world."

Daylon slumped down in his chair, his hand over his eyes for a moment. With a tone more pleading than commanding he said, "Please, do whatever you can."

CHAPTER 18

MISSIONS

Donte bided his time.

For a day he returned to the farm and oversaw what was turning into a tiny enterprise. While this farm would never make anyone wealthy, it would provide shelter and food for the littlest children. The older children were toughening up a bit as they were being taught the finer points of brawling, eye gouging, blows to the throat, kicks to the groin, all designed to give a smaller fighter a moment's advantage to escape. None of the youngsters was likely to grow up to be a proper brawler, though David was putting on a little weight with steady food and exercise.

Mark showed some signs that he might do well at picking pockets, sleight-of-hand street grifts, and anything requiring dexterity and a good eye. The others would make decent farmers.

Tommy, the boy who had taken Donte to meet Healer, was showing remarkable quickness but he lacked size. Donte considered him a future night thief, but hardly fit for a fighting crew.

Now he was back in the Red Starfish, again trying to blend in. He had found a base at the Four Ravens and had paid Shad just enough silver to secure him a room on demand, but not enough that the innkeeper might try to poison him for his coin.

Pug had been generous with the purse, but his funds were dwindling, so he began looking for his own opportunities to replenish his means. And now he was beginning to fully comprehend what the kids had been up against.

When he recognized a street grift, the Mockers had ample muscle nearby to prevent a mark from causing harm to the grifter. He had witnessed some fairly sophisticated robberies, with teams of perhaps as

258 RAYMOND E. FEIST

many as four individuals working together. Whoever this Upright Man in Krondor might be, he had well-trained thieves in his employ.

Donte assumed that whatever other rackets the Mockers were undertaking were well in hand. His wanderings through the richer quarters of the city had shown him a lot of high walls, guards at gates, iron bars at windows, and an annoyingly loud population of barking dogs. At least the children had enough sense that their only play was a quick cut-and-run purse-grab in a busy market.

Still, Donte knew that nothing worthwhile ever came easily. If he was to see some success here in Port Vykor, he needed to upset the balance: as he often said, "out of chaos comes opportunity."

This was Donte's fourth trip to the Red Starfish and the second time he had encountered Burt. The burly worker was affable company. Donte kept the conversation trivial and still managed to draw out bits of information from him. He was getting well versed on local customs and attitudes. Port Vykor, and Donte assumed the Kingdom of the Isles, or at least this part, seemed like some cities on the mainland of North Tembria had been before the attack by the Pride Lords.

The population was varied from the rich and powerful down to the dregs of society, the majority being working people laboring away for their own goal. And that goal was simple: survival. Donte hadn't finished exploring the entire city, but he had visited most of it, and as cities went, this was a modestly prosperous one—for a shipping port. Other than ship-building, there were no industries here. No heavy manufacturing like King Daylon was undertaking in Marquensas, with foundries, kilns, carpentry shops, tanners, dyers. From what Donte had learned, all of that was up in Krondor, an ancient city compared to Port Vykor. Wagons, alone or in trains, left and arrived between the two cities almost daily. Again, Donte decided he would eventually need to take a trip to Krondor.

Since first coming to this inn, he had not spied the fancily dressed man he thought of as the boss of this crew from Kesh. But he had spent enough time watching the various members of that crew drift in and out to have some sense of whom he should approach when the time was right.

Burt said, "Got an early start tomorrow, so I'd best be off."

Donte glanced out of the door and saw the light was only fading a little and said, "Must be damned early if you're heading home now."

Lowering his voice, Burt said, "Got one rolling in on the morning tide and tomorrow's will be sweeping in before dawn. It's a damned three-moon pull, so you know how that is."

Donte nodded. He had no idea what a "three-moon pull" was, though it clearly had something to do with the tide.

After Burt left, Donte kept watch on the Keshians until there were only two left, one of them being the man he had marked as his likeliest contact. He wandered over and caught that man's eye, and with a slight motion of his head, indicated he'd like a moment with him.

The Keshian's brow furrowed, but he indicated that Donte should approach and sit with him.

When Donte did so, he said, "What?"

"Business," replied Donte.

"We don't do business," the man replied. His accent was slightly difficult for Donte. He prided himself on having a good ear when it came to cutting through accents, but this man spoke as if he had pebbles in his mouth.

"I know you don't," Donte answered, "but the man you work for does. I would like to speak with him."

"I don't know what you mean," said the smaller of the two men.

The other spoke in harsh tones, and Donte realized whatever magic Pug or Magnus had used so Donte, Hava, and Hatu could understand languages here appeared to have worn off somewhat. He understood the languages he'd heard on Sorcerer's Isle, and here, but he didn't understand the language these two spoke.

He interrupted and said, "Tell your boss I know where the Mockers are holing up and it's a good bet they still have the loot they took from you tucked away there. If he's interested, I'll be here tomorrow."

Before anything more was said, Donte rose and left the inn as quickly as he could—without running.

MAGNUS LOOKED RELIEVED WHEN PUG stepped through the rift from Garn. He sat upon a stool in the otherwise empty chamber. "Should we shut this down now?" he asked.

"With Hatu still there, I think so."

"Good," said Magnus and the rift blinked out as he waved a hand. "I've had that portal watched every minute. It's a little difficult staying alert when things are so quiet, but something horrible might pop through at any time."

"I understand," said Pug. He looked at the stool and said, "You could have fetched in something more comfortable."

"And risk dozing off?"

Pug, with a smile, conceded that *was* a risk. Then he asked, "How goes everything else?"

Magnus got up and they started to walk. "As we should have expected, your returned early memories have sparked a lot of questions about how we are running the island."

Pug turned to look at the man who was both his son and his mentor, and said, "I haven't forgotten my memories as Phillip just because I remembered my earlier life. I remember your admonitions when teaching me, and yet I now remember admonishing you when I was telling you." He chuckled as they continued to walk. "It's a puzzler, as Kulgan used to say."

"So many memories returning must be difficult at times," Magnus suggested.

"Not really. The years I had none of those memories give me a distance today. Well, to the pain anyway. I remember losing your mother. If I tried, I know I could return to the feelings of horror in that moment, watching that demon feigning death leap up and kill her, but I suspect that memory is more painful for you than for me."

"I resist comparing my personal pain to that of others," said Magnus as they reached the small garden with a fountain outside what had been Pug's personal portion of the villa and was now occupied by Magnus. "Do you want a bite, or shall we sit and talk here?"

"Your mother always liked this garden," said Pug, sitting on the long bench. Magnus sat next to him. "We can work out the confusion over my being who I am eventually, I'm certain, but for the moment I'm very comfortable with your leadership, as it's what I've known for years. I certainly have no desire to return to my dark state of mind during the last confrontation with the Void. As we have no idea how much time we have before the assault on Garn truly commences, let's put aside morbid introspection and look forward as much as we can.

"The problem seems to be that even with Hatushaly returned home, the level of magic there is low by our standards. I'm not sure moving every magic-user we can muster there would help much."

Magnus said, "I believe you're right." He looked out over the meadow and said, "It's hard to remember the fury of that final battle, and how I survived is still a mystery to me. One moment everything around me was exploding out of the ground. Even with my shielding spells, I was thrown into the sky so fast I blacked out, only to regain my wits a little while after, almost a mile away without a mark."

Pug had bargained with the Goddess of Death, his life in exchange for Magnus's, but felt no need to share that with his son. "Sometimes we get lucky. Remember the Followers of Chance?"

Magnus nodded. "Strange cult, putting themselves in harm's way, so if they survive it's a sign of the Goddess of Luck's favor."

"They may be a bunch of mad heretics, but perhaps they know something about luck we don't. In any event, let's focus our minds on the problems at hand, and leave such speculations for another time. You may never know how you survived the battle at Magician's End while I did not."

Magnus looked at Pug and said, "Or why you're back?"

"Especially that. And Nakor? Of all the improbable things we know, including my return, his manifestation is the most remarkable. Even he seems to be at a loss to explain how it's possible."

Magnus chuckled. "Knowing him, even if he did know he might keep that to himself."

"True," said Pug, conceding the point. "He isn't exactly the most forthcoming person we know. So, what else around here needs addressing?"

Magnus stood up. "Come with me. Something I was told about while waiting at the rift, and I think you'll want to see it as well."

Pug followed Magnus and said, "What are we going to see?"

"The young adept from Garn—Sabella—has come up with an idea that got Wejuan excited."

Pug barked out a laugh. "Wejuan? Excited? This I must see."

They walked quickly around the hill to the entrance to the library and, once inside, saw Wejuan directing some of the students, urging them to hurry along.

"What is all this?" Magnus asked.

Wejuan frowned and said, "Finished guarding the rift, I see. Come along." She turned and headed toward what both men knew was one of the larger study spaces.

Once through the door to the study area, they saw Sabella sitting alone at a long table with a dozen different books, scrolls, and one clay tablet arranged around her, while she was writing on a large piece of paper. She looked up at the two magicians and smiled, then turned her attention back to what she was writing.

"What's this?" Pug asked.

"This marvelous child you brought over from that other world—"

"Zaakara brought her over," Pug corrected.

Wejuan's expression darkened and, ignoring his correction, she continued, "—has contrived to investigate something you idiots never considered."

Magnus seemed amused by this exchange but kept silent.

"What exactly is she doing?" Pug asked.

Without looking up at him, Sabella said, "I'm cataloging all the similar elements in a spell, like 'find water,' which while simple seems to have about a dozen different and elaborate incantations to get to what works. Zaakara mentioned something to me, and I realized—" She interrupted herself and grabbed the document she was studying, and then wrote a note on the paper before her. Continuing, she said, "Zaakara explained that almost everything you know about magic is from trial and error. So, one of your problems in teaching is that each student has to . . . flail about trying to discover which version of these spells best suits that student's nature. It seems to me that by having only the common elements of the spellcraft to learn, the process will go much faster, more smoothly, and safer."

Pug and Magnus exchanged surprised expressions. Both knew the other was thinking: why didn't we think of this?

Wejuan said, "Now, you two go away. Leave her to work," and she shooed them out of the door. Once outside, she said, "I don't care what sort of horrible menace you're worried about. You go deal with that, and when we survive whatever it is, she doesn't go back to that other world. I'm keeping her!" She turned around and walked back into the study room.

Pug and Magnus looked at one another and Pug finally said, "It's been a long day. I need a drink."

Magnus said, "I won't argue."

They headed out of the library and back toward Magnus's quarters, where Pug knew that his son had at least one good bottle of something stashed away. "That was impressive," Pug said.

"Very," Magnus agreed.

"I need to talk to Mal and Eliot, as soon as I find time."

"The geomancers?"

"I need to see if they might be willing to travel to Garn and help King Daylon build a stone road."

Magnus nodded.

"Before the Church launches its war against them."

Magnus visibly sagged a bit and said, "Yes, it is most definitely time for a drink."

DECLAN WATCHED HATUSHALY DUPLICATE WHAT he had seen Pug do, effortlessly lift trees out of the ground and toss them away. He'd watched for two days since returning to the building site of the new redoubt, and still he was amazed.

He remembered how not too long ago they were two young men, about to wed the women they loved, leading relatively mundane lives. He was a smith, and Hatu was the new owner of Gwen's father's inn, struggling to learn his new trade in an almost comic fashion, yet somehow succeeding. Those were much simpler times. He felt that to his bones. Now Hatushaly was some kind of master of magic, and Declan was to be the next King of Marquensas.

Or a footnote in history, he thought bitterly.

He might be little more than the next victim of the Church of the One. In their onslaught, they'd already burned one king at the stake.

A dark foreboding rose in him, and Declan felt mounting dread when he considered it might be some other horror he didn't fully understand.

He pushed aside those numbing fears, took himself away from the traps of his own mind, and returned to his fundamental belief: deal with what's before you, not what may come one day.

When Hatu finished, he turned to Declan and said, "That took more than I thought." Workers were rushing with picks and shovels to start filling in the large hole left by the tree. "I now understand what the differences are between here and Midkemia that Nakor told me about."

Declan looked around. "Speaking of Nakor, where is he?"

"Who knows?" replied Hatushaly. "I don't know him well, but I think I'm safe in saying he's the most capricious person I've ever met. He makes Donte look predictable."

"Well, I hope wherever he is, he's doing something useful." Declan surveyed the work and said, "Between you and Pug, we've halved the time needed to create a defensive position." He looked to the sky. "If the rains hold off, we'll have this redoubt finished in a week or less."

"That's good," said Hatushaly. "I hope whatever Pug is doing back on Midkemia gives us what we need . . ." He let that thought go unfinished.

Declan knew he wasn't referring to the coming confrontation with the Church, but the conflict with the Void. With a curt nod, Declan acknowledged the point.

Declan was pleased that the work was going well. The first embankments were finished, and stonework and woodwork were being overlaid artfully. The freed Church engineers were hard at work building a well-protected firing position for Marquensas archers. Attacking Church soldiers would have to scale a head-high berm, then cross a ditch, before being confronted by a ten-foot-high wooden wall. A riser behind this gave archers a second position from which to fire down upon attackers. The Church might breach the wall, but they'd pay a vicious price to do so.

The pathway from the east remained as Declan had found it. The Church would have to come out of that narrow trail no more than two men at a time and would be within the archers' range as soon as they appeared.

Still, it wasn't a stone fortress with stores and water enough to withstand a siege. At this point, it was a choke point to force the enemy to withdraw and find a longer route around the forest to attack Marquenet. If the attack came within a week, Declan knew he could bloody the Church army, but defeat it? Out of the question.

Turning to Hatushaly, he said, "Do you need more rest before we return to—?"

Before he could finish, they were standing in the throne room in the castle. Declan almost lost his balance and just caught himself. He looked around with an expression of amazement. "I thought you had to touch me to carry me here!"

Hatu looked around in his turn. "I did touch you, with my mind."

Declan saw the one guard before the door to the king's chambers was trying to regain his composure after the sudden appearance of the prince and his companion.

"I will never get used to this," Declan muttered as he motioned for Hatu to follow him into the king's study. He knocked once and began opening the door before Balven's voice bade them enter.

Balven sat back as the two came in, and said, "How goes it?"

Declan sat opposite his brother and Hatu took the next chair. "Better than we could have hoped. Between Pug and Hatu we've gained weeks in preparation. If the Church lingers for another month, we'll hold the forest without question. Perhaps even if they wait two more weeks."

"If Pug can persuade those rock magicians, whatever they're called—" said Balven.

"Geomancers," Hatu supplied.

"—to help, and we can finish that road, we can start patrols between the north and south garrisons and the Darkwood and hit their army in the flank if they skirt the forest."

"Where's Daylon?" Declan asked.

"Out riding with the cavalry. He said he had a few ideas to improve their training, but I think he just needed to get out of the palace and get on a horse."

Declan let out a long breath. "I fully understand."

"So, what news from that magician friend of yours?" Balven said to Hatushaly.

"No word from Pug as yet," he replied. "He should return soon: he's not one to be careless in important matters. And I'm certain those things he and Nakor warned us of are very important."

"Speaking of that funny little man," said Balven. "I haven't seen him with you for a while. Did he return to the other world?"

Hatu gave an uncertain gesture, and said, "Actually, I have no idea where Nakor is."

NAKOR SAT IN A TREE, eating his last orange. He scolded himself for not having discovered the whereabouts of a fruit vendor in Marquenet. Marquensas was rich with groves and the oranges were good. He preferred the deep-red fruit pulp of his native Isalani blood oranges, but they didn't seem to exist on this world.

Licking juice off his fingers, he peered down into the village below in the southern branch of Garn's Wound. He'd been observing people called Eaters for the better part of the day. He knew as soon as he reached this area that very bad things were happening here. This part of the valley had been rigorously avoided by the men Declan had discovered stranded in the northern part of Garn's Wound. With good reason, Nakor thought. Freakish magic had played havoc with this region, and Nakor was at a loss to explain how the events on Midkemia at Magician's End related to this world. He usually found odd questions delightful, but not this one. This one involved a massive threat to everything, and that was not amusing.

He was missing many of his memories. He imagined that he might have seen other things as sad as this, but he couldn't bring any to mind. He was still puzzling out what was missing and had given up on why. Some power had decided he needed to be here, and maybe he'd find out why and who, and maybe not.

He had borne witness when Pug defeated the Void's attempt to invade Kelewan from a higher energy reality. The most powerful creature of the Dread had been rising through that reality on its way to destroy the mortal realm. The only way to defeat the Dasati had been to destroy Kelewan, which was being overrun by the more powerful invaders.

The last thing he recalled was dying on the Dasati world, and then he had found himself walking the Hall of Worlds toward the door into Garn. It was as if only a moment had passed.

The memory of that destruction had been bouncing around in the back of his brain ever since. He had a germ of an idea how to fight the next battle, but it wasn't properly formed yet. He'd let it keep bouncing around.

His attention was now focused on some bloody rite the people below were conducting. This area abounded with odd animals: a pig-like creature with quills like a porcupine seemed to be a staple of the people's diet, and several were being slaughtered and thrown into the pit to the creature below.

Nakor could feel only sadness at what he saw. These were a people in thrall to dark forces from the moment of their birth. Whatever joy they felt must be savage, and there was nothing of love in their being. They were damaged beyond imagining, and he could see nothing less than divine intervention could save them. And, as Nakor well knew, the gods' benevolence was in short supply.

He surveyed the parts of the valley he could see from his perch and decided that the sun was setting low enough that he might find himself stuck here all night if he didn't leave. That would not be a good thing. Besides, he had seen enough.

Climbing down the tree quietly took a bit of time. Once on the ground, Nakor knew where he needed to go. His oak staff was where he had left it in order to climb the tree, so he shifted his rucksack and grabbed the staff.

He started his trek up a trail that led to the centermost point of Garn's Wound. As he hiked, remaining alert for trouble, he reflected on the moment he'd stepped through the door into Garn and discovered he stood right outside the library on Sanctuary Island. And to his delight, he'd sensed that an old friend stood nearby. When he had seen Pug, it had taken him a moment to recognize him, because he had a new body.

Still, it was Pug. Nakor's delight had immediately been tempered by the realization that if it was Pug, then trouble was certainly at hand. As much as he had enjoyed his time with Pug, Magnus, and the others he had known over the years, he always found some catastrophe or another swirling around Pug.

Nakor reached the spot he sought, a stand of trees just south of where the trail intersected with the east-to-west trail, and he spied the doorway behind a tree. Those who could see such portals were rare on each world, but there were seemingly endless worlds, so there were a lot of people using the Hall, and that, in itself, represented danger. Many of those using the Hall were simple travelers, some occasional merchants, but there were also predators. The attraction for many traveling the Hall was a lack of time passing, so they didn't age, which meant there were some very ancient and practiced predators to avoid.

He gripped his staff and stepped into the Hall of Worlds.

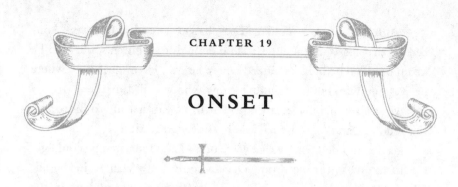

CHAPTER 19

ONSET

D aylon read the message.

"It's begun," he said to Balven and Declan. "Scouts report an army of the Church has been sighted west of the Dangerous Passage. Church outriders almost took one of the scouts by surprise, but he escaped. He estimates from the road dust it's a large force, perhaps a thousand men."

"No more 'reconnoiter in force' nonsense," said Declan.

Balven said, "If they're on the road from the Dangerous Passage, do they intend to strike at Beran's Hill?"

"Once the scouts got away, one brought the message here, and the others began shadowing the Church army," said Daylon, putting down the report. He was silent for a moment, then said, "At least we know they're not coming through the Narrows. Church ships would have been sighted days ago and we have no word from our fortification down there.

"So, we muster our forces and ready to move either east to the redoubt or north to Beran's Hill. We leave the city defense brigade and militia here.

"I want the mercenary companies outside the city at muster," he added. "I don't want them inside the walls while we muster regular soldiers outside. The city watch has enough on its hands without the added confusion. They won't have time to deal with a bunch of drunken mercenaries brawling in some tavern."

"I wish we could use Hatushaly's jump ability to scout them out," said Declan.

"Too dangerous," said the king.

"Agreed," Declan replied. They had discussed it but were concerned that Hatu might appear close enough to Church soldiers to be taken or killed before he realized where he was. He might know where he was jumping, but he wouldn't know who was already there.

After a moment, Declan said, "Still, he can get me to Sixto and the redoubt, and I can be back here if needed in time."

Daylon nodded, and with a wave of his hand indicated he could go.

In the main throne room, Declan could feel a change in the air. The scout had almost certainly said something to the soldiers in the garrison and word had spread. Each soldier he passed was a little more tense, a bit more on edge, and when he was saluted, it was a more formal bracing and slapping fist to chest than he was used to.

They knew war was coming.

Declan hurried to the king's library, which had been established by his great-grandfather, to find Hatushaly. It was nothing compared to the library on the other world, or even the Sanctuary, but it contained some interesting volumes, according to Hatu.

As he had expected, the spy-turned-innkeeper-turned-magic-user was engrossed in a book that looked older than the castle. Hatu looked up and smiled.

"I thought you could read those in an instant," Declan said, snapping his fingers for emphasis.

"I can, but I've discovered that my memory of a page is somehow 'fixed,' so it's not quite the same as rereading it, where I might discover something new."

"I'll take your word for it," said Declan. "Reading has never been a big part of my life."

"True of most people," Hatu replied, "Since most people can't read. Your education at Oncon was unusual."

"Edvalt taught me so I could see if we were being cheated on contracts."

Hatu laughed and put the book down. Standing up, he said, "The life of a blacksmith."

"Indeed. Can you take me to the redoubt?"

"When?"

"Now would be good."

"Very well," said Hatushaly. "But time is growing short to inter-cept Bodai and bring him back."

"Should we do that first? It shouldn't take too long, right?"

"We can hope," said Hatushaly. "When I was on Sorcerer's Isle, my energy seemed endless. Here I find I tire more quickly, and my abilities grow weaker when I do. I just took Hava down to the Sanctuary so she could reclaim the *Queen of Storms* and sail to the island of Shechal to see about ships. Three trips in so short a time? We run the risk of getting to Bodai's ship, then finding I can't return all three of us . . . or worse."

"Worse?"

"I don't know what might happen if I try to return here and we jump short."

"Short?" Now Declan's concern was evident.

"End up swimming in the Narrows or standing on an empty road in Ilcomen. Sharks, or bandits?"

Declan squinted at him. "Are you joking?"

Hatu laughed. "Only a little." He put his hand on Declan's shoul-der and said, "I think if I get too tired, it just won't work—the jump, I mean."

"And we would be stuck on a ship heading in the wrong direction?"

"Yes, and ships are hardly a great resting place. I've slept on them before, but I think I need more than sleep. I need quiet and perhaps some contemplation. I don't know. Even Pug is unsure of what my tal-ents are. From what I can tell, he probably knows as much about magic as anyone, but he often seems baffled by my abilities."

Declan considered. "The weather's good and it's a two-day ride back from the redoubt now that the way has been cleared and you don't have to ride all the way around. If you take me there, then come back at once, how long before you can go after Bodai? Until we really un-derstand what's happening, getting the Kingdom of the Night involved might not be our best choice."

"Nor Bodai getting his throat cut," added Hatu. "I can take you there, return here, and with two days' more rest, I can go and fetch Bodai before he reaches any port in the Kingdom of the Night."

"Let's do that, then," said Declan. "I'll grab a pack and some travel clothing and be back shortly."

"I'll be here," said Hatu, sitting down again and reopening his book.

Declan hurried to his own quarters. As he crossed into the wing of the castle where he and his brothers lived, he muttered, "I wish I could jump from place to place like he does."

HAVA DRUMMED HER FINGERS ON the table. She had convinced Hatu that she needed to be here, and he knew better than to argue. So now she was sitting in a bar and brothel called South House in a town named Shechal on an island of the same name, across the table from Red Sweeney. "Well?" she said.

The older man smiled. The fringe of grey hair surrounding his bald pate was neatly trimmed, he wore a freshly washed shirt, and he still sported rings on every finger, but he did look a bit more fatigued by life. "You know, you've pretty much put everyone here out of business." He sat back and gulped down a shot of rum, signaling to the barkeep to bring another.

"Not much smuggling going on?"

"Without the Pride Lords and those damaged Azhante, you could bring in any cargo you could imagine and land on the docks of any port in Nytanny, have a parade, and no one would care. You've reduced brilliant smugglers to ordinary merchants!"

Hava had spent enough time with him to recognize that Sweeney was only half joking. Almost everyone in Nytanny was overjoyed at the end of the Pride Lords' rule. The Pride Lords might be gone, but more critical to the smugglers was the absence of a market.

What the Pride Lords had called the "slave nations" were now city states, tribal regions, and contained warlords frequently at war with their neighbors. Their appetite for luxury was on the wane, since constant warfare was their main concern these days.

"I have a possible solution, for the short term at least, to your friends' problem," Hava said. She knew that Red Sweeney had "retired" before she met him, but still cared for the people he had sheltered and done business with for years.

"What would that be?" he asked.

"How many ships and reliable crews can you muster?"

He laughed. "How soon do you need them? I can have a dozen here in ten days. Give me a month, and I could have a hundred."

"A dozen good-sized ships will be plenty," she said. "But the hard part is I need captains and crews who are not afraid of taking risks."

Red Sweeney laughed. "They're smugglers! They take risks every day."

"This is a different kind of risk," said Hava calmly. "We're going to need calm minds and steady hands."

"What do you have in mind?" he asked as a barmaid brought over a fresh bottle of rum.

He started to pour a second drink for himself and offered one to Hava, who shook her head, then said, "As impossible as it may seem, I need a small fleet of cargo-haulers to sail to another world and back."

He stopped pouring. "What?"

"I said—"

"I heard what you said," he replied, putting the bottle down. "Another world? Sail there? Too much sun on the quarterdeck without your hat?"

"Seems mad, I know," she said, "but I'm as serious as I was about ending the Pride Lords. You still doubt me?"

"Girl, I doubt my own senses. For a youngster, you've proven yourself more than once. You're as tough as an old boot. So, how does this magic work?"

She laughed. "Magic is exactly how it works." She motioned for the offered drink.

"Change your mind?"

She nodded and, after he filled her cup, took a swallow and said, "This will take some explaining."

"I'm not going anywhere," he said, sitting back comfortably in his chair.

Hava started by recounting a little of what Hatushaly was doing, and the legend of the Firemanes. She glossed over most of what had occurred during the attack on North Tembria by the Pride Lords. Then she skipped over what Red Sweeney already knew about the Sanctuary and the Flame Guard and spoke instead of Hatu's training there and the arrival of the magicians from Midkemia. She barely understood some of it herself, but Red Sweeney asked no questions, so she was able to get to the point of Midkemia having food to sell, and her needing ships to carry the food to Marquensas.

When she finished, Red Sweeney shook his head slowly and said, "Now, that's quite the tale." He was silent for a long moment, then said, "Another world, and you've been there?"

She nodded.

"What's it like?"

"Not unlike here, but with three moons and rougher seas."

"Three moons!" He sat back, his expression rapt. "That must be quite a sight."

"If you feel a tug of adventure, come along," she said in a teasing tone. "You've often told me what a brilliant seaman you were in your youth, or did you forget how to captain a ship in your old age?"

"Old age?" he said in mock outrage, slamming his hand on the table. "I damn well might. Old age!"

"Good, so that's one ship. I'm taking back the *Queen of Storms* for this voyage and I'm going through alone to test the passage. She's the nimblest ship ever built here, so if I survive, I'll know what ships we need, and how to sail this route."

"You're a bold one, Hava, I will say that." Red Sweeney poured another round, then asked, "How many ships?"

"As many as we can find with crews to match. Gold we have, but it's food we need. If I had four or five barges like *Borzon's Black Wake*, that would do it for a year. From what I've been told, the magic hole we'll sail through could handle that size, but we're going to be dealing with a sudden change in tide and winds, so I'll need smaller freighters. If the shift from one sea to the other is severe, a big wallowing freighter could break deep or capsize. Smaller cargo-haulers should do, as we'll sail only an hour or so from port, go through the rift, then appear back here just outside Port Toranda. We can offload there, get everyone paid, and those that wish can sail back here."

"Assuming we all survive," said Red Sweeney with a deep laugh, the rum obviously starting to have an impact on his mood.

"So, how many nimble freighters, like the coasters that run along here or out to the Border Ports, can you get?"

"I can get you a hundred in two or three weeks, but it's not ships, it's captains and crews willing to give this a try. I can count on three others for certain, and another dozen or so likely. I know some fools who would come, but they're bad enough captains they'll likely run into each other, so we won't ask them."

Hava pulled out a small purse and put two gold coins on the table, then slid them toward Sweeney. "For your time."

Red Sweeney laughed again. "How much we paying the lads?"

"It's loading and unloading that will take time, so tell them we'll pay them a full voyage's pay for two days' work at sea, loading and un-loading, if all goes well."

"That should convince them."

"Good. Time is vital. We're not that far from half the people in North Tembria starving." Hava stood and said, "I've got to sail back to the Sanctuary. Send me word there when you know what we can do."

"Good," Red Sweeney said, lifting his mug of rum in a salute.

"All this depends on me sailing the *Queen* through that hole be-tween worlds and living to tell you about it."

"Good fortune, then," said Sweeney. "If you drown, I'll weep."

She chuckled, and as she walked out of South House she said, "I highly doubt it."

NAKOR LOOKED AROUND AS HE stepped out of an empty warehouse. He wasn't certain where he was, except that it was on Garn. He had taken a gamble on a door to Garn he didn't recognize, rather than return to the Sanctuary. There he could see if Hatu turned up to take him back to Marquenet, or sail for weeks. Besides, he was a gambler by nature and the unknown appealed to him. If the door was a bad option, he could always return to the other door.

He looked both ways and saw that the street was empty. From the angle of the sun, he knew he was east of Garn's Wound, and from the cool afternoon air, much farther north.

From the sounds down the street, he realized he was close to a busy market district in some town, somewhere. The fading light told him it was just before sunset. How long the twilight lasted would give him a rough idea of how far north he was. He paused and watched the sky for a few minutes. Not that far north, he judged, as the light began to fade quickly. But he was fine with that, for if he was going to wander around in an unknown place, darkness suited him.

Nakor walked toward the sound and when he peered around the corner, he saw a market was indeed but one street away. He kept close to the building but, knowing that skulking was only likely to draw attention, he moved at a reasonable pace. Long ago he had given up worrying about blending in, opting instead for the tattered orange robes he had worn for as long as he could remember. To whomever might take notice, he was a traveler from a faraway land. Here on Garn, that was especially true.

He approached the rear of a crowd gathering in a large square, some holding torches and waving them. As it darkened, more torches would appear, he knew. It was a noisy assembly and Nakor felt safe in getting closer. No one was paying attention to another gawker.

Peering over the shoulders of taller men required Nakor to stand on tiptoes. It was only by moving around that he finally made sense of the event. A scaffold with three posts had been erected and he realized the crowd was there to witness an execution. Wood had been piled at the base of each post, so he knew it would be a burning.

A rising feeling of disgust caused him to turn away; he'd seen enough such public theater in a long life to have no interest in witnessing another. At least the burning would prove a distraction as he moved through the town.

He was leaving the scene when he noticed several soldiers walking slowly around the outskirts of the crowd, watching. They were dressed in black livery, their tabards marked with a circle of white in the middle. Nakor also noticed a marked lack of enthusiasm among many of those gathered to witness the execution.

He intuitively knew that attendance to the event was mandatory for adult men—there were no women or children present—and that those who were not yelling insults or cheering loudly would be marked for further watching, and perhaps interrogation. As one soldier drew nearer, Nakor raised his right arm in the air and made a fist, shaking it at the empty scaffold. He shouted a meaningless noise.

The soldier walked by and when his back was to Nakor, the little man scurried farther away. He resigned himself to having to witness this ordeal, for to leave early would make him noticeable, and while he wasn't too worried about eluding a chase, he'd rather not be bothered until he knew exactly where on Garn he was. For the moment, he hoped this was North Tembria, rather than on the Church-controlled continent of Enast. Given the half-hearted behavior of the crowd, he suspected he was. These people were not true believers but recent converts, probably at the point of a sword.

On the other side of the scaffold a wagon appeared, and three bound prisoners were roughly forced to their feet and offloaded. Guards half-carried them up wooden steps to the three posts where they were quickly bound atop the piles of timber.

A man in a black robe waved the crowd to silence. Then he spoke in a loud, well-practiced voice. "Heresy will be torn out, root and branch, never to be spread."

Nakor ignored the rest of the litany of charges: he had unfortunately heard the like before, in many places. He had no idea if the three unfortunates were guilty or not. He also suspected the Church didn't care, if it needed to make examples of them.

The first prisoner was an old man barely conscious after a beating, evidenced by the cuts and bruises on his face. The next was a man of middle years, who seemed stoically accepting of his fate. He put up no struggle and stayed silent. The third was barely more than a boy, a terrified and confused youngster, who was crying as he kept repeating he was sorry. The latter two also showed clear signs of recent beatings.

Nakor started looking for his best route away from the market and decided he'd head west, if he could be certain which way was west. Given where the light had faded last, he had a rough notion, but he'd prefer a more certain idea of where he was. Going off even slightly north or south could end up leading him a long way in the wrong direction.

He glanced up. None of the stars looked familiar, of course. It was not a familiar sky.

Once the three victims were secured, the guards moved away, and torches were brought out and the pyres were set afire.

Nakor had seen countless deaths since his birth. It was the nature of life that it always ended in death, but dying in flames was as bad as it got. The sudden smoke informed him that the wood had been treated with oil, perhaps creosote, to hasten the flames. Nakor hoped it rendered the three prisoners quickly unconscious, as a slow fire without smoke was horrible torture before death.

The three all started coughing, and the old man went limp first. The skin on his bare legs began to bubble, then ignite. The flames rose quickly as his clothing caught fire.

The boy's crying turned to screaming and he gulped air and coughed. Then his screaming fell away as he also went limp. He was also soon engulfed in flames, and his unconscious body became a dark silhouette within blinding flames which ate him away, parts of him falling off as ash.

The man who attempted to remain silent was at last overcome by pain and started screaming. The dreadful sound was interrupted only by coughing and gagging sounds, then abruptly falling silence.

Nakor pushed down a deep disgust. He knew he could change nothing and lashing out against the Church officials in attendance would likely bring retribution on the innocent citizens of this town.

The crowd waited, attempting to sound enthused, but when the robed priest and guards left the scaffold, the crowd immediately started to disperse. Nakor elected to follow an old man who was alone. Half a block down the street, Nakor stepped up beside him. "Hello," he said, "I am a traveler and chanced upon this town at sundown. Can you tell me where I am?"

The old man stopped and stared down at Nakor, who was a full head shorter, and laughed. "You don't know where you are?"

Nakor grinned. "That is frequently the case. I set out, find a road, and sometimes just follow it to see where it leads."

"You are in the town of Jantaroo."

Nakor nodded. The name sounded vaguely familiar, as if he might have heard it before. Taking a guess he said, "Sandura?"

Pointing, the old man said, "That way."

"Thank you," said Nakor, turning in the indicated direction.

Once he was out of the old man's sight, he stopped. The citizens of this town obviously got off the streets early, as there were no sounds of a lively tavern or even people chatting as they strolled around. He judged that the Church frowned on fun.

He paused for a moment and considered it lucky he was in North Tembria. He then considered it unlucky he was on the wrong side of the continent. Walking to Marquensas was possible but would take far too long. He decided to double back the way he had come and enter the Hall of Worlds again, seeking out another exit to Garn. Failing that, he could always return to the Sanctuary and take a ship back to where he needed to be.

As he carefully walked back, staying in the shadows as much as possible to avoid Church soldiers on patrol, he decided that while the coming fight with the Void was inescapable, until it fully manifested it was imperative to end the Church. He was certain they were an instrument of the Void. He was firmly convinced everything evil that had happened on Garn since Hatushaly's birth was connected to the Void. Its influence was insidious and far reaching.

DONTE SAT MOTIONLESS, KNOWING THAT any move he suddenly made would be the wrong move. He was sitting at a table surrounded by agents of Kesh, in the Red Starfish, when the man he thought of as the boss entered.

Saying nothing, he waited until the man sat down. The boss looked him up and down then finally said, "You know where the Mockers are hiding?"

Donte said, "I do, and you do as well. Somewhere in Sad Landing. But I know exactly where."

"How is that?" The boss leaned forward. "None of my men got close."

Donte smiled, resisting the urge to laugh. That told him a great deal about whom he was dealing with. Smugglers and fighters, but not a decent thief or spy in the bunch. "I have experience that perhaps your men lack. In any event, let's get to it. I'll happily tell you exactly where your loot is hidden and the best way to take it back."

"In exchange for what?" asked the boss, leaning back in his chair.

"Consider it a gesture of friendship. I am looking for certain business opportunities here in Port Vykor, and it's in my interest to have dangerous men like you . . . inclined to feel they have a reason to keep me healthy."

The boss smiled slightly at that, and said, "Perhaps a wise choice. What sort of business had you in mind?"

"I hail from a distant city, one I doubt you've even heard of, so I'm unsure of which opportunities here are best for me. I have dealt in goods with questionable provenance, and also in rare goods, over the years."

The boss's gaze narrowed, and he said, "You hardly look old enough to have done anything for years."

"Where I come from, we start very young. And one thing I know is that the most valuable thing is information. I have often dealt with that."

"What do you propose?"

"If you and your associates allow me to explore opportunities and then venture where I think my best opportunities exist, I will happily provide you with any information that comes my way which may be beneficial to you."

"You seek protection, then."

"In a manner of speaking." Donte relaxed a little as he realized that the odds of having his throat cut tonight had just declined. The boss was interested.

"From what I understand, these Mockers have been in the city longer than your . . . enterprise. They hold the advantage in snitches and locals inclined to curry favor. They are dug in and have an area of control, and you are trying to catch up. Is that about right?"

"Close enough," said the boss. He looked around the inn to see who else might be near and then said, "They have a more diverse crew and greater numbers. We are at a disadvantage."

That told Donte this crew was self-contained, not supported by anyone back in Kesh. He was delighted to hear that but kept his near-elation in check. He said, "Then information will suit your needs."

The boss nodded.

"On the westernmost boundary of Sad Landing, the street that empties to the center of the abandoned wharf, the broadest street, at the other end it empties into another broad street. Across from that intersection lies the entrance to the old underground market's basement levels, where fish were once delivered. It's there your loot is stored until they can move it, perhaps up to Krondor. I was told that all the old other entrances have been sealed off, except for one, a bolthole. If you can stop that up so they cannot escape, you have them trapped."

The boss nodded. "What you say is in keeping with what we already know." He sat back, seeming to relax, and his tone of voice shifted. "Even if we trap them, they outnumber us at least three to two. Rats in a corner, and all that, you see."

"Perhaps it's best if you let a few of them escape?" Donte offered.

"Then we have a street war. We need to drive them back to Krondor."

Donte considered for a silent moment, then said, "Give me more time and perhaps I can help with that as well."

"What do you have in mind?" the boss asked.

"My thoughts are not fully formed. I need some more information, but if you give me time, I can get it."

"If they move our loot out of the city, we will suffer greatly. My men are loyal, to a point. I still need to pay them."

"Understood," said Donte. "I will be quick."

"How quick?"

"Give me three more days," said Donte, standing up.

As he rose, the Keshians tensed, and Donte realized none of them understood the common language he and the boss were speaking. He saw that the man he originally spoke with was absent, so he assumed he was the boss's second in command.

The boss signaled for his men to relax, and they did. "What do they call you?" he asked Donte.

With a chuckle, Donte answered, "That depends on where I am. Here I am Peter."

"Very well, Peter," said the boss. "I am—"

Donte interrupted. "I think of you as the boss."

The man smiled broadly. "I rather like that!"

Donte said, "Three days, here?"

"Three days here."

As he left, Donte felt a sense of accomplishment that a first step had been taken. Now, if he could only work out what to do in the next three days . . .

CHAPTER 20

INCEPTION

Pug made his way to the bow.

The *Queen of Storms* was slowing, now that all her sails were reefed. Hava gave the order to drop anchor. When the ship was motionless save for a slight rise and fall with the combers, she went forward to stand next to the black-robed magician.

"Still enough?" she asked Pug.

He smiled. "It will have to do. Nothing's perfect." He looked around and said, "Though you did not exaggerate the quality of this ship. I'm not a sailor, but I've traveled on a few, and this is quite a beauty."

"I didn't build her," she said lightly, "but the second I saw her at anchor, I knew she was mine."

"You stole her, you said."

Hava nodded with a smile. "From a murderous band of men who deserved their bloody ending."

"I'd like to hear that story at some point," said Pug. Turning to look forward, he said, "But now I think it's time for me to get to work."

They were anchored a half-day's sailing from the Sanctuary, and Pug surveyed the horizon. "The trick," he said, "will be to test the relative levels of the two oceans. If they are not closely aligned, we'll see a waterfall, one way or the other."

"Then let's not get too close, agreed?" said Hava.

Pug nodded. "A moment," he said.

He stared ahead, then closed his eyes, and Hava saw his lips move, though he was silent. Then he made a quick gesture with his right hand and muttered again.

After a few minutes, Hava saw a silver oval appear, hovering in the water, the two-thirds in the air appearing to be roughly large enough for a rider on horseback to pass through it. Pug nodded, and said, "We can start."

"It's a bit small to sail through," said Hava dryly.

He smiled. "First a small boat. I need to get close to the rift."

Hava ordered a longboat lowered and four rowers shimmied down lines to the boat, with Hava following. Pug simply jumped—as Hava thought of his transport—to stand next to her. One of the sailors looked surprised, but the others appeared to have become used to his displays of magic.

They rowed to where the rift had appeared, a silver shimmering oval mainly above the water. As they got close, Hava had the men reverse their stroke, backing water to stop the boat, and said, "No waterfall on this side."

"That's a very good thing," said Pug. He untied a knot in his rope belt and loosened it, then deftly pulled his robe off over his head. Standing in a white breechclout, he stretched and said, "It's been a while since I've swum in the ocean. I hope I haven't forgotten how."

She gave him a dubious look, "You're going to swim through?"

He nodded. "Only way to be sure. If there's a waterfall on the other side, I can protect myself, and on Midkemia my powers will easily allow me to elevate myself to come back. Once I see if this works, we will establish where you want the rift to open in both worlds and how big it needs to be. Likely I'll need to do that from the Midkemian side as it will require a great deal of energy."

Without another word, Pug stepped up onto the gunwale and dived into the sea. He swam smartly toward the rift and vanished from Hava's view.

A sudden sinking feeling hit him in his stomach and Pug felt himself fall several feet and almost shoot out of the Midkemian side of the rift, for Garn's ocean was elevated perhaps six feet above the Bitter Sea. Fortunately, Pug was able to simply halt his fall and he hovered with water showering around him. He moved himself by will beyond the torrent of water and glanced around. The rift on this side was where he wanted it to be, a short distance from the west side of Sorcerer's Isle. Elevation was going to be trickier. Any stout ship could handle an easy drop of six feet or more, though it might rattle the cargo, but going the other way, trying to climb even six feet on inertia alone would be impossible without a strong wind. He might need Magnus's help to get it right, but at this point he judged the task doable.

He oriented the location and attempted in his mind to adjust the height. Somewhere in his past, his first life as Pug of Crydee, he had intuitively managed to create rifts at ground level, without having to think about it.

This challenge was fascinating, for the rift not only had to be large, but enough of it had to be underwater so that a ship could sail through.

He now fully appreciated the danger that long ago had driven a Tsurani Great One to attempt a rift during a storm on Kelewan. That failed attempt had carried his ship onto the rocks at Crydee. Pug felt slightly annoyed with himself that it had taken him two lifetimes to fully appreciate the problem.

And he was now aware that he was hanging in the air, dripping wet, and getting chilly. He transported himself to the entrance of the rift and started swimming upstream.

Immediately he was in calmer water and swimming toward the boat where Hava looked at him with a questioning expression. "Well?" she asked as he clambered aboard.

He shook off as much water as he could and said, "We can do it. I'll need more trial and error, and perhaps help, but it can be done."

She handed him his robe, which he lifted and dropped over himself. Tying his rope belt, he said, "Sometime I'll tell you a story about the first time I saw a ship that had tried this. I believe I made the same offer to Declan. One day when we're all together."

Hava said, "Good, but for now, let's get back to the ship." She gave the order and as the longboat began to swing around, Pug caused the rift to vanish.

"I know where to anchor that rift near Sorcerer's Island, but you'll have to show me where the other side needs to be here."

"Outside the port of Toranda," she answered. "Nearer to North Point is too shallow for a fleet of ships to appear suddenly and Port Colos is just too far away."

"Good," said Pug. He sat on the second seat ahead of the first pair of rowers and said, "I'm going on ahead to the Sanctuary, if you don't mind."

"In a hurry?" she asked, half joking.

"No. Hungry," said Pug with a laugh, then he vanished.

Shaking her head, she chuckled and said, "You and Donte."

NAKOR HELD AS STILL AS possible, pressing his back against a wall. The sound of footfalls grew fainter as the creature headed away from his location. He cursed himself silently and looked upward. There was a faint line in the ceiling, indicating the path through this maze.

He was almost certain he had passed through this way before, but it was so long ago and given the gaps in his memory he wasn't entirely certain where this particular way led. He knew there would be a door back to the Hall of Worlds somewhere nearby, but the creatures wandering around were very distracting.

When it was completely quiet, he took a breath, glanced upward again, then set out. As he walked, he wondered what the monsters ate when people didn't blunder into this maze. Each other?

Nakor cursed the powers that had brought him back to this existence. He knew he'd lost his humanity ages before, perhaps even before his death on the Dasati home world, Kosridi. He knew his very existence was something contrived by unknown agents. Perhaps the Midkemian gods, and prime among those suspects would be Ban-Ath, also called Kalkin, the trickster god. Or it could be some other agency. But whatever it was, which memories he kept and which were omitted seemed maddeningly random at this moment.

He knew he had entered that particular door in the Hall of Worlds for a reason, but he had no idea what that reason was. He could be given to foolish choices, occasionally dangerous ones, but never suicidal.

He had been trekking through the maze for some unknown time: it was hard to judge with no passing of a sun or movement of stars, and he had never been one to count his own heartbeats—that was too unreliable, given the heart sped up when one confronted danger. Still, he knew he had made some sort of progress.

Turning a corner, he realized he'd come to the end of the maze. A doorway hovered before him, and instantly he knew where he was. Mixed emotions touched him momentarily, as fragments of memories returned then faded before they could be fully apprehended.

Nakor pushed through the door and found himself once more in the Hall of Worlds, a seemingly endless roadway, marked on both sides with doorways that led into different worlds. Each had a sigil hanging above it, glowing against the dark grey of the void.

Nakor now remembered exactly where the maze he had encountered was: the "lost world" of Nokama, which was neither lost if one knew where to seek it nor, in fact, a world. Rather, it was an odd reality of disjointed places, somehow strung together apparently at random, yet it maintained a certain cohesion. He had fled through it before, he recalled, though was at a loss to remember why he had been fleeing. Nevertheless, while Nokama was as close to being the most impossible place he had once visited, it put him across the hall from a gap between two doors which appeared to be another view of the void.

He paused for a moment and considered. Why was the Void, an entity which seemed to be hell-bent on destroying all living beings now, and the void, the empty place, called the same thing? He found the question intriguing and decided he'd return to it later.

He stepped into the gap and manifested inside an entranceway.

Nakor knew that within the known reaches of the Hall of Worlds there were 1,117 known entrances to Honest John's Saloon. So, with knowledge of the Hall, the farthest one might travel was three weeks before finding an entrance. The entranceway was short, emptying into a slightly gaudy, but lavish, common room. Nakor relaxed.

"Kwad!" said Nakor, greeting the saloon's bouncer, a Coropaban giant nine feet tall and covered in black-spotted white fur. Ape-like in form, with a canine-type face, Kwad regarded Nakor with large, deep-blue eyes, grunted his reply, and held out his hand. Nakor nodded, and gave him the walking staff he carried, knowing he could retrieve it when he exited. One oddity of Honest John's was that all doors led to this one entranceway. Upon exiting, one merely had to tell Kwad which door one wished to travel through, and there you were. Nakor had long ago abandoned any hope of understanding exactly how everything in the universe worked, but this place still tickled his curiosity every time he passed through.

His last journey had been with Pug and Magnus, seeking to find a means to change their energy states and visit the Dasati home world. "How long ago had that been?" he wondered. Dying and returning seemed to play havoc with his sense of passing time.

One of the seemingly endless games of chance was underway, and Nakor resisted the urge to sit down at the table. Whatever other gifts he possessed for petty larceny and the like, Nakor considered himself first and foremost a gambler. Most of the time he was good enough that he didn't need to cheat. And he was a good enough cheat that most times he didn't get caught—but when he did get caught, he was very good at escaping.

Scanning the room, he caught sight of the owner, Honest John. It was by common consensus that Honest John was honest, and John was likely not his real name. As the establishment was the only oasis of life in rift-space, people felt the need to simply accept Honest John's identity.

Nakor wended his way through the crowd, some of whom were people who never left the Hall, because one never aged here; there were beings here who were virtually immortal as a result. There were predators who roamed the Hall, a threat to travelers and the lost, but Honest John's was neutral ground. He was about to slap away the hand of a would-be pickpocket when a creature resembling a shadow swooped in and carried the malefactor away. Honest John was a being who took the name seriously. Nakor grinned. There was a great deal about this place he profoundly enjoyed.

Nakor approached Honest John, who was sitting at his usual seat at the high stakes table. John was one of the few gamblers Nakor had met whom he held in high regard. His skills were prodigious, and he was able to smell a cheat before he could even sit down.

Glancing up, Honest John smiled. "Nakor! I thought you were dead."

"I was," Nakor replied. "May I have a moment?"

John glanced at his cards, folded his hand, and said, "Sitting out."
He pushed back his chair. "What do you require?"

"Does Vordam of the Ipiliac still do business above in the gallery?"

"He does," said Honest John. "He shared much of his dealings with
you and your friends when last you visited. It was quite a tale, lost gods
returning and all that."

"Then his shop is my destination."

"Do you have other needs? A room, companions? A game or two
perhaps?"

Nakor grinned. "Still trying to catch me cheating?"

"To live up to my name and be honest, I am still convinced no one
can be as lucky as you are without cheating, Nakor, yet every defense I
have against it, magic and mundane, shows me nothing."

Nakor said, "Time does not permit me to stay now, but should it be
possible, I'll return and relieve you of more of your wealth."

"I think I'd enjoy that," said Honest John. He watched as Nakor
moved deeper into the crowd until he vanished from sight and, with a
pleased expression, returned to his chair and resumed the game.

DECLAN AND HATUSHALY APPEARED IN the clearing, to be greeted
by a frenzy of activity. A soldier turned and dropped his axe at the sight
of his prince and the black-robed magician standing before him.

Declan saw Sixto and without a word hurried in his direction,
Hatu a step behind. He was impressed by the amount of work that had
been done in his absence. The redoubt was fully finished and now the
soldiers and engineers were working on a surrounding ditch, which
was almost fully dug, and were sharpening stakes to be planted between
the ditch and the wall.

Seeing Declan approaching, Sixto said, "Good, you're here. I just
dispatched a rider yesterday. The Church is moving this way."

"If they still think we're a troublesome patrol or small force they're
going to be shocked." Declan looked to the west. "How goes the road?"

"Still underway, but serviceable unless we get heavy rain. If your
magician friend can get those stone magicians you told me of, maybe

we'll be fine. But if the Church doesn't come through that narrow passage to here, and circles around to strike at Marquensas, and the rains hold off, we can hit them in the flank while they march."

"How many?" Declan asked.

"Perhaps two thousand, maybe more."

"Enough to lay siege to but not storm the city," Declan said. "They think we're still short of food, and perhaps of men—it depends on how many agents they had who got word back to Sandura. If they brought enough provisions for a siege, knowing that foraging is poor here . . ." He stopped and after a moment said, "If they do come down the narrow path, even with archers greeting them as they come into range, we'll run out of arrows before they run out of men."

"I can help," said Hatushaly. He still had not mentioned to Declan how he had aided him in Garn's Wound when he escaped the pursuing Eaters, or how he had stoked the flames that had destroyed the great doors to the Pride Lords' keep.

"How?" Declan asked.

"I can throw trees at them," Hatushaly said, only partially joking. "I have ways to move things, and I can start fires. Perhaps other things I haven't tried yet."

Declan seemed intrigued, but after a moment shook his head and said, "No. I don't fully understand, but what little I have gleaned from those black-robed magicians and that funny little man is that you are too vital to risk with even a remote chance of a stray arrow. By the time the Church's army gets here, you need to be far away."

Hatu seemed on the verge of arguing, but seeing Declan's and Sixto's expressions he ignored the impulse. "Very well, but if you think I can make a difference, I'm willing."

"I thank you. We've both come a long way since meeting in Beran's Hill, but I will always consider you a friend."

"As do I," said Hatu.

"And as a friend, I want to know you'll help save Marquensas even should I fall."

Sixto seemed about to say something, but Declan's expression caused him to remain silent.

"I will do everything to help," Hatu answered. But in his mind he knew that so much more was at stake than just the existence of one kingdom, and he also knew exactly what Sixto was thinking: without Declan there would be no future for Marquensas.

NAKOR MOVED THOUGH THE ALWAYS crowded main floor of Honest John's. Several hundred yards wide and twice as long, it was populated by as diverse a population as found anywhere in the universe. Most were humanoid and bipedal, but many were not, and over the centuries Honest John had fitted the place out to entertain any who entered his establishment, so long as they had the means to pay.

At last, he reached one of several large staircases to the upper gallery, a broad walkway that was flanked by shops, some vast, others tiny, and a few that were difficult to find. Had he not visited the shop of Vordam of the Ipiliac before, he might have spent days trying to locate it, but once in the gallery he made his way quickly there and entered.

As before, there was nothing remotely familiar to most humans denoting a shop. Rather than a counter, shelves, or cases, there were many large cushions littering the floor. Picking one close to the door, Nakor sat down.

Within a minute, Vordam appeared. He was tall, slender, and almost human, despite a long face, longer-than-human fingers, and a slight blue tint to his skin. He paused for a moment, studying his guest, then said, "Nakor the Isalani?"

Nakor used his staff to get to his feet. "You remember," he said.

"I remember all I do business with, no matter how long ago," said Vordam. "It is a gift of my race to have good memories, and those of us in trade hone it as finely as we can." He paused for a moment, then said, "Word came that you had died on the world of Kelewan when it exploded."

"Actually, I was between Kelewan and Kosridi, but close enough that I died."

"Apparently, things improved for you since then."

"That remains to be seen," Nakor replied.

What Nakor took to be a smile crossed Vordam's face. "How can I be of service?"

"It occurred to me that in reviewing what you told Pug on his first visit to this shop, and what you said to all of us when we returned, that you perhaps more than anyone I have met may know something about a problem Pug and I now face."

"Pug lives? We heard he died in the war with the Dread."

"He did," said Nakor with a wave of his hand. "He's back, too." His expression showed he didn't wish to explain. "When we traveled to Delecordia to stay with Kastor"—the magic apothecary who prepared them for the Desalt home world of Kosidri—"while we got ready to travel to the realm below this one, I was given the impression that the best analogy to how energy differs between realms is that of water running downhill."

"That is exactly the analogy I used when I first explained the planes. The concept of the seven heavens or hells is common to many worlds and peoples. And from what I have gleaned over a very long lifetime is that all reality is—"

"Like an onion," Nakor interrupted. "Pug told me that bit. Peel away a skin, and there's another layer below, and so on and so forth. But why seven? In each direction?"

"I can only surmise that is because wherever you live, the limits that perception and understanding can possibly bridge lies at fifteen levels, with your level being the center, and seven above, seven below."

"That seems reasonable," said Nakor, "especially as there's no means to test the theory. Just getting to the Dasati realm was difficult enough, and that was one below." He paused, then his brow knitted in thought. "Belog, the demon with my memories . . . He and Child walked . . . here. That's four levels!"

"I have no understanding of that occurrence. Was that during the war with the Dread?"

Nakor nodded and sat down. "That's a story. If you wish, I can share some of it."

Vordam said, "I'd like to hear it." He sat on a cushion opposite Nakor.

Nakor began by saying, "I have some memories that are not mine, and some of mine are missing. I may not even be Nakor. I may be a memory or echo, though it feels as though I am me."

Vordam said nothing, just nodded.

"When a demon named Belog gained my memories, he was smart enough to realize that a great battle was coming, and he set out with another demon, Child, who now possessed the memories of Miranda, Pug's dead wife."

"This is becoming unusual, even for me," said Vordam.

"It gets worse," Nakor said. He shared the story of the conflict that had concluded at Magician's End, with the time-frozen conflict between the greatest Dreadlord created by the Void, and the revived mind of Ashen-Shugar, last of the Valheru, the Dragon Lords, in the body of Tomas, Pug's lifelong friend."

When he finished, Nakor added, "I am convinced that struggle was not the last, and a bigger threat awaits us all."

"Us all?" asked Vordam. "All of Midkemia?"

Nakor said, "If only it were just that. I mean all of reality, all the realms," and with a sweep of his hand, he added, "Even here in this oasis in the rift-space."

"That strains credibility," Vordam said.

"I understand," said Nakor. "But if what we know about the Void proves to be accurate, this place, Honest John's, floats in the center of the very thing that seeks to destroy it."

"The Void is aware and has purpose?"

"The Void," said Nakor, emphasizing the name, "is nothing remotely like any life as we know it—it may not even be alive—yet it exists, is aware, and has fashioned . . . beings, that have come to harm us in the past. Wraiths, specters, wights, death dancers, demons, spirits: the names are endless, but they are all Children of the Void."

"For the first time in ages, you bring me disquiet."

"A reasonable reaction," said Nakor. "Have you wondered how this"—he waved his hand, indicating all of Honest John's—"came to exist in the middle of the Void, rift-space?"

"Few who've found their way here have not," Vordam replied.

"No one knows, as with the City Forever and the Garden, the Hall of Worlds itself. Existing within this void, but not consumed by it. Yes, we have all wondered at one time or another."

"Mysteries."

"Very much so," Nakor acknowledged. "Now let me ask this, where are we? By that I mean, where is Honest John's within rift-space?"

Vordam pondered the question for a few moments, then he said, "All here assume this is somehow at the center of the Void, a place linked in numerous places to the Hall."

"You said 'assume,'" Nakor observed.

"Mortal minds are limited first by perception, second by logic, and last by imagination, yet much exists beyond our ability to comprehend, and beyond that, our ability to be aware of that existence. We must again be willing to accept the existence of realms higher and lower than the seven above and below those we imagine." Vordam looked at Nakor, his expression one of concerned interest. "Just because we're limited in our perspective doesn't mean reality is also limited."

"Yet we know one thing: that energy, mana, juju, whatever it's called, flows downward like water."

"That is the prevailing theory."

"More than theory," said Nakor. "When Pug, Magnus, Ralan, Bek, and I traveled to Kosridi, both Pug and Magnus felt their powers diminished. Yet, Bek, a being of that realm, brought prodigious powers with him from our realm, the one above Kosridi."

"You have an idea, then?"

"One is forming. Before I share it, another question. Why are there low- and high-energy worlds in any realm?"

"My best surmise would be that within any level of reality, energy ebbs and flows like currents, but maybe in such a leisurely fashion as to seem ages from a mortal perspective. Perhaps, to use the water metaphor, swirling mountain lakes between cascades. Water levels may rise or fall gradually, but in a mortal's life span show little change."

"Ah!" Nakor sat up straight. "That is exactly what I wished to hear. I think I shall be returning, and when I do, I may need a guide to another realm."

"Again, to the realm below?" Vordam's expression was quizzical. "Kastor, who prepared you before, died ages ago, living in a mortal plane. There are a few others on Shusar who can enable you once more, but that will take time. Perhaps I can find you another guide."

Nakor pulled himself up and said, "A guide, yes, but preparation? Not this time. If what I believe is possible can be done, we'll need to go the other way, to the next realm above, the first heaven."

Without a word, he turned and departed the shop, leaving Vordam speechless for the first time in centuries.

CHAPTER 21

UNFORESEEN

Donte crouched low.

He had found a decent vantage point to observe the expected attack. This was his third night awaiting the Keshian assault on the Mockers. He'd met with the Keshian boss earlier, who again said the attack would be "soon," but Donte knew time was running out. If the plunder was moved out of Port Vykor before the Keshians struck, his plan would fail.

If the Keshians didn't move soon, he knew exactly how weak their position was. He assumed the last two days had been spent reconnoitering, possibly recruiting some extra fighters, and planning the best time for the raid.

The middle-of-the-night vigils, on top of a quick trip to the farm and back, had him close to exhaustion. Part of his training had been staying alert when his body demanded sleep. Lessons and life-threatening reality were two entirely different things.

A noise alerted him to something changing. The surprise quickened his pulse and drove off the drowsiness. He shifted his weight and duck-walked to a better position to see if anyone was moving along the street below.

Shifting darkness, movement barely seen, alerted him that the Keshians were striking tonight. Now all fatigue washed away.

A few minutes of barely heard movement were followed by silence. Then the sound of bow strings twanging preceded arrows striking.

Two fallen guards lay motionless: the Keshian bowmen must be deadly accurate. Donte scanned the rooftops and saw no hint of the

Mockers' sentries having been alerted. He saw dark figures hurrying across the intersection, stopping before the entrance to the underground market. He wished he had a cat's vision, because he could hardly make out the stream of black-clad fighters racing to enter the tunnel.

He sat back and took a deep breath. There was nothing more to see here, so he decided it was time to return to the Ravens and get some rest.

Keeping low, he walked to the end of the building, moved to hang from the eaves of the roof, then dropped to the street below, landing lightly on his feet.

Distant sounds of struggle barely reached him: the fight was underground and a long way away. He moved from building to building, staying in the deepest shadows.

Donte emerged from the Sad Landing quarter and hurried to the inn. He now had the Mockers and Keshians fully at war, and it was time to contemplate his next move. The more conflict he could orchestrate, the more opportunities would manifest.

He worked his way through the city until he reached the Four Ravens and was surprised to see Burt, his drinking companion from the Red Starfish, standing outside. The big man smiled and said, "Ah, just the lad I was looking for."

A sudden internal warning sounded within Donte and he stopped, but at that moment another man appeared behind him. Donte spun around in a crouch, a dagger appearing in his hand. The man hit the back of Donte's hand with the flat of a sword, hard enough to break Donte's grip on the dagger. Donte began to leap to his left away from the front of the inn, but a boot to the back of his right knee collapsed him. The kick wasn't hard enough to break anything, but Donte slammed into the ground. Just as he started to scramble away, the swordsman placed the point of his weapon at Donte's throat and said, "Stay still and you live."

Burt came back into Donte's view and said, "You're quick for a well-muscled lad, I'll give you that. Now, someone wants to meet you, and he doesn't care if you walk in, or we carry you in. Which will it be?"

Knowing that any sudden move on his part might end in a serious wound, Donte stayed motionless. After a second he said, "I think I'd rather walk."

"Smart choice," said Burt, extending his hand to help Donte to his feet.

Donte reached up and as Burt pulled him to his feet, Donte felt a blow to the back of his head, and lost consciousness.

HAVA CAME ASHORE AT THE Sanctuary and saw Nakor and Pug standing at the end of the dock. Moving toward them, Hava said to Nakor, "Hello! Where have you been?"

"Around," said Nakor, grinning. "Finding out some things."

"Care to share?" asked Hava.

"Soon," said Nakor. "I could use a meal and a drink. I had a bit of a scuffle in the Hall getting back here."

Hava's brow furrowed. "The hall? Which hall, and who were you scuffling with?"

Pug made a sound halfway between a scoff and a chuckle. "I don't think he means any hall here in the Sanctuary, but the Hall of Worlds."

"What's that?" she asked.

"I'll tell you while we eat," said Pug. He asked Nakor, "What were you doing in the Hall?"

"Getting back from Honest John's." He moved his right shoulder slowly in a circle. "I think I strained a muscle swinging my staff at a Nolian thief."

"Honest John's?" asked Hava.

"Later, over lunch," said Pug again. "Why were you walking the Hall? You've been here and have a fixed point of reference. Once out of Honest John's you'd be free of his magic-dampers and could have transported here."

Nakor's eyes widened. "From the Hall to this world? There are a few, like you and Magnus, who can use tricks like that. I doubt I'd have the power, even if I knew how."

Pug bent to look Nakor in the eye. "Even if you know how? You know how. Miranda trained us all together, me, you, and Magnus, at the same time back on Sorcerer's Isle. You're as adept at jumping from place to place as Magnus or me. I've seen you."

Nakor's expression darkened. What looked to be tears of frustration began to well up in his eyes. "Damn it!" he yelled. "Why do I have so many missing memories?" He seemed to be shouting at some unseen presences and scanned the skies as if he expected an answer. Eventually, his exasperation lessened, and he looked at Pug. "I can transport?"

"You can," said Pug. "Over there." He pointed to the far end of the dock, and suddenly that was where Pug stood.

Nakor stood looking at the magician and stared for a long moment, then abruptly he was standing next to Pug. "You're right. I know that trick."

For a moment he seemed fully on the verge of tears, then he took a deep breath, composing himself, and abruptly his cheerful smile returned. He chuckled. "It's a pretty good trick."

"Maybe more of your memories will return," Pug said.

"One can hope," said Nakor. "I never worried about such things before, but lately I find I'm fretting a lot."

Pug laughed lightly. "For a very long time I was one person, and now I'm . . . the same, but different. I think I understand."

Nakor found that amusing enough to grin. "I wager you do." He transported himself next to Hava and gave a slight bow. "Sorry to desert you. That was rude."

Hava took a slow breath and said, "I may eventually get used to you two, but it will take some time."

Nakor laughed. "Probably not, but you're very young, so perhaps if I'm still around in ten or twenty years . . . Now, Pug, he's easy to get used to. Despite all his worry, he's a very nice man."

Hava slowly shook her head and smiled. She glanced around the dock and said, "The hell with lunch. Time for a drink."

Pug appeared next to Nakor, saying, "I didn't know if you were coming back or not."

"Once was enough," said Nakor.

"Make that several drinks," said Hava, turning toward the dining hall and walking away.

DECLAN WATCHED AS THE SCOUT ran into view, leading his horse by the reins through the narrow passage. Declan understood why he didn't try to ride from the east side of the forest; with the path still littered with fallen branches and stumps in the forest shadows, there was far too much risk. The horse was exhausted, and a single misstep could kill either horse or rider.

"They're here," said the scout before Declan could ask for a report.

"How far?" he asked.

"A half-day, no more."

"Are they coming straight on, or moving to the north or south?"

"Straight on, highness."

Declan nodded. "Go tend to your mount, and then eat and rest."

Sixto had seen the rider approach and overheard the exchange as he came to stand next to Declan. "So, they'll come up the path?"

"So it seems," Declan answered. "Send the fastest runner we have to wait at the far end. If he sees them, he's to come back at once, or if he doesn't see them, to be back here by dusk."

Sixto waved over a young soldier and gave him the prince's orders. The young man took off at a brisk trot toward the eastern edge of the forest.

"It makes little sense," said Sixto. "Either one of the Church's scouts made it back and warned them, or no one came back, and they got suspicious. Either way, they should expect trouble here."

"Given the way they fight, I think we're looking at some arrogant bastards who don't care how many men they send out to die as long as they get what they want."

"I wonder what sort of faith does that," said Sixto.

"The same faith that burns people alive because they don't share their beliefs. They burned King Lodavico and half the royal court of Sandura," Declan answered. "It's the same faith that convinced Lodavico to destroy Ithrace, then turned on him."

"Bad people," said Sixto with no humor. "Very bad people."

"Indeed," Declan replied.

"Even if they get to the forest's edge before sundown, they can't be foolish enough to try to get through the trees in the dark."

"We can't take anything for granted," said Declan.

"Traps?"

"Good idea." Declan looked around, saw one of the engineers taking a drink from a barrel, and motioned him over. When the engineer approached, Declan said, "Jaden, isn't it?"

The engineer who had been forced to labor for the Church seemed pleased that Declan had remembered his name. Despite being exhausted and covered in grime, he brightened noticeably and said, "Yes, highness?"

"How long would it take for you and some men to create a nasty surprise for someone coming along that eastern trail in the dark?"

"Not long if you only want to slow them down a little. A serious trap, like a deep pit, would take almost a full day. They'd have to build a makeshift bridge to get across, or retreat."

Looking at the position of the sun overhead, Declan said, "You have half a day. Take as many men as you can and get it done before sundown."

"Yes, highness!" The engineer put his fist over his heart and then ran off to gather workers.

Sixto said, "We'd better send word to that scout we just sent off."

"Wish I'd thought of that," Declan said. "Send another runner, and have Jaden put a long plank across the pit, and tell the scout to be careful, and pull the plank after him."

Sixto smiled. "We'll figure all this out."

"I certainly hope so. What's the biggest fight you and I have seen?"

"Down in Abala, Bogartis's fifty against, what? Two hundred raiders?"

"How many men have we here?"

"About five hundred, here and out on the western edge of the forest," Sixto answered.

"And maybe two thousand Church soldiers headed this way," Declan said, his expression grim.

"Same odds," said Sixto.

"Same odds," Declan echoed.

"Well, this time we have a fortification, we're not out in the open, and there's no surprise."

"Let's hope it's enough," said Declan. "Go and alert Captains Renfore and Markam and have them set up skirmishers to the north and south of their positions. I don't want even a small Church squad hitting us from the flank."

Sixto nodded. "Then we wait."

"We wait," said Declan.

SABELLA SAT BACK WITH A look of frustration. "I can't find a thing," she said to Zaakara.

"We still have a lot more books and scrolls to consult," he reminded her.

"I don't think we're going to find anything that will help. If there was any lore about moving mana, juju, whatever we call it, from place to place, someone would have made mention of it, even a hint, don't you think?"

Zaakara said, "You make a good point. Still, here the energy is abundant, and it's reasonable to expect that those who wrote these books, scrolls, and tomes were also from worlds with enough energy for them to practice magic. So perhaps the question has never come up."

"That's also a good point," she conceded.

"You're tired. Between your studies and the work you're doing here, you'll wear yourself down to a nub. You should get some food and rest."

"You're probably right," she said, pushing back her seat and standing. He stood also. "It's just that I could feel energy flowing from here to Garn when Magnus opened the rift. The others felt it, too. We all gained energy we never had before. It was as if it was flowing from here to there."

"So perhaps a permanent rift?"

"I don't think that would be helpful," she replied as they left the study room and moved toward the entrance of the library. "The best analogy I can imagine is that of enough water coming through a hose to keep someone from dying of thirst, and many people lined up to drink from it being revived, but not enough to fill . . . an ocean . . . all of Garn."

"Or even a pond," he agreed. "Perhaps if you rest for a day or two, we may find another way. Now, as much as I enjoy your company, I also have some duties to attend to. Let me know if you discover anything useful."

"I will," she said, turning to the dining hall, while he moved back toward his quarters in the villa.

As she walked, she muttered, "There must be a way."

DONTE REVIVED IN A DARK room, with barely a hint of light, save what he could see coming under the door from the next room. By the yellow color and flicker, it was torchlight. Which meant it was night. His head throbbed from the blow, and he knew he had a serious knot on his skull but couldn't reach up to touch it. His hands were tied behind his back.

"Awake, at last," said a voice Donte recognized as Burt's. "Go tell him," he said to someone else in the room. The door quickly opened, and a man stepped through, and in that moment of illumination, Donte could see that Burt and two other men were standing between him and the door.

Donte was on a stone floor, near a wall. He scooted back a foot and got himself sitting upright.

"Take it easy and you might live through this," said Burt in an almost friendly voice. "I genuinely would hate to see you dead; you're pleasant drinking company."

The door opened again and this time a man with a torch entered, followed by another. The second man came to stand before Donte and said, "Get him up." He was the biggest man in the room, and Donte sensed he was probably the biggest threat. You didn't get to be leader of a rough bunch like this without being the most dangerous.

Two men came over, one on each side, gripped him by the arms, and got Donte on his feet. From the torchlight, Donte could tell he was dealing with a very seasoned crew. These men were relaxed, but ready, and he was outnumbered five to one. Not only was he groggy from the blow on the head, a bitter aftertaste in his mouth suggested he had also been drugged. He was at the mercy of these men, so his usual bravado and impulse to act rashly were absent. But if they had wanted him dead, he would be lying face down in his own blood outside the Four Ravens. So, they wanted something. He forced himself to breathe slowly, evenly, moderating his heart rate. He knew that fear made you stupid, and he used to joke to Hatu and Hava that he didn't need any help being stupid. At last, he said, "I'm here, so what do you want?"

The last man to arrive, who seemed to be in charge, said, "You're the lad who's been mucking about with the Keshians and the lads from Krondor, right?" He turned his face toward Burt, who nodded.

"Pointless for me to say otherwise, isn't it?" Donte replied.

"Smart lad," said the man. "Now, can you give us a good reason for all your goings-on?"

"Seems to me sort of obvious," said Donte, "but if it isn't, I had in mind a bit of enterprise in Port Vykor. When I arrived, I found two gangs working against each other. Seemed to me that if I let them bleed each other, that made more chaos. I've often heard out of chaos comes opportunity."

"A bit of an entrepreneur, are you?"

"A man's got to make a place for himself." Donte now thought he saw where this was going.

"You picked a bit of a mess to step into," said the man in charge. "Generally, we just do away with intruders, but Burt here thinks you have a knack. He's our man to watch what's going on with the Keshians, so when you turned up, he saw you were watching them, too. Rather than sort you out, he decided to keep an eye on you and judged you to be a clever one."

Donte glanced at Burt and said, "You run a very good con. I thought you were exactly who you said you were."

"Years of practice," Burt said.

"Now, what are we to do with you?" said the big man.

"Getting untied is my first idea," said Donte. "My arms are starting to go numb." He turned around.

"Cut him loose," said the big man. "You're a cool one," he said to Donte.

"No point in being stupid, is there? So, what is it you want?"

The rope was cut, and Donte gave out a sound of relief as he moved his shoulders and stretched to relieve the pain. He turned back to face his captor. Whatever drug he had been given was wearing off, and he was thinking more clearly.

The big man studied Donte. "Where are you from? You said you were a stranger to Port Vykor, and I'm pretty certain if you'd been running around anywhere else in the Western Realm, a lad like you would have drawn our attention pretty quick."

"I'm from about as far from here as you can imagine," Donte said. "I'm sure you've never heard of it."

"Somewhere down in Novindus?"

"Farther."

The man laughed, a short bark and then a scoff. "There is nowhere farther away than Novindus."

Donte said, "Let's say there is, and leave it. Back to my question. I'm alive, so what do you want?"

"Here's the problem," said the big man. "The lads mixing it up with the Keshians—"

"The Mockers from Krondor," Donte interrupted.

That brought a surprising reaction. "No," said the big man. "We're the Mockers, and you're in Krondor."

DECLAN HAD THE MEN STOP working early. He ordered food and rest as the sun was lowering in the west. There was a fight on its way, and he wanted every man fit for battle. For a moment he wished Pug or Hatu were still here, to throw some trees or whatever at the Church soldiers when they arrived, but Pug was off with Hava discovering how to get ships from one world to the other, and Hatu was back at the castle in Marquenet.

Sixto and the other captains were inspecting every emplacement and ensuring that the men would be ready the next day. Sixto came to stand next to Declan and said, "Everything is as right as we can make it."

After sunset, the scout he had stationed at the east side of the forest returned. He jogged over and saluted. "They're out there, highness, but they've camped for the night. I could see sun glinting off armor and weapons, and heard horses and wagons as they arrived, and as the light faded, I could see fires."

"Good," said Declan.

"We need to be alert," said Sixto, "So let's be wary of assassins wending their way through the trees. A single man can get through the forest if he knows his craft."

"In the dark?" Declan asked.

"It's possible. I stationed sentries around here and there, just in case."

"Wise," Declan replied. "Let's try to rest."

Both men returned to the campfire next to the cooking shack, and took the same meal as the fighting men, a bowl of stew and a large hunk of bread. Declan choose plain water over a mug of ale. He wanted to be as alert as possible tomorrow, for everything rode upon him not failing in his mission.

DONTE SAID, "KRONDOR? HOW LONG was I out?"

"A day," answered his chief captor. "After you were clubbed, they slipped a sleeping draught into you, so you'd be no problem along the way. They got you here a few hours ago, before sundown."

"Sorry about messing with your lads down in Port Vykor" was all Donte could think to say.

"Well," said the big man, "that's the thing. They're not our lads, or at least no longer." He waved his hand to his men and said, "Let's move this to the other room."

The two silent men stood on either side of Donte, as Burt followed the big man and the fifth man out the door. Donte moved and his escort moved along with him.

The next room proved to be well lit, with four torches in wall sconces, a table, and half a dozen chairs. Two men moved the table to a corner and pulled two chairs around so Donte could sit opposite the big man.

"Let's start with why you chose Port Vykor," said the leader as he sat down.

"Came there with a friend on business and decided to stay. Looked like a nice little city."

The big man laughed. His surprisingly pale skin was marked by lines of age, yet he showed no signs of weakness in his posture or movements. He might be older, Donte thought, but that didn't make him any less dangerous.

"So, those lads in Port Vykor are just claiming to be the Mockers of Krondor?" Donte already knew the answer but playing for time to think had been drilled into him since childhood. He anticipated he was in a situation where he'd be given some sort of choice, and if he didn't like either option, he needed to find a way out. Time to think was vital.

"They were," said the big man. He learned forward and said, "We run a very disciplined operation here in Krondor, and we have been around for years, since before my great-grandfather was a boy. The Mockers have existed almost as long as the city itself, and we are what you might call an institution."

Donte slowly nodded in understanding. "My family, much the same. My grandfather is a master of crews in many places, as was his grandfather."

"Where did you say you were from?"

"I didn't. As I told you, you've never heard of it."

"Try me."

"It's called Coaltachin."

The big man sat back, his face now openly amazed. "You're one of the off-worlders!"

Donte was genuinely taken aback. For a moment he remained silent, then slowly nodded. "You must have some very good spies," he said.

"Let's say we have a lot of friends in many different places. As I said, we are something of an institution here in Krondor. We've come to an accommodation with the Crown, so long as we keep . . . our business, shall we say, from becoming too much of a burden. We try to keep out of each other's way."

"You're the Upright Man?"

The big man laughed. "No, there are only two men in Krondor who know who he is. I am one. I am the Nightmaster."

Donte nodded. "That would explain why you're rather pale. I suppose then the other is called the Daymaster?"

"You're a sharp one, I'll say." He looked hard at Donte, then said, "Even if your answers are wrong, I think I'd like to keep you around a while just to learn how that place you hail from works. We have only a few rumors about you and your two friends from that world. But that can keep," said the Nightmaster, standing up. "I was to decide if we should kill you or take you to meet the Upright Man."

"I thought you said only two men knew who he was," Donte said.

With a chuckle, the Nightmaster said, "I should have said, we take you so he can get a look at you. You won't see him." He looked at Burt and said, "Bag him. We need this done before sunrise."

Donte looked toward Burt, who approached with a dark bag which he put over Donte's head, plunging him into darkness again.

"At least," Donte said through the cloth, "I don't get another bang on the head."

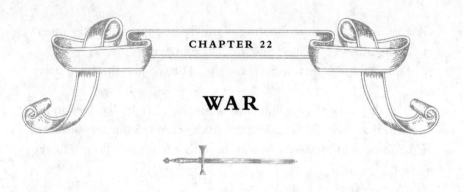

CHAPTER 22

WAR

Declan dozed.

Sleep had escaped him all night, but he had rested. He'd been through enough conflicts to know that rest was vital, for that last bit of energy during a fight might be the difference between life and death. He came awake as he felt a sense of urgency fueled by the sound of men hurrying. He opened his eyes just as Sixto was about to awaken him.

"They're here," said Sixto. "We had a man near the pit, and when he heard men fall into the trap, he fired a whistler into the clearing."

A whistler was an arrow with a small, shrill whistle tied to it. Declan had decided that a flaming arrow, while better to see in dim light, brought too much risk of fire, given all the dry debris in the clearing.

Coming to his feet, Declan said, "I hope it didn't hit anyone."

Sixto appreciated the dark humor, and said, "Came close."

"So, they didn't turn back?"

"Worked around the edge of the pit and found the board. Our scout said they came across in single file but gathered into squads before moving forward. They should be here—" A shout from the pathway was answered by the sound of arrows being loosed. More shouts and screams followed.

Declan gathered his wits and saw that the sun was visible behind the trees and judged it to be perhaps half an hour after sunrise. "They must have started at first light," he said.

He hurried up the ramp to the wall behind the earthen redoubt and saw that his archers were shooting at any figure appearing at the opening of the pathway. "Target practice," he muttered.

Sixto said, "Something's not right. They're just throwing away men."

The sky was growing lighter. It would be a bright day. Declan felt thankful that they weren't doing this in the rain, but the deep shadows of the forest still masked anything beyond a few yards deep into the trees.

"A diversion?" he asked.

Sixto looked around, quickly scanning one side, then the other. "For what? They can't send enough men through the forest to attack in force."

Abruptly, the flow of Church soldiers stopped, leaving scores of corpses littered around the entrance to the eastern trail.

Then the sky began to darken.

Declan looked up and saw no clouds.

"Gods of our fathers," said Sixto. "What is that?"

"Nothing natural," said Declan. "The light is just fading."

The soldiers of Marquensas were also looking around in all directions as the very air around them took on an almost tangible feeling of evil, a miasma of anger and despair.

"Stand fast!" Declan shouted. "Be ready!" To Sixto he said, "Get a runner to the west, and have the captains bring up every man. This is where we will stand!"

Sixto ordered a runner to carry out the order, having to shake him by the front of his tunic to get his attention. After he had gone, Sixto said, "We're about to lose some men if it gets darker."

Declan saw that some of the men were already starting to move back from the wall, and those at the rear of the redoubt were looking for a path of retreat. "Stand fast!" he shouted again. "If you break, we all die!"

Then the older veterans, some who had been with Declan and Sixto in Garn's Wound or had served with Declan fighting the Pride Lords, also began shouting encouragement to the younger soldiers. Declan felt the mood slowly shift back toward one of resolve.

As the daylight kept fading, Declan shouted, "Torches!"

Sixto softly said, "So much for them not attacking in the dark."

Declan said nothing, waiting for what came next.

HATU SAT IN THE LIBRARY inside the castle at Marquenet, engrossed in a book detailing the history of the region, slightly amused at how a bandit had elevated himself to the role of first baron, with a ridiculous amount of puffery in the narration. He'd read every book there and was now circling back to those which had either interested or amused him the first time around.

As he had discovered, a second reading of something he knew by heart still gave him an improved perspective. The second time he'd read this history he had been utterly amused. As he had learned as a child in Coaltachin, history was written by the victors.

He felt as if something cold had touched him. Putting the book down, he sat motionless, listening for something, a sound on the edge of his perception. He felt more than heard anything, like a vibration that should have been a note of music but wasn't quite audible.

He closed his eyes and used his ability to envision lines of energy stretched between opposing furies, and within a moment had found the source of his odd feeling. There was something so twisted and wrong about it that he felt a prickling on his skin as it turned to gooseflesh, the hairs rising on his arms and head. He distanced himself from the source of that terrible presence and opened his eyes. One familiar note remained: Declan.

Hatu hurried through the palace to Balven's quarters and motioned to the sentry to knock for him. The sentry did, and Balven said, "Enter."

Hatu walked through the door and before Balven could speak, said, "Any word from Declan?" His expression was urgent.

Balven said, "A rider this morning brought a message, after riding all night." He picked it up and read, "'Church forces within sight. Camped and apparently ready to attack tomorrow,' which is today."

"They're attacking now!"

Hatu's expression made Balven alarmed. "How do you know?"

Hatushaly looked at Balven with a pained expression. "It hurts!" He had tears welling, then suddenly he vanished.

Balven sat back, eyes wide. He paused for a moment, then ran to find the king.

DECLAN STOOD ATOP THE WALL, looking down at the carnage littering the clearing between the first defensive trench and the trees to the east. He estimated that over two hundred Church warriors lay dead less than half the distance from where the path intersected the clearing and the first line of defense.

Sixto said, "Utter madness. The skies are black, and the dead never had a—" He stopped. "Look, that man is only wounded."

Declan looked where Sixto pointed, and saw that one Church soldier, his body sporting half a dozen arrows, was twitching. "Death throes," he muttered.

"No, he fell too long ago—" Again Sixto stopped, for another corpse had also begun to move.

"What?" Declan asked.

Slowly the corpses strewn across the clearing began to twitch, then tremble and, after a moment of thrashing, started to rise.

Declan's forces stared on in collective horror at the sight of the dead standing. After long moments of stunned disbelief, a few archers began shooting at the animated corpses. When they were struck, the force of the shaft would knock them down or turn them, but they kept moving.

The corpses grabbed fallen weapons, hefting them with purpose, and turned for the redoubt. At first, they stepped slowly toward the men from Marquensas. Then they began to pick up the pace. After a few strides, the dead advanced at a shambling trot.

Arrows flew furiously, knocking some of the dead over, but they just sat up then got to their feet.

Declan shouted, "Save your arrows! They're useless! Swords and axes! Pass the word!"

Several soldiers threw down their weapons and turned to flee, but at that moment the reinforcements from the west arrived. Captains

Renfore and Markam both brandished their weapons and shouted, "Stand!"

A few hesitated and were almost overrun by the soldiers behind the captains. The other soldiers turned and went back to their positions.

The first wave of the dead struck the base of the redoubt and began scrambling up the earthen incline, ignoring the protruding, sharpened stakes that would have injured or killed mortal men. A few became impaled on the stakes and thrashed as they attempted to release themselves, but the rest kept coming.

The first who breasted the earthen wall began swinging at the nearest living soldier. Corpses with dead eyes, covered in blood from their own wounds, some with helms gone, arrows protruding from their bodies, were a sight to terrify even the most battle-hardened warrior.

Fear drove rage, and the men of Marquensas slashed at every creature within reach. A few were beheaded and fell back, only to try to regain their footing and resume their attack. The headless creatures felt blindly around in the dirt seeking a weapon or, if not finding one close, just returned to climbing back up the redoubt.

Sixto put his hand on Declan's shoulder and said, "I think it's time for the prince to move to the rear."

"No," Declan said. "I'll not run."

"You are the only one here who is not allowed to die!" Sixto shouted. "Get to your brother and warn him."

"Look!" Declan said, pointing to the fight below.

Sixto turned and saw what had caught Declan's attention. Some of the dead were falling back, collapsed by wounds to their legs. Unable to rise, they flopped around like fish on a dock. A few rolled over and started crawling back toward the top of the earthen fortification.

"Chop them up!" shouted Declan. "Cut their legs out from under them!"

Sixto repeated the order, then said, "We need to drive them back."

Declan turned to the two captains who were waiting for his orders. He pointed to the still-open gate behind their company and said, "Markam to the right, Renfore to the left, circle and take them from the sides. Chop them into pieces, but do not let them over the top."

As the two captains turned and divided the company into squads and began the ordered maneuver, Sixto shouted, "Look!"

It took Declan a moment to see what Sixto was pointing to. Then he recognized that a dead Marquensas soldier was now moving, turning to attack the living defenders. "The more of us they kill, the stronger they get!" Declan shouted. He stared around frantically, seeing other Marquensas corpses starting to join the army of the dead.

"We need to chop them to pieces," said Sixto. "Or burn them to ash."

"Fire, here?" Declan shook his head. "We set this forest ablaze and we're all dead."

"Not if we set it on fire and run like hell," said Sixto. "These dead men are unrelenting, but they are not fast."

"Last resort," said Declan.

"That may not be long in coming," said Sixto. He turned, grabbed a young soldier who was close, and said, "Get to the camp to the west and have the horses there saddled and ready. I want six riders ready to escort the prince back to the city. Do you understand?"

The soldier's expression was halfway between terror and anger, but quickly resolved to a calmer state and he said, "Sir!" He hurried off to carry out his order.

"If we set fires," said Sixto, "you will be on a horse, even if I have to knock you out and drape you across the withers myself."

Declan did not look pleased at this, but he didn't argue.

The sky continued to darken, so now it was dusk everywhere, and Declan knew that evil powers were now orchestrating this fight. He pushed away a feeling of dread, and sought the power he knew was within him, when the rising anger slowed down the battle and gave him the almost inhuman ability to fight. And if ever he had needed such an advantage, this was the time.

Pug and Hava looked at the slowly assembling fleet, smugglers that Red Sweeney had judged reliable, with crews fearless enough to try something that most would think folly.

"Nicely done," Pug said. "This tidy fleet should bring a year's provisions or more to the city."

Hava nodded. "People are starting to notice we're only a few weeks away from running out of sugar, honey, salt, grain, a lot of what they need every day." She looked around and smiled. "Not to mention everyone but the fishermen are getting tired of fish. We bring food now, and next time cattle, sheep, ducks, chickens, and seeds, lots of seeds . . ."

Pug said, "Marquensas will be back on a solid footing—" Suddenly his expression changed.

Hava looked at him and said, "What?"

"I don't know. A sudden feeling . . ." He cocked his head as if listening. "I . . . Something is off."

"What is it?" she asked again.

He shook his head. "I really don't know. If that feeling returns I'll see if I can find the source."

Red Sweeney approached from the town and, reaching the end of the dock where Pug and Hava stood, said, "Five good ships and crew is all I could gather without risking fools and idiots." He glanced at the black-robed magician and said, "This the fellow you told me about?"

"Red Sweeney, this is Pug."

Red Sweeney extended a hand and Pug shook it. "I've heard a lot about you," Pug said.

"And I've heard only a little about you," said the old smuggler. "Apparently, you can take us all to another world." His tone was a mix of humor and disbelief.

"I can," said Pug calmly. Then he added, "And I'll try not to drown you doing it."

Red Sweeney laughed. "That would be much appreciated."

Abruptly, Nakor appeared next to Pug.

Red Sweeney's eyebrows shot up and he stepped back reflexively. He was saved from falling off the wharf by Hava grabbing his arm.

When the shocked smuggler was safe, Hava said, "Red Sweeney, this is Nakor."

Nakor nodded in his direction, then turned to Pug and said, "Did you feel it?"

"I felt something," said Pug. "Faint, but noticeable."

Nakor nodded emphatically. "It's bad."

"Are you certain?" asked Hava as she let go of Red Sweeney's arm.

"For us," said Nakor, "stuff is muted, so our tricks, our senses are . . . less . . ."

"Less acute. Things we would recognize on Midkemia are hard to recognize here," Pug said.

"It's bad," Nakor repeated. "We need to go see."

"Where?" asked Pug.

"Somewhere over there, I think," said Nakor waving in a general northwesterly direction.

Pug looked at Hava, and asked, "Marquensas?"

Hava nodded and said, "That's the general direction."

"I'll be back," Pug said to her. To Nakor, he said, "King Daylon's palace?"

"Good place to start," said Nakor, and he vanished.

Red Sweeney stood mutely astonished. Hava grabbed his arm again, just in case.

Pug said, "I'd better go." Then he, too, vanished.

After a moment, Hava asked Red Sweeney, "Are you all right?"

The old smuggler took a deep breath, his eyes still wide, and he said, "Now I believe we can go to a different world."

SIXTO AND DECLAN STOOD READY as more of the dead crawled up the wall, trying to reach them. For the time being, the men of Marquensas were holding their own, literally chopping up the animated corpses to the point at which they were unable to pose a threat. Declan saw that it was a struggle for his men to be turning blades on men they had fought beside just minutes before. More than one man fought back tears as he tried to cut up a man wearing Marquensas colors.

A few soldiers here and there had fallen, only to rise and join the attack, but once the defenders understood the peril, and realized their advantage was speed and mobility, the battle became more stable.

Declan said, "If we start gaining an edge, we can end this soon."

"I hope you are right," Sixto said as an arm came over the top of the wooden wall. Before the dead enemy could pull himself up, Sixto lopped the arm off at the elbow and the creature fell silently back.

Of all the elements of horror confronting them, it was the corpses' silence that troubled Declan the most. There were no cries of battle or pain, not even a grunt or the sound of heavy breathing. Just dead men moving toward them with silent purpose.

"I now think going and fetching the special sand for these swords was an excellent idea," Sixto said. "A lesser blade would be getting quite dull, I'm thinking."

"You've hacked off a lot of limbs."

"Bone tends to blunt the edge," Sixto observed.

"So it does," said Declan as he decapitated another dead soldier trying to clamber over the wall.

"Now, if we can just keep our arms from falling off," Sixto said while slashing another arm from a shoulder, "we may just get out of this without having to burn the forest to the ground."

A quick survey reassured Declan that his forces were slowly making headway, as the soldiers of Marquensas had discovered their courage and were now methodically hacking up every dead foe that they could.

A sudden blast of air struck, as if someone had opened a door in a warm room on the coldest day of winter and let in a frigid wind. Declan felt the cold cut to his bones, and every exposed inch of his skin puckered as gooseflesh raised the hair on his body.

He faltered and barely got his sword up to dispatch the next corpse climbing the wall. He glanced at Sixto, who stood, eyes wide and shivering, and then he saw every soldier of Marquensas had also been numbed by the blast. Suddenly, they were freezing as the dead kept coming.

Declan turned to Sixto and asked, "Are you all right?"

Both men saw Declan's breath condensing in front of his face as he spoke.

"Far from it," answered Sixto, and his breath also formed a cloud of icy mist.

Declan saw his men falter, look at one another, expressions of panic everywhere. He shouted, "Hold!" But even as he shouted, he felt every fiber of his being rebel against this sudden shock.

Sixto echoed the command, "Do not stop!"

Declan could see his soldiers resume their fight, but the freezing wind and the darkness were undermining their resolve. He looked at Sixto and said, "Get ready to start the fires."

Sixto nodded and headed for the steps down to the central court of the redoubt. Declan turned his attention back to the fight below and felt a stab of fear. His men were faltering, and he had no idea what he could do to change that.

Then a ringing filled the air. A tone of evil that caused men to drop their weapons and cover their ears. Declan bent over, barely holding on to his sword, and felt his stomach flip, as if someone had punched him unexpectedly. He felt his gorge rise and only just kept himself from vomiting.

His eyes watered and he felt dizzy, and for the first time in his life Declan was certain he was about to die.

PUG ARRIVED MINUTES AFTER NAKOR, who was standing with Hatushaly, while the king looked on with a stunned expression. Nakor turned to Pug. "Something terrible is underway."

Pug nodded. He looked at Hatushaly and asked, "You felt that, too?"

"Like a blow to my heart," Hatu answered. "Something evil is visiting us."

Pug said, "Where?"

It was Hatu who said, "East," and he pointed. "Where Declan is."

The king looked appalled, then shouted, "Go!"

Hatu had been arguing that he should go and help Declan, but till now Daylon had held to the position that Hatu was too valuable to risk accidental death. But the horror that now visited them all, the nameless terror they felt to the core of their being, was too severe to ignore.

Pug said to Hatu, "Can you show us?"

Hatu said, "Yes," and suddenly both Pug and Nakor had a vivid vision of Declan atop a battlement, with a battle raging around him.

Then Hatu vanished.

Pug looked at Nakor, who said, "I know where we're going. Look for me."

Nakor vanished.

Pug extended his senses. He again recognized that the range of his powers on Garn were diminished, yet he could sense where Nakor was.

Pug vanished.

Daylon, King of Marquensas, sat mute, his emotions overwhelming him as he realized that for now, nothing he did would matter, and the fate of his nation, his home, and his family were in the hands of people he hardly knew, whose powers he barely understood.

Pug APPEARED ON THE BATTLEMENT next to Nakor and it took only a moment to see that things were far worse than he had imagined possible. Where he had expected two human armies in battle, he found evil unleashed, a chaotic struggle in a dark and freezing landscape.

The wailing noise had the army of Marquensas in disarray and the dead soldiers were oblivious to it. Men were unable to defend themselves and were dying, only to rise again moments later.

Pug closed his eyes and discovered the source of the horrible noise, darkness, and cold. It was an evil presence that felt both alien and vaguely familiar. He ignored any questions that might be answered later and attempted to counter the spell. After a moment of struggle, he found what he sought: the handiwork of magic, the source, that dimmed sunlight, robbed heat, and created noise.

Tentatively at first, he engaged the dark forces he could feel, pushed back slightly at what he perceived as the boundary between the normality of this world and the intruding evil. Summoning everything he could from deep within himself, he lashed out with the most powerful counterspell he could manage on Garn. He could almost feel a physical resistance as he gathered his will and unleashed every scrap of power he could muster.

The noise ceased.

Pug opened his eyes and saw that the sky was again blue, with daylight flooding down. He steadied himself as his knees threatened to buckle.

The soldiers were in disarray, but the return of sunlight and warmth on their faces and the ending of the ear-shattering din seemed to revive them a little. A few rallied, and after a few minutes order began to take hold. Still, Pug could see the soldiers were worn down, fatigued from a long fight. He couldn't see Hatushaly, and with a hoarse voice shouted, "Where is Hatu?"

Nakor pointed upward, and Pug looked and saw the young man hovering in the air directly overhead, observing the battle. Then Hatu descended to stand next to Pug. "There's something happening that I don't understand," he said. "I tried to see what was causing the darkness, but . . ." He blinked. "Something here is confusing me. I couldn't see the lines of energy I needed to see. The darkness hid everything. How did you end it?"

"I'll tell you later," said Pug, turning his attention to the battle. His breathing was heavy, but he seemed to be regaining his composure.

Nakor gripped Hatu's arm. "It's a trick to stop you from seeing. It's something we can train you to overcome, but not here or now." He looked at Pug and said, "Something very dark is near."

"I can still feel it," Pug said.

Pug extended an arm toward a knot of fighting corpses and a lance of energy erupted from his hand. Instantly four of them flared in a scintillating shimmer of light, then turned to dust. "I'm weakening," he said. He looked at Nakor with a questioning expression.

Nakor said, "I can't do that trick. But I can do this!" He waved his staff over his head, causing Hatu to duck as it barely missed striking him. The little man pointed with his left hand while twirling the staff with his right, and where he pointed a swirl of air manifested and suddenly a ten-foot-high whirlwind appeared. Nakor guided it through another group of dead Church fighters, who were caught up in it, swept off their feet, and carried high into the air. With a flick of his wrist, he caused them to be thrown up and over the top of the trees and out of sight.

Declan shouted, "Thank you!" over the sounds of battle. "We are exhausted."

Sixto said, "But where is the rest of their army?"

Hatu said, "I'll find out," and he shot up into the air, high enough that he was barely visible.

After a few minutes, he returned.

Declan asked, "What did you see?"

"They are just sitting there. The Church army is all ready, but they . . . they look as if they're waiting for something."

Declan looked around and saw that with Nakor's and Pug's help, his men were finally overcoming the dead. "Waiting for what?" he wondered aloud.

Pug directed another beam of energy toward half a dozen dead and they, too, vanished into light and dust.

Hatu closed his eyes, put his hand on Pug's shoulder, then said, "Oh, that's how you do that!"

Hatu then extended his right arm and a flash of energy identical to Pug's took a Church corpse and flashed it away.

Pug said, "Thank you. I'm nearing the end of my ability to help."

Between Nakor's and Hatushaly's magic, the fight turned quickly, and a few minutes later it was over. Every dead soldier was now gone or hacked to pieces. Some body parts twitched or moved slightly, but the fight had ended.

Pug took a deep breath and looked at Declan. "The lack of energy here weakens us. I could have ended this in minutes back on Midkemia."

"That's why we have to fix the problem," said Nakor. His expression was unusually somber. "I have an idea, but I don't know if it will work."

"Once we clean up this mess, we can talk about it," said Pug.

Men of Marquensas were slowly leaving the field of battle, some helping injured comrades get to where their wounds could be tended. Many paced around, still wary, as if unsure that they were safe. Many were drained of color, horror at the battle still vivid in their minds. A few simply sat where they were, regaining their strength before they attempted to leave the field.

"What was that gloom?" asked Sixto.

Pug said, "It was a simple enough spell, but who cast it?"

Declan had sheathed his sword and was wiping his brow with the sleeve of his tunic. "We've had no reports ever of the Church using any sort of magic. Until I met him"—he pointed at Hatu—"I didn't believe magic existed."

"Not a lot here," agreed Nakor.

"Let's get the wounded cared for, rest, and wait to see what the Church does next," Declan said.

A small tent in the center of the new fortification held most of the supplies already delivered from the wagons west of the forest. Declan led the others to it, and said, "We should have a bottle of wine somewhere in here."

In the tent, Declan moved a box and found the wine. He drew his sword and deftly sliced the neck below the cork and looked around. Seeing no cups, he shrugged and put the bottle slightly above his mouth, poured a little, and swallowed. He handed the bottle to Pug and said, "Mind the glass."

Sixto laughed. "Sword's still sharp, master smith." He tapped the hilt on his own blade. "I am grateful we survived to get that damned sand up here to make these blades!"

Declan laughed in return and said, "There are still a few things I can do well."

"More than a few," Sixto said seriously. Then with a note of levity, he added, "You turned me into a bloody officer!"

"A good thing, too," said Declan as he saw Pug hand the bottle to Nakor.

They all drank and soon the bottle was empty.

Declan said, "Get someone in here to organize things, while I go see to the wounded."

Sixto said, "Yes, highness."

For an instant, Declan looked to see if there was any hint of mockery, as Sixto knew better than anyone how the use of that title still grated on Declan's nerves, but he saw nothing but respect from his long-time friend.

Declan looked at Pug, Nakor, and Hatushaly, and said, "Without you this day would have been lost. I thank you."

"It was the right thing," said Nakor. "Bad things are happening, and whatever starts here will not end here."

Declan felt as tired as he had ever felt, but said, "I think I understand. I need to rest, but first I must see to the men."

As he moved off, Hatu said, "He's like that."

Pug said, "That's why he may be a great leader."

With a bitter note, Nakor said, "If we live long enough."

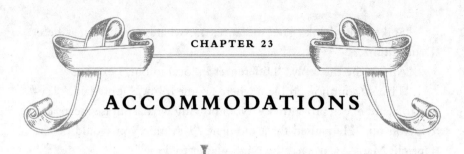

CHAPTER 23

ACCOMMODATIONS

Donte blinked.

Tears were filling his eyes from the harsh light he faced. The hood had been unceremoniously pulled off, and he was staring at two very bright lanterns with polished reflectors that completely blinded him to anything else in the room. As no light was reflected off the walls, Donte assumed the room was painted black specifically for this arrangement.

Damned clever, he thought as he finally blinked away the tears and got his eyes adjusted to the blinding illumination.

He felt the ropes binding him to the chair, not as tightly as before, but hardly comfortable. He twisted as much as he could so the light wasn't directly in his eyes.

A voice said, "It sometimes helps if you close your eyes and just listen."

Donte said, "Seems like a good choice," and he closed his eyes. He still saw a red hue from the light though his eyelids. "That is a very bright light," he said matter-of-factly.

"Yes," replied the voice. "Now to the reason you're here."

"Yes?"

"What you told the Nightmaster, how much of it was true?"

"All of it, I think," Donte replied.

"You think?"

Donte realized it was not a good time to be overly clever, and said, "I got a pretty good knot on my head, and someone slipped me a spike."

"A spike?"

"Spiked my drink, gave me an extra, whatever you call it here. Drugged me."

"Ah," came the reply. "Differences in local idiom, I expect."

"That's a common problem where I come from," Donte said. "Trying to blend in can prove tricky. Not knowing what a phrase means can trip you up." He paused for a moment. "I assume you would be the Upright Man, given what the Nightmaster told me."

"A fair assumption. I rarely speak directly to anyone unless I feel the need. And you are a special case, so I felt the need."

"Not that I object to having people think I'm special," said Donte, "except for the bangs on the head and the rest of it. I will say, Burt's a talent. I pride myself on not being obvious unless I want to be, and him having made me the first day makes him one clever spotter."

"I take it from what you said previously, and what you're saying now, you're not unfamiliar with the dodgy path."

Donte laughed. "I like that. No, I'm not what you might call a law-abiding citizen on my world."

"Care to explain?"

Donte gave a sigh. "Lots of history, there."

"We have time," said the Upright Man.

Donte gave as brief a rundown as he could on Coaltachin, avoiding what he felt was unnecessary. It still took almost half an hour to tell his tale. When he finished, the Upright Man said, "So, something of a criminal empire."

"Hardly an empire, but a nation, yes. A lot of what the masters of Coaltachin have accomplished is through guile and deceit. People fear us because we convinced them to fear us. The truth of what we can do enlarged by a lot of tales and rumors, most of which we created. So, while we have crews in a lot of cities, we don't seek to rule, but we do like to run the grifts, get a cut from others like the brothels, gambling halls, smuggling, whatever we can get a taste of."

"How do you fit in there?"

"That's another long tale," said Donte. He explained his grandfather being one of the Seven Masters, the Council of Coaltachin, and that he was considered a likely heir.

"Then, if you are to become one of these masters, how did you end up here, on another world?"

"I like to travel," Donte replied.

There was a moment of silence, then a burst of laughter. Donte heard a few chuckles from behind. He assumed there would be guards, and now he knew there were.

"There's travel and then there's this," said the Upright Man. "Our history teaches us about other worlds. We've had wars with invaders from them, more than once. The Great Disaster is suspected to be the result of one such, though there is little true history about that. So, again, why did you, the heir to a high position at home, come here?"

Donte realized he was sliding into his old habit of defiance, and it would not serve him here. He took a long breath, exhaled, and said, "My two best friends—hell, my only friends—were brought here by some magicians for some reason I'm still not clear on. I wasn't invited, but at the last moment I jumped through that magic hole to come with them. So, that's how I got here.

"They're doing whatever it is they're doing with those magicians—"

"At Stardock?" asked the Upright Man.

Suddenly Donte wondered if the Mockers knew about Sorcerer's Isle. So, he said, "Yes, I was at Stardock, then we went to Port Vykor."

"Why?"

Again, knowing keeping as close to the truth as possible made lying easier, Donte said, "To commission a ship. My friend is a sea captain."

"I'll look into that at some other time." There was a momentary pause, then the Upright Man asked, "So why did you stay in Port Vykor?"

"I'm not much for sailing after an accident once. I do if I must, but I don't like it." He decided that trying to explain his captivity by the Sisters of the Deep was too complicated a story. "But a port is a different matter. I've worked some good grifts in ports, cut a few purses, broken a few windows, picked a few locks since I was a lad. I noticed a decided lack of organized talent beyond the two gangs, and neither of them was local."

"Ah," said the Upright Man. "To the heart of the matter. You sought to create a local mob."

"In one sense," said Donte. "Maybe not a mob at first but say a tidy crew to start."

"Explain," said the Upright Man.

Donte tried to keep his experiences with the kids and his other observations to a minimum but give the overall conclusions he had reached. When he had finished, he said, "So I then played the Keshians on getting their booty back."

"Clever."

There was silence for a few moments, until Donte asked, "So now what?"

"Now I think it was wise to keep you alive. The lads you thought of as Mockers were once, but they decided to head south and begin their own little mob. Once, ages ago, my predecessors would have sent a squad to crush them for disobedience. Since the Great Disaster, our resources are more limited. Once, the Mockers controlled every harbor and dock from Yilith to the north in Yabon, west to Land's End, and had agents in Kesh and the Free Cities. Now we just do well enough to control various enterprises here in Krondor and a few nearby towns.

"But that doesn't mean we lack ambition," said the Upright Man. "It is logical that the first place we'd expand into would be Port Vykor, as it's the largest Kingdom harbor in the west. Sarth, Land's End, and the rest would follow if trade warranted. My concern is twofold: our future expansion, and not allowing another rival gang to rise up and challenge us before we're ready to move in."

Donte said, "Makes sense, getting rid of them before they dig in."

"So, as I said, I'm pleased we kept you alive. Because I want you to return to Port Vykor and continue creating havoc for the Keshians and my wayward lads. In particular, the self-styled leader of those false Mockers, a boy named Lester Ving. I personally would love to have him sitting where you are now so I could explain in detail why his end was coming, slowly and painfully."

"I understand," said Donte, relieved to know he would live to see the dawn.

"Short of that, I'll settle for his head. Send me that and I'll reward you richly."

"I'll see what I can do," said Donte.

Suddenly the bag was placed over his head again and his restraints were cut. Two men put firm grips on his arms, and he was half-lifted from the chair before he could get his feet under him.

"THEY'RE JUST WAITING," HATU SAID to those gathered in the king's throne room.

Too many people needed to hear everything, Daylon had decided, so they all sat around the head dining table. Pug, Declan, and Nakor sat next to Hatushaly at one end, while Delnocio, Collin, Baldasar, and Balven sat at the other end. The king took the centermost seat.

"How can you know?" asked General Baldasar.

Balven said, "He has this ability to see things at a great distance. How he does it, no one knows."

"I just do it," said Hatu.

"How is a question for another time," said the king. "What we need to know is why the remaining army of the Church of the One is sitting on its haunches in formation a few miles away from . . ." He looked at Declan. "You tell them."

"We fought against the dead," said the prince. He was barely clean, having only had time for a quick wash and fresh clothing, while Pug, Hatushaly, and Nakor were still covered in dirt and dried perspiration from the fight.

Declan gave a concise summation of the battle, sparing little of the horror he and the men under his command had faced. He finished by saying, "It was the intervention of these three"—he indicated Pug, Hatu, and Nakor—"that saved our men." He looked at Pug and asked, "Can you explain more?"

Pug saw doubt and fear on the faces of those gathered. His strength was slowly returning, and he was again fully alert. He said, "There is an enemy out there in the universe. It is something vast, and it seeks the end to everything you know, from all of humanity down to the smallest creature that flies or crawls. It seeks to obliterate all life." He had anticipated their questions, so he added, "We only have a vague idea of its motives, why it wishes to end everything living. It's a complicated theory, so I'll share it with you later if you wish, but for now I will say that Nakor and I have faced this threat more than once, and we have managed to fend it off."

"For a while," Nakor added. Seeing the expressions of Collin, Baldasar, and Balven, he added quickly, "We will have to do it again."

"Just what is this threat?" demanded General Baldasar.

"We call it the Void," said Pug. "Again, after this council, I can attempt to explain it all, but understand I will be speaking of things you believed were myth and fable just hours ago."

"Explain now," said the king. "We will try to understand."

Pug glanced at Nakor, who gave a slight shrug of resignation, and the magician took a breath. "To understand the Void, first you must know something about the universes around you." He tried to give as simple a summation as possible, given the complexity, history, and unknown aspects of the nature of the Void.

After a few minutes, it was clear that the subject was beyond the comprehension of those from Garn, except for Hatushaly, so Nakor interrupted. "At the start of this universe, I mean the very beginning, everything split into good and bad. We are the good, living things. The Void is the bad, something that wants to end life. Understand?"

Collin and Baldasar both looked relieved.

It was Delnocio who said, "That's basic Church canon. The One is good, everything that's not the One is bad."

Nakor grinned. "That's ironic. You see, your 'One' is the Void, and the Church serves it."

Even Pug looked surprised by that pronouncement. "The Church worships the Void?"

Nakor gave a quizzical expression. "They don't know they do, but yes. That feeling at the battle, a strange . . . presence. It's the Void. It's here."

Pug was motionless for a moment, then slowly nodded. "There was an alien presence . . . but it felt familiar." Old memories returned and he said softly, "Sethanon. I felt it there."

"That other time, too, I think," said Nakor. "The big fight where you—"

Pug held up his hand, not wishing to have to explain his two incarnations to those at the table who were ignorant of that fact. "I know."

He looked at Nakor and silently wondered what powers had brought them both back from death. "I know you're right."

Nakor said, "And there's someone or something else out there, that services the Void. That darkness and noise . . . somewhere the Church has a necromancer, or someone wielding death magic."

Delnocio said, "I barely understand half of what you're explaining, but I know the Church and have lived within it most of my life. One thing does make sense. The actions of the Church Adamant and some of my brethren made no sense when I first was betrayed. These were men in power, men with almost nowhere to go above their current stations. Episkopos and generals, men who sometimes were at odds with me and my allies, but only in terms of expanding the Church. It was more about how to do it, nothing else.

"Those serving the Church Adamant prefer to bludgeon people into obedience, to force them to their knees whatever the cost. Fire and blood are their tools of choice. We of the holy orders preferred persuasion. From the accounts of wholesale killings throughout Sandura, after the betrayal of me and my allies, it's clear the Church Adamant is now fully in control. The carnage will only get worse."

"You saw this coming?" asked Balven.

"I knew there was something afoot, and my agents were trying to uncover those secrets for years before the sudden upheaval that drove me here. This I know: if the betrayers were working on behalf of this Void, that finally makes sense of what seemed sheer madness to me."

It was the king who spoke next. "What you say is beyond my ability to fathom, but for the moment, my forces in the Darkwood have an army that outnumbers them—what? Four to one?—just a few hours' march away. I don't care who they worship, only how to defeat them."

"As long as they wait," said Nakor. "You don't have to do much."

"Which brings us back to my first question," said the king. "What are they waiting for?"

Nakor shrugged and looked at Pug.

Pug slowly pushed back his chair. "Waiting to be told what to do next. I can return and see."

"Wait." Hatushaly stood up. "I've rested longer, and I can see from here."

It was Nakor who said, "When they do something, we'll know. Still, we now know that we have a big job after any fight in the Darkwood."

Balven asked, "What's that?"

Nakor smiled and said, "We must destroy this Church. All of it."

PUG TOOK A SIP OF wine, considering what had been unfolding over the last few days. Nakor also seemed lost in thought, which seemed a rare condition. Hatushaly sat, quietly waiting to hear what they had to say next.

Eventually, Nakor said, "At first I thought we had to deal with this Church because it was a distraction to the larger conflict, but now I see I was wrong. It's an agent of chaos, designed to obscure the real threat: the Void."

Pug seemed about to speak, but Nakor waved him to silence and continued, "The Void has worked its will on others before. The entire war between the demons and the Saaur, the conflict among demons, the imposter-advisers in three different nations, all were at the behest of the Void. We cannot assume this Church isn't a major weapon."

Pug looked slightly annoyed. "What I was about to say is that the Void tried to rid this world of all magic." He pointed at Hatushaly. "But he survived."

Hatu looked at Nakor. "The Flame Guard was dedicated to preserving the Firemane line, and they saved me, so perhaps this Void is unaware that I'm here."

"Who knows?" said Nakor.

Pug nodded. "We've opposed the Void and its agents for centuries. Yet we still understand little about it, or its capabilities."

"You've said a few things," Hatu remarked, "but I'd like to know more."

"When the universe was created—" Pug began.

"Created by whom?" Hatu interrupted.

"That is a wonderful question," Nakor said, grinning. "If you find an answer, I would like to know."

"Forces beyond our understanding," Pug said. "It began when I was still serving the Duke of Crydee, and apprentice to the magician Kulgan. A storm brought us to Sorcerer's Isle for the first time. That's where I first met Macros the Black."

Pug explained the evolution of his relationship with the Black Sorcerer. "As fate would have it, it was his daughter I wed." He glanced at Nakor to see if he was going to inject something gratuitous, but he was surprisingly silent.

Pug told Hatu about Tomas. "On the same journey, my foster brother, Tomas, became separated from the duke's party in the vast dwarven mines we were using to travel under the Grey Tower Mountains." He detailed how Tomas had eluded a wraith, Pug's first encounter with one of the Children of the Void, and how he had eventually found his way to a dragon's lair. At the mention of the blind dragon Rhuagh, Hatu's eyes widened. "The dwarf leader Dolgan found him, and both witnessed the final passing of that great dragon. As a gift, Tomas was given the magic armor of Ashen-Shugar, last of the Dragon Lords, and eventually gained the mystic powers within that armor."

Despite all he had come to know about magic and other worlds, Hatushaly was captivated by the story. By the time Pug had explained their search for Macros, to find aid in confronting the Darkness, Hatu was riveted. He hung on every word, and seemed eager to ask questions, but remained silent.

Pug told his story for almost an hour, reaching the part about the time-trap concocted by the Pantathian Serpent Priests, and the flight backward through time.

At last, Pug said, "When time stopped—"

Hatu blinked. "Time stopped?"

"Well, we stopped our flight backward in time," said Pug. "And all of reality stood before us as a . . . very large ball."

"A ball?"

Pug waved his hand. "Since then, I've learned that our perceptions are limited: everything is a matter of how we see things and our perspective."

Nakor grinned and nodded. "Before I died the first time, in between realms, I saw things—"

Pug held up his hand. "As did I. More than once in my life I've learned it's vanity to assume what we see is 'real' and not just what we can perceive and understand."

"Tell me what you do understand," Hatu asked.

"We reached our goal, the Garden at the edge of the City Forever." Hatushaly's expression was puzzled.

"The City Forever is a place inside the Void . . ." Pug began, and then he stopped. "We need to differentiate between the Void, that grey, featureless place, and the Void."

Nakor shrugged. "We also call it rift-space."

Pug smiled. "We shall call the grey void 'rift-space.'"

Hatu tilted his head. "Rift-space makes sense." Then he asked, "If it's an empty place, why are those other places there?"

Nakor laughed. "A question that has been asked by many, explained by none. One day you will have to visit the Hall of Worlds and Honest John's."

Pug waved this comment aside. "The Garden floats just above the edge of the City Forever. Both places appear to be adrift in time, somehow separate from time itself.

"In any event, we were seeking Macros the Black. We set down in the Garden, and as he tried to warn us away, a time-trap was sprung, hurling us into the past. I still don't know how that trap was fashioned. Macros and I used our magic to increase the speed of travel, doubling it repeatedly until centuries flew by in moments. When we reached the beginning of time, the trap ceased to exist; back then, time had no meaning. Then we saw the creation of this universe.

"That ball exploded with the brilliance of countless stars and spread out in all directions. It was the birth of this universe. Once out of the time-trap, we were able to return to our current time."

Hatu was silent, considering what Pug had just said, then he asked, "How did you return without waiting for . . . billions of years?"

Nakor looked at Pug and said, "That is a very good question."

"Macros had opposed the Void before I was born; he and a dragon named Ryath together made the journey possible. It was she who could breach the barriers of time and space. Macros and I accelerated the passage of time, using the same magic as before."

"So, you traveled to the past, then again to the future?" asked Hatu.

"Yes," Pug answered.

"Ah." Hatu looked at Pug and said, "Then I think maybe I need to speak with a dragon, perhaps this Ryath?"

"A great many dragons perished in our last confrontation with the servants of the Void, the Dread. We barely survived, and the world of Midkemia paid a terrible price for that victory."

Nakor pointed at Pug. "He died."

Pug looked annoyed and continued, "During my second incarnation, before my earlier memories returned, I spent years traveling Midkemia with Magnus, and not even rumors of dragons were heard. I know not all perished, but it seems likely they chose no longer to reveal themselves to the other races."

Nakor said, "Still, if they're out there, we might be able to find one for you to talk to."

Pug went on, "The Pantathian Serpent Priests constructed the time-trap. At least that was our assumption, but if they also served the Void, even unknowingly, that would answer questions I have had for a very long time. They were a race without natural magical abilities, we learned, but when they found magic it . . . robbed them of both intelligence and any sense of right and wrong. Perhaps it was from the Void these powers came. The most powerful of the Serpent Priests were all but mindless and blindly obeyed orders."

"Perhaps like an army sitting, waiting, in the middle of Marquensas?" Nakor suggested, raising his eyebrows.

Pug nodded slowly. "That is very possible."

"Maybe that's why I was sent back?"

"So many questions," Pug replied.

"That's why I think this Church must be ended," said Nakor. "The Pantathians were enough of a problem and there were only a few of them. But this Church? They control nations, and armies. They can put dead people in the field by the thousands."

Pug sat back, took another drink of wine, and said, "I'm at a loss what to do next."

"Do what we know we need to do," said Hatushaly. "Get that fleet

Hava is taking to your world, keep looking for where the Church attacks next, and hope we come up with a means of confronting the Void when it next appears."

Nakor grinned. "The energy of youth! How I miss it."

Pug chuckled. "I've never noticed you lacking energy in all the years I've known you."

Nakor smiled again. "You should have seen me when I was a young man."

"The mind boggles," Pug replied. He stood up and said, "Hatu, you should return to Declan and the king, and if you can use your far-seeing ability to spy out the Church's army, please do. Information is key.

"Nakor, you and I have some work to do, back on Midkemia."

"What?" asked the little man.

"I need to see if any geomancer is willing to travel here and hasten King Daylon's roadbuilding. I've been putting it off, and now's the time. And then, we both need to start looking for a dragon."

Nakor nodded his head enthusiastically. "I like that. I may have met dragons before, but if I did, I don't remember, so it will be my first time. That is very interesting."

The three left the room, and Hatu moved back toward the king's chamber.

Nakor stopped and touched Pug's arm. Pug looked at him. "Yes?"

Nakor took a breath, grinned, and said, "I guess we go find a dragon."

CHAPTER 24

SEARCHING

Pug stepped through the rift.

A young magician named Helena sat in a chair in the rift chamber. She put down a book, stood up, and said, "Welcome back." She was petite, with close-cropped light brown hair and dark eyes, and a winsome smile. Pug knew her to be a gifted student, though a novice.

He smiled back. "Where's . . ." He almost said "my son" but caught himself at the last moment and said, "Magnus?"

"He's here, in the meeting room by his quarters," she replied.

Pug thanked her and left the chamber. Magnus must feel comfortable, leaving a youngster to watch the rift. Since Hatu had detected a tiny gap at the rift's edges, suggesting that was where creatures of the Void came through when rifts were left open too long, Pug and Magnus had fixed it. After that, nothing unwelcome had slipped though.

Pug hurried to the meeting room and found Magnus in discussion with Zaakara and Sabella. Magnus said, "We're discussing something interesting. You're just in time." As Pug sat down, Magnus looked at Sabella. "Why don't you fill Pug in?"

She nodded. "We just started a little bit ago, and you already know most of what I've discovered, that energy flows from Midkemia to Garn. Just enough that Zara, Daria, Eefe, Beryl, and I could aid Zaakara in opening a small rift back here after Hatushaly left Garn."

"Yes," said Pug. "What have you found that's new?"

"If you could find a world with even more energy available than here, I think it might be possible to channel that energy to Garn."

Pug was silent for a moment, then said, "Not a bad idea." He looked at Magnus. "Honest John's?"

Magnus considered that for a moment. "We've never found worlds significantly higher in mana than here, but that doesn't mean they don't exist. It shouldn't take long to question a few of the better information sources there."

Zaakara looked at Pug and asked, "How stand things on Garn?"

"Badly," Pug replied. "Nakor is convinced the Church of the One is serving the Void, and I think he's right. He says the Church must be eliminated before the Void's next attack, and I see nothing faulty in his logic."

Zaakara's expression was troubled. "You've more pressing matters to address, but Sabella has done a remarkable job in simplifying several common spells. It will make teaching the new students much easier, I think."

Sabella smiled and lowered her gaze. "Once I see the common elements in the rituals and what is unnecessary, it's fairly easy to do."

Pug smiled broadly. "And yet, with all the brilliant minds"—he glanced at Magnus and Zaakara, and his voice held a hint of irony—"we've had here for centuries, you were the first to think of it. Well done."

Magnus stood up. "We'd best be about our respective tasks." Zaakara and Sabella rose from their seats and left. Magnus looked at Pug. "Those two seem to have formed something of a bond."

Pug gestured agreement. "He seems to have taken to her more like a daughter than his student." Then he chuckled. "What she has in mind, I have no idea."

"So, he may be in trouble?"

Pug laughed. "I enjoy squeezing every moment of humor possible out of life given how much horror and pain we confront."

"Given his parents, it's no wonder he's a bit aloof with women."

"Gods, they did fight, didn't they?"

Magnus also smiled. "One good thing about having your memories fully restored—I don't have to explain a great many things to you anymore. Now you remember Amirantha and Sandreena in their prime, not as an old couple quarreling all the time."

"Not all the time," Pug corrected. "They did love each other a great deal."

"True," Magnus agreed.

"I came back to tell you things are moving apace. Hava is, as I once said, exceptionally gifted. She is very hard to say no to."

Magnus chuckled. "Does she still remind you of Mother?"

"More now than ever. Hatushaly is a rare young man, and I think that's in large part because of her." He paused, then said, "We have known some remarkable women in our lives."

"That we have," Magnus agreed.

"So, how goes buying what Marquensas needs?"

"It goes well. I've got our agents arranging many small deliveries at various ports. Our captains can pick them up without creating undue curiosity. It will take longer that way, but it's safer. I'm a little more concerned about organizing things here to have Hava's fleet pick everything up in an orderly fashion, but among ourselves we have enough ability to make up for a lack of stevedores and barges. Unloading in Marquenet will be more conventional. If it works out, we can perhaps manage one or two more shipments before anyone beyond our confidants starts noticing."

"Good," said Pug. At this point he had assumed no more authority on Sorcerer's Isle than previously, but now Magnus was deferring to his judgment more often.

"Where to now?" Magnus asked.

"I think it best if I go back to Garn and see how the two geomancers you sent through are doing with that road between the redoubt and Marquenet, and how Hava's doing with organizing that fleet." He glanced around. "By the way, Nakor?"

Magnus slowly shook his head, and said, "Who knows? He comes and goes like the wind, and has it ever been different?"

Pug agreed. "Never. I'll be back as soon as I have new information."

Magnus gave him a quick hug. "Be safe." The embrace was unexpected. Even as his son, Magnus was always a bit distant.

"I will," said Pug, leaving his son and mentor behind as he returned to the rift chamber. He entered, nodded to another student watching the portal, and quickly walked through.

For a moment, he blinked, as the light changed from a slightly overcast day on Sorcerer's Isle to brilliant sunlight at the Sanctuary. He hurried quickly to discover Nakor, Hatushaly, and Bodai in discussion at a table in the dining hall.

"There you are," Pug said to Nakor.

"I got bored," said Nakor, as if that explained everything.

Pug nodded a greeting to the other two at the table, and said, "What's going on?"

"I fetched Bodai off the ship—" Hatu began.

"Obviously," said Nakor. "Get on with it."

Hatu's furrowed brow showed his reaction to the interruption. "We returned to Marquensas and conferred with the king and Declan, and decided we needed to wait upon enlisting the aid of Coaltachin in facing the Church."

Bodai held up a hand in greeting. "It was well-timed. I was less than a day from changing ships for the last leg to the home island. The last ship would not be a merchant, but a Council ship, and everyone would have known who I am. Now, if anyone misses me, they'll probably assume that another passenger managed to fall overboard at night. Besides, I still had no idea what I was going to say to the other masters."

"The truth often works." Nakor grinned. "Though sometimes it doesn't."

Bodai nodded. "True."

"So, what have you discovered that has you all agitated?" Pug asked.

"We're receiving rumors of odd goings-on in Nytanny," said Hatu. "Hava left this morning to return to Shechal to continue putting together a fleet. I pop over here when I know she's due back."

Pug nodded. "You miss her. I understand."

Hatu's expression was a mix of humor and resignation. "I also do not want her to think I'm ignoring her. I've had to deal with her mood after getting lost in my own studies far too often."

"Wise man," said Nakor.

"The rumors?" Pug asked.

"The entire continent is still in chaos, but something unusual is starting to happen." Hatu's concern was obvious.

Nakor's expression betrayed impatience. "What is happening is that the Children of the Void may be stirring."

Pug stepped back in shock. "That rumor must be investigated!"

"That was what I was about to say when you turned up," said Nakor.

"Where is this?" asked Pug.

"In the center of the continent is a massive plateau, a mile above everything else, surrounded by mountains. There's some sort of stone city there, and it's full of these creatures—"

"Full of?" Pug asked. "How many?"

"Hundreds," said Hatu. "Maybe more."

Pug's expression was grim, and his complexion paled. "One wraith alone can be a challenge for all but the most powerful magic-user on Midkemia! Here? I would be cautious facing one alone."

Hatu's expression was determined. "You're not alone."

"I understand," said Pug, looking at Hatu, then Nakor.

Nakor indicated that he, too, understood. "They're all stone statues up there. It does no one any good to sit and worry about them now. Maybe later it will. I went snooping down in that big canyon . . ."

"Garn's Wound," said Hatu.

"There's a village there, full of very sad people, who are in thrall to a Dreadlord."

Pug's eyes opened wide. "A Dreadlord? Why didn't you say something immediately?"

Nakor lifted his shoulders. "Didn't seem important."

"Not important?" Pug was incredulous.

"It's not moving. Just there," said Nakor. "There seemed to be other things to worry about first."

Pug could barely contain his irritation at Nakor's capricious approach to sharing information, but he knew that arguing with him about what he should have done was a pointless exercise. Pushing aside his incredulity at how Nakor set his priorities, he pulled out a chair and sat down. "Tell me everything," he said to Hatu, giving a sidelong glance to Nakor. Barely controlling his anger, he said, "I mean *every-thing*!"

IT WAS BODAI WHO LOOKED as if he was going to faint when Hatu finished detailing everything he had discovered with Ruffio, Zaakara, and Nathan. Bodai trembled, and perspiration dotted his brow.

"Are you all right?" Hatu asked his former teacher.

"No," said Bodai. "I've seen many terrible things in my life, but creatures that can suck the life out of you with just a touch?" He took a slow breath, calming himself. "How do you fight something like that?"

"Well, they don't like the touch of cold steel," offered Nakor. "Hit them enough times and they go away." Then he paused, and added, "But they only have to hit you once, so it's tricky."

Pug scowled. "Ignore that. Simply put, on my world I can easily destroy as many as three wraiths, specters, wights, or other creatures from the Void singlehanded, but here?" He sat back and crossed his arms and said softly, "I would dare to face one. Two or more? I would likely flee."

Bodai looked as if he was wilting. "That's not reassuring. There are what? Four, five of you magicians?"

"More," said Nakor. "Many more on Midkemia, and some other places, but none as good as him or Magnus."

"Not helping!" Pug looked at Nakor with a scowl.

"I'll be quiet now." Nakor tried to look contrite and failed.

Pug turned to Bodai. "I know this can be overwhelming, so I understand your disquiet. If I said not to worry, I'd be insulting your intelligence. But I will ask you not to panic. Hatu and Hava both praised your wisdom, and you have more knowledge about the local politics of this planet than anyone else we can trust. So, please, marshal your resolve and help us."

Bodai took a deep breath and appeared to summon some strength. "I'm an old man who's given up much to serve a greater power. It's clear to me now that the Flame Guard was created for a purpose far beyond what we were led to believe." He took another long, deep breath, then added, "Of course, anything in my power to do, all you need to do is ask."

"Good," said Pug, gripping Bodai's shoulder. He turned to Hatu. "You said Ruffio, Zaakara, and this Nathan traveled with you?"

"Not traveled, literally, but witnessed through my vision."

Pug looked at Nakor with a raised eyebrow. "Nathan?"

Nakor put up his hands. "Don't look at me. I'm not him." Then he muttered, "At least I don't think I was." He looked at Pug and said, "I don't remember a lot of things."

Pug sighed. "If Ruffio or Zaakara mentioned a group of Children of the Void to Magnus, why am I only hearing of it now?"

"People forget?" There was no hint of humor in Nakor's remark. "Or someone made them forget?"

Hatu said, "Through my vision they looked like stone carvings, not . . . alive, if that's the right word for these things. I'm not even sure what it was we all saw." He sat back, and added, "Perhaps Ruffio and Zaakara saw them differently?"

Pug forced himself to calmness. "This entire situation is fraught with the unexplainable." He looked at Nakor: "Your return . . ." and then at Hatu: ". . . and generations of your family becoming the sole conduit for magic on Garn." He put his palms down on the table and softly said, "We are but the tools of agencies unknown to us. They will reveal themselves to us—"

"Or not," Nakor interjected.

"Or not, but whatever truth is to be found, for the moment we must deal with the menaces before us." He stood up. To Hatu he said, "Can you guide me to this place of evil?"

Hatu said, "Easily. There is the Curb, a barrier of death surrounding this area—" Pug was about to say he could use a spell to shield them, but before he could speak, Hatu continued, "—but I can protect us."

Pug realized he had to stop underestimating what this young man, barely older than a boy, could do.

Hatu reached for Pug's arm, gripped it firmly, then they both vanished.

Nakor looked at Bodai.

"What?" Bodai asked.

"I'm out of oranges."

"We can find some in the kitchen," said Bodai.

Nakor looked at Bodai with a serious expression, then grinned. "I think this time I'd rather have a drink, before I catch up to those two."

Bodai got up and moved toward the kitchen. "I won't argue."

DONTE SAT WATCHING THE CHILDREN who were tending the sheep but half-playing with them. The sounds of shouting and laughter was punctuated by the bleating of sheep as they moved away only to be chased by happy children. The afternoon sun bathed the scene in a warm glow as glistening sparks shone off puddles left by earlier rain.

Lyndon said, "They were here for three days of cold and wet, so they're just happy to be outside."

Donte tried to mask his disappointment as he said, "I wanted to build a crew and I get sheepherders." Sighing, he sat on a stool and said, "It's my own fault. I should have stuck with pigs."

Scully tried not to laugh and failed to hide his amusement. "It may not work out as you planned, but at least it's a better situation than we hoped for. If the Mockers are not going to meddle, we can keep pitting the Keshians against the boys from Krondor for a while."

Robertson straddled a reversed chair, his arms folded across the top of its back. "And if we can deliver Lester Ving to Krondor, there's a sizable bounty for us."

Donte was tired and he wanted to think. "I need to know more about those false Mockers. From what little I've seen, I'd have guessed maybe they were thirty or forty strong before the Keshians hit them. Guessing when someone else is risking a sword point is one thing, but when the blade's pointed at your own throat, that's a different matter."

"Agreed," said Scully. "So, what next?"

"Information," said Donte. He almost grimaced: so much of his life had been spent acting out against the discipline and lessons his training demanded, yet here he was taking those very lessons to heart and, by utilizing them, acknowledging their wisdom. Still, survival was paramount, advancement next, and if this was the way to get to those goals, so be it.

"How so?" asked Scully.

"Who's ready to mingle in the streets with open ears?"

"David, easily," said Robertson. "He's a quick one. Catches on fast. Mark, as well. The older lads have a better knack for staying alive."

"Where's Healer?" Donte asked.

"Got an ill sheep. Trying to see if it's something might turn the whole flock sick."

"Wonderful," said Donte sarcastically. "Just what I need now, a plague." He stood up and said, "Get David and Mark ready to travel. They'll be leaving with me in an hour."

Donte made his way to the large shed used to store tools and found Healer with a circle of children tending to a ewe that was lying on her side. "What's this?" he asked.

"They found her like this, and I dragged her here to keep the other sheep safe," said Healer.

"How long ago?" Donte asked, pushing past the children.

"Less than an hour ago."

"Let me see." He knelt and saw the ewe's abdomen was distended, as if she'd swallowed a balloon. He nodded and said, "Kids, go to the house." When they hesitated, he shouted, "Now!"

They scurried to obey, and he pulled a knife from his belt.

"You going to kill her?" asked Healer.

"No," said Donte. "It's simple bloat. I worked at a farm as a young-ster for a few months and saw this before. Now watch." He felt her ribs and between the last rib and hip, he put two fingers down with his left hand. Then with a quick downward jab with the knife punched a small incision. A hiss of released gas and a foul stench were accompanied by an indignant bleat. Donte pressed down to hold the incision open as the gas escaped and, after a moment, the ewe started kicking with her back legs. Then she scrambled up and fled out of the open door back to the pasture.

"It's all that damned wet grass. They eat too fast, and they can't belch out the gas. Have the kids watch the others for distress, and you saw where to cut: between the last rib and hip; and don't go any deeper than when you hear the gas."

"Smell it, you mean," said Healer.

"Whatever gets it done," said Donte. "Keep a watch for the cut festering, but if it doesn't, the sheep will live. If this wet weather keeps up, we might have to cut some of this grass. Fat mutton is good, but dead sheep aren't."

An hour later, Donte had the two oldest boys ready to leave with haversacks over their shoulders. Each boy wore nondescript, simple travel wear: loose-fitting tunics; baggy trousers tucked into the top of their boots. Each had a small assortment of daggers secreted about them, one in the belt, one at the small of the back, and a pair of smaller blades, one each in a boot.

"I'll ride, you walk," said Donte, mounting his horse. "We'll stay together until we're in sight of the city and then I'll head in before you. As soon as you're near the gates, you'll split up. Come on now, let's get to it."

A few of the children with Healer stood watching as the three set off toward Port Vykor.

"Now," said Donte as he walked his horse so the boys could keep up, "we start with your legends."

"Legends?" said Mark. "What's that?"

"The lie about who you are. You need to learn it like it's truth, so you don't accidentally say something to botch the con. Got it?"

David nodded, but Mark looked doubtful.

"This may be a very long ride," Donte muttered.

HATU SAID, "THE LAST TIME I saw that city, or whatever it is, was in a vision. Even then I felt the Curb encircling it and I had to defend against that harming us through my vision. This time we're going there physically, so I don't know what to expect."

Pug looked first at Nakor, who nodded his understanding, then at Hatu and said, "Get us to a location close to this barrier and we'll examine it before we cross."

Hatu nodded and said, "Ready?" He reached out and put his hands on their shoulders and immediately they stood on a windswept granite ledge atop a rocky precipice.

"I can feel it," said Nakor.

"As can I," Pug said.

Hatu looked toward a cliff face which rose hundreds of feet. He pointed to the west and said, "That way lies the Curb. I feel it, too. I think we'll all know when to stop moving toward it."

Pug peered at the next escarpment and said, "I judge that to be less than a few miles, so we should be able to walk it." He glanced around. "Not a lot of plants." He paused to listen, closed his eyes for a moment, then added, "I don't sense any animals of size nearby."

Nakor said, "Feels dead to me."

Pug silently nodded.

They began walking and each felt a rising sense of risk with each step they took. Finally, when they were a few hundred yards short of the next cliff face, they all stopped.

"Any farther and we're taking needless risk," said Pug. He looked at Hatu. "When you used your vision, what precautions did you take?"

"I don't know if I can fully explain it, but I sensed how . . . energy moved between the furies, one way or the other. I felt that this Curb was designed to draw the life force out of us, so I . . ." He paused. "I guess you could say I just wouldn't let it."

"Impressive," said Nakor.

Pug motioned for him to stand close, then cast a spell. He asked, "Did it feel like this?"

Hatu extended his senses and said, "Something like this, yes."

Nakor grinned. "As I said, impressive."

"Protection wards need to be as powerful as what they are shielding us from, Hatu," said Pug. "This is a very powerful defense and to fend it off takes great mastery. Like many other things, you did it intuitively." He reached out and put his arms around Hatu's and Nakor's waists. "While we investigate, I think it best if we stay close."

Without waiting for a reply, Pug elevated them straight up until they could look down into the plateau's center. A flat ring of empty land circled a massive structure, seemingly fashioned out of the heart of the plateau, carved into the stone. It was an open maze, but punctuated with domes and square edifices, without apparent purpose.

Pug cautiously moved closer and downward, and as he did so, more details became apparent. Most terrifying were frozen figures Pug knew all too well. "Children of the Void," he said.

"That's what Ruffio called them," said Hatu.

"They look like stone," said Pug. "I can see why you may have thought them statues, or no threat."

After they descended more closely, Nakor said, "They aren't stone!"

Pug reached out mentally and gently probed a figure of what he took to be a wraith close by, and after a moment he softly said, "It's alive."

"Or as close to that as these things get," said Nakor.

Pug steered them down until their feet touched the stone and all three felt a strange tugging, as if something was seeking to suck them down.

"The life-draining force here is fierce," Nakor said.

"Worse than anything I've seen before," agreed Pug.

"What is this place?" asked Hatu.

"I have no idea," Pug admitted. "It resembles a warren, an alien imitation of a city, perhaps?"

"We're only going to find out by looking," Nakor said.

Pug moved toward the nearest structure and they descended through an opening. They settled on the stones and Pug said, "Stay close. Let's see what's here."

They entered the structure, and Hatu created a circle of light around them, and they found a ramp leading downward. The walls were featureless, as if somehow carved out of solid stone by some device or agency that created perfect tunnels.

They descended to a large room with a vaulted ceiling. Across the floor lay a lattice of stones, tilting slightly downward, toward another tunnel on the far side. Walking toward the tunnel, they inspected the chamber. Upon the walls were dozens of odd symbols carved into the stone.

"What is all this?" Pug wondered aloud.

"It's not any language," said Hatu.

Pug and Nakor both looked at him, and Nakor asked, "If not any language, what is it?"

Hatushaly stepped closer and examined the multitude of lines that ran from the floor to the ceiling, some branching off to the right or left. He stared for a few seconds. "I have no idea." He turned to look back at Pug and Nakor. "Everything here is . . . different." He closed his eyes and after a moment, opened them again. "I can barely see any of the normal threads of energy that surround us out there." He pointed in the direction from which they had come. "I can sense the protective spell you cast around us, Pug, and am sure that's what's keeping us alive."

Nakor said, "This place is . . . ungiving. Not a blade of grass, not an insect, nothing within the . . . whatever it's called."

"The Curb," Pug answered. "Come, I have an idea." He motioned for them to stay close and continued walking across the chamber and up an incline opposite the one by which they had entered.

Lines and geometric designs were carved everywhere, and finally when they emerged aboveground they could see hundreds of motionless figures, shadow creatures of various sizes and shapes. As they passed close to something taller than any of them, Nakor said, "Wait!"

He dropped to his knees and half-crawled until his face was down above the stones, mere inches from the bottom of the figure. It was of roughly human shape but appeared as if it were created out of smoke, partially translucent, and frozen in an instant.

"What are you doing?" Pug asked.

Nakor sat back on his heels. "There may be no spiders or insects, birds or grass here, but there is dust. Look closely. This thing is moving."

Hatu got down next to Nakor, while Pug used his magic to look closely at the bottom of the figure, which looked something like the hem of a long robe that swept the ground. Behind it was a tiny, thin line containing noticeably less dust than everywhere else around.

"How did you notice that?" Hatushaly asked.

"Noticing things is how a gambler stays alive as long as I have . . . or did. You know what I mean." Nakor stood up. "Time here did not stop, it just slowed to the point at which a second may take years, or even longer."

Pug's brow furrowed. "I used a similar spell to slow time around Princess Anita when she was poisoned, so Prince Arutha had time to travel . . . to find a cure." He cut short the story. "Come close," he said.

When they were close, Pug again put his arms around their waists. "Hatu, you have the power. Take us up for a better view, please." Suddenly they were rising into the air. Abruptly, the sun shone brightly.

Hatu said, "Letting more light in helps."

Looking down, Pug asked, "What do you see?"

Nakor said, "A very odd-looking city full of evil things."

Hatushaly took a moment, adjusted his senses to the energies that now flooded his senses, then said, "It's a dome!"

In an instant they again stood at the edge of the plateau.

"What is all this?" Hatushaly asked.

"I don't know," Pug answered. "But at some time in the past, the Void or its agents created this horror, and someone else froze it."

"Macros," said Nakor.

Pug's eyebrows rose and his eyes widened, but before he could speak, Nakor said, "This world has no apparent divinities, or celestials. Of every mortal we have met, human or otherwise, he is the only one who might have had the power to do something like this. Imagine appearing here, with all your skills, and doing this while fighting off those creatures, or the Dread?"

Pug said, "With the low energy here? Impossible."

"Perhaps that was before, when stuff was . . . more . . ." He shrugged. ". . . abundant? I don't know what I'm saying." He pointed at Hatushaly. "Him, all the stuff to do tricks ends up in one family, then just in Hatu?" Again, he shrugged. "How did all that happen?"

"There's a design to all this I certainly do not understand," Pug admitted.

"Then we should find someone who does," said Nakor.

"Who?" asked Pug.

Nakor waved his hand in a circle. "This place must be known to someone who wrote history. We just need to find out who."

Hatushaly said, "Declan and the king were here fighting the Pride Lords. Most of the army of Marquensas was here. Someone may have seen something."

"I'll go," said Pug. "You return to the Sanctuary and see what's in that library, and perhaps Bodai knows something."

"I have an idea!" said Nakor, and he vanished.

Pug gave out a long sigh. "He does that."

CHAPTER 25

DISCOVERIES

Nakor floated.

He hovered above the dark sphere he had visited with Hatushaly and Pug. He rose slowly until he could observe the entire area clearly. An occasional cloud drifted between, but he found that only mildly annoying. In his left arm he held a large piece of wood, extending from the crook of his elbow to beyond his fingertips. He had affixed a cord to the back and wrapped that around his wrist in case he lost his grip. In his right hand he held a long stick of drawing charcoal.

He drew.

It had taken him a few minutes to get to this height and working out how to anchor himself above it had taken a bit of experimenting. Before that, he'd used the same trick he had seen Hatushaly employ to rid the dome of the darkness and had been pleased to discover it was a very easy trick. Then he again wondered if he had already known it before and had just forgotten it. He had armored himself against the cold at this altitude, and while the air was thin, he could cope with it—he'd endured higher mountain peaks before.

He had been drawing as much as he could see from above, wishing he was a better draftsman, but content that he was getting enough detail to convey a good idea of what this place was to anyone who might understand the design.

Dark clouds were coming up from the western side of the escarpment and the sun was moving toward the horizon. Nakor glanced down to see if there was some important-looking detail he might have missed, then decided the light was failing too quickly for him to be certain what was a feature and what was a lengthening shadow. And his arm was starting to ache, so he put the charcoal stick in his rucksack and vanished.

A moment later he stood before the doorway at the Sanctuary that entered the Hall of Worlds. Farther to the east than a moment earlier, he arrived at twilight. He took a moment to enjoy firm ground beneath his feet and the luxury of unfolding his arm and flexing it a little. He had no idea if he was who he thought he was, if this was truly a mortal body or some construction of energy created by an unknown entity. But however he had come into existence this time, he certainly felt every ache and pain as if he were mortal.

And hunger. He realized he hadn't eaten all day and had nothing in his pack to eat. He balanced the need for food against the urgency of discovering the secret of that alien place; then he decided to eat.

Entering the dining hall, he saw it was virtually empty, with only a handful of students getting ready for the evening meal. Nakor hurried to where the plates were stacked, grabbed one, and quickly filled it with food. He elected for some fruit, tossing two oranges into his pack, a large portion of dark bread, and a thick slice of cheese. Juggling the board over one shoulder, his rucksack over the other, and a platter, he managed to grab a flagon of ale and get to a chair without spilling anything.

Halfway through his meal, he saw Pug and Hava enter the hall. Pug said something to Hava, and they both approached the table.

"Where did you go?" Pug spoke in even tones, though his expression betrayed his annoyance.

Hava tried to conceal her amusement. "I'm going to grab some food." Looking at Pug, she added, "Can I fetch you something?"

He shook his head. "Thanks, but I'll be along shortly."

Nakor motioned toward the large board leaning against the table. "Look at that."

Pug picked up the board and inspected the drawing.

"Don't smudge it," Nakor warned.

Pug studied it for a moment and asked, "Is that the place under the dome?"

"As well as I can draw it," Nakor answered.

"I think you got it close."

"I just need to show this to someone I think may know what it is." Nakor shoved the last piece of cheese and bread into his mouth, chewed, and swallowed, then said, "It's not a city."

"It's big enough to be one."

Nakor said, "Damn!"

"What?" Pug asked.

"I left my staff there. This damned low-energy place. Still, I better get on." He grabbed the drawing and his rucksack, then vanished.

Hava returned just as Nakor disappeared, and said, "I will never get used to that, I swear. Where's he off to?"

Pug looked at her. "I don't think even the gods know where he goes."

"Better get something to eat," she advised, as she sat down. "A swarm of hungry workers is about to descend and if you want any of the good food, you need to be quick."

Pug smiled. "There are moments when you do very much remind me of Magnus's mother."

"Is that a good thing?" Hava asked.

Pug smiled. "It's a very good thing." He turned and moved toward the food tables.

DONTE HALTED HIS HORSE AND dismounted. In the distance lay Port Vykor with the sun halfway to sundown. "Now, any last questions?" he asked the boys.

David glanced down the road. The boys knew that from this point Donte would ride ahead and they would enter the city after him. He slowly looked around and said, "My name is Davie, from a village near the edge of the border, Ilbundi, closer to Landreth than here. I'm looking for my brother."

"What's his name?" Donte studied David to see if there was any hint of lying.

"Tommy. He and our father got into it over him staying on the farm, so he ran away. We know he went north."

"And . . . ?" Donte kept his eyes fixed on the youngster.

"Our father died, and our mother sent me looking for Tommy while she and my little brother work the farm."

"What type of farm?"

"Sheep," said David.

Donte pointed at Mark. "You."

"I'm Micky from Landreth and I want to go to sea, so I needed to get to Port Vykor."

"Good. Makes for why you're acting like a dock rat."

Donte asked a few more questions, then said, "I guess you're as ready as you'll ever be. Now, keep your secret purse inside your trousers secret! You know Port Vykor well enough to stay out of needless trouble. Remember, with Healer at the farm, you're on your own. Try to avoid anyone who might remember you, and if you need me, leave word at the Four Ravens and we'll set up a meet." He mounted his horse and without another word rode toward the city.

He entered the city an hour later and found his way to a reputable boarding stable where he arranged for his horse's keep and getting his saddle and tack cleaned. It was nearing sundown as he set out for the Four Ravens. On arrival, everything looked exactly the way it had the last time he had been there.

Not unexpectedly, Shad's first words were, "Buying a drink?"

Donte muttered, "It's nice to know that in an uncertain universe, some things are predictable." He raised his voice and said, "Yes, a mug of ale."

When the mug was placed before him, Donte took a long swallow, then said, "If I go up to my room, will it be empty?"

"Should be," said Shad. "Kept it like you told me."

"Somehow I doubt that," said Donte. "Just make sure the sheets are clean." He turned and looked around. "Now we get to work."

DECLAN READ THE REPORT THE king handed to him. "Have you seen this?" he asked Balven.

"Of course." Balven had a troubled expression. The message from the redoubt had arrived while Declan was making an inspection of the forges and speaking with Edvalt Tasman on what was needed to continue arming the kingdom. Word of the rider reached him there, and he had hurried to the king's chamber without being summoned.

"They're dead? All of them?" He tossed the message back on the table in King Daylon's council room.

"You read it," said the king. "The Church soldiers in the field before the forest, and those in the big encampment behind them. Corpses everywhere."

"I left after the battle over two weeks ago," said Declan. "They should have been provisioned for a long march, so food and water would have been ample. Why are they dead?"

"I sent back word that we need more information," said Balven. "Retreating I would understand. Quitting the field to regroup, plan another attack, seek another course of action, but to just sit there and die?" His distress was obvious. "It's as if they don't need this army."

Declan considered that for a moment. "They don't. Or at least they don't need a living army. I know that all too well." Daylon and Balven looked at him expectantly. "Dying of thirst and starvation is obvious, but this part about the dead just lying there, it . . ." Then he sat up, almost leaving his seat. "The bodies should have stunk enough that any breeze would have washed the stench to the redoubt, and the carrion birds and scavengers should have descended in flocks. Those corpses would have been mutilated by now."

Daylon recalled the scene after the Battle of Betrayal, when the last King of Ithrace had been murdered. "Crows would be swarming; vultures would be soaring above to swoop down upon the dead. The field would be overrun with carrion eaters: wild dogs, foxes, right down to beetles and ants."

"I must go and see," said Declan standing up. "If Hatushaly turns up, have him find me. I'm leaving by horse now!"

He departed before the king formally gave him permission to depart, which hardly surprised Daylon. Things remained informal when the brothers were alone. He turned to look at Balven. "I'll be relieved to learn what he finds there."

Balven said softly, "I won't. I have a sense of foreboding."

Daylon drummed his fingers on the table. "Yes, 'relieved' is the

wrong word. There is too much here of dark magic, especially when I
didn't believe in magic only a year ago."

Balven said, "That is indeed my foreboding."

NAKOR HAD FOUND HIS STAFF where he'd left it, outside the dark
dome on Nytanny, and had recovered it without incident, then had
gone back to the door from the Sanctuary to the Hall of Worlds. Once
in the Hall, it had been a short jump to the entrance to Honest John's.
He entered, and again was greeted by Kwad, the large Coropaban who
had been the door bouncer for as long as Nakor could remember. He
gave over his staff and a small dagger in his robe, then entered. As with
every time before, he took a moment to inspect this improbable establishment.

A vaulting roof of four stories rose overhead, each floor revealing
an open gallery overlooking the main floor. This main floor was a
massive casino displaying games of chance from a multitude of worlds,
offering almost numberless opportunities to lose a fortune. Interspersed
were open cafés and moneylenders' booths, and around the edges were
brothels, sleeping quarters, tailors, and other common places of business. The galleries above were populated by purveyors of rare goods,
skilled craftsmen, illicit merchandise, and any service imaginable. The
massive and varied architecture of Honest John's constantly evolved,
and getting lost was a common hazard. The decor was bright, slightly
chaotic, and still managed to come together in a style Nakor thought
he'd seen before, though he couldn't recall the name for it.

Brightly painted walls were trimmed with white crown molding
at every level, and the dome of the ceiling was adorned with paintings
he had never bothered to inspect closely, but he expected them to be
grand, tasteless, or both. The floor was a nicely carpeted expanse in a
deep wine color, which somehow was always clean.

He made his way through the crowd, avoiding many who were indifferent to his passing, twice almost being stepped on, and once avoiding
someone from across the room he did not wish to waste time speaking
with—a short man with a wide smile and a slightly deranged look in

his eye. Nakor was unsure if he was someone to whom he owed money or someone he just didn't care to spend time with. That part of his memory was missing, but in any case, he felt the need to avoid him. So, he adroitly made his way through the gaming tables and curled back around to the grand staircase to the upper levels.

Nakor hurried up the steps and dodged among the many beings working their way up and down, then entered the first gallery level. Quickly, he reached the shop he sought.

He entered Vordam's establishment and found the Delecordian dusting the room with a strange-looking contraption of feathers. "You know, you could hire someone to clean up for you."

Vordam smiled. "It gives me something to do while waiting for clients, and besides, it saves me money."

"There is that," Nakor said.

"What have you there?"

"Something I am going to show to Ificad, if his shop hasn't moved."

"The Darlanian? He still works with his toys in his shops. You know time has no meaning here, and many of us stay as long as there's trade. Ificad has always done brisk business."

Nakor looked pleased. "Good, then I'll go in a moment. I first wanted to ask what progress you've made regarding my request?"

"To visit the level above Midkemia?"

"Yes, that plane of reality."

"Lacking any familiarity with the realm above yours, I was at a loss as to where to look, so I sent out inquiries. I have asked many sources, and there is perhaps one being who may be able to help. Apparently, there is a celestial, by the name of Eleleth, from the very realm you seek, who is in the realm in which you reside."

"That sounds promising. Where might I find him?"

"Therein lies a problem." Vordam's expression was usually difficult for Nakor to read, but now he was clearly struggling as to what to say next.

"What problem?" Nakor's gaze narrowed.

"His location is fixed, as he is now on the world of Cynoth."

"I know that world, or at least word of it." Nakor's brow furrowed, and he looked distracted for a moment. "I don't know if I've been there." He returned his attention to Vordam. "What else? What don't you wish to tell me?"

"He's a prisoner. In the Vault."

Nakor was silent for a moment, then a memory returned. "The Vault!" He let out a long sigh. "Now I remember Cynoth! The Vault is in the Kingdom of Assala. A dungeon under the palace."

"One can hardly call it a dungeon, though living beings have been imprisoned there. It's more of a trophy gallery for the king."

"Why's he being kept there?" asked Nakor.

"I have no idea."

"It's a hellhole, no matter how fancy the decor," Nakor said. He was silent for a few moments, then he said, "So at least we know where he is. Thank you. What do I owe you?"

Vordam smiled, his white teeth made more dramatic by contrast to his bluish complexion. "Consider this a favor."

Nakor smiled warily. "In exchange for . . . ?"

Vordam laughed. "For returning and telling me just how you conclude all this . . . adventuring. Rumor is that few, if any, ever escape the Vault, and if you manage to do so, the how is valuable information."

"Done!" said Nakor with a broad smile. He gave Vordam a bow, turned, and hurried out.

Making his way down through the crowds to one of the lower levels of Honest John's took a bit of time. Eventually, he reached the level where most of the manufacturing shops were. It was noisy, replete with pungent odors and acrid fumes that brought tears to the eyes, and a carpet of litter—fragments of metal, ashes, bits of char, and innumerable scraps. As he wore his usual cross-gartered sandals, Nakor stepped cautiously.

He reached the shop of Ificad and entered. The interior smelled even more polluted than the hallway of this lowest level of Honest John's. John claimed to have put in proper ventilation ages ago, but Nakor found this to be a dubious assertion. He saw cases along each wall full of odd devices and gadgets, most of which were alien to him, their functions and purpose obscure.

Toward the rear of this open shop, he saw a pair of workers sitting at benches on the left side, and on the right a small furnace that seemed to be a kind of kiln or forge.

Leaning over a bench on the other side of the furnace was the person Nakor sought: Ificad, a Darlanian tinker, a master of mechanical and other devices, with an apparently encyclopedic knowledge of apparatuses and instruments of all types, from many worlds.

Nakor approached. "Ificad!"

The named being looked up, saw Nakor, and said, "Is that really you? I thought you were dead."

"I was," said Nakor. "Can you look at something for me?"

"What?" Ificad rose from his stool, coming to his full height, which was a good deal taller than Nakor. He was humanoid, his features resembling a human whose chin and scalp had been tugged just enough to make the face oddly thin and long, the jaw protruding a little; his skin was pinkish-white, and his hair was a flowing crown of black with lavender highlights when struck by light. He wore a simple grey work suit from ankle to neck, with a long fastening down the front. Pockets full of tools covered it from chest to knee.

"What have you there?" Ificad asked.

"A drawing I made. I hope it looks like what I saw." Nakor laid the wooden board down where the tinker could see it, and added, "It's really big."

"How big?" asked Ificad, kneeling so that he could inspect it more closely.

"About the size of a small city," Nakor said casually.

Ificad nodded slowly. "Well, it looks like it could be something. How deep down does it go?"

"A few levels, maybe more. Tunnels here and there, with strange lines all up and down, this way and that."

"Lines painted or cut into the walls?"

Nakor considered. "Maybe both? Etched lines with paint in them?"

Ificad stood up. "Not paint, but dried liquid metals, perhaps. Well, it does resemble an engine."

"Engine?" Nakor said. "Something used by an engineer?"

Ificad made a clicking sound with his tongue and lower teeth, which Nakor knew was a Darlanian laugh. "Come," he said, waving

Nakor to follow him. "Engineers fabricate all manner of things using tools and mathematics, all sorts of knowledge. They build bridges, raise castles, dig out canals, and construct any number of objects. But an engine is another thing. Let me show you."

He led Nakor to one of the shelves along the wall and took down an odd-looking device. It was a small metal ball, with two bent arms protruding from opposing sides, fitted between two arcs of metal that held it high enough off the shelf that the arms could move freely. This device he set down on a table near the shelf, then moved across the room and returned with a pitcher of water and a lit candle.

"I fill this device with a little water," he said, pouring the water through a tiny hole which he then stopped up with a small rubber cork. Then he put the candle under the orb. "Observe," he repeated.

In a few moments wisps of steam came out of the two small openings at the end of the bent arms. After a few more moments, the steam started to whistle, and the ball began to rotate on the stand.

"This is an engine. It's a child's toy, but it uses the same principle." He pointed as the steam lessened and the ball slowed. He removed the candle.

"What I saw was no child's toy," said Nakor.

"No, it isn't," agreed Ificad. "What an engine does is to take energy and convert it into something else. In this case, motion. Imagine a device a great deal larger, anchored firmly to the ground, with a huge fire below and a large volume of water within. Now, imagine that whirling engine has a wheel connected and it turns a mill, to grind grain somewhere with no running stream, river, or waterfall."

Nakor's eyes widened as he began to comprehend the concept. "So, a ship's sails?"

"In one sense, yes. The ship is an engine that converts wind energy to motion through the water. A windmill uses wind energy to grind grain. A water wheel uses energy from a river to do the same."

"What type of engine do you think I saw?"

Ificad said, "I don't know. I might speculate if I knew what sort of energy it was to convert, fire or heat, light, or even electrical lightning."

Nakor suddenly went pale, and things he had learned from those who had seen the carvings of the Pride Lords, and those who had told him of the lore, came flooding back, and at last he said, "Human lives. The tales said instead of simply draining victims, the Children of the Void would sweep down and carry them off." He sighed. "They took them up to the plateau and drained their lives into that place. It's a death engine."

Ificad moved his hands suddenly in a gesture that appeared to be a superstitious warding against evil. "If this thing is a death engine, that big, I can only guess it's a creation for massive evil. Necromancy is the most unholy and foul of the magic arts, and those who wield it are beings with the darkest hearts."

He took another look at the drawing and asked, "These three round spots"—his long finger pointed—"look as if they are aligned in a triangle."

Nakor looked again at his drawing and said, "I was floating in the air a thousand feet or so above it, so the proportions may be a little off."

Ificad seemed unfazed by the statement, and said, "If they are exactly equilateral, then when energy is pulsed through this massive engine, whatever that energy is transformed into will burst forth and strike a point in the sky above."

"What will that do?"

"One can only guess," offered Ificad. "But it can be for nothing good. And depending on how many lives are sacrificed into that thing, it could rip open the sky."

"Sky?"

"That very thing you seek to do: reach a higher plane of existence. This device could possibly rip open a massive passage between realms, either up or down."

Both stood in silence for a moment, then Nakor said, "My experience with the human life force is limited, but it seems to me that a lot of lives would have to be sacrificed at the same time to make this work. Am I correct?"

"Not necessarily," Ificad responded. "If they are stored—"

"Stored?"

"In a cell, battery, or other means to hold energy . . ." Ificad stopped, and then said, "Those lines are . . ." He blinked. "Nakor, that entire structure is an accumulator!"

Nakor was silent, then his eyes went wide. "I must go!"

He hurried out of the shop, almost knocking over people in his haste to climb the stairs up to the main floor of Honest John's. Ignoring greetings from acquaintances, he hurried to where Kwad stood, retrieved his staff and dagger, and said, "The Sanctuary at Garn!"

The black-spotted massive being operated a device next to him, then waved Nakor in. He stepped through, seeming to appear from between two other doors from rift-space, and across from the door leading to the Sanctuary.

A quick glance showed him no other being nearby, and he quickly crossed the wide hall to the door, opened it, and stepped into the library at the Sanctuary.

Glancing around, he saw that the library was empty, but the torches were not lit, so he assumed it was still daylight outside. He hurried to the meeting rooms, found them empty, then outside and to the dining hall and saw this was also empty but for the servers.

A young worker was clearing away what appeared to be remnants of the midday meal. "Are Pug or Hatushaly nearby?" Nakor asked.

The young worker shrugged and returned to cleaning.

Outside, Nakor saw no one near enough to speak with, so with a sense of desperation, he willed himself to the docks.

A dockworker almost fell into the water when Nakor suddenly appeared next to him, and Nakor had to reach out and grab his arm to stop him from falling. "Sorry," he said.

Looking around quickly, he saw the *Queen of Storms* wasn't berthed at the dock, and if that ship was gone, so was Hava, and Pug probably with her.

He vanished, only to reappear a moment later in the king's throne room in Marquenet, outside the door to the king's chamber. A pair of guards outside the door both jumped at the little man's sudden appearance. "Declan? Is he here?"

One of the guards gathered his wits, and said, "He left a while ago." He pointed toward the exit to the marshaling yard.

Nakor went to the door, stepped outside, and saw a pair of guards chatting at the entrance to the stables. He hurried over and said, "Prince Declan?"

One of the guards looked at Nakor with a confused expression, but the other said, "He rode out of the eastern gate a—" Before he could finish, Nakor had vanished.

Nakor stood on the road outside the eastern gate and fixed his gaze on the horizon. The trick, as he thought of it, was to transport to what he could see. He jumped, and jumped again, and after half a dozen jumps saw a company of horsemen down the road. With a deep breath, he gathered his strength, then appeared a few yards ahead of Declan.

Declan held up his hand, signaling a stop. "What?"

Nakor said, "We need to find Pug!"

Declan pulled on the reins and his horse circled. "Last I saw, he was arranging the transfer of food from your world to this. What is this?"

"Things best discussed somewhere else." Nakor looked around, and said, "What are you doing?"

Declan quickly explained the information about the entire Church army lying dead, and Nakor said, "We must find Pug. We must send for Magnus, and you and I need to see this dead army."

"We're a day away from—"

Before he could finish, Nakor came to stand next to his horse, grabbed the bridle, and suddenly the two of them were outside the redoubt.

The horse whinnied, beginning to buck, and Declan had to use every trick he knew to calm it. After getting his mount under control, Declan gave Nakor an evil look. The little man was unsteady, obviously weakening. Declan looked around and saw Sixto. He dismounted and grabbed Nakor by the arm. Half-dragging the little man to where Sixto stood, he said, "What do you know?"

Sixto said, "Since I sent the message, I've had scouts trying to reach the main Church position on the far side of where the dead lay, but they couldn't seem to get close. They became lightheaded, felt weak, and were barely able to get away to regain their strength."

Nakor said, "We must go there now." He pointed to the entrance from the eastern passage. "My energy is very low now, so I can't take us there." He took a deep breath, then added, "So we must run."

"Run?" asked Sixto, but Nakor was already three steps away,

adroitly running through the debris strewn across the clearing between the redoubt and the trees.

"Slow down!" Declan yelled as he and Sixto set out after the nimble little man.

They quickly caught up with him and stayed with him despite the litter of debris along the path. Once out of the forest, Nakor slowed.

Slightly out of breath, Declan asked, "What are you looking for?"

Nakor halted, pointed at the field of sprawling bodies, and said, "That."

"What?" asked Sixto, squinting.

"Don't look at the bodies, or the ground. Look at the air, through the air. Let your eyes relax."

Declan did as instructed, trying to relax his vision as if seeing the air above the dead. Suddenly a movement in the air appeared, but the moment he tried to focus on it, it vanished.

"What was that flickering?" he asked.

"That is like the dark air which was all around when you were fighting the dead," Nakor replied. "We can go back now. No need to run."

"I'm glad about that," said Sixto.

Declan looked at Nakor as he started walking back toward the path through the forest. "What does it mean?"

Nakor made an uncertain gesture. "I need to talk to Pug, but I think I know."

"Know what?" Declan asked.

"That maybe the Void is going to let every soldier in the Church die to give it more power."

"More power to do what?" Declan's expression was a mix of confusion and aggravation.

"That's what I need to talk to Pug about. I'll rest a while and when I can, I'll take us both to wherever Pug is."

Sixto stood still, trying to comprehend all he had just heard. He closed his eyes, took a breath, and when he spoke, his voice was weak and tired. "I like the rest part."

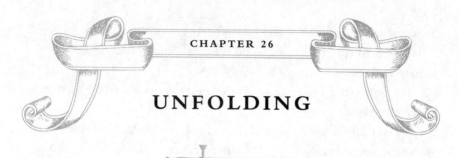

CHAPTER 26

UNFOLDING

Magnus listened closely as Nakor finished his explanation. He looked around the table, seeing puzzled expressions from Bodai, Declan, the king, and Balven. Only he and Pug seemed to grasp what Nakor was saying.

"So," said Magnus, "the sacrifice of the hundreds of soldiers is to supply this . . . accumulator?"

Nakor nodded. "That is what I think."

"To power this . . . engine?" asked Pug.

The king put his hands on the table and said, "Enough!" He pushed himself back into his chair and added, "I am completely confused by all this."

It was Pug who said, "Apologies, Majesty. To sum up, Hatushaly discovered what he imagined was a strange city belonging to the Children of the Void atop the plateau in the center of Nytanny. We didn't realize exactly what the threat was until recently. That is not of the moment. What is vital is that there seems to be what we have been warned of: a massive device that may prove to be the ultimate weapon to destroy everything. Magnus will find Hatushaly, while we"—he indicated himself and Nakor—"continue with more immediate projects, foremost being getting that fleet of ships from Garn to Midkemia, and back with foodstuffs."

Daylon looked baffled. "It looks as if I have to accept that there are many things beyond my understanding." He stood up and everyone also rose. "I'll focus on the tasks before me." His frustration at the limits of his ability were obvious. "I will personally oversee preparations for war with the Church. As for this dark magic threat, I'll leave it to the rest of you to do what you must. Balven will coordinate with you."

He departed, heading through the door that would take him to the marshaling yard.

Balven waited until the door was closed and said, "My brother is a man who finds leaving things to others difficult. Delegating tasks was a hard lesson to learn. Especially when he's unsure as to exactly what those others are doing. Now, I think I comprehend a little of what you've said. Let me reiterate, there's a device the size of a small city atop a plateau in Nytanny. It is something called an engine, that takes life and turns it to a weapon of indescribable power, and somehow it's . . . paused? Is that the right of it?"

Pug nodded. "Hatushaly saw it first, and two magicians from my world shared his vision. The creatures look like stone carvings, alien statuary, but they are not. Hatushaly has little understanding of the Children of the Void, which is why he thought that massive construction was a city. The turrets and domes do resemble one on casual inspection, and he wasn't there physically, but seeing it through a distant viewing. Now we have a better understanding."

"Can it be destroyed?" Balven asked, his expression suggesting he didn't want to hear the answer.

It was Nakor who said, "Anything built can be destroyed. It's just sometimes very hard to do that."

Magnus intervened. "The king is correct. He, the general, Master-at-Arms Collin, and Prince Declan can only fight as they know how. In the matter of the Darkness, the Void, that's best left to us magic-users. We must proceed as planned." He spoke quickly, but calmly. "If that device suddenly activates, then fate has taken a turn, and we will do what we can. Until then we can investigate. But while I go and find Hatu and then see this place for myself, we'd best concern ourselves with what we are able to do.

"Livestock, grain, and everything you need: it's all gathering in Midkemia, and we need to bring it here. You can aid your brothers in preparing for attacks from the Church. They may have sacrificed a small army just days ago, but from what Delnocio has said of them, they still have a big army out there."

"Correct," said Balven, "on all counts. Let us each do what we can and deal with what is before us."

Pug turned to Nakor and Magnus and said, "I'm off to the Sanctuary to get Hava's fleet organized. Good luck in finding Hatushaly."

Nakor grinned. "It won't be hard. There aren't that many libraries here."

Magnus nodded.

Pug said to Bodai, "Where do you think you can serve best?"

The old teacher looked pale. "I have no idea." After a moment, he said, "If you're seeking Hatushaly, I think I'll go with you. I've known him long enough to sense when he may act rashly. Without Hava, he can be unpredictable."

Pug smiled at Bodai. "Your contributions have already been important. Without your guidance, Hatushaly might not have survived long enough for us to find him." Pug vanished.

Magnus said, "Let's see if he's in the library here, then we'll move to the Sanctuary."

Nakor smiled. "If he's not there, Sorcerer's Isle."

"Likely," said Bodai.

The three of them walked to the king's library and found Hatushaly hunched over a very old and dusty book. Without looking up, he said, "I found this in a corner, under a pile of old parchment."

"What is it?" asked Bodai.

"It's a story, I think," said Hatushaly. "Or a historical narrative but containing a prophecy. It reads like a story. If it's history, it's important. The language is new to me. It's Hagallan."

Magnus reacted with wide eyes. "That is . . . impossible."

"Why?" Hatu asked.

"This is a dead language from Midkemia. The Hagallan kingdom fell as Kesh rose. That book is perhaps a thousand years old."

Magnus looked amazed. "How could that tome end up here?"

It was Nakor who answered. "Whatever powers are playing with us put it here!" His expression was unusually angry. "Kalkin, or another unknown power, is somehow leading us into a confrontation none of us wish. Call it fate."

Pug shared Nakor's anger but controlled his words. "We'll worry about how later. What does it say?"

Sensing their anger, Hatushaly looked uncertain and glanced from face to face, worrying he'd done something wrong.

Suddenly Pug realized that despite his incredible abilities and powers, Hatushaly was still very young. Not yet twenty-six years old, he was facing four people who measured their lives in centuries.

Pug took a breath, then smiled to reassure Hatu. "You've done nothing wrong. We are simply frustrated about what we don't know."

Hatu relaxed. "Well do I know that feeling. Ask Hava about my temper as a boy when denied knowing things."

Pug continued: "We can only deal with what we know is threatening now, not an unknown future. We have never been able to predict what the Void creates. To guess is a waste of our time."

Bodai asked, "What is this book about?"

"As far as I can tell," Hatu answered, "there was a prophet who was captured by some king in Hagalla, the city the kingdom was named after. It's unclear why he was taken prisoner, or I'm not understanding something, but the prophet was brought before the king, who demanded that the prophet prove he wasn't a charlatan."

Hatu took a deep breath, and then went on, "There was a lot of 'this king will beget that child who will fight this war and his enemies will flee,' and so on. But the part that caught my attention is this." He began to read. "'The kingdom shall crumble, and another shall rise, but the order shall continue.'" He paused. "I have no idea what 'the order' is: command, an organization, some sort of system . . .'" He went back to reading. "This is the part that I was talking about. 'Then shall come a darkness which will engulf worlds.' Worlds, not just Midkemia. 'He who must travel against time's wind will halt the darkness before.'" He looked at Pug, Magnus, and Nakor and said, "I don't know what that means."

Pug was silent for a long moment, then he said, "I think I understand part of it. Centuries ago, when I first lived on Sorcerer's Isle, my daughter, Gamina, came to us. My wife Katala did not bear her, but we took her into our home and hearts. She had traveled with a kind blind man, a seer named Rogen, who was the first to warn us of a coming darkness. That ended in our first battle with the Void and its agents, at the Kingdom city of Sethanon.

"Some ancient seer in Hagalla foretold of the Void's coming." Pug sighed and looked down at Hatushaly. "I think I know where we must go."

He turned to Magnus and said, "We will not be long, but I must take this tome and Hatu to—"

"The Oracle," Magnus finished. "I've known you too long not to know what you're thinking. I'll continue to work with Hava in anticipation of your return and getting that fleet through the rift."

Pug looked at Hatu. "If this is a clue of some sort, it's that a seer predicted the Void. On Midkemia, there is only one who might have that ability—"

Nakor interrupted. "The Oracle of Aal!" He grinned at Pug. "I'll go too!"

Pug looked resigned. After all these years he knew better than to argue. "Bring that tome," he said to Hatushaly.

"Where are we going?" Hatu asked.

"First to the Sanctuary, then to Midkemia. Then to the abandoned city of Sethanon."

DONTE WAVED DAVID OVER TO his table, and asked, "What word?"

The youngster glanced around and then sat down, and Donte was pleased to see he was checking his surroundings instead of automatically assuming he was safe because Donte was here. "I think I'm in as a boy looking for a lost brother and have avoided being seen by anyone who might know me." He smiled. "I'm a bit taller than when we left here, and I've got a lot more weight on me. Besides, nobody pays attention to a street boy."

Donte asked, "Any word on Lester Ving or the Mockers?"

"Not that I heard, but I'm just the new boy. I can work as a slop boy at the Red Starfish, like you suggested, so if the Keshians say anything about the Mockers or their own business, I should catch a hint."

"Slop boy's a nasty enough job, but the good thing is no one will look twice at you. You'll be furniture with ears. One thing: if you see a big, burly fellow by the name of Burt at the bar—looks like a laborer— ignore him. If he says anything to you, play stupid and tell me as soon as you can. He works for the real Mockers, but you don't know that, understand?"

David nodded.

"I trust him up to a point, but knowing you work for me is beyond that point. So, you get out of here and get to work."

Without another word, David left the table and Donte sat back. Throughout his upbringing, he and the other children, many younger than David, had been constantly at risk, even while still in school. They were often sent from the school to train with a crew in any of a dozen towns and cities, and occasionally a child did not return.

Donte hadn't minded losing another child when he was a student: it was the risk they all took. Now that he was the one sending children into harm's way, he discovered he wasn't happy with that responsibility at all. He cursed himself silently for growing fond of the kids. They were not like the children of Coaltachin. The girl, Sarah, had blossomed at the farm, loving the sheep and excited for the coming lambs. She worked all day without complaint and sang in the field and the kitchen.

"Damn me," Donte muttered to himself, "if I'm not turning into some soft-headed mark ready to be conned by a bad trickster."

Scully came over, sat down, and said, "I have a line on that fellow, Lester Ving."

"What?"

Scully said, "The Keshian payback hit them Mockers hard. So, he's looking for reinforcements. Wants some leg-breakers."

Donte considered what this might mean; then he said, "Has he looked for new muscle before?"

"Not that I've heard. I might have considered working for him if he had. I guess the Keshians made him change his mind about only working with the boys he brought with him from Krondor. He's got religion." He smiled.

Donte wasn't quite sure what that last remark meant, but then said, "The religion of survival?"

"Yup," said Scully, motioning to one of Shad's new girls and ordering a pitcher of ale.

Donte decided that meant Scully planned on staying a while and found himself darkly amused. Between his sudden concerns over the kids' welfare and his mild annoyance that Scully assumed Donte was paying for the ale, he decided being a crime lord might not be all it was cracked up to be.

"So, leg-breakers," said Donte. He paused, then looked at Scully. "Did he ask for leg-breakers, or did you just say that?"

"I don't know what you mean," Scully replied, sucking down a gulp of ale.

"If he wants muscle, it could be for his personal safety. If he wants leg-breakers, he's looking to lean on businesses for protection, or to bust back at the Keshians."

"I think I heard . . . muscle. I just said leg-breakers."

Donte nodded. "Then you have a career opportunity. If he's looking for new muscle to replace the lads he brought here from Krondor, it means the Keshians hit him really hard. It means we might be able to put you inside."

"Me?" Scully said, pushing his chair back slightly.

"You, Lyndon, and Robertson are stout lads who can thump a skull, but Robertson looks Keshian and has no idea how to pretend to be anyone else, and Lyndon gets giddy and talkative when he drinks, right?"

Scully chuckled. "Too right. So, I go spying?"

"Something like that. You've been around and know the risks, so I'm thinking two things. First, you only send me messages that are really important. I won't need a 'this is how many times he visited the jakes to piss,' or how he plays cards. We're not setting him up for a confidence trick. Just anything about his business. Clear?"

"Absolutely," said Scully. "I'll steer clear of here and only seek you out when I have something solid."

"Excellent." Donte smiled. "It's a good thing I didn't break your neck."

Scully laughed. "I agree."

Donte took a long swallow of ale. He still had a little gold and silver to spread around, informants in place, and was clear what his next move should be. Things were coming together, if slowly, but as alien as patience was to him, he embraced the need for it.

Eventually, when the pitcher was drained and Donte made no move to order more, Scully said, "I'll be off."

As Scully turned to leave, Donte said, "Try and avoid getting killed if you can."

"Too right," Scully replied, and he left.

Donte picked up his flagon of ale, which he'd been nursing, took a deep drink, then sighed. He'd been captured by evil sea hags, washed up on a shore with little memory, and now was in a different world, with no masters to placate. Life wasn't turning out the way he thought it would when he was younger. He'd expected to get a crew, then take over a city operation for his grandfather. Maybe end up being one of the Council of Masters. Nothing like being on another world, working a game with two warring crews, and trying to look after a bunch of kids. No, nothing like he imagined, Donte thought. He took another drink.

PUG, MAGNUS, NAKOR, HATUSHALY, AND Bodai appeared out of the rift at Sorcerer's Isle. Jaroly was once again sitting beside the opening and smiled at seeing familiar faces.

Bodai was wide-eyed, adjusting to the wonder of moving through a rift to another world.

Pug motioned to Jaroly. "Bodai, this is Jaroly, one of our best young adepts."

Bodai looked around the chamber, still uncertain what he had just experienced. "Hello," he muttered.

Exiting the chamber into the open air, Pug saw that it was now just after nightfall. "Come. Let us eat, rest, then begin tomorrow."

Bodai looked around the area between the rift chamber and the villa. The evening was soft and a light breeze off the Bitter Sea filled the air with a slight salt pungency. He looked to Hatushaly, and said, "This place reminds me of the home island."

Hatushaly laughed. "It is an island, but there the similarity ends. Sorcerer's Isle is nothing like Coaltachin." He pointed upward.

Bodai looked, and when he saw two moons above, his eyes widened.

"There's a third one which hasn't risen yet," Hatu said. "When time permits, you must see the library here."

"That would please me."

They made their way to the dining hall, with Bodai stumbling several times trying to look at everything they passed. Entering the dining hall, they heard a delighted shriek from across the room. All of them looked to the source, to see Sabella hurrying toward them.

She threw her arms around Bodai's neck and gave him a vigorous hug. "I wished you could see this place, and here you are!"

Her enthusiasm was infectious. Bodai laughed and, stepping back, said, "You've put on some weight! Good. And you've a bit of color in those cheeks."

"I feel wonderful," she responded. "This place is amazing. Wait! Let me show you!"

She elevated herself a foot off the floor, her grin as broad as he'd ever seen. Bodai's eyes welled up and he wiped away a tear. "You have magic," he said in astonishment.

"There is so much energy here compared to home," she replied as she touched down lightly on her feet. "I'm learning more every day."

A regal-looking man, perhaps seven feet tall, came into view and Bodai recoiled reflexively, bumping back into Hatushaly, who steadied him.

"Easy," Hatu said quietly. "There is no being here who would do you harm." He chuckled. "Here there are many who are not like us."

Pug said, "That's Noromendis, an elven geomancer. His father was an ally the last time we faced the Void."

"Elven?" Bodai asked in a hoarse whisper.

"Elves," said Hatu, amused at his former teacher's befuddlement.

"The stories . . ." Bodai took a breath to regain his composure. "They're little creatures that flit around on tiny wings . . ."

Pug laughed and clapped Bodai on the shoulder. "One mystery a teacher such as yourself will find fascinating, I think, is how so many myths are commonly held from world to world. The details, however, tend to vary widely."

Bodai stared at a short, stocky man with dark-green hair who was hurrying past.

Pug again laughed. "That's not any otherworldly being. Martak just likes to dye his hair that color."

Bodai joined in the laughter. "This is an amazing place," he said, somehow relieved by a man's vain choice of hair dye.

"Come along," said Magnus. "Let's rest and we'll plan for tomorrow."

DONTE MOTIONED FOR SCULLY TO approach the moment he entered the inn. By the time he had reached the table, Donte had already pulled out a chair and was leaning his elbows on the table expectantly. He had sent Scully out to infiltrate the false Mockers only three days previously and hadn't expected to see him this soon.

Scully sat down. "It's important."

"I assume so, or you wouldn't be here. Did you get into the gang?"

"No need," said Scully with a grin. "I was nosing around, trying to get a hint of where to go and join up, when I saw three men heading out of Sad Landing, so I tagged along. Lester Ving has a gal stashed away in a little house just outside the turf they control. Two nights running he went down there, and the two guards stayed out front for a few hours, then he left and went back inside the Landing."

"You know it's to see a woman?" asked Donte.

"Second night I hung about until dawn, then as the markets began to open, this gal comes out—pretty little thing—so I followed her to the market, and she did some morning shopping. She got enough food for one person for a day or so, then strolled around looking at this or that."

"You stayed out of sight?"

"Not my first time, you know," said Scully, looking a little annoyed. "I reckoned it was a good bet Ving wouldn't leave her on her own, so I played it safe, and I saw a big fellow keeping close watch on her, one of those Mockers making sure she was untroubled."

Donte sat back. "The two guards stayed in front of the house?"

"The place is set back-to-back with another on the next street over—no alley between—so they're only worried about someone coming in from the front."

Donte's face was a mask of contemplation. After a moment he asked, "Roof?"

"Best way if you're looking for a stealthy way in, but it might be tricky. Falling through old shingles is a risk. These are broken-down buildings, and a wrong step might land you in somebody's kitchen."

"Then the front is the way in," said Donte. He glanced out of the door and said, "We have plenty of sunlight. Show me this house."

Donte followed Scully out of the door and down the street to an intersection. He recognized this was just before the street where he would turn right to approach Sad Landing, but Scully led him straight on. Two more streets, and Scully turned right and, halfway down the street, stopped. Turning his back to the house on the right, Scully looked down as if to examine something. "Other side, third house up from here, with the faded green door."

Donte looked down as if examining something Scully held but gave a sidelong look across the street. It took him only a few moments to see how best to hit that location. "Let's head back."

Once they reached the Four Ravens, Donte grabbed a pitcher of ale from Shad and went back to the table where Scully waited. Pouring out two mugs, he said, "Go fetch Robertson and Lyndon. Four of us should be able to handle two of Ving's lads."

"That'll take me a couple of days, you know?" said Scully.

"I'll keep watch on Ving. I want to see if he goes every night and if it's always two with him."

Scully nodded, drained the goblet, and said, "Horse?"

Donte opened his purse and handed a pair of silver coins to him. "Even if you were stealing my horse for a silver, the lad at the stable would let you. But tell him it's me. Richard's the name I used. And don't ruin my horse."

"I'll be gentle. I'll push through tonight, then rest tomorrow. Me and the lads will be back here in a few days."

Donte said, "Before you get the horse, see if you can grab the boys. Have Mark and David find me here."

Scully nodded and left. Donte sat back and considered. The simplest approach was direct, but before he committed to that course in his mind he reminded himself: the simplest was not always the best. Again, he realized this whole being-in-charge thing was an annoyance.

PUG SAT WITH MAGNUS, WAITING for the others to arrive. Magnus said, "I'm getting a little apprehensive about this visit."

Pug smiled. "You, apprehensive?"

Magnus rolled his eyes: he knew he was about to be teased.

Pug added, "You could be as good a card player as Nakor—except for the cheating. You almost never show your feelings, let alone admit to them. Years ago, I worried about that, when you became very distant after losing Helena. Over the years, I've realized that it's simply who you are. Not everyone is gregarious. Caleb was far more at ease with people than you were."

Magnus relaxed a little. This was more his father speaking than Phillip. The youngster he had taught for years, that personality was fading, and his father's character was becoming dominant. Phillip would not have ignored the opportunity to sling a barb. Magnus said, "One doesn't visit the Oracle of Aal uninvited."

"Chalmers, the Oracle's servant, said that we are always invited."

Magnus nodded. "What about the others?"

"Stop Nakor from coming along?" asked Pug.

Magnus smiled slightly. "Not likely."

"My other concern is Hatushaly."

"You think he should go?"

"Absolutely. That youngster is unique and has a critical role to play in what is coming. Of that I am certain. I've encountered countless users of magic. The Assembly on Kelewan numbered hundreds, as did the Academy at Stardock. And among practitioners of magic, you were the most powerful, with arts like mine and your mother's combined. But Hatushaly already has abilities to rival ours, and more, the ability to see, do, and understand things we can hardly imagine. And he's hardly more than a boy!"

Pug was silent a moment, then added, "Look how long it took for

you to come into your full power." Then he smiled, "It was your ten-
dency to be so cautious that slowed you in manifesting your powers, I
think."

Magnus chuckled. "The fire I started that got Mother so upset
when I was a boy, I think that was the cause of my . . . becoming cautious."

Pug laughed. "I thought of that the exact moment Ruffio told me
the story he'd heard from Bodai, about Hatu burning a ship to the
waterline."

"Anger will do that," Magnus agreed.

Hatu and Bodai entered with Nakor a step behind. They arrived
at the table and Pug said, "Let's eat, then get on with a very busy day."

They all got their food and returned to the table. Pug stayed silent
while they ate, listening to Bodai asking questions which were mainly
answered by Magnus, with Hatushaly and Nakor occasionally chim-
ing in.

Eventually, Pug said, "Bodai, we need to visit somewhere I fear
you would be unwelcome. But I think you can lose yourself very easily
in our library for a while. You'll no doubt find Sabella there if she's not
in class. If not, make yourself known to Wejuan, who is in charge, and
ask her nicely if she has a moment to show you around."

Bodai said, "I know better than to turn up where I'm not invited
unless I'm ready for trouble."

Both Pug and Magnus looked at Nakor upon hearing that.

"I'm going," he said flatly.

Pug and Magnus exchanged resigned looks, and Pug said, "Hatushaly, it is vital I think, for you to come, for there is much about
you yet to be discovered, and I hope some of those mysteries may be
revealed when we reach our destination."

Hatu said, "I'm willing to come."

Pug looked at Magnus and said, "Hava is expecting me to join her
soon before she sails to Shechal to gather the fleet. Would you visit her
and explain the reason for my absence?"

"I'll do that," Magnus said, standing up.

Pug said, "Return here and wait for us. I don't think this will take
very long."

"I will." Magnus nodded good-bye to them, then turned and headed toward the rift chamber.

Pug looked at the others, and said, "Let's be on our way."

They stood. Bodai said, "I will most likely be in the library when you return."

"Follow the path past the villa—" began Hatu.

"I know the way," Bodai said with a smile. "Be safe, all of you."

After the old teacher had left, Hatu said, "After what Bodai said, will I be welcomed by this oracle?"

Glancing at Nakor for a moment, Pug looked at the young man. "Welcomed? I am certain you will be expected."

Nakor grinned. "She's an oracle, after all."

Pug rolled his eyes. Then he motioned for them to step closer and put his hands on their shoulders.

Suddenly they stood in a massive cavern illuminated by a huge wheel of lights which hung from a great chain. The walls had been smoothed and crafted into arching rings from one side to the other and scintillated with flickering lights. The ancient stone floor had been replaced by smooth marble reflecting the light from above, illuminating the entire chamber far more brightly than the last time Pug had visited. A shimmering wall of light stretched across the immense chamber, which also danced with colors.

"Oh, pretty," said Nakor.

A robed figure stood a few feet away and with a bow said, "Pug, you've returned." The man had his hood thrown back, revealing a bald pate, high forehead, and dark eyes. His narrow face was set in a neutral expression, neither friendly nor hostile.

Pug returned the bow. "When last we spoke, you granted us leave to return at will. We seek counsel." He looked around the chamber. "Some fine changes since last I was here."

"When the oracle sleeps, we who attend her have little to do, so using our magic and a great deal of labor to create a more commodious home seemed a clear choice," said the robed man. "Welcome to all. I am Chalmers, first attendant."

"You are different than I remember," said Pug.

"As are you," the robed man said.

"True."

"We both possess different bodies, but the essence within remains the same." Chalmers turned to Nakor. "The gambler," he said with another bow. Then to Hatushaly he added, "And the Master of Furies, who can bend energy to his will."

Hatu's expression was one of awe as he spoke in a near-whisper. "We were indeed expected."

"We serve the greatest oracle ever known," said Chalmers. "Surprises are exceedingly rare."

"Where is the oracle?" Nakor asked. "This place is pretty empty."

A smile crossed Chalmers's face. "She is here." He waved his hand toward the rear of the vast hall, and the shimmering wall of light vanished, revealing a massive, brilliant form.

The dragon sat upon a mound of cloth the size of a hill. Her body was covered in scales that seemed fashioned of gold embedded with thousands of gems of all colors: sapphires, rubies, emeralds, opals, diamonds of all shapes, cuts, and sizes. Her body was enormous, her shoulders easily four times Hatushaly's height. Her head was the size of a huge freight wagon, and her long snout had a downturned beak-like shape. The tips of two fangs protruded to overhang her lower jaw, and black eyes the size of doorways peered down at the three visitors. A silver crest ran from the crown of her head down her spine, and her claws were like ebony.

She rose up and slowly unfolded, then extended her gigantic wings, as if in greeting. She lowered her head almost to the floor and a voice sounded in their minds. *Greetings.*

Pug bowed deeply and spoke aloud. "Greetings. Are you well?"

"As well as can be expected." This time the words sounded out of nowhere, hanging in the air.

Hatushaly regarded the dragon with wide eyes, his mouth open. He was visibly shaking.

Nakor grinned in delight. "I once saw a dragon flying toward the Dragon Mere when I was a boy. No one in my village believed me."

"The Darkness returns," said Pug.

"I know," the voice in the air replied.

"We must know anything that will aid us." Pug's tone was pleading. "When we fought and won here against the servants of the Void, I thought the world safe. Then, when I died at what is now called the Battle of Magician's End, I again thought us safe, and the Void vanquished. But now we find the Void manifested on another world."

"What you call the Void," said the dragon, "is a manifestation of the very fabric of all reality. You cannot vanquish that part of reality any more than you can vanquish air, or sunlight, or the soil beneath your feet.

"You could destroy Midkemia and the sun around which it circles, but there are countless other worlds with air, sunlight, and soil. Stars are being born, worlds are forming even as we speak. The vastness of multiple universes cannot be comprehended, even by me."

"Is our task hopeless, then?" Pug asked. "Are we fated to end in oblivion?"

"There are outcomes beyond my ability to see," said the oracle. "Again, we come to a fixed nexus, and beyond that is only uncertainty. Endless possibilities that exist as potential, until that point in time is passed. Only then will the future reveal itself to me."

"Then what do we do?" Pug asked.

"Listen," came the voice in the air, *and witness*, said the voice in their minds.

They plunged into darkness.

CHAPTER 27

REVELATIONS

Donte waited.

He peered around the corner, then pulled back. The two guards outside the door of the small building appeared to be at ease, chatting as if nothing threatening had ever occurred on their watch.

Lester Ving was upstairs with his lady, and Donte was getting ready to ruin his night. He turned to Scully and Robertson and whispered, "Should be about now."

At the other end of the street, two shadowy figures appeared, running toward the two guards. The guards both turned and quickly had knives out. The two runners slid to a stop just yards away from the guards. Donte could now see Mark and David in the dim light.

One guard shouted and charged, and the boys set off as fast as they could run.

"Hey!" the remaining guard shouted, vainly waving for his companion to return.

"Now," said Donte, leading Scully and Robertson in a rush toward the lone guard. By the time footfalls alerted him to turn, Donte had slammed into him and slashed him across the throat.

The guard who had chased the boys turned to see three men running toward him. He hesitated for an instant, then spun, and fled.

Donte shouted, "Enough! We don't want him." He led them past the guard bleeding out on the ground and up to the door.

Donte put his thumb on the door latch and pressed down. It yielded without protest. He inclined his head and opened the door. In the dark it was difficult to see anything other than vague shapes.

"Light?" whispered Scully.

"No," Donte whispered back. "Wait."

After a moment, their eyes adjusted a little and Donte made out stairs opposite the door and a faint light from above. "Follow me," he whispered. He trod lightly on the stairs and moved upward.

At the top of the stairs was a single door with a pale glow showing below and above the edges. Donte paused to listen and heard grunting and the sound of wood creaking.

He slowly opened the door and saw a naked man's backside. With a quick step he moved behind the man who lay atop a young woman and struck him hard on the back of the head with his dagger hilt.

The young woman shrieked as her now-unconscious lover rolled off the bed and pushed herself back against the wall, her eyes wide in terror. She was young, barely older than David, he judged, but in the streets they often started young. She had large brown eyes, dark hair, and otherwise resembled many girls Donte had known in the gangs. He suspected that she was a lot tougher than she looked.

Donte smiled and said, "Not to worry. We're here for his scrawny arse. You'd best skip out. When his lads come looking for him, they may decide you were in on this."

Her expression went from fear to relief, followed quickly by a calculating look. "I'll need a bit of help," she said.

Donte realized she might be young, but there were years of experience in her manner. He turned to Scully and said, "Let's get some trousers on this rascal, then get out." He turned back to the girl. She sat in the bed covered by a small sheet that barely hid her thin frame from view. He dug into his belt pouch and fetched out a pair of coins. Smiling, he said, "If you're traveling, starting now would be a good idea." He looked at his two companions. "That fleeing guard is probably on his way out of the city, but he may be fetching his mates to head back here. So, if that's the case, we'd all best be gone before they arrive."

Scully and Robertson hauled the unconscious form of Lester Ving upright while Donte got his feet into the trousers that were on the floor. With a quick lift he had the man half dressed, grabbed his legs, and picked him up. "Don't drop him," he said. "I think he's worth a bit more alive than he is a head in a box."

Donte glanced back to see the girl dressing, unashamed of her nudity. He muttered to himself, "Too skinny for my taste."

They carried the unconscious leader of the false Mockers down the stairs. Once on the street, they stopped, and had Robertson sling Ving across his shoulders while Donte and Scully got their daggers out, ready for trouble. "I hope Lyndon is ready," Donte said.

They lugged Ving down a street, turned north, and in a few minutes found a wagon waiting.

Lyndon jumped back into the wagon bed and helped haul Ving up into it. He had laid a carpet across the wagon and quickly rolled Ving into it.

"You stay in the back," Donte said to Lyndon. He smiled as he grabbed Scully's arm, saying, "Find the boys and get them back to the farm. Tell them I'm very happy with them. When I return, we shall have a feast!"

Almost giddy with how smoothly the operation had gone, Donte climbed up to the seat next to Robertson and took the reins. With a flick and a soft grunt, he moved the horses forward. Heading toward the north gate, he said. "Lyndon, if that lump behind us begins moving, smack him a good one across the head. I doubt the Upright Man cares if he's a bit damaged when we get to Krondor."

Lyndon laughed and said, "No worries."

PUG, NAKOR, AND HATUSHALY WERE on a wide, white stone road, one Pug and Nakor both recognized. Nakor glanced around. "We're in the Hall!"

"But no doors," said Pug.

Hatushaly peered above and then around. It was a seemingly grey universe with the single white stone road beneath their feet. "Where are we?" he asked hoarsely. His expression was a mix of wonder and fear.

"I think we are still in the cavern with the oracle," Pug said softly. "I think this is a vision we are sharing."

Hatu gripped his left wrist with his right hand, then knelt to one knee and touched the stones. "This feels real to me."

Nakor grinned. "This is a very good trick."

"Where are the doors?" Pug asked.

"What doors?" Hatushaly looked confused.

Pug said, "The heart of the Hall of Worlds consists of countless doors which lead directly into different worlds."

"There's that one in the Sanctuary, into the library," Nakor said.

They looked both ways and could see nothing but open roadway. "What happens if you step off?" Hatu asked.

"Don't," Nakor said.

"That puts you in what we call rift-space. Those little gaps you discovered between each edge of a rift? This is what that is."

"Where's the light coming from?" Hatu then asked.

"That's a good question," answered Nakor.

Pug looked around again. "If this is a vision, as I expect, it would do us little good if we couldn't see."

Nakor laughed at that, despite the exceedingly odd place in which they found themselves. "If this is a vision, there's not much to see."

Pug extended his hand. "Except that."

Both Nakor and Hatu looked down the hall to where Pug pointed and saw what appeared to be a cloud of dense white smoke or dust swirling and moving slowly toward them.

"Should we go there?" Hatushaly looked at Pug.

"I'm certain this is a vision. I think we stay here and let it come to us," Pug answered.

Nakor sat down with a grin. "Let's see what's next."

The white cloud hovered for a moment, then moved toward them. Hatu glanced at Pug with a concerned expression.

"It's all illusion," he said in a reassuring tone. "The oracle would not place us in harm's way."

"Pretty sure," said Nakor in a wry tone.

The cloud came closer until it enveloped them, replacing the surrounding grey with a white cocoon. They were barely able to see the stones beneath their feet. The white mist began to darken, then continued until their vision was black, save for the white strip of stone below them.

Abruptly, lights sprang into existence across the dome above them.

Scintillating points of brilliance, massive clusters of radiance, began slowly to swirl around them. More clouds of glowing colors—orange, pink, brown, blue—formed and within it points of lights appeared, all circling in rhythm.

Hatushaly looked down and, except for the white stones, the vision of the universe surrounded them. It felt as if he was floating in space. He gasped audibly. "When I first learned to use my distant vision, I would stand on a hill and stare at the sky, trying to see stars up close. This is beyond what I imagined."

The swirling lights above and below them were countless, blazing brightly, enormous blue and red spheres of light with flickering prominences erupting from them. "The pointy ones are stars," said Nakor. "Like the suns above Midkemia and Garn. They're like the little yellow dots."

"What are those softer swirls?" Hatu asked.

Pug put his hand on Hatu's shoulder. "Those are galaxies, collections of billions of stars."

"So tiny?"

"No, just incredibly far away from us."

The starscape that surrounded them picked up speed, clearly establishing their perspective at some sort of center point. Then other images appeared. Faint at first, then abruptly lines of energy emerged, massive ropes of color stretching between distant points in the sky.

"Furies!" Hatu turned around in a full circle. "You can see them, too?"

"Yes," said Pug. "But this is a vision. Is this how you perceive them?"

Hatushaly fell silent for a moment as he surveyed the growing lines of energy between the galaxies. At last, he said, "I see countless fine lines between everything in the world. These are . . . seem more like ropes in size to the threads I see. If all the threads of energy on Garn or Midkemia were spun together into . . . twine . . . and thousands of those strands of twine were woven into ropes . . ." He paused, and softly added, "No, not ropes. These are cables woven from millions of ropes. This is the power of the universe."

"We see pretty pictures," Nakor said. "It's what we can't see that fascinates me."

Suddenly their vision moved swiftly, the illusion so vivid that Hatushaly reached out to grab Pug's shoulder to steady himself. Nakor laughed. "Just remember where your feet are, and you won't fall over."

The movement stopped so suddenly that Hatu swayed before he took command of his own senses, realizing that Nakor's advice was good. He laughed quietly in relief to discover nothing beneath him was moving.

At intersections surrounding them, like a net of impossible size, forms began to take shape. Hatu calmed himself and took a slow, deep breath, then asked, "What is this?"

"Gods," said Nakor with an ironic chuckle. "Celestials, divinities, higher beings, whatever label pleases you."

"The human mind interprets what it can't understand—" Pug began.

Nakor interrupted. "And creates all sorts of nonsense about what it can't even see!" He laughed.

Pug gave Nakor a dark look, then continued, "It's part of who we are. I've learned that our gods on Midkemia are what humanity expects them to be. We do not bend great power to our will, but rather we influence how they appear to us."

"We have no gods on Garn," Hatu said, "but we still believe in them. At least, some do."

"It's the lack of stuff," said Nakor. "Midkemia has a lot, Garn only a little, so you don't have great power turning up uninvited."

Pug looked exasperated. "This is very much like what I saw on the Tower of Testing on Kelewan, when I came into my power and gained my black robe. It was the history as known there, from their chronicles, but it's much the same."

"But from whose history?" Hatushaly wondered.

"That we will probably see soon," said Nakor.

"From everyone's history," said a voice from behind them.

All three spun to see a slender man clothed in green-and-gold diamond-patterned garb. A fool's hat with two points ending in bells sat rakishly atop a thick crop of dark hair. His face was inhumanly perfect, a straight nose above full lips, and dark eyes set widely in a face of chocolate hue. His smile was dazzling in contrast to his skin, and he moved like a dancer, his lithe body seeming barely to touch the floor below his feet.

"Who are you?" Pug asked.

"I am called Piper," he answered.

Suddenly, Nakor's eyes widened. "I remember!"

"What?" asked Pug.

"When the Sven-ga'ri trap sent us to the higher realm!"

Pug's eyes narrowed. "You're Belog?"

"I don't know," Nakor answered in hoarse tones.

Piper laughed. "You mortals live in such confined ways of seeing, understanding . . . thinking."

Nakor said, "When we were trapped, each of us had a vision."

Pug nodded. "I saw my old teacher, Kulgan."

"And Belog saw Lord Borric," said Nakor. "I have that memory now!"

Pug said, "And Miranda—Child—saw . . ." He pointed to Piper.

"In a fashion," said the green-clad being. Abruptly, his form changed into that of a young woman, slender and blond. Then again into a youngster, a boy barely past a dozen years. "One of these forms perhaps. When I am needed, I leave the Bliss and acquire the knowledge I require for whatever task the One sets before me."

"The One," said Hatushaly. "You serve the Church of the One?"

Piper twirled on his left foot, his other leg off the ground, knee bent, then laughed. "The Church of the One serves the enemy of the Bliss, and the Church's name is an evil joke. The One needs no servants, no worship, no allegiance, for it simply exists and all are but parts of it."

"What are we here for?" Pug asked.

"To see what is needed," answered Piper, who now appeared as an older woman with grey hair and piercing blue eyes. Her pale skin was almost as translucent as parchment and yet there was an energy about her manner that belied any suggestion of age or infirmity.

"Why do you keep changing your appearance?" Nakor asked.

"Because it amuses me," she answered with a laugh.

Nakor appeared delighted. "That I fully understand!" Then his mood turned more somber. "Am I who I appear to be, or am I—"

She interrupted. "You are an echo of all you have ever been before, Nakor the Isalani. Time and distance have no meaning in the Sphere of Bliss. Only once past the Realm of Emergence, upon whose boundary you now stand, are such things meaningful."

Hatu's eyes went wide. "Tell me about time!"

She smiled and suddenly became a young man with brown hair and freckles. His youthful laughter was pleasing to their ears, and he cried, "It is but another illusion!" He spun on his toes and sang. "Come follow!"

Piper skipped along the road below them, away from where the white cloud had formed, and they followed. Doors were shimmering into existence, barely visible. Piper said, "Behind is the Crystal Highway, a path no mortal can perceive or endure. Now we travel the Star Walk, the Gateway Path, what you know as the Hall of Worlds."

Pug said, "It was without doors a moment ago."

Piper again laughed. "Illusions! Before, the path existed, and after, it will continue to exist."

"Before and after what?" Hatushaly asked.

"Everything!"

Nakor nodded, his expression set in consideration, lacking any of his usual signs of mirth. "I begin to understand."

"Where are we bound?" Pug asked.

"Here!" Piper sang, and abruptly they floated in the grey of rift-space.

An enormous structure hovered below them. It stretched in all directions, surrounded by emptiness. Directly below them was a circle of green. Pug whispered, "The City Forever."

Piper said, "And the Garden."

They drifted downward, and when their feet touched the grass lawn in the Garden's center, Pug tensed slightly, half-expecting the time-trap.

"What is this place?" Hatu asked, eyes wide.

"It's still an illusion," Nakor reminded him.

"It feels so real," Hatu replied.

"The good tricks do," Nakor said with a hint of admiration in his tone.

Pug spoke softly. "No one knows what these places are. The City

Forever, the Garden, Honest John's are all places within rift-space, but somehow able to exist."

Piper laughed. "You know what they are. You just don't know yet." Now a young woman, she said, "Time confuses me."

Hatushaly was about to ask a question, but the illusion vanished and abruptly they stood before the Oracle of Aal. Again, Hatushaly almost fell over, as if his balance was betraying him, but he caught himself in time.

From the air came the oracle's voice. "You have seen."

Pug took a slow, deep breath and said, "I have witnessed some of that before. I think I know where we must go next."

"Seek wisdom and knowledge from ancient times, magician, from those who were here before. Know the truth. The Aal are not the eldest race. We are the eldest, the first race, in this epoch, but there are some who linger from before."

Nakor laughed delightedly. He turned to Hatu and said, "Don't ask."

Hatushaly stepped back slightly. "What?"

"Before! Because it's the same answer. 'Everything!'"

Nakor gave the oracle a low bow. "I thank you, for you have given me a great deal."

He reached for Pug and Hatu and they were suddenly back on Sorcerer's Isle. "I really have gotten good at this trick, haven't I?" he said with a chuckle.

Hatushaly looked around, pale and shocked. "What now?"

Pug looked at Nakor and said, "I think we need to eat."

Nakor grinned. "Then we need to go find some elves."

DONTE GUIDED THE WAGON THROUGH the streets of Krondor. He stayed on the alert for anyone who might be a Mocker lookout, since he was sure eventually word would reach the Upright Man that he was back in the city. Lester Ving had revived twice, and Lyndon had quickly rendered him senseless again with a thump to his head. The second time he groaned and moved a bit, but then fell back into unconsciousness.

"I think this is it," said Donte, pulling over to the side of the road. He left enough room on his right for pedestrians to pass, and enough on the left for another wagon. This was a rather nicer quarter of the city than he had anticipated. "Watch yourselves," he said to his companions. "I'll be back shortly." He jumped down from the driver's bench and muttered, "I hope."

Donte crossed the street and stopped at a small shop door. He looked to his right and saw stairs leading to a top-floor entrance. He counted the steps—sixteen—and gave himself a nod of reassurance.

He glanced both ways to see if he was being observed and saw no one obviously watching. He returned to the door and opened it, stepped through, and saw a large man behind a table with a device Donte didn't recognize. The man regarded him with dark, deep-set eyes. He sported a full beard, dark with some grey, and Donte saw enough old marks and faded scars to know this man had been a scrapper in his youth. His broad shoulders and his seated position made it difficult for Donte to judge if he was fit or fat, but just to be on the safe side, he stood with his back to the door.

After a silent moment the man pushed his chair back a bit. "Yes?"

"I have your package," Donte said, motioning with his head that it was outside.

The man was silent for a moment. "What package?"

"The one you asked me to deliver," said Donte, "when we last had a chat upstairs." He pointed at the ceiling.

The man looked at him, then asked, "Are you sure you're at the right shop?"

Donte grinned widely. "Now I'm absolutely certain. See, you made two mistakes. First, you drugged me bringing me here from Port Vykor, but you only bagged me when you turned me loose. I learned how to blind-trace a route by counting steps and turns, and your lads never even tried to hide the route. Second, you didn't disguise your voice.

"Ving is in a wagon across the street. He's a little the worse for wear, but you can still have whatever sport you like with him. So, you said there would be a reward."

The man behind the table crossed his arms and said nothing, then finally stood up. Donte saw that he was heavyset, but that there was still a lot of strength under his fat was apparent just by the way he moved around the table. Donte tensed slightly, his hand drifting to the hilt of his dagger.

"You use that, do you think you'll live as far as the city gate?" the Upright Man asked.

Donte hid his apprehension and patted his dagger. "I use this, and I might just take over the Mockers."

The big man stopped, looked Donte up and down, then laughed. "Nothing shy about you, is there?"

"Where I'm from, you train all your life, or you run out of life. It's just how it is. I don't know about your boys, but those lads following Ving were . . . disorganized. Bad training and easily disposed of."

"Show me Ving," said the Upright Man. Before Donte could open the door, he added, "And to anyone else, I'm a go-between. Understand?"

"Completely," said Donte. Trusting he wasn't going to be knifed from behind, he stepped through the door and indicated the wagon where Robertson and Lyndon waited.

They crossed the road and Donte said, "Show him."

Lyndon pulled aside the rug and revealed Lester Ving lying there. His face was a collection of black-and-blue lumps, but he was still breathing. "Some blood," said Donte, "but no permanent damage."

The Upright Man nodded and put his hand in the air. From a short distance away four men hurried to them.

"Get off the wagon and I'll buy you another."

Donte waved for his two companions to leave the wagon. Robertson and Lyndon jumped down and the four men who had arrived quickly mounted the wagon and drove it off.

The Upright Man waved Donte and the others to follow him, then at the door to the shop he motioned for Robertson and Lyndon to wait outside. Once inside with the door closed, he turned to Donte and said, "Who am I?"

"A fence for the Mockers. They'll accept that."

"You're too clever to kill." The Upright Man circled around the table and sat down. "But you're only the third man alive who's seen my face."

"I can be a loudmouth, foolish, and short-tempered," said Donte. "But I can also keep my mouth shut and, if I must, think before I act. I do like to stay alive."

"Good," said the Upright Man. "Then I think I can use you."

Donte's brow furrowed a little, but he said nothing.

"I think I'd object to you trying to take over the Mockers, so let's put an end to that conversation." The Upright Man leaned forward, elbows on the table. "But I've thought about what you said, about how your masters have conspired to run gangs in cities all over your world."

Donte had never claimed that agents of Coaltachin worked worldwide on Garn, but he decided this was not the time to correct the Upright Man.

"Let's do this. Return to Port Vykor and rid it of the Keshians, set up the crews, and get the merchants sorted out. Send me a tenth of what you collect each month. If you can do that in a year, I'll get you up to another city.

"The Daymaster and Nightmaster each manage Krondor in my name, but outside the city we've lost all control. It's time to return the Guild of Thieves, the Ragged Brotherhood, the Mockers to its former authority."

Donte grinned. "Ambition? That's good."

"You're willing?"

Donte laughed. "Do I have a choice?"

"No," said the Upright Man with a chuckle.

"I'll need help," said Donte. "You've met two of the three men who work for me. I'll need more if I'm going to rid Port Vykor of the competition."

The Upright Man sat back. "Three? You only had three helping you round up Ving?"

Donte nodded.

"You are dangerous." The Upright Man sounded impressed. "I've tried to track down the traitor for four years."

Donte nodded. "Training. You don't train your people."

"Training?" He considered that, then said, "We will talk more. What do you need?"

"A little coin, always, but six men. Give me three of your best, and three youngsters who can be trained to become the best. I'll do the rest."

"You can take over Port Vykor with nine men?"

"I can do it with six, but nine does it faster."

"Done." The Upright Man said, "Wait here."

He stepped through a curtained doorway and after a few moments returned with a heavy pouch. He tossed it to Donte, who jingled it and then stuck it inside his shirt.

"Not going to count it?" asked the Upright Man.

"It's fair, I expect. You'd kill me before you'd cheat me." Donte smiled broadly. "I can't say I understand you fully, but I'm getting there."

The Upright Man sighed, smiled, and sat back. "You finish in Port Vykor, and we'll have a long conversation about training up the Mockers. We lack that . . . precision."

Donte gave a shrug. "It's brutal, but effective."

"Where do I send the six men?"

"Find me at the sign of the Four Ravens. Have them ask for Richard." With a smile he said, "And when you're not up there"—he pointed upward—"what do I call you?"

"Leon the Chandler." He gestured at the device on the table that had been there since Donte entered. Now Donte could see it was a sort of navigational device. "I fix things."

Donte smiled and left without another word.

Outside, he stopped and considered. His original plan had been to sow chaos and seize the opportunity to set up a small operation in a city still reeling from an ancient war, a commerce port with little commerce. Now he had the opportunity to become important in the rebirth of a criminal organization. He smiled as he thought that even his grandfather might be impressed.

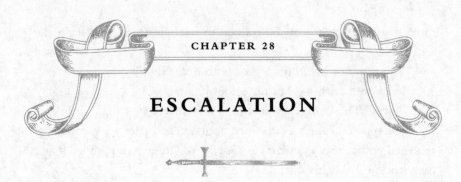

CHAPTER 28

ESCALATION

Hava gripped the helm of the *Queen of Storms*.
The sea was choppy as the ships were breasting combers in a rhythmic up-and-down motion. Every sailor balanced as they moved about their tasks. She marveled at how all this had become second nature to her over the course of only a few short years.

The core of her crew comprised those who had survived the slave ship from which she had broken free, then captured. The Pride Lords' raids on the west coast of North Tembria had been vicious, and only her training and ability had spared her a lifetime of slavery. She had taken freed slaves and homeless men and women and built a crew around a few experienced sailors. By capturing ships and freeing prisoners, she had turned that first ship into a fleet. That fleet was becoming the heart of what was now the Marquensas Royal Navy.

Magnus stood to her right, looking toward the bow, balancing like an experienced seaman. He might not be a sailor, she concluded, but he had obviously spent a great deal of time aboard ships in his long life.

"Do you think we can do this?" she asked him.

"From what Pug told me and you've shown me, I think it will be fairly uncomplicated, once the rift is opened. The trick of it will be quickly communicating to those behind us what we encounter."

She pointed to a sailor holding two pennants. It was a simple system. Each ship could quickly see if they were to bear right—a red pennant—or to the left—a blue pennant. No pennant shown meant straight on.

Magnus had spent an hour using his arts to jump from the ship to the rift in Garn, through that to Sorcerer's Isle, then back. As far as he could judge, the sea on both worlds was navigable.

"Let's see if this is folly," Hava said as they moved through the chop toward a massive rift oval which was large enough for the ships to sail through. Magnus had created it with the aid of Ruffio on the other side.

Turning to Magnus, Hava said, "Pug had to swim around to calculate matching currents, tides, and levels." She almost winced: she had already expressed her worry about Magnus taking over this task from Pug. She hated that she felt the need to repeat herself.

Magnus barely hid a chuckle. "I think you'll be well served. My father may have more experience, but he'd be the first to admit I have more power."

"Father?" she muttered to herself. Out loud, she said, "Well, if we need muscle, more power is better.

"Sails!" she shouted, having decided what she needed, given the day's winds. Everyone aloft was ready. Within seconds, reefs were loosened, and sails tumbled downward, to be filled with wind, snapping loudly as they pulled against their sheets.

She turned the wheel and headed for the rift. Glancing back, she saw the other five ships behind, lowering their sails. The interval looked wide enough that they would not pile up one on the other. Hava looked forward and took a breath as the bowsprit entered the rift.

For an instant she felt as if she was about to float off the deck, but before that sensation completely registered, she felt the ship lurch and the sky changed from a light overcast to a brilliant blue. A motion to starboard told her that the current was different, but nothing to cause a problem. She looked at the sails and shouted orders to trim for a shifting wind.

"No pennant!" she shouted to the sailor waiting to signal behind. "We're heading straight on!"

She saw the north side of Sorcerer's Isle off the starboard bow and recognized they were just a short distance from the docks. Looking aft, she saw the silver oval shimmering, then the ship behind them emerged. She watched as it settled and saw sailors quickly correcting for the changes.

"Damn, but this is working," she said. Judging by how far she needed to travel to stay clear of the other ships, she shouted, "Ready to reef sails!"

People were gathering along the shore, and she could see a crowd assembling ahead near the bend in the coast that would be the jetty where the goods would be loaded.

The men aloft had been instructed that after dropping the sails they were to stay in place; they wouldn't be needed to trim unless ordered. They knew that it was now time to end this very short voyage. After the *Queen of Storms* had passed by the docks, she ordered the sails reefed. Once the sails were taken in, the ship slowed. The anchor was released, and the ship came to a gentle halt. Turning to Magnus, Hava smiled and said, "I think we're there."

He returned her smile. "We're halfway there." He looked skyward and said, "We have half a day to load the cargo, then finish tomorrow morning. While that's underway, Ruffio and I will work together to create another rift to Marquenet." He looked aft and said, "The last ship is through."

Hava followed his gaze and saw the five ships following and slowing as they all came to rest in a safe anchorage. "Some of those lads will be talking about this journey to their grandchildren."

"It's all part of a great struggle, and everyone is doing what they can," Magnus said. "After you get the barges underway, you can find me in the dining hall. I have some things to see to, but after that I'll be hungry."

"As will I," she said. "It's already been a very long day. But I still have to ensure that no one crashes a ship into the rocks or otherwise creates havoc. If time permits, I'll find you at the dining hall."

Magnus vanished.

Hava turned to see how the crew was doing and was pleased that everyone was taking this strange journey in their stride, briskly going about their tasks. Then she realized she was getting used to the magicians vanishing. While some of the crews might still be flustered by passing through the rift, enough were attending to the ships' needs that

she felt good about this half of the passage. Maybe she would have time
to eat.

HATUSHALY, NAKOR, AND PUG APPEARED near the bank of a river.
Pug said, "Now we wait."

"For what?" Hatushaly asked.

"To be invited into the elven forest," Pug answered, kneeling, then
sitting back on the woodland ground. "This is the River Boundary,
and we sit here on the northwest border of the Duchy of Crydee and
wait."

"What's a duchy?" Hatu asked. "I've read the word, and know it's
political, but I've never fully understood it."

"They have no dukes on Garn," Nakor said, sitting next to Pug.

"We have kings and barons," Hatushaly said.

Nakor laughed. "Humans! They organize so many ways to split
up the spoils from pillaging the commoners." Looking at Pug, he said,
"I forget which world it was, but I once visited a kingdom that had
fifty-four ranks of nobility." He smiled and shook his head. "Greater-
this, arch-that, a rank with this order, same rank with a different order,
which was higher than the first order. Then there was another place
where peasants owned the land, but 'servants' owned the peasants . . ."
He sighed. "It all seemed very important to the humans."

Pug looked at his old companion. "You speak of humans as if you're
not one of us."

Nakor grinned. "I might not be. I'm an echo of . . . ?" He shrugged,
seemingly amused by this mystery.

Pug smiled, then lightly punched Nakor's shoulder, causing him to
almost fall over. "You certainly seem real enough," he said.

Nakor laughed loudly. "So, Phillip hasn't gone away completely, I
see."

Pug laughed with him. "Never."

From across the river, a voice said, "This is a wonder to behold."

The three looked across the river to see a tall, blond figure standing in the late afternoon sun. His hair fell to his shoulders, and he wore
green-dyed leathers and held an elven longbow. Behind him were two

other tall figures dressed alike, one with reddish-blond hair, the other with raven-black hair.

Nakor leapt to his feet. "Calis!"

Pug stood, as did Hatushaly. "May we enter?" asked Pug.

"Welcome," said Calis, and Nakor waded quickly across the river.

Pug took Hatu's hand and jumped to stand next to the tall half-elf. Nakor came ashore, holding his now-soaked robe and laughing. "I got so excited, I forgot to do that!"

Calis said to Pug, "You are different. I don't know what to call you."

"Call me Pug," he said. "I have all my memories back so am my essential self."

Calis looked at him in wonder. "I mourned your death."

"Me too," said Nakor. "But you know how these things go."

Calis slowly shook his head. "Not really." He took a deep breath, then said to Pug, "It's been a very long time."

"Yes and no," Pug said. "While I am again Pug, I am still Phillip." He paused, and then said gravely, "The Darkness returns."

Calis's brow furrowed. "We have much to speak of, then." He turned to his companions and said, "Continue without me."

The two elves nodded and silently set off on what Pug assumed was a routine patrol, and quickly vanished between the trees.

Calis slung his bow over his shoulder. "Magnus never openly said he suspected who you were, but as much time as we have been together . . ." He let the thought go unfinished.

Pug nodded. "We have a long history. I remember the first time I met your brother, when your mother rode to Crydee to share news of the Tsurani with Lord Borric. He was generous with his wisdom to a very young boy, a boy who was unsure of himself, especially when it came to what he should do regarding a young princess." His smile faded and he said, "We can reminisce later. For now, I must meet with the king and the eldar."

Calis said, "Since the battle at Magician's End, few humans have come to the River Boundary. Fewer still were welcomed to Elvandar."

"I know," said Pug. "The war was harder upon the long-lived

than upon us humans. Many elven warriors and Spellweavers sacrificed themselves to save us all." He paused and said, "And now the Darkness is back."

Calis was silent for a moment, and his expression changed so subtly that few humans other than Pug would have noticed. In that change of expression, Pug saw a hint of fear and anger.

Calis said, "Your need is understood." He looked at Hatu.

Pug said, "Hatushaly, this is Calis, Warleader of Elvandar and brother to King Calin. Calis, this is Hatushaly from the world of Garn. He has magic like no other, which is why we need to speak with an eldar Spellweaver."

"Come," said Calis. "I expect you can get us to the king's court faster than if we run for three days?"

Pug smiled. "If Elvandar is in the same place as it was last I was here, yes."

"It hasn't moved," Calis said dryly.

Pug reached out and the four formed a circle. There was a sudden whoosh and they stood in a clearing. Hatushaly's eyes widened.

Before them, across the clearing, a city of trees rose upward. Towering boles, dwarfing any oaks Hatu had ever seen, were linked together by huge arching bridges of branches. The bridges were flat across the top, and elves were crossing from tree to tree.

Hatushaly looked up and up and saw that the trunks rose above the bridges until they were hidden by leaves and branches. The leaves were mainly a lush green, but golden, silver, or even white foliage was visible. In this late afternoon light, the leaves were aglow with a soft radiance.

Pug put his hand on Hatu's shoulder and simply said, "Elvandar."

Hatushaly was speechless.

Calis said, "Let me carry word to my brother-king and then you should walk to the court. You'll arrive just in time to be feasted." He smiled at Pug. "Then we can catch up."

"Before you go," Pug said, "how are Ellia and the boys?"

Calis appeared to be genuinely delighted. "My wife is hale and will welcome the return of an old friend. For a city-dwelling elf from across the sea, she has come to be at ease here. The boys, as you called them, are fully grown men."

Pug seemed embarrassed as he said, "It has been a while, hasn't it?"

"As usual, a father will always think of them as boys, but they are well past that. Both are wed, and I am a grandfather."

"It has been a very long time," said Nakor. "The Crimson Eagles."

Calis nodded and said, "I think of them from time to time. Now I must go. Wait a short while, then take the high path. Pug remembers the way."

"I do," Pug said.

Hatu watched as Calis set off at an easy jog, heading toward what appeared to be an entrance to the city of trees. Pug clapped him on the shoulder and said, "I think you will find this a wonderful place to learn some new arts."

Nakor grinned. "The Spellweavers know a lot of good tricks."

As they neared the entrance to Elvandar, Hatushaly could see a busy community. Hunters were dressing a deer. Next to them stood two younger elves, ready to pull a cart piled with the day's meat. Two large hunting hounds waited patiently nearby for permission to devour the leavings. A few yards away, a group of elven women were finishing the day's work at a massive loom, where a shimmering cloth was being carefully taken down from a giant head roller, while two heddles the size of a man's arm were pulled away.

"Elven crafts are much like our own," said Pug to Hatu, "but so much finer."

Nakor chuckled. "They've had a lot more years to learn how to do things."

"Which is exactly why we're here," Pug replied.

They continued until they reached a wide staircase spiraling up the side of a huge tree. As they climbed, Hatu realized there was no handrail or safety line on the outer edge. After a single circuit of the tree, he looked down and saw they were now a good thirty feet above the forest floor.

"Good thing we know how to fly," Nakor joked.

"Yes," said Hatushaly nervously.

Pug looked at the young man. Smiling broadly, he added, "Elves are very sure-footed."

"Apparently," Hatu said as they continued to climb higher.

DONTE LOOKED OVER THE SIX men the Upright Man had sent to Port Vykor. He sat in the common room of the Four Ravens and silently waited until the new serving girl had poured seven mugs of ale. When she left, Donte inclined his head and picked up his mug.

The three younger men glanced around, unsure of what was expected, and Donte laughed. "Drink up, lads." He took a long swallow from his mug, then set it down.

The three older men also drank and when their mugs were returned to the table, Donte pushed his chair back. "Either you are the best the Upright Man could send, or people he wants to get rid of." He laughed. "Either way, he wishes to extend the Mockers' reach and get rid of the Keshians."

The three older men glanced at one another and were silent, but the younger trio looked very worried. "It doesn't matter," Donte said. "We have an opportunity to take over this city." He took another drink and continued: "I have a different way of seeing things than you do, I am certain. I come from a distant place that has been running cities since before my however-many-grandfather's time." He smiled. "So, let's all get to know one another." He pointed to the oldest-looking man, who had greying dark hair, a sunburned face, and muscle softening with age. "You?"

The man he had singled out looked around as if uncertain what to say, then after a long silence said, "I'm Janos. I was a day-bull on the docks. I'm the best."

Donte gave a nod. Muscle, but with some brains. He pointed to the next man, a brawler by appearance, more muscle than Janos and enough facial scars to show he wasn't especially adept at ducking. "Fredrick, but everyone calls me Freddie." Donte smiled. "I guard." Donte didn't bother to ask what he guarded, as he already knew the answer: anything that needed guarding. Given his appearance as a human *makiwara*—the Coaltachin word for punching bag—he was obviously tough enough to take a beating and survive.

Donte looked at the third man: older, wiry, his grey hair cut short, and dark eyes that darted around the room. Donte said, "Roof-runner?"

The man said, "Hillman. People call me Hilly." He nodded. "I'm the best thief in Krondor."

One of the younger men laughed. "So he claims," he said with a mocking expression. He was also a slender man, with a dancer's frame and a cunning air about him. Dark hair and eyes and a dusky complexion suggested he had some Keshian or desert blood in him, from what Donte had learned. His clothing was also what Donte would expect from a practiced night thief.

Hilly looked as if he was ready to stand and confront the youngster, but Donte prevented that with a curt "Don't!" Looking at the young man, Donte said, "And you?"

"Name's Stanley, but everyone calls me Shadow."

It was Hilly's turn to scoff. "Nobody but Stanley calls him Shadow."

Donte looked at Hilly, then Stanley, and said, "Am I going to have trouble with you two?"

Hilly shook his head. "I just do what I'm told. That lad thinks he's the next Jimmy the Hand."

Donte shrugged. "Whoever he was." To Stanley he said, "And you? Do you do what you're told?"

"More," Stanley answered. "If I see an opportunity, I take it. If I'm told to steal a prize from a merchant, I try to come back with more."

Donte sat back and considered this for a moment, then said, "Ambition. I like it." Stanley's expression brightened. "And sometimes I hate it," he added. Stanley's pleased expression faded. "You've always got to balance risk against reward, especially if you're on a pilfer alone."

Hilly nodded.

Donte said, "Here's the thing. The Upright Man intends to take over Port Vykor. I delivered Lester Ving to him last week, so he put me in charge here. So, consider me the Upright Man of Port Vykor, without all the secrecy. Or the Nightmaster or Daymaster, whatever time it is, or simply your boss. Understood?"

All of them exchanged looks and Donte laughed. "Ah, so he sent you here without bothering to let you know what's coming." He shook his head. "I guess that means he didn't tell you this city is your new home. Look, spare yourself any notion of running back to Krondor first chance, because you won't be welcomed back. So, let's make the best of this."

Donte stood and said, "Where I'm from we run things differently, so we're going to make some changes from what you're used to. According to what I've been told, you all come in and out of somewhere called Mother's and get instructions from whoever's in charge at that hour."

They nodded.

"Well, where I'm from, we're more spread out, so we have crews. That's how we'll do it here. I'll give orders to three lads you'll meet soon enough, by the name of Scully, Robertson, and Lyndon, and they'll be the ones to keep you informed of what we want done. In between times, you get to take advantage of whatever brings in some booty, just enough not to get the city watch frothing at the mouth. That means no unnecessary blood, broken bones, brawling, abusing people for sport, anything that gets us noticed. Right?"

They all nodded that they understood.

"So, here's how I see it. Janos, you get the harbor. Which one of these lads do you choose?"

Janos glanced over and pointed to a young man who looked enough like him to be a relative: stocky and with a thick neck, clearly a strong brawler. "Pytor. I've done work with him before. He's good in a dust-up and he does what he's told."

"Good," said Donte. He pointed to the last youngster and said, "Your name?"

"Andrew," he answered. He was a nondescript-looking fellow, which Donte liked in someone who was trying to blend in. He had light brown hair, brown eyes, was not too tall, short, fat, or thin.

"You're with Freddie." Donte looked at the older man. "I don't need much guarding these days. I need people who can blend in and stay quiet, and who listen. You two may be told where to go and who to follow, but most of the time I want you wandering among the merchants and listening. I'll have runners around who can carry word should you need to reach me.

"That leaves you two," he said to Hilly and Stanley. As both stared at him, Donte held up his hand to halt any protest. "I don't care if you have problems. You put them away." He pointed at Hilly. "You have skills he needs to learn." He then pointed at Stanley. "You want to be called Shadow? You earn it. You listen. That's how you learn."

Donte fought down the urge to laugh uproariously at saying all the things that had been said to him as a student, and that he had routinely ignored. He continued speaking to Stanley. "If you have a hunch, share it. Act rashly and you'll pay the price for that rashness if it brings any heat down on the rest of us."

He motioned for them to stand. "Start by cleaning up around here. It may not be Mother's, but it's our home for the time being. From this point on, we are the Mockers of Port Vykor." He moved toward the door. "I have other business, but the three men I told you about will be rolling in here in a few hours. See that they're not disappointed in how much work you've done today."

Donte left the building and turned down the street that led to where his horse was stabled. He was overdue to visit the farm and catch up with Healer on what was happening there. As side hustles went, sheep farming was rarely profitable, but given how much trouble building a criminal empire was becoming, he might just give it up and become a sheep farmer full-time.

DECLAN READ THE REPORT AND threw it on the table. "We need Hatu or one of those other magicians here," he said to his brothers.

King Daylon said, "Where are they?"

"At least one of them will be returning shortly with Hava and the fleet bringing food from Midkemia," said Balven. "Until then all we can do is wait and watch."

Declan's expression was clearly one of frustration. "No decay, no scavengers, bodies just lying there, looking as if they fell only moments before. It's nearly a month now. I should get back to the new fortification."

"To do what?" said the king. "To look over everyone's shoulder, waiting for the dead to rise up and attack again?"

Declan appeared to be on the verge of an argument, but he made a noise of frustration and sank back into his chair. "I just need to do something."

"Then something to do you shall have!" said the king with a laugh. "Seriously, little brother, I think you need to take a ride down to our fortress at the Narrows and see if everything looks as good as the reports suggest. We expect the Church to come through the forest, but that doesn't mean we should neglect our flanks. I've already sent Collin up to Beran's Hill since he's familiar with the region."

Declan said, "Well, that's something. Four days out, one day to poke around and then back. This is when I wish one of those magic-users was here to pop us down and back."

Balven chuckled. "At times it has made things much easier. If I understand what Hatushaly and the others have said, it's possible we may have a magician or two here after all is said and done."

"One can hope," said Daylon.

Declan rose from the dining table, gave his brothers a bow, turned, and exited. After the door closed behind him, Balven said, "He's learned some court manners at least."

The king let out a long sigh, and said, "Now if we can just prevent him from getting himself killed."

"Or us, when he gets to meet his future wife."

Daylon fixed his brother with a narrow gaze and said, "You still haven't mentioned the baron's daughters?"

"One battle at a time," said Balven.

PUG, NAKOR, AND HATUSHALY APPROACHED the center of Elvandar, the king's court, as the sun fully set. Now the forest was alight with globes glowing with a bright inner light. The leaves of white, gold, or silver were brilliant in comparison to the more muted earth tones that were evident everywhere. Elven art and crafts were on display, with tapestries of fine weave used to divide areas they had passed. Flowers were abundant and the air was redolent with their scent. The aroma of spices accompanied the night breeze from cooking fires somewhere nearby, and the faint hint of smoke was a counterpoint that Hatushaly found pleasant.

The shock had worn off, but not the wonder. He gawked at everything as they passed, but when they reached the court of King Calin, he nearly stumbled in awe. The king's throne was a massive chair of finely carved wood. As a carpenter's apprentice in one of his early assignments for the Kingdom of the Night on Garn, Hatu had seen enough of woodcraft to appreciate that this was a magnificent work of art, sculpted out of a solid block of wood as tall as a man and half that size on the sides. The artistry was exquisite: it was a paean to nature in wood. Deer, foxes, and other animals were carved in relief on the side he could see, with vines and leaves intricately fashioned as a decorative frieze.

The king wore a simple circlet of gold on his head, open at the brow. Calin looked just as Pug remembered, with perhaps a tiny bit more weight and a hint of grey in his brown hair.

Seeing the three humans enter, Calin rose with a smile and said, "Pug. Welcome, old friend."

Pug bowed from the waist, and Nakor and Hatushaly followed his example. "Greetings, King Calin. It has been too long."

The king descended from his throne and gave Pug a warm embrace. "I sense you are now more than you were when we last met."

"All my memories have returned," Pug said. "From before the Battle of Magician's End."

"Ah," said the king. "That explains much. When you and Magnus came to honor my taking of my mother-queen's place after she journeyed to the Blessed Isles, I sensed you were growing in your power. This, however, is something unexpected. We have a great deal to discuss and shall do so over a feast. First, my brother says you have a warning."

"The Darkness," was all Pug said.

Calin nodded. "There has been growing unease among our Spellweavers that something evil is gathering. We will hold a council tomorrow."

"I need first to speak with the eldar."

"So few remain," said the king, "but they will also be with us in council. But for now, who is this newcomer?"

"Hatushaly, from the world of Garn. He is both the last in the line of kings known as the Firemanes and a wielder of powers unlike any I've seen."

Calin looked surprised, an expression rarely seen in an elf, whose emotional displays tended to the nuanced. "Unlike any? You've seen more than any being I've encountered."

"More than me, too, sire," said Nakor.

"The gambler," said Calin with a smile. "Once again you seem drawn toward trouble."

"It's my nature, I guess," said Nakor.

"Let us celebrate your arrival. Our concerns about coming troubles can wait until tomorrow." He looked at Pug and they exchanged knowing glances. "We've faced such before and must again, but we may steal a moment or two between to appreciate old friends."

They all bowed as Calin turned to walk from the portion of the court used for formal occasions to a large platform set aside for dining. They followed him around a circular table with four breaks to allow service from the inside. Calin indicated that Pug should sit to his left, as Calis arrived and took a cushion to his brother's right. Pug recognized some faces, but there were many younger elves who were now members of the court, and too many older friends no longer here.

Pug felt a passing sadness for the absence of those he had come to cherish as friends: Aglaranna, Calin's and Calis's mother, the elf queen who had married Pug's childhood friend Tomas, for years a foster brother; Tathar the old Spellweaver, who had taught Pug so much. They and others were gone.

Pushing aside his melancholy musings, Pug smiled at those he did recognize and turned to Hatushaly and said, "You are doing well for someone who did not know these people even existed before you came here."

Hatu smiled and said, "It's wonderful."

"We must endeavor to keep our sense of wonder if we are to keep our resolve," said Pug. "Now, enjoy this evening, for tomorrow we begin to unravel mysteries."

CHAPTER 29

MYSTERIES

Pug awoke.

Elvandar was never dark, but the soft glow was all that remained after the illumination globes had been dimmed. Calis knelt next to the sleeping mat, removed his hand from Pug's shoulder, and with a single nod indicated that Pug should get up and follow him. Calis had been stealthy: the others slept on.

Pug adjusted his robe and followed. Once outside, he glanced skyward and estimated there were still three or more hours to sunrise. Soon some members of the Elvandar community would be rousing, those whose duties included preparing the morning meal, hunters setting out in the predawn hours when game was about, and patrols and sentries relieving the night watch.

Pug followed Calis to the king's private chambers, which he had not seen since Calis was a baby. There was a poignant moment as he recalled standing there with Calis's parents, the elf queen Aglaranna, and Pug's boyhood foster brother, Tomas.

Within that relatively small chamber, the king waited with two old elves Pug recognized. Calis moved to sit next to his older brother. The two eldar sat side by side on cushions in front of the king.

Pug inclined his head toward Calin, then said, "Abadin, Jacinta, it's good to see old friends." Phillip had only known those elves whom he had met the one time he had visited Elvandar with Magnus. These two had not been among them. But now with Pug's memories fully returned, he knew them both very well and was struck by the changes time had wrought.

Elves aged slowly, but they did age, and it was centuries since he had last seen these two. The vigor of elves in their prime had been replaced by grey hair, faces lined with age, and a slightly less energetic demeanor, though, like all elderly elves, they were still alert, with lively expressions and bright eyes.

Abadin and Jacinta had been among the youngest members of the eldar when Pug had found them on the Tsurani world of Kelewan. Once servants of the Dragon Lords, the eldar were living in a forest under the ice cap, protected by magic, a place called Elvardein, a smaller, twin forest to Elvandar. The eldar had lived there for centuries until Pug offered them the means to return to their home in Midkemia.

The two old elves greeted Pug warmly, his change of appearance clearly of no matter to them.

King Calin said, "I deduced from what you said that while you wish to consult with our Spellweavers, you wished to speak with the eldar first."

Pug suddenly felt a drop in his stomach and said, "Are you all that's left?"

Abadin smiled, his deep wrinkles in sharp contrast to his bright blue eyes. "We are the last descendants of those tasked with serving the Valheru who were born on Kelewan." The Dragon Lords had eldar with them when they raided other worlds. "Our children born here are simply eledhel. The only distinction left is that we still hold knowledge from that time."

"It is that lore I seek," Pug said, sitting on a floor cushion. "I found Elvardein because of a hint of what I witnessed on the Tsurani Tower of Testing, when I finally mastered my arts and was granted a Great One's black robe. When humans knew you only as 'the Watchers.' Finding you was my first step in learning many things beyond what I learned at the Assembly on Kelewan." He paused, gathering his thoughts. "I spoke to the Oracle of Aal, as I have done before, and remembering when I first encountered them on their dying world, the legend of them being the oldest race in the universe seemed fitting. Ancient in knowledge and gentle wisdom, and with the power to see the future. But I am faced with a conundrum: elves are the oldest people of Midkemia since the Valheru vanished into rift-space, but legend says that the Dragon Lords were the first people, so how is that reconciled?"

Jacinta studied Pug for a moment. Her face was a match to her husband's, aged and weather-beaten, framed by long, flowing grey hair, yet her eyes also were alight with youthful energy. Pug knew that the elves lived for centuries, barely showing their age, before looking as these two did. Elves suffered no elderly infirmity, unless caused by an injury, but when death came, it was unexpected and sudden.

After a few moments, Jacinta said, "Even the Valheru are not the oldest race here. The dragons came first. Then the Valheru, then the edhel." She used the word applied to all elves—light, dark, sun-elves, elves from across the sea, and the star-elves. All were edhel. She regarded Pug's puzzled expression and continued: "You have power, and those of your race with spellcraft live a long life but compared to the edhel it is short. The king's mother, the blessed queen, lived for five centuries before you were born. She would have lived longer, I think, save the grief at losing Calis's father hastened her to the Blessed Isles." Like all elves, she did not use Queen Aglaranna's or Tomas's names, in the belief it might summon them back to life unwillingly. "So, you must understand, we speak not of years, decades, or even centuries."

Abadin nodded in agreement. "We speak of millennia."

Jacinta went on, "We can only surmise from the lore of our ancestors that at the beginning, when all was created, the first life to arise was perhaps simple: small plants, creatures, swimmers in vast oceans. But as little as we understand the nature of the Enemy, the Void, we do know that it is capable of mimicking life, even if it doesn't truly understand life. It's a mockery of life. It destroys life needlessly, as if life itself is the Void's foe, through countless attacks. We can assume that its essence limits it in significant ways here." She spread her hands, indicating the world around them. "If it is a thing of rift-space, also known as the Void—perhaps they are one and the same, or perhaps a fragment of the Void itself. We may never understand."

Abadin said, "It is limited in what it can do here, just as we have limits on what we can achieve in rift-space. You know well it takes prodigious spellcraft for life to survive in rift-space. Life is of this realm, while the Void is apart, alien to life. It may use life but is incapable of creating life. So, it must manipulate life for its own purposes."

Pug nodded slowly. "Black slayers, death dancers, shadow assassins,

the Children of the Void: all were servants of the ensorcelled Dread-
lords, who are ruled by the Darkness." His face revealed deep dismay at
the thought of those beings. "I have battled many of them."

Abadin nodded. "We have heard all the tales. We know of the false
advisers to human rulers before the last great conflict. We know of demons summoned from other realms, some corporeal, some created out
of human flesh for spirits to control, and some dark spirits possessing
still-living beings. All of these are servants of the Void."

"You say dragons were first?" Pug's expression was puzzled. He
looked at Jacinta, who looked to King Calin.

"This lore is hidden," said the king, "known only to our ancients."
He indicated the two eldar. "My parents knew, as did I when I was
named Warleader." He nodded toward Calis, indicating to Pug that this
was also true of Calis. He added, "Younger lorekeepers have also been
given this knowledge."

Abadin said, "When Jacinta and I journey to the Blessed Isle, the
lore will endure. Our descendants may have not been born on Kelewan, but that knowledge remains with them. You must understand this
universe is ancient, billions upon billions of years old. Unimaginable
forces were unleashed in its creation and beings of immense power
sprang into being."

"The gods," said Pug.

"A name," said Jacinta. "There are other names. Some of these
beings are things of the mind, invisible to the senses, and others are
of flesh and blood like you and me. More have withered and perished
since the dawn of this universe, and more came into existence who
abide today; some will be born long after we are dust. Such is the span
of years.

"To your questions, dragons came first, and as it is with their kind,
they begin as little more than animals, like their lesser kin, the wyverns
and drakes. However, as dragons age they acquire intelligence, then
spellcraft. They have unique abilities."

Abadin said, "It may be that some part of their creation was fashioned by both life and the Void, for dragons above all other creatures
can enter and leave what you call rift-space at will."

"The Valheru, whom humans call Dragon Lords," said Jacinta,

"were the first mortal race corrupted by the Void at their creation, so says our lore. Elves were created to serve them. You've seen others—the tiger-men, serpent-people—those who were raised up by the Valheru as servants and playthings."

"Elves were created by the Dragon Lords?" Pug asked.

"Unlikely," Abadin answered. "The Void can possess, corrupt, or influence; all these things the Void is capable of doing, but creation? Tiger-men and other such beings began as simple animals, and the Valheru used their arcane arts to mold them into what they became, but they did not create those lesser creatures."

"We may never know how the edhel came into being," Jacinta said, "but our belief is that life itself created this form. Life finds a way, and for reasons we may never know, we were created as an echo of the Valheru before they were corrupted. But when Calis's father came to us bedecked in the armor of a Valheru, we discovered we were no longer servants. His influence on us was powerful, but he could not command us all. We had evolved.

"At the height of his rage during the war with the Tsurani, some here were willing and able to oppose him. That never would have been possible in ancient times."

Pug remembered Tomas's battle within himself against the magical legacy of Ashen-Shugar, the Ruler of the Eagle's Reaches, whose armor he wore. It had been a close thing before Tomas obtained dominance over the memories of the ancient Dragon Lord.

"You humans," Abadin said, "are from other worlds, and, like the goblins, dwarves, trolls, and other races, came here during the first advent of the Chaos War."

Pug was silent for a moment, then said, "My vision on Kelewan also showed the arrival of many races escaping from chaos on a golden bridge though a massive rift."

"Yes," said Abadin. "The legend of the golden bridge is common to many worlds and shared by many species. As the Valheru raided across the universe, they crushed advanced empires and primitive tribes indiscriminately. These were the Chaos Wars in our history, when races were forced to leave their home worlds to seek sanctuary elsewhere."

"Think of it as a metaphor," said Jacinta. "We do not believe there was a single bridge of golden light stretching from one side of the universe to the other. Perhaps there were portals through the Hall of Worlds to places unknown to those who fled. But eventually the combined might of spellcasters of all types accomplished one thing."

"Closing the door behind them before the Dragon Lords could follow," said Nakor from the doorway.

King Calin stood up, his expression stern. "You were not invited, gambler."

"I was not told to stay away, either, king," Nakor answered blithely. Then his tone turned serious. "I was brought back to life for a reason, and this is it." He pointed to where Pug and the two eldar sat.

Pug was skilled enough at reading elven expressions and movement to see that Calin conceded Nakor's point. The king sat down again without comment.

Nakor came and sat next to Pug. "The question that is plaguing Pug here is, if the Aal are not the first race in this universe, who is?"

Abadin answered. "Dragons are the oldest race in this universe, having changed over the ages, rising to become beings of unequaled power and intelligence, yet unique in that they must evolve within their own life cycle to attain that status. Moreover, they are able to traverse both rift-space and time, and no other being we know of can do that."

"What of the race of the Aal?" Pug asked.

Jacinta said, "We do not know. My speculation is that if they wanted to share the answer to that mystery with you, they would have done so."

"Or perhaps they're waiting for the right moment," said Nakor, without his usual humor.

"Some things are unfolding, some things are being revealed, yet much is still hidden," Abadin offered. He looked at Pug. "What do you know?"

"Not as much as I'd like," Pug conceded. "There is a thing that Hatushaly discovered through his arts." He waved toward Nakor. "Identified as a death-machine, a collector of life force." With a nod he indicated that Nakor should explain.

Nakor adopted an unusually straightforward narration, explaining what he had seen, and his discussions in Honest John's with Ificad about the nature of the gigantic accumulator. He finished by saying, "Ificad speculates that with enough life energy stored, the device could be used to rip open the sky. He meant—"

"Tear a massive rift through the heavens," interrupted Jacinta. "It is . . . familiar."

Pug's expression was questioning.

Abadin nodded. "As I said, dragons are unique in their powers, and opening passages through rift-space is different to the passages you create to travel to other worlds. The Void is powerful, but limited, and perhaps we can surmise this accumulator is the means to reach the world of Garn on some massive scale."

Jacinta said, "It is speculation, but I can see little other purpose for what you describe."

Pug was thoughtful for a moment, then asked, "Have you anything else you can share with us?"

"Nothing we think will aid you in the next confrontation with the Darkness," said Abadin. "We always return to the reality that things are not always as they appear to be, and it may be foolish to accept the first explanation of things as the only one."

Nakor stood and said, "We need to do two things."

"What?" Pug asked, looking up at the little gambler.

"At some point we must have a chat with a dragon," Nakor said. "The Oracle is impressive, but she's not a true dragon. But before that we need to go to the world of Cynoth."

"Why?" Pug asked.

Nakor's expression became mischievous, and his eyes lit up. "We need to break into the Vault below the Palace of Assala to free a prisoner."

"Who?" Pug asked, his expression already revealing apprehension in proportion to Nakor's glee.

"An angel named Eleleth!"

Pug was speechless.

"He can show us a way into heaven."

Even the four elves could find no words.

"Heaven?" Pug asked.

"If the lower levels are hells, then the upper levels are heavens, right?"

Pug could only nod.

MAGNUS LOOKED AT HAVA AND said, "Ruffio and I are ready. He's at Sorcerer's Isle, waiting to deal with any unexpected problems there."

Hava took one last look at the line of ships ahead and said, "The nice thing about this rift business is not having to turn the ships around." She looked over her shoulder, and added, "Those ships are damn near wallowing, they're so loaded with cargo."

Magnus smiled. "Once we get the cargo ashore, you can get these ships back to the Sanctuary or leave them in Marquensas as you please. I'll speak to the king about doing resupply by wagon. A dozen wagons a week from here to there should keep Marquensas fed until their farms, flocks, and herds are fully restored. We shouldn't have to do this by ship again."

Hava laughed. "I know just the fellow. He had a thriving freight business before the Pride Lord raids. He works for the king now, and he'll be glad of the work. All people here will have to do is learn to endure Ratigan's constant complaints."

Magnus inclined his head. "Most here have lived very long lives. We're familiar with whiners."

"He's a bit more prickly than that." She judged the wind and said, "Let's be off."

Magnus closed his eyes and held up a hand, and a moment later the rift opened a hundred yards ahead of the ship's prow.

Hava ordered the flag-bearer, "Signal that we are getting underway!" Then she shouted, "Raise anchor! Drop sails!"

The crew went about their tasks efficiently, and soon the ship was moving toward the rift. It quickly picked up speed and entered the rift without incident.

The sudden shift from Midkemia to Garn was far less tranquil than the transition had been the day before. A brisk wind with rain spray hit them hard from starboard. Hava felt the ship lurch and yelled,

"Trim those sails!" as she pulled hard on the wheel. "Signal to port! Blue pennant!" she instructed the sailor behind her.

A moment later she felt the ship's motion smooth out, and while everyone was rapidly getting chilled by the unexpectedly cold, wet weather, the ship was in no danger.

She looked behind until she saw the next ship come through. Despite the warning, that ship lurched, and it was clear the captain and crew had a struggle getting it back on course.

"Damned lugger is carrying too much cargo!" she shouted.

Magnus closed his eyes and abruptly the ship righted itself and came into alignment with the *Queen of Storms*. He opened his eyes and said, "Just a little push."

"You may have to push again," she said, returning his smile. "The wagon idea is a good one."

"Still, we need these provisions today." He pointed to a promontory to the south. "I'll watch from there." He vanished.

Hava kept the ship steady, and it moved parallel with the peninsula that ran west from the port of Toranda, where they'd anchor and offload cargo. Wagons from there up the King's Highway would be only a little slower than sailing up toward Marquensas, as the ships would be fighting seasonal winds and tides, at far greater risk.

Hava easily navigated to a point just a little north of the harbor, dropped anchor, and furled the sails. She watched until the last ship could be seen safely making its way to an anchorage. Abruptly, Magnus appeared next to her. She turned and said, "I've been meaning to ask, what happens if you did that where I was standing?"

He smiled, genuinely amused. "I'm sorry to say you'd probably be knocked overboard." Then he added, "The trick is to not appear inside a wall."

Hava winced. "I can see how that might be a problem."

"The key is knowing exactly where you want to appear. Make a mistake, it's your last problem."

Hava saw that several figures had appeared on the docks. She pulled out her spyglass and inspected them. "Looks like they're ready," she said, lowering the metal tube. "Ratigan's there, so Balven got everything organized from here to Marquenet. While they're loading the wagons, you'll have time to set up his traveling to Midkemia and back. Going to another world will hardly bother him if there's money to be made." She tapped Magnus on the chest lightly with the spyglass. "And do not ever start discussing payment with him. Just tell him to take the matter up with Balven when he gets to Marquensas."

"Good," said Magnus, gently pushing the spyglass aside. "I'm very bad at haggling. I almost never have to do it. One of the benefits of magic."

She laughed. "I can see that. In my thieving days, magic would have saved me a great deal of running and hiding." She relayed a few instructions to her mate, then said to Magnus, "Let's get over there."

He reached out and put his hand on her shoulder and a moment later they stood on the wharf. A pair of people she didn't know instinctively moved backward. The two figures she did recognize were Declan and the newly appointed commander of the garrison at Toranda, a captain named Ressler.

Declan and Hava greeted one another, then Declan said, "Magnus, thank you. You may not have saved the kingdom in one act, but your magic has given us hope."

Hava smiled at that, then turned to Declan and asked, "You worried I might wreck the ships on the rocks?"

He smiled. "Hardly. Trying to stay busy and keep my mind off the coming fight."

"What fight?" asked Hava.

Declan said, "The next one." He glanced at Magnus, who nodded.

She said, "Magnus said you had an encounter." She looked at the magician, her brow furrowed. "What didn't he tell me?"

Declan explained the situation at the redoubt in the Darkwood, and Magnus listened attentively. He explained the attack and victory, then the appearance of the soldiers who had waited and then died in place. He finished, "Now more dead are simply . . . waiting. Nothing happens, no decay, scavengers, anything. Just there. Whatever's coming will be worse."

Again, Hava looked at Magnus, with a clearly disapproving expression. "You didn't think to tell me this?"

Magnus said, "I didn't wish to distract you from the matters at hand. Traversing the rift with a small flotilla is hardly a trivial matter. This necromancy—death magic—is the darkest of arts, and as soon as we've finished here I will travel there and see for myself what more can be discovered."

Declan said, "To hell with inspecting the Narrows. It's the last place the Church will attack. Take me with you. I was hoping that you or Hatushaly might come so I could get up there in a hurry."

Magnus nodded agreement. "Hatushaly is with Pug and Nakor on Midkemia, seeking more knowledge. They should return shortly."

Declan said to Hava, "If your husband seeks you out before coming to Marquensas, can you inform him of what's afoot?"

"I'm not happy sending him away the moment he turns up, but I understand."

"Good."

Hava said to Magnus. "I'll talk to Ratigan and travel with him to the king's palace. He and Balven have butted heads before, so Balven will see it done. You go now."

Declan turned to Captain Ressler. "Give my horse to Lady Hava here to ride to Marquenet." He turned toward Magnus and said, "Now?"

Magnus nodded, put his hand on Declan's shoulder, and instantly they vanished.

Hava took a deep breath and muttered, "Now I'm a lady? What's next?"

DECLAN AND MAGNUS APPEARED ON top of the viewing platform set high above the redoubt. New walls were under construction on every side, and the foundation of a new keep was evident behind them.

Declan looked to the west and saw one of the geomancers from Midkemia had created a stone road as far as he could see. He looked around and saw Sixto below with a clutch of soldiers receiving orders. He tapped Magnus on the shoulder and pointed. "I hate to presume . . ."

Magnus gripped Declan's arm and suddenly they were standing just far enough from Sixto not to startle anyone. Sixto saw Declan and Magnus and stopped what he was doing. "You're here!" he shouted.

The soldiers turned as one and, seeing their prince, saluted. Declan waved them aside and said, "What news?"

Sixto said, "Our scouts report something behind the Church encampment to the east. Church skirmishers forced them to retreat so they had to circle widely around that base to get here. They don't know what's coming, but from road dust alone, it seems like a large force."

"When?" Declan asked.

"They were spotted five days ago west of the Dangerous Passage. A messenger to the king should reach him today. The Church forces could be here in two days, three at the most."

Declan said, "Maps?"

Sixto said, "The pavilion."

Before they could move, Magnus grabbed both by the arms, and they were in the pavilion.

Sixto went pale and faltered, before Declan grabbed his arm to keep him from falling. Sixto took a breath and said, "I would appreciate a warning next time."

Declan moved to the large table, and said, "Show me."

Sixto traced his finger on the map. "The north road," he said. "Moving in force, and more movement from the east. None of our scouts could get close enough to see how many. I sent a galloper to the hills above the road just east of Copper Hills to see if he can estimate how big an army is heading this way. He might get back soon. Not that it will make much of a difference. We have what we have, and we're working as fast as we can to bolster this defense."

Declan was silent for a moment, studying the map. Then he said, "They may try to skirt around us and drive straight to Marquenet, but that would leave us at their rear, nearly a thousand men."

Sixto said, "I've been in sieges before, inside and outside the walls. Inside with food and water is better. Outside with another army behind you is bad. So, I'm assuming they'll try to end us first."

"I can take a look," said Magnus, and he vanished.

Sixto was startled. "Do you ever get used to that?" he asked Declan.

"I pretend I do," he said. "How are we on stores?"

"Until the food from Midkemia gets here, we're good for another week, longer if we cut rations."

"The ships are at Toranda, unloading as we speak."

Sixto nodded. "That will be good if no army turns up before the provisions get here."

Declan said, "Agreed. Water?"

"All the barrels are full, but we still haven't hit enough groundwater for a well yet. We're bringing up mud now, so a few more days. We've got a lot done, but there's so much more to do." Sixto smiled ruefully. "Life as a mercenary was simpler," he said with a tone of regret. "Turn up, fight, get paid, get drunk, find a woman, go to the next fight."

"Living from day to day is for the young. What would you do in your old age?"

"Be an old mercenary?"

Declan chuckled. "I have an idea." He motioned for Sixto to follow him and left the pavilion. He climbed up a scaffolding where a wall was being erected, men hauling stones up with baskets, where they were set with sand and gypsum cement.

Looking at the wall for a moment, Sixto said, "That stone-making magician, from the other world? He said on his world he could build this wall in two days. Here his magic is weaker, so I set him to working on the road. He may be finished with the first section tomorrow."

Declan said, "How does the wind usually blow here?"

Sixto shrugged. "Onshore, as always in the city. Here only a breeze, but still mostly easterly. It will start blowing south off the mountains near Copper Hills when the weather gets hotter." He pushed Declan's shoulder gently. "As you know as well as I do, given that you've lived here longer than I have."

Declan nodded. "Just reassuring myself." He waved toward the trees, and said, "You've given us another fifty yards of clearing since we started."

Sixto said, "We needed a lot of timber for scaffolding and fires." He pointed to the unfinished wall's eastern end. "There'll be a ballista platform there, but with a catapult in the marshaling yard below, we can keep enemies farther away. I assume claiming the western half of Ilcomen, you'll need a large road that way." He indicated the remaining forest to the east.

"Eventually." Declan motioned for Sixto to follow him and led him back to the pavilion.

Once inside, Declan sat in a chair next to the map table and asked, "Wine?"

Sixto nodded and moved to a corner table, where he grabbed a bottle and two goblets and filled them. He gave one to Declan and pulled over another chair.

"Tired?" Sixto asked.

"Everyone's tired. If it's not the fighting, it's the building, the travel . . . the worry."

Sixto nodded. "You've learned a lot since you joined Bogartis's company. Hard to believe that was only a few years ago. Anyway, you still haven't learned how to rest when you can."

"Some can sleep on the eve of battle, some can't."

"True."

Magnus appeared suddenly, and Sixto almost spilled his wine.

"What did you see?" asked Declan as he stood up and helped Magnus sit in his chair. It was obvious that the white-haired magician was on the verge of exhaustion.

"A moment," said Magnus as he gathered himself.

Sixto went to the corner table, poured another goblet of wine, and brought it to Magnus.

Magnus drank and said, "I've done a lot of work today, and I forget how quickly I become weak here. Three transports with others and now I can barely stay awake."

"You can nap on my pallet," said Declan. "Just tell me what's coming."

Magnus said, "I flew above the enemy's army and saw perhaps three thousand men and two hundred horses, supply wagons, and mules hauling siege engines. It looks likely they'll attack the city."

"How far away?"

"At the rate they're traveling, about four days. I must rest, then find Pug. This dark magic confirms the Church is serving the Darkness, either willingly or by manipulation. The dead to the east are there for a purpose, which I can only guess at. They'll attack here while the large army attacks the city."

"That will prevent us from attacking their rear," Sixto said with a sigh of exasperation.

Declan said to Magnus, "Rest, and Sixto and I will come up with a plan." He indicated a curtained-off area of the pavilion.

"My thanks," said Magnus, rising and crossing to the sleeping section.

"Plan?" Sixto looked dubious.

"I have a bad one," said Declan.

With a wry smile, Sixto said, "A bad plan is better than no plan at all."

CHAPTER 30

BATTLE

Pug listened.

Thala, an older Spellweaver, had been asking Hatushaly questions for almost an hour, and was learning a great deal about the young man's abilities from the exchange. Elven magic was an organic use of energy, so in ways Pug barely understood it seemed more naturally in harmony with Hatu's manipulation of the furies' energy.

The old elf smiled and said to Pug, "This youngster wields enormous power at a thought. He is unlike any user of magic we have ever encountered. You did well in bringing him here." Her face was alight with excitement.

Hatushaly said, "Thank you for helping me understand myself more, but there are so many more questions."

"There always are," said Nakor with a smile. "The more you learn, the more you understand how little you know."

Pug nodded and stood up. "We must go. The Darkness menaces Garn, so we need to return."

The old elf rose from her cushion and said, "Young Hatushaly, should we weather this coming struggle, you will always be welcome to come and study here should you wish. Pug has always been generous with sharing his knowledge and many of us have been welcomed at Sorcerer's Isle. I myself spent a lovely year there, ages ago. We learn much from one another."

Hatu gave her a bow. "If fate allows, I would love to return. This is perhaps the most amazing place I have ever seen. Just being here fills me with energy."

Thala said, "What you call magic—"

"Stuff," Nakor said playfully.

Thala seemed amused. "Labels are meaningless. Do you know the old adage, 'The map is not the terrain'?"

Nakor laughed. "Yes, it is true."

Hatushaly looked confused, and Pug reached out and put his hand on Hatu's arm. "Think about it and you'll understand." He looked at Thala and said, "Thank you, and good-bye."

"Back to Sorcerer's Isle?" Hatu asked.

"And then to Garn," Pug replied.

After a moment, he touched both Hatushaly and Nakor and they were standing in a clearing west of the villa. Hatu spent a moment surveying the scene. Students were hurrying past nearby, and a few recognized Pug and waved.

Hatu said, "In understanding my powers and magic, my life on Garn seems barren compared to what I have experienced here."

"Perhaps that's why we all met," said Nakor. His tone was again serious as he looked directly at Hatu. "How you came to be the pre-eminent wielder of power on an entire planet is a question still to be answered, and how you can return that power to others without loss to yourself, yet another question."

Pug put his hands on both men's shoulders in a reassuring gesture. "We have much ahead of us that is rife with peril. But knowledge can always be shared. So, we share as much as possible whenever we can."

Nakor smiled and shrugged. "When not running from danger."

Pug gave his shoulder a playful shake and said, "True. Now, let's return to Garn."

They walked the short distance to the rift chamber, entered, and again found a student watching the entrance. "Still no trouble, Jalain?"

The young woman smiled and said, "This is a very good place to read—it's so quiet."

Pug looked at Hatu. "I wish someone had found those gaps in rift boundaries centuries ago. It would have saved us unimaginable suffering." Then he remembered Tomas fleeing from the wraith in the mines and realized it would never have happened, and Tomas never would have found the ancient Valheru armor. He pushed aside such musing as a waste of time.

"Come on," said Nakor. "I want to see what's happening."

"You in a hurry to find trouble?" Pug asked.

"Always," said Nakor as he jumped into the rift.

Pug and Hatushaly exchanged glances. Pug said, "He'll never change."

They followed Nakor through to just outside the library at the Sanctuary. Hatushaly looked around and asked, "Where is he?"

Pug laughed. "The gods only know. He'll turn up. I'll check the library and then the dining hall. You should go and look for your wife."

Hatu smiled broadly at the mention of Hava, and then closed his eyes briefly. "She's up in North Tembria. I can always sense where she is . . ." He laughed. "Assuming we're on the same world."

"I'll see you soon," said Pug.

Hatushaly vanished. Pug paused, remembering how long it had taken him to transport himself by thought even to a place he remembered well, and again reflected on just how powerful this youngster was.

Then he brought his attention back to the present, and decided he'd better go and look for Nakor.

DONTE WATCHED AS HEALER CONDUCTED a small class with the children. He was teaching them to read.

Donte had never considered that might be a useful skill, despite it having been demanded of him in the Coaltachin school. Playing the role of an ignorant peasant who could just happen to read whatever was on someone's desk or table was useful spycraft, but he'd never thought about it for these kids.

When the children were dismissed to see to the chores around the farm, Healer came to sit next to Donte in the farmhouse kitchen. "Reading?" Donte asked.

"Whatever your plans were for a gang of little thieves and informers, many of these children would not survive a week. But if you are going to expand into other areas, like this farm, or other trade, you will need people who can read, write, and deal with numbers in ledgers."

Donte sat back, his brow furrowed in thought, and after a moment said, "I hate it when you're right."

Healer laughed. "You amuse me. Thank you."

"Well, if my life of crime doesn't work out, perhaps I have a future as a jester."

"Why, Donte, you possess depths of understanding I never imagined possible."

Donte swung a lazy blow at Healer that he easily avoided, and both laughed at the joke. "I'm surprising myself," said Donte.

"What are your plans?" asked Healer.

Donte was silent for a moment, then said, "Honestly, I have no plans. The business of driving out the false Mockers is done. I thought at first I'd set up my own little crew while they and the Ferrets chewed each other up. Now that Ving is in the tender care of the Upright Man, the rest of those idiots have either left the city or begged for forgiveness and sworn eternal loyalty to me." His expression was dubious. "The Keshian smugglers are depleted, and I may be able to turn the brighter ones to work with me, run them out of the city, or maybe kill them." He sighed. "I guess instead of my own little crew, I'm now part of a major Bitter Sea criminal endeavor." He scowled. "It's as if my grandfather's plans for me to be a master is a curse on me. If not in Coaltachin, on Garn, then here, damn it!" Suddenly the absurdity of it all struck him, and Donte laughed.

The sound of running feet and laughter reached Donte and Healer. Children were chasing each other or one of the animals. Donte's expression turned pensive.

Healer looked at Donte for a lingering moment, to the point where Donte began to squirm. "What?" he said.

"I've worked with youngsters for decades, and sometimes it takes a while to understand a particular kid." Healer smiled. "I don't know your past, what you endured, how you learned, but at this moment, I can say something in you has changed."

"What?"

Healer again looked long at Donte, then said, "I don't know. That's for you to puzzle out."

Donte sighed again, loudly. "I don't know, either. It's just this building a crime family of my own, without help from my grandfather, is not turning out the way I expected."

"What did you expect?"

"Not this," said Donte. "Something different, I guess. A lot more fun and less . . ."

"Responsibility?" Healer supplied.

"Yes, damn it. I never ran a crew before, let alone tried to take over a city. I mean, my family was one of the seven biggest families, my ancestors were founders of our nation, and . . ." He slumped a little in his chair. "It's just . . . it makes me realize how much my grand-father put up with from me, despite the beatings and lectures about responsibility. There's a lot more to life than simply looking out just for yourself."

"You've spoken of your friends. Looking out for them isn't just looking out for yourself."

Donte nodded. "True. Hava and Hatushaly are like my sister and brother. I would do anything for them, though I'd never admit it to them." He reflected on the witchery used on him by the Sisters of the Deep to find Hatu and kill him, and how that compulsion had simply faded. Part of it was something about waning magic—he didn't quite understand it all—but most of it was that he just wasn't going to do it. He put aside pondering that, as reflection was starting to give him a headache.

"Well," said Healer, standing up. "Leaving the children to their own devices for a long time is never a good idea. I'd best check on them. You have ample time to consider what you wish to do next. Scully and the others you have working for you can oversee what needs to be done in the city, and I've got things pretty much in hand here, so take your time and answer that question: what's next?"

Donte laughed. "I think a glass of ale and a late lunch is next. After that, I have no idea."

Healer smiled. "You'll think of something. And if it means any-thing to you, you've saved these children from a great deal of suffering. Take some pleasure from that, I suggest."

Donte sat quietly after Healer left. He wondered what his grandfather would think of all this and decided he didn't like thinking about
what his grandfather thought. "Damn," he muttered. "Life gets complicated."

HATUSHALY APPEARED ON THE SIDE of the road a dozen yards ahead
of where Hava rode. She smiled broadly and, with a kick, set her mount
to a quick trot, then reined in next to him.

Jumping from the saddle, she barely held on to the reins as she
threw an arm around his neck in a fierce hug. "Where have you been?"
she demanded and kissed him before he could speak.

When she loosened her hold on him, he laughed and said, "Nakor
and Pug took me with them to meet the elves! I have so much to tell
you."

She put her hand on his chest. "Later. I'm certain it's wonderful,
but we have other concerns at the moment."

He took a breath and said, "What are you doing here?" He looked
around and saw that Ratigan was driving the first wagon and waving.

Hatu waved back, and said, "I thought you'd be on the *Queen of
Storms*."

"I was. So, how'd you find me?"

He grinned. "I can find you anywhere, always." He gave her a
quick kiss and said, "So, again, what's all this?"

"The first caravan of wagons up from Toranda. That's where we're
offloading the cargo we brought through from Midkemia. I have Declan's horse and I was supposed to be at the palace if you'd gone there."

"I would have if you were there. What's happening?"

"As much as I hate to tell you, you need to go to the redoubt in the
Darkwood. Magnus is already there. The Church has an army heading
there." Her expression and tone were grim.

Hatu's expression turned serious. "An army?"

"Big one, from what I overheard. And Magnus says there's evil
magic at work. They need you."

Hatu took a moment to think, then said, "Pug and Nakor should
still be at the Sanctuary . . ." He closed his eyes and let his mind seek

out Pug's unique energy, and after a moment opened his eyes. "They still are. If there's magic at play, we should all go there. I love you." He kissed her cheek and then vanished.

As another wagon slowly rolled by, Hava let out a sound of aggravation and then remounted her horse. She set her heels to the gelding's barrel and urged it forward to overtake Ratigan's wagon.

"That was a quick visit," the teamster said.

"Too quick," she replied shortly. Necessity dictated the actions she and Hatu had to take, but she didn't have to like it.

Ratigan knew her well enough to know this wasn't the time to chat. He flicked the reins and stayed silent.

PUG AND NAKOR WERE HALFWAY through the midday meal when Hatu appeared. "We have to go," he said without preamble.

"Where?" Pug asked, as Hatu reached out and put his hands on both men's shoulders.

Suddenly they were at the redoubt, with both Pug and Nakor barely able to keep from falling as there were abruptly no chairs under them.

"I was eating!" Nakor shouted in an aggrieved tone.

"There's food here," said Hatushaly. He quickly explained what Hava had told him, and then took a step back.

The three surveyed the site and saw that a lot of work on the structure had been abandoned, as workers were frantically now working on a barrier around the breastwork below the eastern wall. Others were clearing away as much of the debris near the redoubt as they could. "Where're Declan and Magnus?" Pug asked.

"Declan's over there," said Nakor, pointing to a raised portion of the unfinished wall.

Hatu waved to get Declan's attention as they moved toward him. Declan landed lightly on his feet on the pathway and said, "I'm glad to see you."

"Where's Magnus?" Pug asked.

"He's sleeping in the pavilion. All the bouncing around he did for me wore him out." He scanned the three of them and said, "You look fresh."

Pug said, "We're fresh from Midkemia, while Magnus has had to depend on the energy available here. Let him sleep. What's going on?"

Declan quickly summed up what he and Magnus had concluded, which was that the main army was circling the forest to attack the city, while the dead soldiers would attack the redoubt. Eventually, he said, "If I must, I'll fire the forest to burn the dead soldiers, and hit the attackers from the rear."

Pug considered for a moment, then said, "It's a sound plan, given the circumstances." He said to Nakor and Hatushaly, "We should rest as well, harbor our energy. I think when the time comes, we'll need to play our part and we must use our strength wisely."

Hatushaly looked at Declan. "My wife is on the road from Toranda to Marquenet. Is she at risk?"

"Hava should reach the city from the south well before the Church army arrives from the northeast. She'll be as safe as anyone behind those walls." Declan tried to sound certain, but there was concern in his tone. "There's ample room inside my pavilion, food and drink. Rest and . . . wait."

Pug glanced at his two companions and saw their expressions matched his mood: expectant and unsure.

HAVA RODE THROUGH THE GATE just ahead of Ratigan's first wagon. She urged the horse forward, avoiding people hurrying in the streets. There was no doubt: a warning had been sounded and everyone not detailed to defend the city was either fleeing south past the incoming wagons or rushing about carrying whatever they could find to hunker down and wait out a siege.

The throng in the streets made it difficult to move directly from the gate to the castle marshaling gate. She looked back and saw some of the teamsters having to use the wagon reins as a makeshift lash to prevent people from attempting to loot the wagons. Food was about to become even more precious than it had been the day before.

Hava kicked her mount forward and reached the castle gate. Seeing Master-at-Arms Collin in the distance, she rode to him and shouted, "We've got food wagons from Toranda! Ratigan needs guards!"

Collin shouted orders, and within moments a dozen palace guards were rushing down the boulevard to drive back those menacing the wagons. "The lads on the walls are so busy waiting for an attack, no one at the gate thought to escort the food through the mob," he said to Hava. "I better have a word or two with the lads on the gate."

Hava had no doubt those would be words the guards would not welcome. Still, it was chaotic in the city and panic was rising. In her travels, she had skirted enough sieges and eluded battles by wits and stealth. She could sense that this was a city that had not endured a direct attack in a lifetime. The only advantage Marquenet held was the number of survivors of the Pride Lords' raids on North Tembria who now lived here. Those who fled south would soon be out from underfoot and those who remained were battle-tested.

Hava said, "This is Declan's horse."

Collin smiled. "So, he's off with your lad?"

Hava dismounted. "They jumped to the redoubt. Seems there's some dark magic there." A groom hurried over, recognizing Declan's horse and rig. Hava handed him the reins. "I should let the king know."

"Aye," said Collin. "That would be the correct thing. The king has a galloper stationed to the north and the moment he returns there'll be an army following close after him, so then the gates will be closed. If you need to get back to your ship, I can have a fresh mount waiting once you've spoken to the king."

Hava considered this for a moment, then said, "No, I'll stay. Hatu will find me if he needs to and, not to brag, I have a way with a sword."

Collin laughed. "Indeed you do. Now, I have tasks ahead of me as well." He moved toward the wagons.

Hava hurried over to the side entrance to the castle, used most often to avoid trudging through the large entrance. The guard there recognized her and saluted. "Admiral," he said as he opened the door for her. Once inside, and the door closed behind her, she stopped. She shut her eyes for a moment, calming herself. "First 'lady,' now 'admiral'?" she muttered. "Do I have any say about my life in this kingdom?" Silently she promised herself that once this war was over, she was going to have a long discussion with Hatu about where they were going to live.

She headed toward the king's private chamber to give him the latest news about her journey.

MAGNUS AWOKE AND, AFTER STRETCHING, moved aside the privacy curtain that divided the prince's sleeping section from the rest of the pavilion. He saw Pug and Hatushaly seated at the dining table and Nakor sleeping in his chair, snoring.

Hatushaly brightened at the sight of the white-haired magician. Pug looked up and also smiled. "Are you rested?" he asked.

"Well enough," said Magnus. He sat down next to Pug and surveyed the food filling half the table. "I'm hungry," he added, reaching for a pear. "One of those annoying questions: why do so many worlds have the same fruits and vegetables?"

Nakor opened an eye and laughed. "I thought that would be obvious."

Pug smiled. "Your theory?"

"If people were fleeing from a single world in what the elves called the Chaos Wars, they'd have taken whatever they could with them: seeds, cuttings, livestock, pets. Not all the same, you see. Garn has no blood oranges, like the ones from home. The Tsurani had no chocolate, and Midkemia no chocha, but both had tea." He shrugged. "Sometimes things change, too."

Magnus smiled. "Seems logical. And we really don't know how long people had to prepare. They might have been running with what they could carry, or they might have had time to load up wagons and leave at their leisure."

Hatushaly looked at Pug. "I saw enough of what the people went through after the Pride Lords' raids to know that they are usually resourceful. It's what we're seeing here, now, with the rebuilding of Marquensas."

Pug said, "Bright lad."

Nakor lay back again. "It's nice to think about such questions. And I think the question of time is always a good one."

Hatushaly took a breath and said, "Time is always a . . . thing in all this, isn't it?" His expression became distant, lost in thought.

"How long does something take, how quickly can we get some-where," said Nakor, sitting up. He cocked his head and said, "Is it me, or did it get very quiet outside?"

Pug's brow furrowed and he walked to the entrance of the pavilion, and looked toward the construction. Men were sitting, some eating, others attempting to nap. All were now in battle dress or had missing pieces of armor and weapons close at hand.

Pug turned back to the others. "They're getting ready for battle."

"How soon do you think?" asked Hatushaly.

"That pesky time thing again," Nakor said with a laugh.

Hatu said, "I'll look." He closed his eyes and the other three could almost feel him using his far-seeing ability to seek out information. Suddenly, he opened his eyes. "They're here!"

Pug looked out of the entry again. "It's getting dark!"

By the time all four got out of the pavilion, the entire garrison was in motion. Shouts and alarms sounded loudly, and men who were not rushing to their posts were finishing putting on armor and getting weapons ready.

Declan stood atop the highest portion of the newly erected fortress wall, overlooking the eastern side of the redoubt, as archers scrambled to their assigned positions. There was no hint of movement from the far treeline or along the trail from the east, but the slowly darkening skies heralded an imminent attack.

Pug said, "Save your energies. Climb up there." He pointed to Declan's vantage point. "We are as strong as we can be here since returning from Midkemia, but even a short jump up there will deplete us."

Hatushaly put his hand on Pug's shoulder and said, "That's true for you, but I carry the magic of Garn within me. Stay here." Suddenly he was no longer at Pug's side but standing on the wall with Declan.

Declan seemed unfazed by Hatushaly's sudden appearance and said, "I'm pleased you're here." He looked down and saw Pug, Nakor, and Magnus, and said, "And them as well. Whatever is coming is more than mortal men can face, I fear."

Hatu gave Declan a smile, put his hand on the prince's shoulder, and said, "You and Gwen were our first true friends in Beran's Hill, and I will always be at your side when you need me."

Declan showed a brief moment of strong emotion, but he fought it down and simply said, "You're a good friend, Hatu."

Both men stared at the distant treeline as it faded into the advancing darkness. Torches and watchfires were being lit around the redoubt and everyone waited.

Above the trees, something stirred. A vague shape, slightly darker than its surroundings. "What is that?" Hatushaly asked.

"Something very bad," said Nakor as he approached them, Magnus and Pug a step behind him.

The darkness resolved slowly into a humanoid figure, a deep-black form against the shades of grey above the treetops. It hovered in place, raising its arms and moving them in a circle forward. A loud thrumming filled the air, and the soldiers of Marquensas took a step back, glancing around, exchanging questions, looking hesitant.

"Stand ready!" Declan shouted as loudly as he could.

Sixto and the other captains repeated the order.

As the visibility lessened, a strange rustling came from the distant forest, followed by a loud cracking noise, and the trees began to shake visibly. Timber emitted a shrieking sound as if torn apart by a massive invisible hand. The ground shook.

"Hold!" Declan yelled.

Trees opposite the defenses were twisting, as if trying to pull themselves from the ground. Splinters flew and clouds of wood dust filled the air, and as the light continued fading, figures began to emerge from the forest.

Shambling dead carrying weapons appeared and purposefully moved toward the defenders.

"Hold!" Declan repeated.

The figure floating above the trees took form, and Hatushaly shouted, "What is that?"

Pug put his hand on the young man's shoulder and said, "Stay here!"

Nakor said to Hatushaly, "That is a thing of the Dread."

Hatu recognized it as something akin to the creature in the pit that he had seen in Garn's Wound. He tensed and felt energies starting to rise, but Nakor gripped his arm and said, "Do nothing. You have no idea what you face."

"Archers! Ready!" Sixto called out from below where Declan, Hatu, and Nakor watched.

"All arrows will do is slow them down," said Declan.

"Slow is better," said Nakor. "Let Pug and Magnus deal with the Dread. That is the true danger." Then he smiled, and it was without warmth. "I can help with the dead soldiers if they get too pesky."

Hatushaly looked at Nakor. "I need to help."

"When the time comes," Nakor replied. "Remember, you are the only one here who has his full powers, because they reside within you. The rest of us"—he gestured to himself, Pug, and Magnus— "will quickly lose strength. You must be ready and do as you're told."

Hatushaly's expression turned confrontational, and he felt old angers coming to the fore, feelings that echoed his childhood tantrums, emotions he barely remembered since marrying Hava. He was on the verge of challenging Nakor, who read that expression and said simply, "Don't!"

For a moment Hatu struggled, then he let his feelings flow through him instead of taking control. Without a word, he nodded and slowly pulled his arm from Nakor's grasp.

"Remember the dragon?" Pug asked.

Hatushaly said, "How could I forget?"

"That was the dragon who fought a Dreadlord and almost died defeating it. What's floating over there is a lesser creature of the Dread, but still deadly beyond anything you've faced."

Nakor said, "Watch, learn!"

Hatu turned his attention to Pug and Magnus as they waited for the Dread to move. He focused his mind and listened closely.

Magnus said, "I have not seen its like before."

"Neither have I," Pug replied. "I've faced Dreadmasters, wraiths, death dancers, conjured demons, wights, and the rest, but this is something else."

The shadowy shape continued to swirl like a figure of smoky darkness, with tiny flashes of energy, pinpoints of red sparks, flashing within its form. As they watched, Pug said, "Look!" They saw more corpses were filing through the trees to take up position.

"Is it directing them?" Declan asked.

Pug said, "I'm going to risk finding out." He put out his right hand and a beam of brilliant blue light shot out, striking the floating creature in the middle. The black figure exploded into fragments which swirled in a large orb of smoke and lights. The fragments picked up speed and slowly moved back toward a center point. A humming sound reached them as the Dread figure re-formed.

Pug said, "The dead kept moving. This thing is not controlling them."

"It reeks of evil," said Magnus. "What's its purpose?"

"Perhaps just to keep us here," said Pug. "To prevent us from defending the city."

Hatu closed his eyes and let his attention shift to the shadowy figure. He began a meticulous examination of the fury-energy flowing around the Dread. In his mind he saw a vortex of violent colors crashing down and around the alien silhouette, a void rather than a shadow, an emptiness that drank in that rush of power. He let his attention grow more confined as he focused on lines of power a thousand times smaller, and the Dread being became a monstrous thing towering above, like a mountain to an insect.

He found a boundary, a barrier where the lines of force he was so used to contemplating simply vanished. He let his vision sweep completely around the Dread. Every line of force, every color he could imagine that defined the source, earth, air, life, sunlight, all just stopped.

He quickened his examination, letting his magical sight sweep up and down, around, and finally as close to that boundary as he could— and then he felt it. At the tiniest focus in his perception, he saw it, a shutter for an instant, repeated everywhere as energy reached the monster. Countless infinitesimally tiny threads were pushing back!

His vision vanished as he opened his eyes. He looked at Nakor. "It's out of time!"

Nakor asked, "What?"

"It's not in our time!" Hatu said loudly.

"What?" asked Pug.

"This creature is trying to be here, but it exists a moment behind us. I don't know if I can explain, but time is working to our benefit. Unless the Dread thing can overcome this, it's cocooned in a . . ." He fumbled for words. "Whatever that thing does, it's always going to be too late!"

Magnus asked, "How do you know?"

"I can see the energy surrounding it! I see normal lines between furies, but this thing is . . . an intrusion. It doesn't belong here." He waved his hand and said, "Our universe is not letting it catch up to us in time! Our universe is pushing back!"

Pug said, "We can't assume it will stay that way."

Magnus said, "I have an idea." He closed his eyes and, after a moment, opened them again. "Sense it!" he said to Pug. "Don't look at it. Close your eyes and sense as you would something invisible!"

Pug did as Magnus suggested and said, "It's not all there!"

"Not completely," said Magnus. "It flickers in and out of phase."

Across the clearing, the gathered army drew their weapons and started to advance toward the redoubt.

Hatu said, "What do we do?"

"Find a way to help Declan," Pug replied. "You have more power but lack experience if this thing fully materializes."

Magnus said, "We'll stay ready!"

Hatu turned and saw that Declan was on his way down to where Sixto stood behind the rank of archers. He looked at Nakor and said, "Are those corpses pesky enough?"

Nakor grinned. "I think so."

"Save your energy," Hatu said, grabbing Nakor's arm, and instantly they stood next to Sixto and Declan. The attackers were within bow-shot range, and Declan shouted, "Loose!"

As before, when arrows struck legs, or hit with enough force to cause the dead soldier to fall, the corpse slowly regained its footing and lurched forward.

Hatu said, "I have an idea." He closed his eyes and again sought to explore all lines of energy before him as the first wave of dead soldiers reached the bottom of the redoubt's earthwork. After a minute, he opened his eyes and said to Nakor, "If you can help here, I must speak with Pug again."

Hatu vanished and appeared a moment later again next to Pug. He shouted, "It's stuck!"

"What?" said Pug.

"You're waiting for the Dread to attack. It can't. It's stuck."

Pug sat down, his face showing relief for a moment, and he said, "Explain."

"When I found those tiny gaps between the end of one rift gate and the other, you closed them." Pug and Magnus both nodded. "That's how—" He stopped.

"What?" Pug asked.

Hatu took a breath and calmed himself down. "It is time: it's out of . . . rhythm. I can try to explain later, but for the moment my guess is creatures from rift-space, Children of the Void, need a way to slip into our . . . reality. Maybe some get through by accident, or because of those things you told me about rifts attracting them, but this one seems to be trying to push itself into this world by force. I said earlier I thought this world wouldn't let it in. I was right. It's stuck."

Pug and Magnus exchanged looks, and suddenly Magnus laughed. "That is madness, yet it makes so much sense."

Pug nodded slowly. "There's an irony here that begs understanding."

The sounds of fighting grew louder. The dead made no outcry, just the sound of swords hitting shields or pole arms crashing against armor, and the cry from the wounded living.

"First we need to deal with this," said Hatu. Standing, he said, "Rest, because once we're finished here, we will need to stop the attack on the city."

He vanished.

Magnus looked at Pug and said, "His power is growing."

"His potential is unimaginable. I'm very glad that he considers us friends."

Magnus nodded.

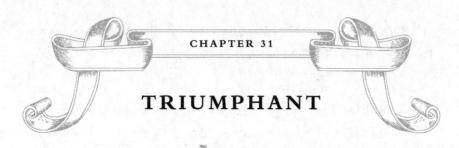

CHAPTER 31

TRIUMPHANT

Hatu appeared on the battlement.

He saw Nakor using his limited power to sow destruction. A flame on the leg of a dead soldier caused it to fall, and others tripped over it, also igniting.

Declan looked at him and said, "We are holding . . . barely."

Hatu took a deep breath, his face set in an expression of resolve, and said, "I will end this!"

He closed his eyes, and his whole body tensed, as if he was about to take a blow. Suddenly a high-pitched sound that cut through the noise of battle rang out. It was harsh and bone-grinding, and many of the Marquensas soldiers faltered, some dropping their weapons to cover their ears.

As soon as the sound rang out, the attackers froze in place. Some fell over in mid-step, toppled like unbalanced statues.

Hatu said, "Have your men fall back."

Pug and Magnus both appeared next to Nakor, looking around.

Declan's eyes were wide with astonishment, but he gathered his wits and shouted, "Retreat to the wall!"

Some of the soldiers were slow to appreciate what was occurring and others were wounded. Those able to follow orders quickly took charge of helping the others fall back. Sixto repeated the order to retreat.

The fallen dead lay on the ground quivering. After the Marquensas troops were safely back, Hatu spread his arms and at once a wave of air slammed along the ground, tossing the dead into the air a few inches. They stopped moving, then fell back to the ground.

"What did you do?" Nakor asked, his usually playful manner replaced by an expression of open surprise.

"I'm not sure," said Hatushaly.

Declan said, "Is that it?"

"I think so," Hatu answered. "I just felt something, and I knew that if I could . . . cut off a . . . tie, a connection between . . ." He began to lose focus and Nakor grabbed him around the waist.

Hatu's eyes rolled up and he collapsed into Pug's arms. Pug slowly lowered him to the stones of the parapet, while Declan and Sixto knelt beside Hatushaly. "He's breathing," said Nakor. "I think he just exhausted himself, doing that trick."

"It was a prodigious act," said Magnus.

"Is this over?" asked Declan.

Magnus studied the dead upon the ground, and then looked at the twisting figure still hanging in the air above the distant trees and said, "A pause, at least. Give me a moment."

The white-haired magician jumped by magic to the clearing below and bent to examine one of the dead. He pulled back instantly, then a moment later was standing next to Pug and the others again. "The putrefaction that was halted is now occurring at an accelerated rate. They're decomposing by the second."

"If the wind was blowing this way," said Nakor, "you'd smell them."

Sixto said, "I'll take whatever tiny mercy I can get."

Nakor smiled.

Declan turned to Sixto and asked, "How did we fare?"

"I see only a few wounded, and only one or two dead carried away. I think we fared well."

Looking at Pug and Magnus, Declan asked, "Are we safe to go and aid Marquenet?"

Magnus said, "As long as that thing is there, I wouldn't say safe." The distant shadow figure was still twisting in some invisible wind.

Nakor said, "I can watch Hatu and keep an eye on that thing. We don't know what it is or what it does, but if it somehow gets through here, I can come and fetch you if you want to go help the city."

Magnus considered this for a moment, then glanced at Pug, who nodded in silent agreement.

Pug said, "Somewhere out there is at least one master of black arts."

Nakor tilted his head. "I can help if a dark magician turns up, or that thing breaks through. Once Hatushaly revives, if he has any of his strength left, that makes two of us." He looked at Declan. "Leave a few swords here just in case, but the rest should go and aid your brothers."

Turning to Sixto, Declan said, "Leave a dozen men to watch the wounded and help Nakor and Hatushaly, and ready the men on foot to leave for the city as soon as they finish eating. The horsemen leave at once."

Sixto said, "Here or there?"

Declan knew exactly what he meant. "Both of us, there. If there's magic here, let these two deal with it, but hard fighting awaits us outside the city walls. That's our trade."

Sixto nodded. "At once." He turned and started shouting orders.

The milling troops seemed energized by suddenly having something practical to do after dealing with the fear of the brief but horrible fight.

"Let's get the boy to the pavilion," said Nakor, who was still cradling Hatushaly's head.

Pug knelt. "I can do that without much cost." He put hands on both Hatu and Nakor and a moment later they were inside the pavilion.

Magnus appeared immediately afterward.

The three of them picked Hatushaly up and moved him to the prince's bed.

"When Declan gets here, tell him we're with the king," said Pug. He nodded to Magnus and the two of them vanished.

Nakor looked down at Hatushaly and said, "What did you do out there, boy?"

He let out a long sigh and sat down at Hatushaly's side.

PUG AND MAGNUS APPEARED IN the king's throne room. A pair of guards half-drew their swords in reaction before Balven waved them back to their posts. A large board had been placed upon a dining table used for celebrations, with the chairs removed so that the map could be more easily viewed.

Pug said, "The situation at the redoubt appears to be under control. Declan should be here with that force sometime in the next two days."

"Where's the king?" asked Magnus.

"Ensuring that the defense is properly deployed," Balven answered. "Daylon, General Baldasar, Master-at-Arms Collin, and a gaggle of captains are running around checking every detail in person. The Church Army is arriving even as we speak, deploying beyond the range of our catapults, hauling up some big machines of their own. We'll see the first assault tonight or in the morning."

"Once we've rested, we can help," said Pug. "We may tire rapidly on this world, but we should be able to destroy any catapults or trebuchets they set up. If we can force them to storm the walls, and Declan takes them from behind, and you then sally out with a large enough company at the right time, you might rout them in days."

"If they lay siege it may be messier," said Magnus.

"You sound like experts," Balven said, a little dubiously.

Pug smiled. "Magnus and I were witnesses to battles and sieges before your grandfather was born."

"I'll take that as a yes," Balven said. "My brother has done remarkable things in a short span of years. We may not have the blind loyalty that Steveren Langene earned in Ithrace, after generations of his line had ruled brilliantly, but Daylon has forged a loyal army out of mercenaries and refugees." His tone became ironic as he added, "It helps that they have nowhere else to go."

"Your brother is a good ruler," said Pug. "I've seen the best, even counted some as family, and I've seen the worst. If the Church can be defeated, in time this will become a great kingdom."

"One can only hope," Balven replied. "I fear that this is just one battle, for now that I've learned of those nightmares you say have caused all this misery, the only logical conclusion is we must marshal our resources and strike across the sea once more." His long face betrayed deep-rooted fatigue and a mood bordering on hopelessness. "This time it won't be a rash act of revenge against pretenders to great power. The Pride Lords were nothing more than what Hava called them: 'jumped-up crime bosses, and not very good ones.'" This time it will be an entire continent that has been under the heel of the Church for generations. The Azhante fanatics of the Pride Lords were a small cadre of their entire army. The Church Adamant is nothing but fanatics willing to die on command."

Pug said, "If we can achieve some semblance of organization, we may be able to glean more about the Church's homeland and what forces they can bring."

"We know already," said Magnus, "that they are a dire threat to everything you are trying to do here. There are dark powers involved, and Pug and I will try our best to uncover what they are."

Pug said, "If we're going to need our powers once the attack here begins, we must rest."

"Whatever you require," said Balven, taking one last glance at the battle map. He motioned a court page over and said, "Show them to our guest quarters and post someone at their doors in case they need anything. They are not to be disturbed unless the king or I send someone."

The young man in the light blue, white, and gold livery gave a slight bow, turned, and said, "Please follow me."

They followed the page to the guest wing and found themselves outside the very same rooms they had occupied on their last visit. Pug smiled at Magnus and said, "Starting to feel a little like home."

Magnus returned the smile, as they both acknowledged that this was a quip Pug never would have bothered to make before his life as Phillip. "At home, we wouldn't need constant rest to recover from simple tasks of magic."

"It's a lesson," Pug said. "Never take things for granted. We struggled on Kosridi when seeking to stop the Dasati, but we assumed that all worlds on this plane of reality would be like Midkemia and Kelewan."

Magnus nodded, then said to his father, "Rest well."

"You too," said Pug.

They entered their small but comfortable rooms as two pages arrived to stand outside.

DAYLON SURVEYED THE DISTANT FORCES of the Church as they set up for a siege. Using a brass spyglass, he could see pavilions and tents being erected behind a line of soldiers positioned in case there was a

RAYMOND E. FEIST

sortie from the city. Clouds of dust from behind the tents revealed the approach of more soldiers, siege engines, and supplies.

Master-at-Arms Collin stood at the king's side and said, "We've got everything ready, Majesty. South gates closed and buttressed, water and food safely stored. It's a stroke of luck those supplies arrived when they did. I wager we can hold fast for months if we must."

Daylon said, "Months will break this kingdom. This city might survive, but the rest of it? We need to end this as quickly as we can. Keep the topmost lookout at the keep watching for signs of Declan's forces. If they hit the Church from behind, how fast can we ride out?"

"I'll have a force standing ready according to who can be out of the sally ports in under five minutes. The rest of the garrison is sleeping with their arms and armor close to hand, and if they don't wish to endure my displeasure, they'll be ready to go as soon as it takes to pull up their trousers, slip on their boots, and grab weapons."

"Good," said the king. "I'm confident you've done all that can be done."

Collin smiled. "It's my duty."

"I understand why Rodrigo had you running his army and that's why I stole you from him. It's more than your duty. It's your gift. I thank you."

Collin's gruff manner softened for a moment, and he said, "You are worthy of loyalty, sire. You've saved so many of us."

In an unexpected gesture, Daylon reached out and gave the old warrior's shoulder a brotherly squeeze. "I wish we could have saved more."

Both men fell silent as they waited for the onslaught to begin.

THEY CAME THAT NIGHT. A shout erupted from beyond the city wall and the first fusillade of massive stones came speeding out of the dark to crash into the stonework.

Watchfires were ignited, torches lit, alarms rang out, and men raced to their assigned positions. Inside the castle, Pug sat up and blinked himself awake. He put on his black robe and sandals and grabbed his staff.

He opened the door to his room at almost exactly the same moment as Magnus. "So much for a good night's sleep," the white-haired magician said.

"Let's see what we can do," Pug replied.

They looked at the two pages, who were regarding them expectantly.

Pug said, "We won't need you any longer. Go to where you're needed."

Both ran off without comment.

"The king will be on the wall," said Pug.

Magnus nodded. He closed his eyes a moment then said, "I'll take us there."

He put his hand on Pug's shoulder and suddenly they were standing on the wall next to Daylon and Collin.

"Keep your wits about you," said the master-at-arms, unfazed by their sudden appearance. "If you see a big stone coming, duck."

Pug looked at the Church Army and incanted a simple spell to see in the darkness. "They aren't attacking."

"They're trying to break down the walls first," said Daylon. "They won't attack until there's a breach."

Collin said, "They must have hauled a lot of stones with them if they intend to break through."

Pug focused on a large trebuchet located far behind the lines and held up his hand. A flame appeared in his palm and grew until his hand was blazing like a torch. He closed his fist and then reached back and threw a ball of fire. It streaked across the night sky, growing larger and larger, to smash into the trebuchet. Flames spread and shouting soldiers raced to fight the conflagration with whatever was at hand.

After a few minutes they had put the fire out.

Magnus said to the king, "On our world, that ball of fire would have been much larger, and that trebuchet would be gone."

Daylon said, "It's still very impressive."

"At least that slowed them down," said Collin. "They have to make sure the wood is still sturdy and replace the burned ropes. That will take a few hours."

Pug said, "Then I'll just throw another."

"Or they may give up on a breach and simply storm the walls with ladders at sunrise," said the king.

"We shall see," Magnus replied.

HATU STIRRED, THEN SLOWLY OPENED his eyes. He raised himself on his elbows and looked around. Disorientation finally faded and he realized he was on Prince Declan's sleeping pallet and that it was dark.

He sat up, feeling lightheaded for a moment, then with feet firmly on the floor, stood up. After a deep breath and a stretch, he shook off the muzzy feeling. He parted the curtain. He found Nakor asleep in a chair before the dining table, his feet propped up between an empty ale mug and a half-eaten plate of food. "Nakor," he said.

The little man jerked awake, almost tipping the chair over backward but caught his balance and got his feet under him. "So, you're still alive," he said with a grin.

"Apparently," Hatushaly said. "Where is everyone?"

"Off fighting a battle at the city. I stayed behind to wake you up if that black floating Dread-thing started something."

"It's still there?"

"I don't know. I fell asleep. Besides, it's dark."

Hatu moved to the eastern exit from the pavilion, facing all the construction works, which now lay abandoned. Half a dozen guards were nearby, but otherwise the entire site of the previous day's carnage was silent.

Hatu took a deep breath to clear his head further and gazed into the night. Closing his eyes, he sent out his awareness to where the Dread creature hung suspended, contained within a lost moment of time, still swirling furiously and even at this distance heralding evil. Hatu repressed a shiver as he turned to Nakor. "It's still there."

"Still trapped?"

Hatu closed his eyes again and returned his attention to the confined Void creation. After a moment he looked back at Nakor. "I can't sense any difference."

"Good. I think we're needed in the city. You rested enough to get there?"

Hatu smiled, put his hand on Nakor's shoulder, and they were suddenly standing in the king's throne room. "I need to see my wife," said Hatu. "Why don't you go find Pug and Magnus? I'll catch up."

Nakor grinned. "Don't take too long." He turned as if he were looking for something, then, with a simple bob of his head, he vanished.

HATU ENTERED THE ROOM HE shared with Hava to find her sitting on the chair next to the small writing desk, honing her sword. She looked up, startled, then dropped the blade and jumped up, throwing her arms around Hatu's neck. After a welcoming kiss, she said, "Are you all right?"

"A little . . . fuzzy, but all right."

"Fuzzy?"

He pointed to his head. "There was some nasty business out in the Darkwood, and I did a couple of things that . . . well, I passed out."

She stepped back a little, her face a mask of concern. "Passed out?"

"I'm all right. Mainly, I just slept. Some odd dreams, too, but when I woke up, everyone but Nakor had come here. I could use something to eat and some coffee, but there doesn't seem to be time." He looked at her sword on the floor. "You planning on joining the fight?"

"Only if I must," she said, bending to retrieve her sword. "It's too distant a ride to Toranda and the ships will sail to the Sanctuary without me if the Church attacks the city. So, I might as well be here. I knew you'd find me."

He smiled. "Always."

"Where are you going?"

"To the battlement, to see if I'm needed. Nakor, Pug, and Magnus are already there."

"I'll go with you," she said, pulling on the leather jacket she wore aboard ship during cold weather. She then sheathed her sword, and they left the room together.

It took them a few minutes to walk through the otherwise empty streets—those not manning the wall were staying inside their homes. They reached the steps to the highest tower by the gate and after a brisk climb found the magicians and the king.

Hatu gave Daylon a bow from the waist and the king inclined his head in acknowledgment, then returned to watching the opposing army.

Hava and Hatu looked out and saw a line of torches in the dark.

Pug asked, "How are you?"

"Well enough," Hatu replied.

"Can you explain what happened back at the redoubt?" Magnus asked.

Hatushaly looked uncertain. "No. That's something I need to discuss with you, when we have less pressing concerns." He motioned to the Church Army.

The king said, "Those trebuchets will probably be throwing again soon."

Hatu closed his eyes and sent his senses into the darkness, across the open field before the city's gates to where the Church Army stood ready. He found the amount of human energy he sensed there confounding, so he paused and simplified his perception until he could map out where things were. He opened his eyes and said, "That dark presence we saw at the redoubt is not here."

"The Dread creature is still stuck," Nakor added.

Pug said, "The story Ruffio told us, about the time you lost your temper and burned that warship down to the waterline . . ."

"Yes?" Hatu asked.

"Can you do it again?" Pug asked.

Magnus looked at him curiously. "Phillip?"

Pug blinked, drew back from Magnus a bit, and said, "I'm very serious."

Magnus looked at Hatushaly and said, "Throwing a ball of fire that far is neither simple nor easy."

Hatushaly gave a half-smile. "I have a different idea."

He closed his eyes again and extended his senses toward the big war engines. He reached the closest of the two trebuchets and could almost caress it, his impressions of it were so vivid. He remembered how he'd increased the energy within the flames the king had used to burn down the gigantic doors of the Pride Lords' fortress, and again sought the fundamental fibers of the wood in the massive frame of the trebuchet. Pulling energy from the soil below and even the air surrounding it, he willed that energy to an excited state and heard an audible gasp. Opening his eyes, he saw a fire swirling on one support of the distant machine, and the shadowy figures of shocked soldiers scurrying away or trying to put out the flames.

He closed his eyes again and found it surprisingly easy to will the flames to become hotter until they billowed through the entire structure. A faint crack accompanied the teetering of the tall engine and distant sounds of alarm.

As the machine fell crashing to the ground, horns sounded and a single stone from the other engine came speeding toward them. It fell short, landing in an empty section of the yard between the outer wall and the tower on which they all stood.

"I guess their commander decided not to wait for sunrise," said Nakor.

Kingdom soldiers were now fully deployed on the wall and the smaller ballistas were ready. King Daylon waited and when the first rank of attackers rushed forward, every fourth man leading a ladder team, he shouted, "Loose!"

At once every ballista on the city wall towers and every archer unleashed a shower of missiles. Church soldiers with shields raised them high, attempting to protect themselves and the ladder teams.

Men fell screaming and the first wave of attackers hesitated, then pressed forward. Again, the order was given, and the archers loosed their rain of fletched shafts, and more Church soldiers fell.

Hatu glanced at Pug, who said, "Do nothing for the moment."

"But—" Hatushaly began.

"Nothing!" Pug cut him off. "Harbor your strength until I tell you it's needed." He then looked at Nakor. "You as well."

Nakor gave a grin, and said, "I'm not always foolish. Just occasionally."

Large shields were carried forward to protect those holding the ladders, and soon half a dozen were propped against the walls. Another massive stone came flying out of the darkness, on a higher arc than before. Pug reached out his hand and with a motion deflected it downward, to crash close to where the first stone had landed. This one rolled into the base of the tower, striking it hard enough that those standing on top could feel it shake.

"Enough of this," said Magnus. He cast a huge ball of flames back toward the fire engulfing the first engine, and it struck the second trebuchet. "It may not destroy it, but it will stop them from using it for a while."

Pug glanced at Hatushaly and said, "Keep waiting."

The sky to the east began to lighten; dawn was less than half an hour away. Fighters clashed at the top of the wall, with the Church forces constantly repelled. Marquensas soldiers used long poles to topple ladders and those few Church soldiers who managed to top the wall were quickly killed. It was a close and bloody struggle, hand-to-hand as more Church soldiers gained positions on the battlement.

Hatu finally succumbed to his rising frustration and said to Pug, "We must help!"

"Not yet," Pug replied. "If my worst fears become real, we will need every bit of power the four of us can summon. Wait."

The fight continued without the Church establishing a foothold anywhere. As soon as one portion of the wall was gained, Marquensas forces retook it, but at a heavy price. Men on both sides fell and littered the ground behind the walls.

"They're spending lives without a thought," Collin said.

King Daylon said, "They're fanatics. We've dealt with such before."

"True, Majesty," Collin replied, "but never in such numbers."

Nakor spoke without humor. "Soon they won't need any ladders. They'll just walk up on the bodies of the dead."

Abruptly, a distant battle horn sounded, and flames appeared in parts of the distant Church encampment.

Daylon leaned forward, his knuckles turning white as he gripped the merlon. "Declan!" he shouted.

Collin barked out a short laugh. "The prince is hitting them in the arse. That'll put paid to them."

"Ready the sally," King Daylon said.

"Form up for the sally!" Collin shouted down to the men below. He looked at the king and asked, "Any change to the tactics, sire?"

"No, as planned," the king replied. "That's my brother and your future monarch out there. He's surprised them, but he's still got a big army between him and us. Get to him swiftly!"

"Yes, Majesty," Collin replied. "To the port!" he shouted, and the order was repeated below.

Hatushaly pointed off to the right, where a section of the wall was being uncovered as a force of men lined up, four abreast, and a sally port was revealed to have been cleverly hidden by the painted cover being carried away.

Collin turned to Pug and the others and said, "We'll hit them from the right; and on the left side of the castle, we'll send the cavalry out of the rear marshaling gate. They'll ride around the enemy's right flank to go and aid the prince. Let's hope our lads on the right distract them enough."

The disguised gate was thrown open and the column of soldiers ran through as quickly as they could. As they left the wall, they spread out, men moving away on both sides. When the Church soldiers became aware of the sortie, their left side began to falter.

Hatu and the others watched as the Church attack fell apart, with those in the van suddenly uncertain of which way to move. From the far left, Pug and the others could see in the approaching dawn a large company of horsemen riding to relieve Prince Declan. "If their commanders are there, the prince can end this soon enough," said Collin.

"You think so?" asked Nakor.

"Look at those tabards." He pointed. "They have a different design. These are regular troops, maybe even mercenaries given their black outfits, but they aren't Church Adamant bastards, I'll wager."

"I hope you're right," said the king.

Hava cleared the last flight of steps to come and stand next to Hatu. "I got bored."

Hatu knew his wife well enough to know that even to suggest she should go somewhere safe would provoke a needless argument he could not possibly win.

The fighting beyond the wall was to Marquensas's advantage, but it was ferocious. As the sky to the east lightened, the scene of carnage became more evident by the minute.

Charging men were struck hard enough to send them tumbling

into their comrades; spears were planted in the ground by desperate men so that horses ran onto them, squealing as they fell. Men screamed in anger and fear, and the battle spread out before the castle as more soldiers from both sides joined the struggle.

Pug and his companions watched in silence as the fate of Marquensas, and perhaps the entire world of Garn, was decided by the men dying below. Hatushaly stood rigidly, fists balled tightly, with Hava's hand on his shoulder as if to calm him.

Suddenly a wave of anguish washed over them all. Pug and the others felt their hair stand on end and their skin crawl with a sudden bite of cold out of nowhere.

Pug looked at Magnus and said, "It's broken through!"

On the field beyond the wall, men were dropping to their knees, some retching, others curling into a ball. Still others were elevated to a battle frenzy, attacking anyone nearby, friend or foe.

Daylon had his hands over his ears as if there was a loud sound ringing, and even the usually imperturbable Collin held tightly to the stone merlon to keep from stumbling, his face drained of color and his eyes tightly shut.

"Declan," Hatu said, choking out the words. "He's here."

Pug motioned for Nakor and Magnus to come close. "Hatu, you have more power than the three of us combined. Can you take us to him?"

Hatu forced aside his rising panic, and with a deep breath closed his eyes. He had found Declan before when he was stranded in Garn's Wound. There had been little to confuse him then, but now the storm of human energy masked his friend's whereabouts. Hatu felt his anger rising again. He refused to let that building rage confound him but instead channeled it as he searched for the familiar presence. Then he felt it: Declan's unique energy. "Yes," he said.

Fighting off the pain, the king cried, "Declan!"

"We will find him!" cried Hatu.

He motioned for Pug and Magnus to come close, and just as he was ready to transport them to Declan's side, Hava reached out and threw her arm around her husband. In an instant they stood in the midst of chaos. Declan and Sixto stood back-to-back, doing their best to ignore their surging emotions, physical pain, and mind-numbing fear.

Pug glanced at Magnus, and without a word the white-haired magician understood what was needed. He raised his arms and a bubble of energy spread out and engulfed the group and a handful of nearby soldiers. Instantly, the mind-numbing sensations washing over them faded.

Declan shook his head to clear it and jumped forward to end the life of a Church soldier about to kill one of the king's own. The few Church soldiers inside Magnus's bubble also shook off the mind-numbing sound. Declan saw one regaining his focus and quickly engaged the man, killing him before he fully recovered.

Sixto, a moment later, was also laying about him, and within moments, the handful of Church soldiers nearby lay dead, and no enemies remained within Magnus's sphere of protection.

Declan looked at Hatu incredulously. "Did you do that?"

Hatu pointed to Magnus. "He did."

"Thank you."

Magnus gave a small tilt of his head in acknowledgment.

Pug looked eastward and said, "Get as many men here as you can."

Declan moved and suddenly Sixto grabbed his arm. "You stay here!" he said in as commanding a tone as Declan had ever heard. "I'll get them."

Without waiting for any comment from Declan, Sixto hurried outside the radius of calm Magnus had created and grabbed a soldier rolling on the ground. He half-dragged, half-carried the man back inside the bubble.

Pug looked at Magnus and asked, "Can you expand this spell?"

Magnus closed his eyes, raised his shoulders as if lifting a weight, and with a force of will, pushed the dome of protection outward.

Soon a cadre of soldiers surrounded the prince, quickly recovering from the magic onslaught that had rendered them helpless. Pug looked from face to face and shouted, "Something is coming! Stand fast and protect the prince!"

The soldiers gathered themselves in a circle around Declan, but beyond the bubble, chaos continued. Men rolled on the ground as if in agony, while others ran randomly, some throwing aside weapons, others just standing and shaking.

To the east, as the sun rose, a cloud of darkness grew larger every moment. Quickly it became apparent that something was approaching.

"It's here!" Pug shouted.

As if stepping out of a cloud of black smoke, a massive figure of evil aspect appeared. It was a black beyond any simple hue, a profound emptiness that drank in light. No feature could be seen, but odd shifts within the inky form suggested a massive human-like form, head, shoulders, arms, torso, legs, all moving with purpose.

Hatu recognized it from his earlier contact. The creature was a manifestation of emptiness, literally a void in the world in a monster's shape. How something not in this world could manifest so that the crush of its footfalls shook the ground was impossible for him to grasp. Yet here it was, a towering horror made real.

Around its head burned four flames, all staying in place as the head-shape moved. The flames were crimson and yellow, crackling and sputtering as if enraged. The monster paused for a moment, then turned toward Declan and those surrounding him. Where eyes should have been, two giant red embers regarded them.

Nakor said, "Pug?"

"It's a Dreadlord!"

Magnus reached out and a lance of blue energy sizzled in the air as it struck the creature in the chest, knocking it back a step. It faltered for a moment, and as it regained its balance, Pug savaged it with another bolt, knocking it farther back.

"Get Declan to safety!" Sixto shouted.

"No!" Pug yelled. "Anyone who steps outside our protection will be like those outside. All will die!"

"What can I do?" Hatushaly asked.

"Grab Declan and your wife and jump to safety!" Pug answered.

Nakor shouted, "No! I'll take them. You two are weakening here. Only Hatu has the power." Without waiting, he grabbed Declan's arm and Hava's belt, and vanished.

Hatu stood uncertain for a moment, overwhelmed by the terrifying closeness of a being like the one he'd seen in Garn's Wound. The difference was that this horror was fully animated with purpose and rage.

A moment later, Nakor reappeared. "Safe," he said. "Though Hava is very angry with me." Hatushaly gave him a momentary look of gratitude. "And with you, too, I think."

"What are you doing back here?" Magnus asked as he struck the Dreadlord with another blast of murderous energy.

"I can't fight from the palace," Nakor answered, and he cast a beam of brilliant white light that sizzled audibly when it struck the Dreadlord. The creature emitted a howl that shook the ground beneath their feet.

Knowing that Hava was safe, Hatushaly composed himself amidst the chaos. Every man outside the protective sphere was now on the ground, some twitching, others trying to crawl, but most lay motionless.

"It sucks the life out of everything nearby," Pug said.

Hatu saw that the ground under the Dreadlord's feet was now blackened and devoid of any living plant. The nearest trees were darkening as if afflicted with blight. He sensed all life was now flowing into the monster. Pug, Magnus, and Nakor's attacks had driven it back, injured it slightly, but it was regaining its focus and purpose.

Hatu closed his eyes and sent his senses toward the creature. As before, when he reached a point just a hair's breadth from the Dreadlord, the lines of energy vanished. This time, there was no feeling of dislocation, no energy pushing back, as he had felt when the Dreadlord had been trapped out of time. Now he felt a drawing of energy, almost as a sponge drinks in water. He paused.

Time seemed to freeze for Hatushaly. He felt as if he was floating between moments. He let his mind slowly expand to touch on more and more of his surroundings. Once before he had investigated threads of energy around a Dreadlord and discovered the tiniest fiber of time embedded within. He hesitated for an instant, seeking an understanding of what he beheld, and saw that it was time that had lingered for a moment after all the other energies had been destroyed. He sensed a balance, something he'd sought to understand now becoming clear to him. After a few more moments, he took a deep breath, and said, "I know."

Pug looked at him. He saw the young man standing motionless, his arms outstretched, his expression relaxed, almost smiling. Then something extraordinary happened.

The Dreadlord froze, not even the flames that crowned it flickering. Suddenly, all energy appeared to have been drained out of the monster.

Pug drew a deep breath, putting his hands on his knees for a few seconds. Then, standing upright, he turned to Magnus and said, "How are you?"

"Exhausted" came the weak reply.

Nakor nodded.

Sixto asked, "What's happening?"

They all looked at Hatushaly, who stood motionless.

Sixto began to reach for Hatushaly, but Pug held his hand up, indicating that no one should interfere with what Hatu was doing.

For long minutes no one moved. Nakor looked back and forth between the Dreadlord and Hatu. Pug and Magnus both focused what was left of their energies on trying to understand what Hatushaly was doing.

Nakor glanced up and said, "The darkness is fading."

They all looked up and could see the sky was slowly returning to its morning brightness. All four then looked to where the frozen Dreadlord loomed, seeing that it was also looking less substantial.

"What is that boy doing?" Nakor asked. "Whatever it is, it's a magnificent trick."

Pug looked at Magnus and said, "Closing the gate between realms destroyed a world. Closing the entrance to Midkemia cost the lives of half of all the magic-users. You and I have faced the Dread. You have more power than I, but together we could not do what we're seeing."

Magnus put his hand on Pug's shoulder. "I think this is not only beyond our ability, but perhaps also beyond our understanding."

Sixto raised his voice. "Look! It's fading!"

Pug could not take his eyes from the Dreadlord. When the silhouette had been blacker than ink, it had drunk in all the light around it. Now it was a smoky dark grey, the color fading by the moment. Soon, Pug, Magnus, and Nakor could see through its form, as it became less and less substantial.

Long minutes dragged by, and Pug looked back and saw a company of Kingdom horsemen halted a safe distance from what had been the scene of mayhem. Bodies were strewn everywhere, the field resembling an abattoir, corpses twisted into impossible contortions. Here and there lay men without a mark upon them. It was obvious they all were dead.

Pug felt Magnus's hand tighten on his shoulder and he looked back at the Dreadlord. It was now fading to a wisp of grey outline, the trees beyond becoming visible through it. Fainter and fainter the thing became; then abruptly it was gone.

All three looked at Hatu, who stood motionless. Pug put his hand out, and pulled it back, clearly unwilling to interrupt what Hatu was experiencing.

Then Hatushaly collapsed.

Nakor caught him before he struck the ground, and they lowered him gently. Pug put his ear to the young man's chest and heard his heart beating. Nakor closed his eyes, and after a second said, "He's all in there."

Pug wasn't certain what that meant, but said, "We need to get him to the palace, to the king's healer."

"I can do that," said Magnus.

"Me too," said Nakor.

"Good," said Pug. "I don't know if I can, and I also want to see what's going on here."

Magnus and Nakor each took one of Hatushaly's arms and, looking at each other, they nodded, and vanished.

Pug turned to Sixto and said, "I think this battle is over."

"Apparently," said Declan's longtime friend. He waved to the waiting column of riders moving toward them. The young captain, Joran, led the riders, and he called out, "The day is ours!"

"Good," said Sixto. He looked around the battlefield, now brightly lit by the early morning sun. He saw the Church banners still snapping in the breeze above empty pavilions. Horses and mules staked out on the other side cropped what plants they could reach. He turned to Pug, and said, "I can barely believe what I just saw."

Pug said, "You are not alone."

Regaining his usual composure, Sixto said to Joran, "We'll need graves dug."

As the young captain started giving orders, Sixto softly added, "Many graves."

Pug could only sigh.

THE KING'S TABLE WAS QUIET. Instead of a raucous celebration of victory, a relieved group celebrated being alive. Hatushaly was still asleep in the quarters set aside for him, and Hava was with him.

Pug, Magnus, and Nakor were at the table with Daylon, Declan, and Balven, Sixto, Collin, and General Baldasar. The conversation had been muted, and at last the king said, "It's not over, is it?"

It was Pug who answered. "Probably not. If I have learned anything about the Void, it is that it is unrelenting. Even though we have defeated it before, we have only set it back. We were amazingly fortunate today. If not for Hatushaly's powers . . ."

Nakor said, "He was supposed to be dead."

Balven said, "What?"

"That story, about destroying all the Firemanes, you saving Hatushaly."

Daylon said, "It was the Flame Guard who saved him. I merely put him somewhere I thought he'd be more likely to survive."

"It all worked out," said Nakor. "If Hatushaly had not lived, no tricks at all would have worked here. This place needs a lot more stuff."

"I'm not certain what that means," said the king. Looking at Pug and Magnus, he asked, "How do we continue to prepare?"

Just then, Hava and Hatushaly entered. Hatu appeared a little wan, but otherwise well. The king stood and said, "How fare you?"

"Well enough, I think," said Hatu. He and Hava sat down when the king waved them to seats. Hatu looked at Pug and said, "Before you ask, no, I do not know what I did, or how I did it. I just did it. Like before with the soldiers. I don't understand."

Nakor grinned. "More questions!"

"We were just discussing what to do to prepare for the next attack," said King Daylon.

Pug was about to speak, but Nakor cut him off. "Two things. You have to completely finish the Church. They are bad people and work for the Void."

"Is that all?" Balven asked with a tone of disbelief.

"Simple is not always easy," Nakor replied. "Then we have to go rescue an angel."

The king, Balven, Sixto, Hatu, and Hava all stared at him in stunned silence.

Magnus asked, "Care to elaborate?"

"If we're going to bring more stuff here, we have to go somewhere that has a lot of it floating around. So, we go up!" Nakor pointed toward the ceiling. "We need to visit heaven and we need this angel to guide us there. But he's in a prison, so we have to get him free."

"Prison?" asked Balven.

"Yes," Nakor answered matter-of-factly. "He's called Eleleth, and the King of Assala has him locked up in the Vault. I was told by a very well-informed fellow by the name of Vordam. If something needs to be known, or found, he's the man to see. I asked about getting to a higher realm, and that's how we do it."

Magnus winced. "The Vault? Is that what I'm thinking?"

"Yes, on the world of Cynoth."

Hava and Hatu exchanged glances, and Hava asked, "Is the Vault a prison?"

"According to legend," said Magnus, "it's not only a prison, but one from which no living being has ever escaped. It's in the lowest basement of the palace of the king, which also happens to be a fortress city."

"Wonderful," said Balven. "I would judge you all mad, if I hadn't seen everything that's already happened since this business began. How do you expect to free a prisoner from such a place?"

Hava said, "As for dealing with the Church, as soon as Bodai gets back, we should send him to Coaltachin. If we're going to defeat the Church, we'll need their help."

"And the other?" asked the king.

Again, Hava and Hatu looked at each other. Then Hatu said, "Breaking out of prison? We know somebody."

Daylon looked around the table and said, "And now I think it's time for more wine."

No one disagreed.

REUNION

Donte looked through the open door as the sun rose. The children were already working at their chores under Healer's supervision. He had spent the previous day consulting with Healer and had been reassured that everything here was running smoothly. The children were thriving, and Donte again reflected on their overall well-being compared to what he had known growing up in a Coaltachin school. He still felt oddly ambivalent about how to proceed. Back on Garn, those children below a certain age judged unfit to serve the Council of Masters would be returned to their families, while older children who had seen too much would simply be disposed of.

He took a deep breath and wondered about his new realization, that being a member of a crew in a foreign city was often fun and always challenging, but being the crime lord of a city was mostly about being an administrator and rather boring.

The false Mockers were gone, either dead, fled, or come over to his side. The Keshians were also gone, dead, or fleeing back to Kesh. There was little to do that Donte considered fun.

He was halfway through his second mug of coffee when, without warning, Hatushaly and Hava stood before him. He almost fell backward in his chair, only catching himself with one hand on the table, pulling his chair upright.

"Damn, that was unexpected," he said with a laugh. He came to his feet and grabbed Hava, half-spinning her around in a hug, then embraced Hatu so hard that he knocked the breath out of him.

"What brings you to Port Vykor?" Donte asked.

"You," said Hava. "But this isn't Port Vykor."

"True," said Donte. He pointed. "You have to ride about a full day that way. How did you find me?"

Hatushaly smiled. "I can always find you."

"That's reassuring," Donte said, then he paused and added, "I think."

Hava glanced out of the open door at the sound of children laughing. "What is this place?"

Donte thought for a moment, then said, "It's a cover for a dodge. I have people thinking I'm a rich sheep farmer."

"You may be the only person I've ever heard use the word 'rich' before 'sheep farmer,'" said Hatu.

"And what are all these kids doing here?" Hava asked.

"I'm . . . training up a crew."

Hava's expression was clearly skeptical. "Really?"

"Trying to, anyway. I have the older ones working in Port Vykor."

"Building your criminal empire?" Hava asked mockingly.

"Trying to, anyway," repeated Donte, his expression darkening.

"We need you," said Hatu.

"For what?" Donte asked.

Hava pulled out a chair and sat down. "How many times have you broken out of prison?"

Donte considered the question, then said, "Counting the ones I've broke out of more than once?"

Hatushaly laughed.

Donte said, "Don't know. I've lost count."

"How would you like to risk your life on a strange world, breaking someone out of prison?" Hatushaly asked.

Donte blinked. "Really?"

"Yes," Hava said.

"What's in it for me?" Donte asked.

"No one has ever broken out of this prison," said Hatu. "It's in the lowest level below a fortress, where lives a king. It's never been done in the history of this world."

Donte gave Hatushaly a sidelong look. "Never?"

Hava added, "Never in the centuries since the prison was built. It's extremely dangerous."

"Extremely?" Donte repeated.

"Absolutely," said Hatu.

"Who are we breaking out?"

"An angel," said Hava.

Donte's lips twitched in a smile, and then he grinned. "I'm in." He stood up. "Let me go tell my man out there I'm going off for a while, and to send a message to my boys in Port Vykor, then we can leave." He hurried outside.

Hava chuckled, then looked at her husband. "Is this a good idea?"

Hatu gave her a crooked smile. "No, but it's the only idea I have."

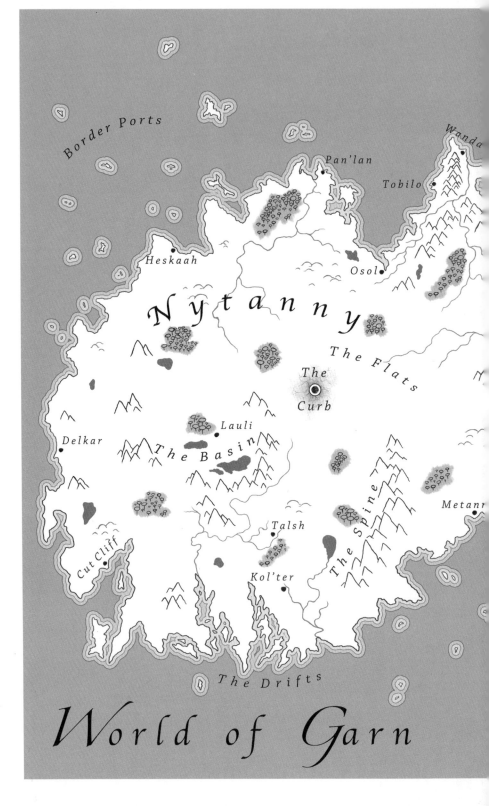

Border Ports

Wanda

Pan'lan

Tobilo

Heskaah

Osol

Nytanny

The Flats

Delkar

The Curb

Lauli

The Basin

The Spine

Metann

Cut Cliff

Talsh

Kol'ter

The Drifts

World of Garn